Studies in Global Science Fiction

Studies in Global Science Fiction (edited by Anindita Banerjee, Rachel Haywood Ferreira, and Mark Bould) is a brand-new and first-of-its-kind series that opens up a space for Science Fiction scholars across the globe, inviting fresh and cutting-edge studies of both non-Anglo-American and Anglo-American SF literature. Books in this series will put SF in conversation with postcolonial studies, critical race studies, comparative literature, transnational literary and cultural studies, among others, contributing to ongoing debates about the expanding global compass of the genre and the emergence of a more diverse, multinational, and multi-ethnic sense of SF's past, present, and future. Topics may include comparative studies of selected (trans)national traditions, SF of the African or Hispanic Diasporas, Indigenous SF, issues of translation and distribution of non-Anglophone SF, SF of the global south, SF and geographic/cultural borderlands, and how neglected traditions have developed in dialogue and disputation with the traditional SF canon.

Stephen C. Tobin

Vision, Technology, and Subjectivity in Mexican Cyberpunk Literature

palgrave
macmillan

Stephen C. Tobin
University of California
Los Angeles, CA, USA

ISSN 2569-8826 ISSN 2569-8834 (electronic)
Studies in Global Science Fiction
ISBN 978-3-031-31155-0 ISBN 978-3-031-31156-7 (eBook)
https://doi.org/10.1007/978-3-031-31156-7

Cover credit: Image Source/Getty Images

This Palgrave Macmillan imprint is published by the registered company Springer Nature Switzerland AG.
The registered company address is: Gewerbestrasse 11, 6330 Cham, Switzerland

To my co-creators Mom and Dad, a.k.a. Alice and Jim Tobin, without whom this book would never have been published.
And to Milo, whose gaze was most present during this work's conception, creation, and revision.

Acknowledgments

Writing a book is paradoxical in that it is fundamentally comprised of a solitary activity, yet no one ever does anything truly alone. Even when a body with a mind sits alone at a desk, looks at a screen and manipulates a keyboard and mouse for endless hours to create fragments that form a coherent whole of meaning, that body is constituted by a multitude of contingent elements and forces that are biological, political, economic, social, and cultural. Additionally, thoughts formulated into words are always already a commixture of words and ideas read and heard, whose meaning is often extracted from and inspired by words of other people. To this end, this book owes a large debt of gratitude to a number of people whose own words have been instrumental in the process of this monograph's creation. They deserve recognition.

Isis Sadek's editorial counseling has greatly strengthened and polished my ideas and their articulation throughout this work. Without her assistance, this book would read much less smoothly.

My dissertation adviser Laura Podalsky graciously offered guidance and encouragement despite the work being a half-formed seedling of an idea. Ana del Sarto's critical comments helped reshape one chapter considerably, and forced me to reconsider how gender works in myriad ways through bodies and subjects in this literary corpus. Joel Wainwright's review of an early draft also offered a formidable reconsideration of numerous aspects of the work.

The vocal support and unyielding encouragement from Chloe Ahmann, Mandie Dunn, and Jenn Trivedi offered operational and emotional assistance.

The following students were instrumental in helping me rethink some analysis in two chapters: Robin Ayala-Barrios, Elena Cawthorn, Christian Erickson, Isabella Fernandez, Stephanie Rivas-Lara, Laura Sainz Merin, Fatima Sánchez, and "Lily" Huiying Wang.

Finally, Patricia Arroyo Calderón, despite never having read a word of this particular monograph, has been there the longest; her presence and interaction have been critical sources of emotional and intellectual reassurance as the book was being written; without her, it would not exist.

Praise for *Vision, Technology, and Subjectivity in Mexican Cyberpunk Literature*

"How do speculative narratives engage with major societal and technological changes? Stephen C. Tobin answers this question through excellent analyses of numerous Mexican speculative fictions. He postulates narrative itself as a mutable genre that constantly adapts as it interfaces with other media, particularly visual culture. In so doing, he shows how, beyond reflecting the debates of their time, speculative narratives also imagines new modes of knowing. *Vision, Technology, and Subjectivity in Mexican Cyberpunk Literature* will be a key text both for scholars of Latin American science fiction and the fantastic and for any scholar interested in the role that the written word continues to play in an increasingly audiovisual society."

—David Dalton, *Associate Professor of Spanish, University of North Carolina,* Charlotte, Author of *Robo Sacer: Necroliberalism and Cyborg Resistance in Mexican and Chicanx Dystopias* and *Mestizo Modernity: Race, Technology, and the Body in Postrevolutionary Mexico*

"Dr. Stephen Tobin's monograph is the first book examining cyberpunk and post-cyberpunk literature written in Spanish. The book shows how Mexican cyberpunk and post-cyberpunk literature not only 'reflects' the way technology is transforming subjectivity, but how it even anticipates new modes of subjectivity that are absent in other types of cultural works. Tobin reads these literary texts in dialogue with works on technological remediation, cyborg theory, and theories of media and visuality, but also carefully provides contextual information as needed. As such, the book will make an engaging read for scholars and non-specialists alike."

—Miguel García, *Assistant Professor of Mexican Studies, Arizona State University*

Contents

CHAPTER 1

Introduction: Entering the Screen

> We are all part of a moving-image culture and we live cinematic and electronic lives. Indeed, it is not an exaggeration to claim that none of us can escape daily encounters—both direct and indirect—with the objective phenomena of motional picture, televisual, and computer technologies and the networks of communication and texts they produce. Nor is it an extravagance to suggest that, in the most profound, socially pervasive, and yet personal way, these objective encounters transform us as subjects. That is, although relatively novel as 'materialities' of human communication, cinematic and electronic media have not only historically symbolized but also historically constituted a radical alteration of the forms of our culture's previous temporal and spatial consciousness and of our bodily sense of existential 'presence' to the world, to ourselves, and to others. Vivian Sobchack (1994, 82–83)

Visceral Scopic Regimes

In Eve Gil's futuristic novel *Virtus* (2008), all of Mexico suffers a sudden blackout one evening, which thrusts nearly all its citizens into total darkness. Everyone—who up until that moment lived immersed within a constant state of digital virtualization, where the totality of their social and subjective experiences comprised of being surrounded by vibrant moving audio-visual images and interacting with holographic avatars—abruptly

S. C. Tobin, *Vision, Technology, and Subjectivity in Mexican Cyberpunk Literature*, Studies in Global Science Fiction,
https://doi.org/10.1007/978-3-031-31156-7_1

finds themselves in pitch black. Without light, all are thrown into a disorienting abyss; shock and confusion abound. The protagonist Juana recounts this experience from her youth, recalling how everyone remained completely still in the first moments, their visuospatial perception suddenly absent. In its place, sound moves to the perceptual forefront: a cacophony of collective cries, both from her and other schoolchildren, renders the void deafening. Juana's mother, who happened to be at the school at the time of the blackout to pick her up, guides them out to the street where the newfound horror of a de-virtualized world continues—the surface of reality stripped of ubiquitous simulation overlays. Once finally back home in their 22nd floor apartment, Juana, her eyes having adjusted, gazes from a window at the city scene unfolding below that reveals the "reality of the unreality" (2008, 17): without the constantly moving and interactive digitally produced simulacra laid overtop the reality of their surroundings, people pinball about like zombies, unsure of where, or even who, they are, and what actions they should take. They appear like a purposeless mass of blind cyborg citizens. By immersing the reader in a jarring commencement that emphasizes the visual in such a manner, the novel makes offers a clear illustration of what I term a "specular fiction," or literature whose principal thematic and rhetorical focus pertain to the dynamics involved in the changing visual sphere of contemporary Mexican society.[1]

Virtus's opening with such a collective shock provides a worthwhile jumping off point to discuss the visceral nature of the literary corpus under analysis. The narratives examined here—Gerardo Porcayo's *La primera calle de la soledad* (1993) analyzed alongside its sister story "Esferas de visión" (1997), Pepe Rojo's "Ruido gris" (1996) and *Punto cero* (first published in 2000; second edition in 2012), Gil's *Virtus* (2008), and Guillermo Lavín's "Él piensa que algo no encaja" (2014)—offer extensive verbal descriptions that shock the reader into the experience of new scopic regimes in Mexico.[2] Christian Metz first coined this term to describe a "cinematic scopic regime" (1982, 61), but it was Martin Jay's "Scopic Regimes of Modernity" (1988) that popularized the phrase in scholarly usage by delineating three different regimes of the modern era: Cartesian perspectivalism, Dutch art from the seventeenth-century, and the Baroque.

[1] The term "visual sphere" brings to mind all that is possible to be seen in a society; a vast, cumulative potential inventory of what is visible. This phrase can be used interchangeably with visual field and field of vision.

[2] These can also be called visual, optic, or specular regimes.

Although Jay provides no clear definition of what constitutes a scopic regime, his work points to dominant visual modes in art history. For our purposes, visual regimes can be considered particular modes of seeing that are expressions of given culture. Courtney Tunis's definition, that these regimes are "an overarching experience of the gaze, as enacted on an entire culture" (2007), connects well with some of Porcayo's narratives, given that his writing privileges a male gaze and buoys heteronormative patriarchy. Rojo's creative work most frequently expresses a televisual regime—where television becomes a site of all-encompassing power, as well as that of this power's rhetorical innovation. Both Gil's novel and Lavín's story articulate a cybernetic scopic regime; the former foregrounds digitally virtualized images such as interactive avatars and holograms, and the latter showcases a regime overrun with the mini-screens of cellular smartphones. The cybernetic scopic regime occurs after, as well as alongside, other regimes, suggesting that a plurality of these exist concurrently. Undoubtedly, other optic regimes exist in Mexico, given that "the visual" encompasses the "the entire multifaceted field of visual experience" (Heywood and Sandwell 2012, 12). Some of the more studied ones include the pictorial arts (such as drawing and painting), photography, film, theater, murals, comics/graphic novels, architecture, dance, etc.[3] But the male gaze, televisual, and cybernetic scopic regimes are the most pronounced and are all expressed through the subgenre of cyberpunk and post-cyberpunk science-fiction literature that appears in 1993–2014. *Vision, Technology, and Subjectivity in Mexican Cyberpunk Literature* offers an analysis of the visual regimes depicted in these literary narratives and examines their complex intertextual links with broad socio-economic changes, political shifts, and cultural transformations occurring in Mexico.

One overarching thesis of this study is that contemporary science-fiction literature from Mexico has become a key genre through which to reflect upon and work through changes occurring in some of the country's contemporary visual practices. The literary works of this corpus highlight the subjective effects brought about by the latest manifestation of the image—the "e-image"—according to José Luis Brea in his work *Las tres eras de la imagen* (2010). He develops this as the final form of three main kinds of images that have emerged chronologically, and include the

[3] A growing number of studies in these fields have appeared since the turn of the century. See "Estrategias para mirar la nación. El giro visual de los estudios culturales mexicanos en lengua inglesa" (Sánchez Prado 2011) for more information.

"material image," "film," and the now-dominant "e-image," which pertains to the electronically generated, moving audio-visual image (2010, 67–76). Interacting and engaging with screens—what Nicholas Mirzoeff calls "visual events" where "user[s] seeks information, meaning or pleasure in an interface with visual technology" (2002, 5)—has become a core component of socially lived and subjective experience, every day more widespread throughout much of the developed and developing world since Mirzoeff wrote that 20 years ago. As a result of this dramatic increase in the occurrence of visual events, we can consider the narratives analyzed here as key signifiers of Walter Ong's notion of the "shifting sensorium" (1991), except that the visual sense is given primacy compared to other senses.[4] This is not to say that other senses are unimportant—Ong himself maintains that television is "sound medium as much as it is a visual one" (1991, 30). Aligned with Ong is W.J.T. Mitchell, who has argued that all media are mixed media, meaning that no media is purely visual (2002, 91, 93, 95). The works highlighted in this monograph foreground visual themes, technologies, practices, etc., which parallel significant changes occurring in the broader social plane; its aim is not to make lofty claims that media are exclusively visual, but rather point out ways in which the screen reaches such a pervasive point in Mexican society that a certain literature begins to register, dialogue, engage, and critique its multitudinous presence in meaningful ways—making visual elements a key feature of its contemporary science-fiction imaginary. These narratives emphasize visual practices, events, technologies, and their related effects on subjectivity attributable to significant alterations to the field of vision in contemporary Mexico. As I detail later, the country has undergone many changes to its media and telecommunications industries in the period under study here—from the early 1990s through the mid 2010s—which has substantially reorganized the sensorium to make television, computer, and cellphone screens ubiquitous throughout urban spaces in Mexico, and even perceptible in rural areas. As such, the authors of these science-fiction texts engage the changing visual sphere of the Mexico of this era; they absorb and assimilate these changes, and then speculate on how these particular

[4] Ong, a founder of Sense Studies, understands the sensorium as "the entire perceptual apparatus as an operational complex" (1991, 28). Michael Bull, Paul Gilroy and others consider all the senses as "an ever-shifting social and historical construct." Most emphatically, and going against what they perceive as the limited assumptions of psychologists and neurobiologists, they maintain that the "perceptual is cultural and political" (2006, 5).

visual technologies and their e-images appear to affect the country and its population.

Given the temporal frame these works share, it is important to recognize here at the outset what has become so commonplace when discussing works of science fiction that it verges upon academic cliché: this genre, so frequently set in the future, invariably comments upon the present in which it is written. Ursula K. Le Guin famously stated that the genre is "not predictive…[but] descriptive" (1976, ii); Argentine scholar Carlos Abraham goes a step further, suggesting that science fiction, by most frequently orienting its narrative temporality toward the future, may paradoxically make it the literary genre that most comments upon the present in which it is written (2013, 9). Along with the fact that these cyberpunk works register their presents, they also prefigure the future in significant, sometimes uncanny, ways. For this, the now antiquated usage that refers to science fiction as "literature of anticipation" (López Martín 2011, 95; Capanna 2007, 38) seems especially apt for these specular narratives of the turn of the twenty-first century. Rather than adhering to the original usage of the term that anticipated a technoscientific utopianism through the realization of organizational structures of society based on reason, these stories anticipate an ascendant world of hyper-visuality where television, computer, and smartphone screens dominate the sensorial experience, with myriad attendant consequences. Their discourses emphasize the visual because the worlds they inhabit become increasingly populated with screens and other ocular mediations between the human subject and visual objects.

Specular Fictions: Towards a Definition

The term "specular" abounds with meaning, and, in order to understand its relevance to this book, a discussion of its etymological roots and usage in Spanish and English is in order. Although the definition "of or pertaining to sight or vision" ("specular" def. 4.2.) has fallen into disuse in English, it is precisely the primary meaning intended for the corpus analyzed here—one which this monograph revives in order to foreground the visually thematic nature of these literary texts. The case for using specular increases further when considering the word's translation in Spanish, for which its usage *especular* carries numerous distinct meanings. Each of the following signifieds possesses some degree of relevance for this study: (i) pertaining to a mirror; (ii) to register or look at something with attention in order to recognize and examine it; (iii) to conjecture about something without sufficient knowledge; (iv) to obtain financial gain from mercantilist exchange ("Diccionario de..." 2001).[5] Insofar as the works interrogated herein reflect upon certain social, economic, and/or political processes occurring in Mexico at the time of their writing, they offer a degree of mirrored likeness in their representations (i). They critically examine visual practices and their related technologies (ii), and were all written in the neoliberal period that saw the heightened return to market-oriented policies, often critiquing them (iv). Finally, they perform their critiques through the uniquely technoscientific speculative framework that science fiction offers (iii). When taking into consideration its usage in Spanish as well as with the broader, archaic definition in English, along with the similarity to the more frequently employed "speculative fiction" as a stand-in for "science fiction," *specular* becomes the most apt term to describe these kinds of works. I consider specular fictions as literary narratives that engage with representations of visual technologies—defined as "any form of apparatus designed either to be looked at or to enhance natural vision, from oil painting to television and the Internet" (Mirzoeff 1999, 2)—such that socio-visual practices become thematically or rhetorically central in these narratives' discourse.

Specular fictions may be present in many eras and across all genres of literature the world over, but they are distinctly characteristic of literature in the modern Latin American context, and most specifically within the broad rubric of fantastic literature so pertinent to the region. Specular themes have arisen in the works of canonical authors such as Rubén Darío, Leopoldo Lugones, Horacio Quiroga, Julio Cortázar, Adolfo Bioy Casares, Roberto Bolaño, Edmundo Paz Soldán, among others. To situate this trend, this monograph acknowledges the work of Valeria de los Ríos, whose book *Espectros de luz* (2011) interrogates the meanings of photographic and cinematic apparatuses that appear in the fictional worlds created by many Latin American writers of the late nineteenth and early twentieth centuries, many of them short stories of the fantastic. These specular fictions foreground these then-new visual technologies within their narratives, revealing a cultural longing and an anxiousness that these devices provoked at the time. As de los Ríos argues, "Podría decirse que

[5] 1:"Perteneciente o relativo a un espejo," 2.1:"Registrar, mirar con atención algo para reconocerlo y examinarlo," 2.2: "Meditar, reflexionar con hondura, teorizar," 2.6: "Procurar provecho o ganancia fuera del tráfico mercantil."

son, al mismo tiempo, fragmentos de la modernidad, espectáculos populares, medios para establecer conexión con el más allá, y prueba fehacientes del fetichismo de la mercancía" (2011, 16) [It could be said that they are, at the same time, fragments of modernity, popular spectacles, mediums to establish connection with the beyond, and the irrefutable proof of commodity fetishism]. Throughout the book, she convincingly argues that these works register unique and critical articulations of larger themes like cultural identity, modernization, desire, appropriation, as well as center-periphery relations (2011, 21).

But *Vision, Technology, and Subjectivity in Mexican Cyberpunk Literature* differs from de los Ríos's work in several important ways. The most obvious departure is that her historically minded, cultural studies approach focuses on the visual apparatuses of photography and cinema, rather than the televisual and cybernetic. For my analysis, the pervasiveness of television throughout much of Mexico reaches near ubiquity in the mid-to-late 1990s, whereas computers begin their perceptible ascent a decade later in the mid-2000s, followed shortly—and then eclipsed—by the smartphone into the early 2010s. Together, these changes in the visual fields of urban spaces bring about an era of, if not screenic omnipresence, then of a sufficiently heightened prevalence to denote scopic regimes. In turn, in an attempt to compete with their surrounding environ some literary works absorb new media as they emerge, perceive these changes, and then engage them by attempting to assimilate them; this makes them, as de los Ríos observes, thematically and rhetorically central in the linguistic and narrative structures of these types of works (2011, 18). Marshall McLuhan noted, "the 'content' of any medium is always another medium" (1964, 23), which occurs here, but unlike digital media's tendency to refashion older media as its content, "older media refashion themselves to answer the challenges of new media" (Bolter and Grusin 2000, 14). For Geoffrey Winthrop-Young and his study of the nineteenth century novel, literature attempts to "describe more, if not everything, in a far more 'life-like', complex and detailed way... [in order to] incorporate, mimic, or co-opt the achievements of competing electric media" (1994, 124). Like the novel of the nineteenth century that competed with the photographic apparatus in the last half of the century, the literature of today continues to "bear the scars" (1994, 124) of the new media of its contemporaneous era. That is to say, in the case of this special brand of specular literature, the electronic image, displayed through the medium of television, computer, or cellular phone screens, infiltrates the content of the older media on the printed page in order to make it central to its stories and themes. In this sense, the image and the text can be seen as existing in tension or engaging in a kind of media rivalry.[6] In all, de los Ríos rightly perceives that "la literatura se presenta como un lugar privilegiado para analizar la impronta de la visualidad en la cultura, puesto que recoge consciente o inconscientemente su impacto, inscribiéndola en el texto de manera ficcional" (2011, 17) [literature presents itself as a privileged site to analyze the imprint of visuality in culture, given that it consciously or unconsciously gathers its impact, inscribing it in the text in a fictional manner].

The present work, unlike de los Ríos, focuses on a shorter temporal scope, as well as a specific national context defined by the ongoing transformations wrought by globalization. These specular fictions show how literary works respond to alterations occurring in a circumscribed visual field within urban spaces. What is more, whereas de los Ríos's primary concern resides with the histories of these visual technologies, along with their ontological and epistemological status as they appear in literature and change over time, my focus remains largely on the subjectivities that these technologies aid in producing (described allegorically in the stories), together with the broader institutional processes that underpin such material transformations unfolding in Mexico.

Critics may ask why I choose to theorize televisuality through literature, a decidedly verbal medium, to the exclusion of other forms of primarily visual cultural production, such as television and film. For one, Andrew Brown has contended that "literature…is a particularly important place to think through the dynamics of culture" (2010, 2), an assertion which I would extend to include "visual culture," given the binary often established between the visual and the verbal (or the image and the text). Literature proves useful precisely because it possesses a uniquely nonvisual vantage from which to be able to take a more distanced, critical perspective towards changes that happen in a culture with regard to image production. As a medium of communication whose dominance occurred within the nineteenth and twentieth centuries, to arrive at the twenty-first century and have print culture witness the dominance of the e-image

[6]As Pulitzer Prize-winning American author Phillip Roth stated in 2009: "The book can't compete with the screen. It couldn't compete [in the] beginning with the movie screen. It couldn't compete with the television screen, and it can't compete with the computer screen. Now we have all those screens, so against all those screens a book couldn't measure up" (Flood 2009). Of note is the fact that the smartphone had not yet fully taken root when Roth stated these words, which would certainly add more weight to his foregone conclusion.

(televisual and digital images) likely puts literary expression in something of a defensive position, given how its own stature as a cultural practice diminishes alongside visual media. Therefore, some works of literature take as their narrative focus visual events, processes, and technologies, in order to underscore how these effect society and its subjects. If it is true, as Winthrop-Young states, that literature contains, imitates, or appropriates achievements of its surrounding electronic environment, then literature, even today, still enjoys at least some privileged perspective from which to consider changes in the visual field of Mexico at this time. That film, television, and digital culture haunt neoliberal Mexican prose is a testament to the extent to which televisual and cybernetic discourses have entered the national imagination. Put simply, even verbal genres have to grapple with the visual hegemony. This gives merit as to why the specular within literary texts are being analyzed apart from other cultural forms which are fundamentally visual. And with regard to those Mexican televisual and cinematic narratives created around the time of this literary corpus being produced, I have not found any that merit inclusion here. It is as if media that is primarily visual in its mode of expression does not consider the specular to be problematic. To use a fitting expression of scopic origin, these media may have a blind spot when it comes to reflecting upon this topic, possibly due to their own mode of expressions' participation in and complicity within their respective mediums.

Also deserving of explanation regards why does this monograph focus on visual aspects of the literary texts when many of the works under discussion could also be analyzed through different critical lenses. For example, given the temporal scope of the neoliberal era in which all the works appeared, it would be possible to treat them largely as *Economic Science Fictions* (Davies and Kember 2018), insofar as they all present stark condemnations of the Mexican instantiation of the neoliberal agenda that began to fully manifest in the 1990s and continues to this day. Indeed, a number of works of this corpus have already been analyzed as harsh allegorical criticisms of the economic order, via Hernán García's articles (2012, 2017, 2018), some parts of Elizabeth Ginway's *Cyborgs, Sexuality, and the Undead: The Body in Mexican and Brazilian Speculative Fiction* (2020), as well as David Dalton's *Robo Sacer: Necroliberalism and Cyborg Resistance in Mexican and Chicanx Dystopias* (2023). Dalton's biopolitical analysis of the cyborg figure ensnared in a neoliberal economic system that monetizes death foregrounds this criticism in the most overt and sustained manner. Another related framework in which Dalton's monograph would fit nicely regards analyzing the dystopian articulations of the works of the corpus assembled here, similar to the approach of Miguel López-Lozano's *Utopian Dreams, Apocalyptic Nightmares* (2008). He analyzes novels by renowned Mexican authors like Carlos Fuentes, Carmen Boullosa, and Homero Aridjis as dystopias critical of the pernicious social and ecological effects unleashed by neoliberal reforms, often to the indigenous. Despite these two analytical categories—economic science fictions and dystopias—as pertinent lenses for this monograph's frame, *Vision, Technology, and Subjectivity in Mexican Cyberpunk Literature* stresses the visual in literature due to the deep sense of urgency with which they articulate their primary thematic preoccupations. The male gaze, a woman's stolen eye, an ocular journalist, a television that consumes a spectator, a holographic president, and virtual glasses that alter the wearer's subjective sense of the world—all clearly foreground the visual rhetoric that are difficult to ignore or relegate to a secondary plane. They emblematize specular fictions more than being primarily economic or dystopian science fictions.

Genre and Gender: Mexican Cyborgs as Sites of Discourse on Sight

The treatment of gender and genre in this corpus merit deeper inquiry. Some texts examined here establish gender as a primary concern.[7] This preoccupation signals that the materialization of these new scopic regimes necessarily entails and highlights the social perception of the male-female gender binary. In particular, who is permitted to gaze and who receives the gaze naturalizes a sense of heteronormativity that underpins the social order and hierarchizes power relations between genders. Perhaps unsurprisingly, a large number of purveyors of this mode of narration tend to pertain to the male gender—the one most frequently associated with the possessors of the gaze. Several hallmarks of scholarly analysis of gender in the twenty-first century reveal gender as largely—if not fully—socially constructed (Marecek et al. 2004, 192), as well as an ongoing process that is subjectively performed by biologically sexed individuals (Butler 1990, 140). The crucial component of gender within the discourse of cyborg

[7] For de los Ríos, the question of gender is left untreated altogether—a curious omission given her analysis of a wholly male-centric corpus, several of which include José Martí, Eduardo Holmberg, Roberto Arlt, Salvador Elizondo, Edmundo Paz Soldán, Roberto Bolaño, Clemente Palma, Horacio Quiroga, Julio Cortázar. In total, 17 authors' works are examined in her book with no substantial discussion of the gender politics present in the narratives, the authors themselves, or the local/national place and time from which they write.

studies developed in Mexico reveal two emerging strands. The first is that comprised of narratives with posthuman characters who challenge heteronormative, patriarchal ideals, be it through the postrevolutionary discourses that Sara Potter has studied (2013), or the speculative fiction featuring cyborgs, queer sexualities, zombies, or vampires that Ginway analyzes from the nineteenth century to the present (2020). On the other side are examples of cyborg subjects that sustain racial and gendered hierarchies, as David Dalton has shown in *Mestizo Modernity* (2018), or reveals posthumans to be born in a laboratory without parents and an origin story but, in fact, yearn for such connection, as Andrew Brown analyzes (2010) in Carmen Boullosa's *Cielos en la tierra*. My own study fits with the latter trend while remaining circumscribed to cyberpunk and post-cyberpunk literature that articulates vision and visual technologies pertinent to the era. To this end, the Chap. 2 demonstrates how foundational Mexican cyberpunk author, Gerardo Porcayo, portrays gender in two separate but related stories, each protagonized by a male and female cyborg—and in service of heteronormative patriarchy. In the Chap. 4, Eve Gil's *Virtus* portrays a posthuman society that is run by men as well, albeit one narrated by a female narrator largely outside cybernetic technology and whose narration is a testimony of feminist resistance to the posthuman patriarchy. What is clear in both narratives is that the scopic regimes that help organize their structure also aid in upholding and seemingly naturalizing gender binaries, rather than disrupting them (Ginway 2020, 29). It bears mentioning that cyborg theories that have originated in the Global North—be it Donna Haraway's cyborg manifesto that imagines female cyborgs as resistance to dominant power structures, or Rosi Braidotti's more recent New Vitruvian Woman (2013, 21) symbol as replacing DaVinci's enduring image that defined and normalized Northern conceptualizations of "the human"—do not fully translate in Mexico.

Moreover, the specular fictions treated here spur a reflection upon the other meaning of *género* in Spanish—that of genre. All these works link directly to literature codified as science fiction, which suggests that such a genre may be, if not a privileged space to think through the dynamics of contemporary visual practices, then one in which the speculative narrative framework—one based either directly or indirectly on a technoscientific rationalism—facilitates such contemplation more easily than others. After all, the etymological root of "speculative" ultimately derives from two Latin terms: *speculari*, meaning to observe, and *specere*, which means "to look at or view." These evolved into Old French's *speculacion*, meaning careful observation with intense attention, and then into one of its current meanings based on the notion of "intelligent contemplation; act of looking" (Harper 2001). Speculation based on hypothesis and extrapolation is obviously inherent to the creation of science fiction narratives, but this monograph suggests another possibility: speculation also inherently connects with the dynamics of vision, and therefore positions the genre to be naturally inclined toward registering and critiquing alterations occurring in the visual plane. Some will rightly point out that ocular themes do occur in realist literature in Mexico, although, with these narratives visual technologies associated with the e-image component is either wholly absent or sufficiently secondary as to be peripheral to the narrative's themes.[8]

Consensus on a definition within the genre of science fiction remains a quixotic quest. This rings especially true in Latin America where science fiction production has for decades remained under the shadow of the region's dominant speculative mode, magical realism (Ginway and Brown 2012, 1). What is more, countries in the region lack clear market segmentation compared to the North, which contributes to writers moving more fluidly between genres both in terms of publishing works across genres as well as hybridizing them. Most frequently, authors have melded science fiction with horror or the fantastic (Bell et al. 2007, 369), a syncretism which we see in the present study with *Punto cero* and "Ex machina." Darko Suvin's notion of "cognitive estrangement," which he sees as critical in underlying the formal framework of the genre (1972, 7), remains the most referenced starting point for scholars of science fiction in the

[8] There appears to be at least three groupings of specular literature without the e-image. First, male authors of non-speculative literature where the gaze is central, e.g. Juan Villoro's *El disparo de argón* (2005); mid-century author Juan García Ponce's "erotic literature" (Ochoa 434; Serur 53) in which he used cats as metonymic for the gaze—"El gato" (1984) and *El gato* (1974); Salvador Elizondo's experimental novel *Farabeuf* (1967) focuses on themes of the gaze, a photograph, and a fragmented narrative that attempts to "eternizar un instante mediante una imagen visual, aproximadamente del mismo modo en que la fotografía lo hace" (de Teresa 1996, 18) [capture/make everlasting an instant in time through a visual image, more or less in the same way a photograph does it]. Second, another more recent tendency that foregrounds the gaze as wholly absent, and where blindness and disability become central: Mario Bellatin's *Carta sobre ciegos para uso de los que pueden ver* (2017), and Guadalupe Nettel's *El cuerpo en que nací* (2011). A final type, related to what is sometimes referred as "Word and Image Studies," looks at the intermedial relationship between texts and images. Some examples include Mauricio Montiel's *La penumbra inconveniente* (2001), Pablo Soler Frost's *La mano derecha* (1993), and Daniela Bojórquez, *Óptica sanguínea* (2014).

region. But even this definition contains problems when examined closely—a point which is often elided in scholarly discussions on Latin American science fiction; as Simon Spiegal has astutely argued, Suvin's own definition suffers from internal inconsistencies, stemming from his misunderstanding and conflating the estrangement concept as articulated by two separate theorists: the Russian Formalist Victor Schklovsky and avant garde playwright Bertolt Brecht; Spiegal states that "the formal framework of sf is not estrangement, but exactly its opposite, naturalization. On a formal level, sf does not estrange the familiar, but rather makes the strange familiar" (2008, 372). To complicate the matter further, the term "speculative fiction" sometimes is used synonymously with science fiction, although consensus is even less consistent with its usage.[9]

My own preference for a categorical definition of science fiction finds useful Guillém Sánchez and Eduardo Gallego's designation (2003), whose clear, structural articulation accounts for the vast majority of texts: "La ciencia ficción es un género de narraciones imaginarias que no pueden darse en el mundo que conocemos, debido a una transformación del escenario narrativo, basado en una alteración de coordenadas científicas, especiales, temporales, sociales o descriptivas, pero de tal modo que lo relatado es aceptable como especulación racional" ("Qué es la ciencia ficción")

[9] In terms of a scholarly consensus and usage, "speculative fiction" is a term whose usage has yet to be settled upon. In the realm of writers, some authors use it as a way of identifying their work as distanced from the stigmatized label of "science fiction," as in Eve Gil when describing her work *Virtus* (see Chap. 4). Robert Heinlein proposed it as an ampler term to rechristen science fiction in the 1960s and 1970s. Mexican author Alberto Chimal sees the term as a "general [classification] that encompass[es] almost any narrative work that one wants to place in them as long as they incorporate the fantastic imagination in some way" (n.d., "On Latin American…"). Some scholars have suggested this is a useful umbrella term for "genre fiction that takes technological advances as its point of departure" (Castillo and Colanzi 2018, 8), although, as Emily Maguire has rightly pointed out, this approach "risks flattening out the different ways in which science fictional elements appear in these texts" (2021, 179). Andrew Brown uses it to describe his corpus in *Cyborgs in Latin America* as a way to signal novels with some speculative characteristics but are not necessarily codified as science fiction (2010, 3). Elizabeth Ginway employs it her recent monograph *Cyborgs, Sexuality, and the Undead: The Body in Mexican and Brazilian Speculative Fiction* (2020) to refer to science fiction, fantasy, and horror, broadly construed. To further complicate the matter, Alessandro Fornazzari appropriates the same term as the eponymous title his book (2013) in order to describe the culture industries in Chile as inextricably linked to economic transformations; speculative in this usage refers to stocks or property invested into a market that involve risk of gains or loss.

[Science fiction is a genre consisting of imaginary narratives that cannot happen in the world we know, due to a transformation of narrative setting, based on alterations of scientific, spatial, temporal, social, or descriptive coordinates, but such that that which is narrated is acceptable as rational speculation]. Suffice it to say, not all works from the region fit nicely under this definition. Some, such as those that pertain to indigenous futurism, are not always underpinned by rational speculation, in part because of a rejection of the Western enterprise of science altogether, thereby sidestepping the epistemological framework comprised by scientific knowledge production. In all, it is useful to note, as Silvia Kurlat Ares has done, that that no definition encompasses all works that fit under the category of science fiction, its aims or sensibilities, despite the apparent stable agreement on the term in the Global North. She writes that "discussions concerning the definition of sf have been a complex and unsolved matter *everywhere*" (2021, 5; emphasis in original).

Post-/cyberpunk

Related to this question of genre is why specular themes occur with some consistency in cyberpunk, as opposed to other variants or subgenres within science fiction. Both cyberpunk and post-cyberpunk are naturally inclined to engage with televisual and cybernetic visualities as part and parcel of their narrative contents, due to predisposition of their themes. Gerardo Porcayo, who many consider to be one of the subgenre's originators in both Mexico and Latin America, maintains in the anthology *Silicio en la memoria* [Silicon in Memory] that one main raisons d'être of Mexican cyberpunk is "el enfrentamiento de las nuevas generaciones a las ráfagas de los *mass media*" (1997, 7) [the new generation's way of confronting the flurry of mass media]. As the media increases in its economic power, political influence, and social prevalence—which begins to precipitously manifest itself in the 1990s—so, too, do the writers of cyberpunk science fiction take what often becomes metonymic of the mass media—the screen—as a critical object of narrative focus. Therefore, the employment of "Mexican Cyberpunk Literature" in the title of this monograph functions as much as a temporal marker as a description of the thematic content that characterizes the subgenre. As I discuss below, post-/cyberpunk continues to be produced in Latin America to this day. However, it should be noted that not all works of post-/cyberpunk contain visual themes as a leitmotif, but it is within this tendency of the country's science fiction that these specular narratives occur with such intensity, as the corpus under examination shows.

Beyond a temporal characterization of what constitutes cyberpunk in Mexico, it is worth considering what defines cyberpunk as a practice within Mexican science-fiction literary production. Much has been written on this topic by both scholars and authors alike and, within the country, the identification of cyberpunk and post-cyberpunk works has been relatively clear and without controversy. According to Frederic Jameson, in the Global North, cyberpunk is "the supreme literary expression if not of postmodernism, then of late capitalism itself" (1991, 419).[10] In the introduction to the anthology *Mirrorshades* (1988), often considered to be the manifesto for the movement, Bruce Sterling states that what characterizes cyberpunk is the way in which "technology is visceral…pervasive, utterly intimate. Not outside us, but next to us. Under our skin; often, inside our minds," and include traits such as "body invasion: prosthetic limbs, implanted circuitry, cosmetic surgery, genetic alteration…mind invasion: brain-computer interfaces, artificial intelligence, neurochemistry" (Sterling 1988, xiii). The body becomes rewired in its adaptation to the emerging cybernetic environ of the 1980s. From this emerges the hacker and/or cyborg figure that frequently embodies a rebelliousness toward the socio-economic and political milieu, which is frequently represented with the dominant multinational corporation. Hence the suffix "-punk," derived from the music rock subgenre and subculture movement that was countercultural to traditional values and lifestyles. The US cyberpunk movement effectively died in the late 1980s, but the literary aesthetic continued through the 1990s and onward—coming by then to be seen as post-cyberpunk. Some traits include a preference for quotidian or domestic narrative settings; the inclusion of mainstream or middle class characters; its attitude has an "adversarial relationship to consensus reality" (Kelly and Kessel 2007, xii) while not necessarily being punk anarchists; the singularity of a time when Artificial Intelligence will surpass humans in intelligence is still present—but without bringing about an apocalyptic end; finally, their use of literary form was more postmodern, self-aware, parodic, and playful (Kelly and Kessel 2007, xi–iv).

[10] Larry McCaffery's *Storming the Reality Studio: A Casebook of Cyberpunk & Postmodern Science Fiction* (1991) remains the paradigmatic exploration between cyberpunk and postmodern aesthetics—pastiche and collage, parody and play, the dissolution between high and low culture, and the simulacra and simulated life supplanting the real.

Like what happened in the United States in the 1980s, a cyberpunk movement took shape in Mexico in the 1990s that was quasi-formalized, self-aware, and self-labeled as such,[11] consisting of at least a dozen authors, all of whom were male. This movement began in the early 1990s in the Tecnológico de Monterrey where many of them studied, and formed the Real Sociedad del Zapato Verde [Royal Society of the Green Shoe] (Trujillo Muñoz 2000, 341). Stories with cyberpunk themes, whose roots can be traced back as far as 1984 with the works of Porcayo and José Luis Zárate, began appearing in fanzines like *Otra cosa*, *Fractal'zine*, *Azoth*, *La langosta se ha posado*, *Nahual*, *Sub*, *Complot International*, etc.; they also began winning national science-fiction prizes from Kalpa and Premio Puebla throughout the 1990s. *Silicio en la memoria*[12] is often cited as the anthology that solidified the movement by making explicit its formation, although José Luis Ramírez stated that there was talk of a movement several years before—around 1995 (n.d., "Cyberpunk…") Similar to the US counterpart in the 1980s, the Mexican cyberpunk movement began to wane as early as 1998, according to Ramón López Castro (qtd. in H. García 2018, 10–11), and was effectively over in the early 2000s.

What are some of the principal characteristics of Mexican cyberpunk? Hernán García's comprehensive and detailed work on the topic provides a solid starting point for recognizing its most recurrent themes, which help convey the contours of the subgenre's locality in Mexico. Some of its most recurrent motifs and settings include:

> [I]mágenes de tribus "pos-urbanas", drogas tecnificadas, edificios abandonados y vandalizados, territorios dominados por bandas, discotecas de ambiente negro enclavadas en un más oscuro barrio, mercenarios con prótesis letales, descomunales fiestas de hackers, prostitutas de carnes flácidas que compiten contra irresistibles *virtual girls*, y el entorno de la realidad virtual como vía de perdición. (2012, 334)
>
> [Images of "post-urban" subculture social groups, technified drugs, abandoned and vandalized buildings, territories dominated by gangs, discotheques as dark enclaves in an even darker neighborhood, mercenaries with

[11] However, Rodrigo Pardo stated that he wrote cyberpunk before becoming aware of the US movement, and José Luis Ramírez stated that this happened to many authors of this moment (n.d., "Cyberpunk: El movimiento en México").

[12] Another anthology, *Cuentos compactos: cyberpunk* [*Compact Stories: Cyberpunk*], was also published in 1997, but had fewer than half the number of stories compared than *Silicio en la memoria*.

lethal prostheses, enormous hacker parties, flaccidly-fleshed prostitutes competing against irresistible virtual girls, and a general environment of virtual reality as a road to perdition.[13]]

The bleak urban setting, disaffected and subalternized youth on the margins of society, along with a heavy presence of technology involving implants and virtual reality stand out in many narratives. Indeed, the character of the hacker and/or cyborg frequently appears in these stories, both of these incarnating archetypal protagonists in many Mexican cyberpunk tales. As H. García notes, their tone and resolution were most frequently apocalyptic (2018, 10).

However, despite cyberpunk's pronounced death (and also like its predecessor in the United States), the literary aesthetic of Mexican cyberpunk reemerged in the mid-to-late 2000s, showing both its contemporaneous relevance and staying power as a preferred mode of writing that continues to this day. There is no dearth of post-cyberpunk examples in Mexico's literary and cinematic production, as Hernán García demonstrates in "Hacia una poética de la tecnología periférica: Post-cyberpunk y picaresca 2.0 en *Sleep dealer* de Alex Rivera" (2017). In this article, he points out that this renewed interest in cyberpunk as an approach does not necessarily adopt the hacker or cyborg as a primary anti-hero, with settings that are less frequently those of obscure, dangerous streets in urban peripheries, nor is technology always an escape or trap. In its place, a fresher vision of the future exists, one with human values, and technology that can be used for achieving positive ends, as Rivera's film shows (García 2017, 330). This cyberpunk scholar is right to consider this part of science-fiction production in Mexico as post-cyberpunk, given both its temporal occurrence after the movement ended and its qualitative evolution as a genre beyond the corpus established in the 1990s. In this sense, cyberpunk continues to be written and published in some form to this day—in both Mexico and Latin America. The reasons for the continued production vary, but Chilean Jorge Baradit succinctly captures the rationale when he states that, at its core, Latin America *is* cyberpunk:

> Latin America, between modern and shamanic, with both democratic governments and old guerrillas still carrying out revolution, with narcoterrorist messianic leaders and ayahuasca. Cyberpunk, as the accumulation of technology rather than the replacement (obsolete technology living alongside cutting-edge technology), as the accumulation of cultures rather than the

[13] The translation is my own. Throughout the book, all translations are mine unless parenthetical references indicate otherwise.

> replacement (indigenous people and technocrats living alongside each other in the same spaces); cyberpunk as overcrowding and overpopulation, violence and ghettos of millionaires and the poor, the great economic interests managing governments, etc. (qtd in Kurlat Ares 2021: 15)

As this quote signals, a provocative discussion has sprung forth in recent years regarding the status and allure of post-/cyberpunk as a loosely construed, narrative framework. Even numerous Latin American authors from literary establishments, such as the ones from the McOndo and Crack movements, experienced widespread use of technology into urban life in the new millennium (de Rosso 2012, 322, González 2018, 214), prompting writers to incorporate into their narratives "science fictional elements in explicitly concrete ways" (Maguire 2021, 172). All of this means that including technoscientific devices—especially small electronic, cybernetic ones—into narratives becomes increasingly commonplace. The experience of everyday life has become intimately conjoined with the technoscientific, bringing about the technosocial. Since a significant portion of the population is becoming accustomed to being surrounded by and immersed in these technologies, then many Latin American people, including authors, are everyday inching closer to being cyborgs, if they are not already.[14]

In all, what links post-/cyberpunk to Mexico, and by extension, to Latin America, is an enduring ethos that corresponds to the region's contemporary social, political, and economic reality. Within that reality resides an abundance of screens from small to medium sizes whose number has precipitously increased in this timeframe, altering the everyday encounters of its subjects with an ever more technologically mediated experience that began in earnest in the 1990s (as demonstrated in section on visibilization below).

[14] It bears mentioning that the use of the term cyborg here refers to the narrower, more transhuman understanding of the term that refers to a hybridized coupling between the organic and cybernetic coupling. It does not take into account the much broader conceptualization proposed by critical posthumanism where the human is understood to be part of an assemblage that is constantly co-evolving with its environment that includes plants, animals, objects, bacteria, etc., and of which technology is but one element among many in its ecological surround. Further, there is the key question of whether or not one need have had a surgical operation with an apparatus like a pacemaker installed into their body to be a cyborg; rather, it is sufficient to consider one cyborgian given the subjective effects occasioned by constant use of a technology like a computer or smartphone.

Of course, these screens and the images they project have been mediating perceived realities well before the 1990s—with film being arguably the most noteworthy and impactful example throughout the twentieth century. But with television, which was first broadcast in Mexico in the mid-1940s and reached notable social presence by the 1960s, it is only in the 1990s that it achieved a near ubiquitous screen presence in the country. This was followed by computer screens in 2000s and smartphones in the 2010s; each device alters the visual field such that they form scopic regimes for each, becoming a hegemonic visual practice and forcefully appear in its post-/cyberpunk literature. But not all science fiction literature accords these objects the same value; some are, at best, secondary, while others are central and become narrative actants, as the comparison below demonstrates.

10 Crucial Years: Comparing Screens in Mexican Science Fiction

In order to clearly show what constitutes a specular fiction, let us consider two examples. Both have the same visual element present in their narrative—television—but one pertains to the specular category whereas the other does not; this is due exclusively to the narrative centrality conferred to the television screen. Ten years separate the publication of two Mexican science fiction short stories— Mauricio-José Schwarz's lauded "La pequeña guerra" ["The Little War"] and Francisco Amparán's lesser known "Ex machina" ["Ex machina"] published in 1984 and 1994 respectively—yet what they articulate about televisual technologies in Mexico, such as their increased proliferation and centrality in society, and the concomitant effects on the production of (imagined) subjectivities, could not be more divergent. Both utilize the television screen within their stories, but to markedly different ends. This difference not only illustrates a larger shift in thematic preoccupations of Mexican science fiction production from the 1980s to the 1990s, but it also correlates to socio-historical changes that occurred in the intervening decade. These factors are a part of a complex interplay with political-economic transformations that began in the early 1980s and culminated with the North American Free Trade Agreement (NAFTA), which reconfigured an important part of the Mexican media industry and increased the presence and usage of certain visual technologies, in particular that of television. Although this medium entered Mexico in the 1950s, the qualitative and quantitative shifts that happened from the 1980s to the 1990s manifest remarkably in the more recent "Ex machina" to show how television, along with the appearance of the video cassette recorder (VCR), become key markers of this transformation. In comparing these two stories, one finds that in the latter any distinction between the subject and object collapses. That is, by the mid-1990s the (human) subject has been fused into the (television) object, marking a qualitative shift in Mexican science fiction's engagement with televisual technologies. "Ex machina" articulates what Nicholas Mirzoeff would call "a new visual subjectivity" (2002, 10)—what I call a tele-visual subjectivity (see Chap. 3)—and pertains more broadly to a unique kind of literary text from this era that merits its own descriptor—specular fiction—whereas "La pequeña guerra" lacks any of these elements. To illustrate this difference, let us look in closer detail at how each story treats television.

In "La pequeña guerra," television is used as a minor and largely innocuous device within the confines of the home. In the story, the state mandates a radical solution to a social problem: in order to curb the boom in urban population of a city-turned-megalopolis and all its attending consequences, such as fewer essential resources like food and water, all ten-year-old children are required to participate in yearly gladiator games[15] as a way to maintain population control.[16] The story's young protagonist, Arianne, looks up from the fighting floor to see her father, Akira, who wonders early on if the training he gave her would be enough for her to win and survive; her mother Guinnivere nervously gasps at the thought of what is coming: her first battle. Outside the stadium, Arianne's eight-year-old brother Jünge is being cared for by his aunt and uncle at their house, where they sit around the television watching the event together. "Jünge

[15] While there are numerous differences between "La pequeña guerra" and the novel *The Hunger Games* by Suzanne Collins (2008), they share a very similar core conflict. This story is yet another example of Mexican science fiction narratively achieving what Universal science fiction would make globally popular some years later. Other examples of this include Eduardo Urzáiz's *Eugenia* (1919) coming before Aldous Huxley's *Brave New World* (1932), and Amado Nervo's "La última guerra" (1906) arriving well before George Orwell's *Animal Farm* (1945).

[16] The city is never mentioned by name, but Schwarz, born, raised, and living in Mexico City since the 1950s, had seen the immense problems brought forth by the massive internal migration of millions of the country's poor such that by the 1980s, the environmental effects were not only visible but breathable. The capital in this decade was considered one of the most polluted cities in the world, and in 1992, the United Nations declared it "the most polluted city on the planet" (Air Quality Life Index n.d.).

había deseado ir con Guinnivere y Akira a ver a su hermana, pero no se lo habían permitido. Ahora, sin embargo, en casa de sus tíos, la veía mejor que sus padres…En la pantalla, Arianne frunció el ceño y apretó las manos" (1991, 128) [Jünge had wanted to go with Guinnivere and Akira to see his sister, but they did not let him go. Now, however, at home with his aunt and uncle, he could her see better than his parents…On the screen, Arianne ruffled her brow and squeezed her hands.]. Here, the primary function of the visual technology reminds us of the literal definition of tele-vision—which means to see at a distance—by connecting viewers to the live event in real time and immersing them within it.

The television screen appears repeatedly throughout the story, always to shift between the narrative spaces of the stadium and the home, where Jürge and/or his extended family surround it. The first clear example here is "Jürge, fascinado ante la pantalla de televisión, miraba orgulloso la triunfante y tierna figura de su hermana […]" (1991, 130) [Jürge, fascinated before the television screen, looked on proudly at the triumphant and tender figure of his sister…]. After her second win, Jürge is eating dinner when suddenly "sin despegar los ojos del televisor, empezó a gritar triunfalmente ante la imagen de su hermana" (1991, 132) [without taking his eyes off the screen, he started to yell triumphantly before the image of his sister]. The function of the television in this story remains minor within the plot; it becomes a linking device between separate spaces and through which the narration travels. In short, the purpose it serves here largely reflects its major social function in the 1980s: television occupies an important place in the house where viewers watch it, thereby constituting a public, as well as a market. But in narrative terms, this seamless inclusion of the device in the story indicates how the medium remains, at most, secondary.

Fast forwarding 10 years to the publication of "Ex machina" by Francisco José Amparán reveals the markedly central position that the assemblage of television, which now includes video, has taken on in Mexico by the 1990s. Rather than being a minor element within the narrative, it becomes primary and pivotal. The story tells of a family that has recently ascended into the middle class due to the father, Roberto, obtaining employment at a maquiladora working long hours. Having entered into the new consumer society, his wife, Milagros, demands that they buy a new Samsung VCR which she saw while out shopping. Once purchased, the new VCR occupies the most privileged spot in the living room—just below the television. As the family quickly adapts to the new machine in the house, watching several movies on videocassette per day, a peculiar event happens: a man in a white suit with a hat and a mustache appears in multiple instances of different films being watched. First, the kids report the sighting, then the father, and soon, the neighbors also report having seen the same man in their own rented films. Milagros finally goes to complain to the videoclub owner, who readily dismisses her as if she was crazy. She eventually has a chance to watch a film on her own one Saturday afternoon while her family is away, and during one scene around half-way through, a man impeccably dressed in white appears wearing a stylish Panama hat. She suddenly realizes who he is: Rico, a lover of hers from 12 years ago before she met Roberto and had children. In a telanovela-esque turn, he says he has come to speak with her and offers to take her away—this time for good. Milagros hesitates, arguing that she cannot just leave her family and house and life in Chihuahua, and Rico looks around from the screen into her living room, stating: "Tu casa no es simple ni bonita sino ordinaria. Tu familia no es normal, es corriente. Y tú…tú no eres sencilla, sino aburrida: una aburrida ama de una casa ordinaria" (1994, 24) [Your house is not simple nor pretty but ordinary. Your family is not normal, it's average. And you, you are not simple, but boring: a boring housewife in an ordinary house]. With these words, Milagros realizes he is right, and, after he beckons her forth to the screen, "Milagros se acercó a la pantalla y sin titubear, extendiendo los brazos anhelantes, se introdujo en ella" (1994, 25) [Milagros approached the screen extending her eager arms and, without hesitating, she entered into it]—a fantastic climax.

In "Ex machina," the place of television is obviously fundamental to the narrative. Unlike "La pequeña guerra" from the previous decade, the television screen has become endowed with supernatural powers—a prime narrative actant. The screen not only fascinates and captivates, but ultimately consumes the subject into it—the story's *deus ex machina* of the title. Milagros's desire to own the VCR early in the story transforms into another desire to leave her routine life that eventually moves the plot toward its fantastic end. It merits pointing out that this impossible climax reveals an intermeshing between the science fiction genre and the fantastic, showing how "[science fiction] is often intertwined with other speculative forms in Latin America (most commonly horror and the fantastic)" (Bell et al. 2007, 4).[17] This ending shares much in common with Pepe

[17] The reasons for this include a) a lack of attention from the established literary centers in their own countries, which allows writers to ignore delineated boundaries of genre (Bell et al. 2007, 4), as well as b) market-driven causes, since literary genres are not as segmented or specialized as they are in larger markets like the U.S. or Europe, authors slide between and hybridize styles without regard to their borders (Gonzalez 2018, 212).

Rojo's *Punto cero* (see Chap. 3), both in terms of a similar climactic event and its irreal, inexplicable nature.

Beyond being the central plot event, the inclusion of this device in this manner signals larger shifts occurring in the Mexican media industries and the impact that these technologies have upon visual practices in the country, both aspects of which make this story a worthy example of a specular fiction. This type of literary text thematically reflects complex interplays between political, economic, and social forces unfolding in Mexico, which at the time of its writing are increasingly tied to global shifts. In this sense, "Ex machina" articulates some core neoliberal transformations that have occurred within the social and economic milieu of its characters, such as the rise in presence of the multinational electronics company, an increased presence and centrality of televisual technologies within private spaces, the growth of maquiladora employment along the border, an expanding Mexican middle class, and the concomitant surge in consumer society. What is more, with Milagros's disappearance into the screen, the story allegorically suggests the ways in which the centrality of these visual technologies has come to affect subjectivity in the country. This is to say that television possesses a vortex-like power around this time, signaling a new intensity in its presence and use. Finally, it bears underscoring how this story—and specular literature more broadly—not only mirrors these changes in its discourse, but also can be read as adopting and adapting new rhetorical strategies in an effort to compete with a social sphere that is becoming overrun with screens.

While some may argue certain families in the mid-1980s may have used television more prominently than others in the mid-1990s, due largely to the emerging presence of computer screens, one key data point underscores the likely validity of my claim that the television dominates in this period as a dominant visual practice of the nation. As I detail in the following section, approximately 75% of homes had televisions in the mid-1980s, whereas around 86% had them 10 years later. By comparison, computers were quite rare in the mid-1990s by comparison, as only 2% of families had computers in their homes (INEGI). As such, there is a clear dominance and centrality to TV as a visual technology and practice in this decade, one that notably increases in volume, presence, and centrality throughout Mexico in the last decade of the twentieth century.

One of the larger questions for Mexican Studies in the 2010s inquires as to how Mexico arrived to the where it is: a country plagued with systemic and persistent violence, feminicide, extremely high rates of crime, a sense of pervasive corruption and rampant impunity, generalized fear among the population, an almost universal distrust of authority, high levels of poverty, and a widespread sensation of social anomie, among others. The specular fictions that comprise this corpus contend with many of these issues in a variety of ways, although they do it through the lens of science-fiction literature. This study reveals that this particular strand of science fiction may also be a favored symbolic space through which to think through some important dynamics of visual culture. Literature shows how the social, economic, and political spheres aid in producing certain subjects, and does so in original, creative, and critical ways. In the case of the specular fictions treated here, they often address pressing issues *as* they are happening and, in some case, *before* the social sciences take up these topics as objects of study from which to collect data and analyze through their numerous disciplinary lenses. In a very real sense, these authors perceived alterations in the country's collective field of vision, and in some cases, anticipated key changes. To this end, the authors of this book's inquiry may be considered to belong to a type of organic intellectual (Gramsci 1971, 5) that sensed and critiqued alterations occurring in the country's field of vision as they were happening.

Visibilization in Mexico During Globalization

Expanding on a definition previously given, visual technologies are either media that have been created for the purposes of being seen or they are media that have the potential to enhance, extend, strengthen or intensify visual capabilities. Examples of this are the oil painting, photograph, film, television, and interfaces with the Internet (computers/laptops, tablets, smartphones), etc. Ian Heywood and Barry Sandwell have extended this description by stating that visual technologies are "the apparatuses and mechanisms that provide the conditions of the possibility of visibilization/s" (2012, 16), where visibilization signifies "the social and material conditions, machineries and processes that make different modalities of visuality possible" (2012, 15). The former does not occur without the latter. Put differently, visual technologies do not appear neutrally but are always the product of larger forces at work in the social, political, economic, and cultural milieu where these technologies appear.

Considering the above definitions, we can say that, for several decades now, the changes in the mode of visibilization brought about the volume, intensity, and kinds of visual technologies that have appeared in Mexico since the 1990s, ushering in significant transformations in their visual practices. This is seen most prominently in the proliferation of new technologies of television, computers, and smartphones, as well as the way in which the media industries have operated. As research on this topic has been plentiful, it is able to offer a rather detailed description of changes in the visual sphere. One of the first studies that reveals this is *Impacto del video en el espacio audiovisual latinoamericano* (1990), written by Octavio Getino. He and a group of researchers from Mexico, Cuba, Argentina, Brazil, Colombia, Peru, and Venezuela set out to study the extent to which visual technologies like video had impacted habits of seeing in cinema and television. What they found was that video cassette technologies, along with other communicational infrastructures such as satellite communications and cable television, had changed the audio-visual sphere in these countries more in the 1980s than in all the previous decades since the advent of film and television combined. The traditional practice of film in Mexico—which starts at the beginning of the twentieth century and its silent era, continues with the Golden Age (1930s–1950s) and continues with the reliance upon proven formula films such as *comedias rancheras*, *churros*, and *melodramas* of the 1960s–1970s—declined precipitously in the 1980s by more than 50%, and, as a result, numerous theaters closed their doors. Television, which has been in Mexico since the 1950s and had its own Golden Age in the 1970s–1980s (Sinclair 1999, 39), also began experiencing changes in the way it functioned industrially and in what images were displayed across its screen. Some of the major conclusions of Getino's study foresaw a growing influence of diverse audio-visual media as well as a tightened interrelation between the local cultural industries of the countries researched and those of the advanced industrial world (1990, 12), both of which proved to be true. A few years later, Nestor García Canclini and a group of researchers set out to map the contours of some of these changes by focusing on the Mexican cities of D.F., Mérida, Guadalajara, and Tijuana. The results were published in 1994 and titled *Los nuevos espectadores*. The study's objective was to produce a demographically clearer picture of these changes with the aim of seeing beyond the simple explanation according to which the introduction of video into the market was the cause for the decline in film-going. One surprising revelation was that more films were being consumed by Mexican spectators than ever before, just not in theatrical venues (1994, 14). This change in visual practices signals a monumental shift away from how films had been traditionally received in the previous half-century. From within the social science disciplines pertaining to urban anthropology and media studies, García Canclini's study focuses on the consumption habits of citizens in relation to film, thus defining an emphasis on spectators. By conducting interviews on the viewing habits of many different kinds of urban citizens from different age groups and socio-economic backgrounds throughout multiple cities, they were able to get a more granular picture at how cultural markets had been reconfigured and who these "new" spectators alluded in the study's title were. What both Getino's and García Canclini's studies showed is that, by the early 1990s, the traditional spectator of Mexico, who would go to the local movie theater with some frequency was giving way to a kind of spectator who increasingly watched films on video and on open-air broadcast through the television set at home. Just as the sci-fi story "Ex Machina" demonstrates, the rise of video with television as a central visual practice was eclipsing movie theaters and becoming *the* focal point of private spaces and the media industries, thereby cohering into a scopic regime.

Outside the scope of these important studies, however, are the dynamics at play in the political and economic (re)configuration of the country with regard to culture industries in Mexico, which have been instrumental in affecting and shaping these specular regimes. Put in the terms of visual studies, changes in visibilization have affected the visual sphere—in visual technologies and practices—which in turn alter the production of subjectivities. It is useful to remember, following Michael Hardt, that "subjectivity is not pre-given and original but at least to some degree formed in the field of social forces. The subjectivities that interact on the social plane are themselves substantially created by society" (1998, 148). Mapping how subjects have emerged from political and economic forces requires considering a broad array of structural adjustments in Mexico. Reacting to global pressures, particularly from the United States, the political economy enabled by the Mexican state in the 1980s and 1990s implemented changes across its institutions; these changes affected the ways numerous industries operated, including the media and telecommunications industries, both of which broadly denote television and information technologies. As detailed below, we see a marked transformation happening in the television industry starting in the early 1990s, which reins as the dominant visual practice throughout the 1990s and through the 2000s. Computers and their screens began to take hold in the 2000s, but they remained outnumbered by televisions in this decade; even by the middle of the 2010s, televisions still outstripped computers in presence. Around the start of the 2010s, however, smartphones appeared and spread with great force and velocity throughout the nation. By the end of this monograph's timeframe in 2014 when Guillermo Lavín published "Él piensa que algo no encaja", smartphones and computers were careening toward dominance, although still had not eclipsed television presence. The following section maps out some of the broader and most impactful changes to the media and telecommunications industries.

Transformations in the Media Industry

For television, three areas reveal where these changes have occurred: (i) the restructuring of the media industries within Mexico; (ii) a higher proliferation of images via an increase in programming; and (iii) the growth of the television market, all of which resulted in the television screen becoming so central as the main visual practice across Mexico and as key components of the specular literature treated here.

The restructuring of the television industry is the combined result of multiple factors. The major elements include: political legislation and privatization; reacting to the expansion of foreign oligarchic media companies (mostly from the United States) that crossed Mexican borders through multiple avenues; changes in internal administration and management; debt; the national peso crisis; and the appearance of new technologies. This is not the place to review of all these aspects in detail, but rather to examine the ones most pertinent to the changes in the images that crossed the screen in Mexico.[18] As such, any study of television must start with Televisa in 1973,[19] the monopolistic behemoth whose presence and growth went unchecked in the country and led to its being called "el quinto poder" [the fifth power] by the outspoken journalist Manuel Buendía in 1984, coining an expression that subsequently became eponymous title of a book of critical articles about Televisa in 1985. Unlike the

[18] For a comprehensive summary of both the US and Mexican culture industries, see *Televisión sin fronteras* [Television Without Borders] by Florence Toussaint (1998).

[19] However, it is useful to note that Televisa's origins go back to 1955 when Telesistema Mexico was founded by the linking of three television open-air stations; if one links it to its origins in radio, then that date must go back to the 1930s when Emilio Azcarrága Milmo opened a commercial radio station in Mexico City (Sinclair 1999, 34).

United States's creation of the Federal Communication Commission (FCC), an autonomous, non-governmental agency whose purpose was to monitor the industries and ensure that no monopolies developed, Mexico has lacked such an agency; despite writing into its constitution that radio and television open-air channels were considered a public good and should be regulated as such, in practice such regulation has largely been overlooked (Toussaint 1998, 175). As a result of this and other factors,[20] Televisa was able to grow into the largest media company in Mexico, as well as in Latin America.

The period between 1991 and 1993 saw a massive sea change in the television industry in this globalized era. Florence Toussaint has characterized the transnationalization of Mexican television as being constituted by a dual move, one with a centrifugal—or outward—force, as exemplified by Televisa's corporate strategies starting in the 1990s, and one with a centripetal—or inward—direction, led by foreign companies interested in staking a claim in that national market. First, Televisa's outward expansion to other national markets began in 1991 and ended several years later. In total, they had purchased ownership shares in a television company or related companies in Chile, Venezuela, and Peru, as well as a programming partnership deal with several stations in the Southern Cone and control of PanAmSat, a satellite it had helped launch in the 1980s (Sinclair 1999, 43). This outward move resulted in Mexico's telenovela being one of the most sold and viewed in the entire region, as well as being successfully exported to Europe and China. This strategy, whether related to NAFTA in spirit or not, is in keeping with a geo-linguistic conception of the region that led Televisa to view its potential market as not limited to the population of Mexico but rather to all of Spanish-speaking America—around 350 million people in the mid-1990s (Sinclair 1996, 26). The second move Mexico undergoes is a penetration *inward* to the country from foreign media conglomerates, especially from the United States. From the beginning, the culture industry in the United States grew separately around each new media, allowing them room exist distinctly until

[20] Toussaint lists a number of factors as to how it grew so large within Mexico, such as i) the cinematic industry was never strong enough to establish conglomerate links into other industries (as it did in the United States), ii) in spite of the occasional invention, like color television, the industry within Mexico was never large enough to establish a strong pattern of patenting, and was therefore forced to import technologies from the United States, iii) Televisa has had strong political ties to Mexico's post-revolutionary ruling party PRI and benefitted greatly from this relationship (1998, 173–175).

they grew large enough for certain industries to begin merging, such as cinema with television, cable with cinema, television with the news media, cable with satellite, etc. The 1980s saw these previous strategies of horizontal integration give way to vertical integration, a move which resulted in the creation of oligarchic corporations that came to exist through mergers that aimed to create multinational multimedia conglomerations. These are ABC-Capital Cities-Walt Disney, Time-Warner-Turner, RCA-NBC-GE and Fox-News Corp (Toussaint 1998, 45). These massive corporations sought to continue their expansion into other markets across the world and, of course, in the United States's adjacent and populous southern neighbor, Mexico.

It is absolutely essential, however, to understand that the that the active participation of the Mexican state allowed and enabled the larger shifts that occurred in the culture industries within Mexico, as it set up the legal framework that made these changes possible. Although NAFTA came into effect on January 1st, 1994, the movement toward neoliberalization in Mexico had begun as far as back as De la Madrid's administration in the early to mid-1980s. For example, during the first two years of his term (1982–1983), in an attempt to help restructure the country's growing debt and stemming from mounting pressure from the International Monetary Fund, the Baker Plan was put into place which allowed US investment in 101 Mexican industries, such as the production of automobiles, medicine, textiles, soaps, electronic devices, detergents, tobacco, hotels, etc. American companies such as Anderson Clayton, Purina, Celanese made from 80 to 500% profit, the majority of which went back to the United States (Agustín 1990, 83). In terms of the culture industries, Carlos Salinas de Gortari announced in 1990 that the government would privatize Imevisión, the state-owned open-air television station, which operated channels 7 and 13. This led to the purchase of the station which would become TV Azteca. Televisa finally had a competitor, but the monopoly that existed in Mexico up until then now became a duopoly, making clear that the only companies that could seriously compete and potentially survive in such an environment were oligarchies with transnational ties. TV Azteca's initial strategy was to begin importing programs rather than produce them, and Fox's "The Simpsons" and "The Nanny" were imported, broadcast, and became big hits in the country. The channel also partnered first with Telemundo and then directly with NBC, as well as its cable news network, CNBC (even though the deal eventually soured). It was the first time a national open-air channel in Mexico had such connections with one of the largest multimedia companies in the United States (Toussaint 1998, 143).

Along with a reconfiguration within the industry, which now had two large media companies competing, technological advances also helped change the visual sphere—particularly in the expansion of available programming through the emergence of cable television, along with the widespread adaptation of videocassette technology. Cablevisión, the cable subscription-based television company owned by Televisa as early as 1966, began to see competition from Multivisión, a company founded in 1989 in D.F. that came to combat and even surpass Cablevisión in audience share. Rather than a single cable station producing original content, it mostly rebroadcast other media's contents, eventually hosting up to 18 channels, the majority of which were from the United States and came to retransmit some of the shows from the networks of Fox, HBO, ESPN, Cartoon Network, Cinemax, MTV, CNN, TNT, and the three big open-air networks ABC, NBC, and CBS (Toussaint 1998, 156). The point to keep in mind here is that none of these were available in Mexico before 1990, and that as the 1990s pressed on, options flourished. The other technology that affected tele-visuality at this time was videocassette technology. Toussaint points out that in 1989 there were only 400 videoclubs in all of Mexico, and by 1991 that numbered had exploded to 10,500 (Toussaint 1998, 90). This number peaked around that year, along with the entry of Blockbuster Video, the then-dominant videoclub from the United States.

This shift from public to privatized television has increased dependence on imported programming, the majority of it coming from the US (Gorton 2012, 467). This has had the predictable result of a strengthened culture industry in both countries, with Mexico piggybacking off its influential northern neighbor. Several commentators on the subject have used the term "media imperialism" or called it the neo-colonial globalization of media (Sinclair 1996, 6; Toussaint 1998, 13). Indeed, such significant shifts were unfolding at all levels in the industry that, by 1997, TV Azteca had reached up to 36% audience share with only its two channels compared to Televisa's four. With this, it seems reasonably safe to conclude that the country's televisual sphere had undergone some drastic changes in its way operating, in the kinds of programs it produced, imported, and broadcast, along with the wide array of other (foreign) media companies with which it was partnered. In addition, another conclusion worth emphasizing is that the field of vision in this era comes to be based on entertainment above all else. Toussaint concludes that what the culture industries in both Mexico and the United States share in common is the tendency to "convertir el entretenimiento y la información para las masas en negocio. Maximizar las ganancias todo lo posible y reducir poco a poco las opciones que el público tiene de disfrutar programas realmente diferenciados. El resultado es una industria concentrada, oligopólica y de alcance internacional" (1998, 173) [to turn entertainment and information into a business. Maximize profits as much as possible and reduce the options that the public has to enjoy truly varied programming. The result is a concentrated industry, oligarchic, and of international reach].

In addition to the intricate shifts in the industry that initiate a qualitative change in the programming, there is also an increase in the presence of television sets in Mexico around this time. Put another way, the human sensorium of Mexican subjects experienced a heightening of audio-visual exposure in the 1990s. The percentage of television sets available in homes throughout Mexico attests to this. The census reported that in 2000, approximately 86% of the population had a television set in their homes (82 million of a total of 95 million); in 2005, this had grown to 91% (91 million of 100 million), and by 2010, 94% (103 million of 110 million) of those who took the census reported having one or more television sets in their homes. With this average increase in television ownership of 3–4% every five years, we should be able to retroactively estimate that in 1990, approximately 78–80% of the population owned televisions.[21] As such, increases of television ownership from 80% to 86% to 94% are shown to be steady and significant with each decade until it reaches near ubiquity throughout Mexico by the 2010s.

Numeralia, from the statistics department in the Universidad Autónoma de México (UNAM) in Mexico City, detailed a report in 2005 that offers a bit more granularity to the aforementioned statistics ("Televisión en…" 2009). Of the 31 states of Mexico, the ones with the higher concentration of urban areas had the highest incidence of homes with television (e.g. D.F. 97.7%, Jalisco 96%, Guanajuato 95%, etc.) and as they begin to decrease in urban population, the numbers notably descend (e.g. Yucatan 90%, Puebla 87%, Hidalgo 84.4%) until reaching the rural, largely indigenous populations where the decline is marked (e.g. Guerrero 79%, Oaxaca 69.6%, Chiapas 69.1%). Clearly, television's omnipresence is proportional to urban density, but still majoritarian in rural areas. These numbers help elucidate why television—along with related practices that affect

[21] I am subtracting 6–8% less from 2000s rate of 86% to get this number.

it, such as video, cable, satellite—has become such a focal point for the media industries of Mexico. It also explains the emergence of a televisual imaginary in the specular fictions studied here, especially in Chaps. 3 and 4.

Beyond this, there is another factor that adds a deeper, more material layer to the presence of televisions in the country: their production. Television assembly plants began relocating to Mexico in 1985 after the yen fell sharply, making the country an attractive spot due to the availability of cheap electronics manufacturing labor. By the end of 1987, Sony, Samsung, Matsushita, Hitachi and Sanyo had moved to Tijuana. By 1993, they had produced a total of 4,940,908 million televisions, two years later this figure reached seven million (Aguilar Benítez 1999, 218). By 1996 up to 16% of all maquiladora labor in Tijuana was dedicated to making televisions, reaching a production capacity of more televisions than any other city/country worldwide (Parfit 1996, 107). Asian multinational television producers changed the face of Tijuana's manufacturing sector during this decade by creating integrated complexes of assemblers and component suppliers ("San Diego/Tijuana…" 2004). Tijuana's manufacturing sector continued to grow through the turn of the century such that by 2009 it produced 16 million televisions; in 2010, over 27 million. All these data support why Tijuana earned the moniker "la capital mundial del televisor" [the world capital of the television set] (Cervantes 2010). This is especially relevant when it comes to Pepe Rojo's "Ruido gris" and *Punto cero* (see Chap. 3); when writing the novel, he lived in this border town with his wife and children. Several photos provide documentary evidence of how televisions have become a part of Tijuana's material foundation in a literal sense. Rogelio Núñez's photograph, "Untitled," in the 2006 book *Here is Tijuana!* shows how a makeshift layer of steps made from television sets appear to have become solidified into the landscape (2006, cover and 167). Pepe Rojo showed me some photos where he was looking inside the constructed art installation that is partially comprised of found-television screens, the whole piece bringing to mind the *rasquache* aesthetic (roughly translated as "making-do with what is at hand"). In a text he later published on Tierra Adentro's webpage, Rojo described this part of the work as such: "Arriba, el techo de uno de los pisos de la torre de Fernando [Miranda] es una especie de tragaluz construido con varios monitores de televisión ensamblados en forma de mosaico" (n.d., "La basura…") [Above, the floor of one of the floors of Fernando's tower is a kind of skylight constructed with several television monitors assembled in the form of a mosaic]. Televisions and Tijuana are deeply intertwined.

As televisions become dominant in the late 1990s and into the turn of the century, another visual technology begins to notably appear around this time: the computer screen, whose contextualization describes more fully the visual sphere in Mexico and lays the groundwork for the fifth chapter in this study. When polled by the National Institute of Statistics and Geography (INEGI), results showed that the percentage of respondents who acknowledge having access to a computer at home was markedly different over time than television: 2001: 11.8%; 2005: 18.6%; 2010: 29.8% (INEGI).[22] As with television, there no data for the 1990, which makes the only knowledge of presence of computer screens around that time an educated guess, likely around 5% or less. The reasons for this lack of statistical data in 1990 directly relate to Mexico's then restructuring of the science and technology sectors within neoliberalism. During the administrations of Salinas de Gortari (1988–1994), Ernesto Zedillo (1994–2000), and Vicente Fox (2000–2006), we begin to see incremental political attention paid to the status, organization, and development of science and technology in Mexico (Thirión and Espinoza 2006, 198). However, it is not until Fox's announcement of his "e-Mexico" plan in 2000,[23] and its implementation in 2002, that the seeds are sown to convert the semi-industrialized country into one whose economic and social formation can be based on information.

Unlike television, which became privatized, the e-Mexico initiative was catalyzed by the state. Its primary purpose was to provide broadband connectivity within the country by utilizing several related strategies, such as increasing citizen connectivity to the internet and providing online content and social programs that are relevant to the citizens, such as e-Health, e-Economy, e-Learning, and e-Government (López Dávila 2006, 2). The

[22] These statistics come from the survey "Hogares con equipamiento de tecnología de información y comunicaciones, según tipo de equipo, 2001 a 2019" on INEGI's website. It is worth noting that the statistics on computers with a connection to the internet at this time are markedly less: 2001: 6.2%; 2005: 9%; 2010: 22.2%; 2015:39.2.

[23] Vicente Fox announced: "Doy instrucciones al Secretario de Comunicaciones, a Pedro Cerisola, de iniciar a la brevedad el proyecto e-México, a fin de que la revolución de la información y las comunicaciones tenga un carácter verdaderamente nacional y se reduzca la brecha digital entre los gobiernos, las empresas, los hogares y los individuos, con un alcance hasta el último rincón de nuestro país" ("El Sistema Nacional e-México") [I have given instructions to the Secretary of Communication, Pedro Cerisola, to quickly commence the project e-México in order to ensure that the information revolution and its businesses have a truly national character, and they reduce the digital divide between the government, companies, home and individuals, with a reach that extends to every corner of our country].

larger purpose of this was to decrease the digital divide—which indicates a nation's overall ability to have access to information technologies, along with the knowledge of how to utilize them—in order to not fall behind other developed societies whose dominant economic and social organization was increasingly based on a proficiency with information technologies.[24] In other words, its purpose was to make Mexico a viable player of the new rules established in the information society. Consequently, it is not until the mid-2000s when some significant data about the connectedness of Mexico begins to appear.[25] As of 2006, Mexico was ranked 66th of 181 countries worldwide, and it was 15th in Latin America. To give this some perspective, the comparison between Brazil and Mexico can provide some clarity. According to the World Information Society Report, "In Latin America, Brazil and Mexico had the same household computer penetration of 18 per cent in 2005, yet in Brazil, 74 per cent of computers were connected to the Internet. In Mexico, only 9.4 per cent of homes had Internet access" (2007, 50). The rate of growth of internet connectivity in Mexico very slowly from 2002 to 2006, and most new users of the Internet accessed from outside the house in internet cafés (2007, 50).

The final screen at play in this monograph pertains to the smartphone.[26] From the outset, and at the risk of offering a banal explanation, this device merits distinguishing from its predecessor, the non-intelligent cellular phone that was used initially only to talk, and later included sending text messages; the smartphone connects to the internet and runs applications with impressive computing power for such a miniature size, offering a visual and tactile interface, often called a touchscreen. The haptic visuality

[24] Manuel Castells's authoritative trilogy of *The Information Age: Economy, Society and Culture*, comprised of *The Rise of the Network Society* (1996), *The Power of Identity* (1997), and *End of Millennium* (2000), has clearly influenced policymaking in many advanced countries.

[25] Irak López Dávila's "Information Society and e-Government: The Mexican Experience" aggregates a number of different data collection sets that help put into the view the reach of some of the government's efforts in the area of Information and Communications Technology (ICT). These sources include INEGI, the United Nations, the World Information Society Report, Network Information Center México (NIC-Mexico), Asociación Mexicana de la Industria Publicitaria y Comercial en Internet (AMIPCI), and the Mexican Internet Society.

[26] It is important to remember that smartphone usage pertains to an older history of non-intelligent cell-phone presence in Mexico. Cell phone ownership and usage began in 1990 with 64,000 subscribers and was mostly a practice of the upper classes, but by 2005 44% of the total population owned one (Bonina and Mariscal 2008, 65–66).

of the smartphone offers users unparalleled interactivity, and remains the heart of this device's ascendant sociocultural significance in the 2010s throughout much of the developed and developing world. In Mexico, the presence of this mini, mobile, and highly interactive screen sees a vertiginous increase in the 2010–2015 period. Consider that in 2005 smartphones had zero of the percentage of cell phone connections, in 2010 only 2%, and by 2015, 50–60% of all cellphone users owned a smartphone (Castells and Stryjak 2021, 5). Such celerity of market growth equates to rapid growth in screen presence among tens of millions of Mexicans both in urban and rural areas—a fact unparalleled in any other visual technology under discussion here.

In 1990, the state initiated a process of major reforms to the telecom sector, with its stated aims as modernizing the country-wide network, as well as opening the market up to international trade and foreign investors (Bonina and Mariscal 2008, 65–66). Here, again, changes made possible through legislation and by altering national and international laws in order to increase the informatization of Mexico, end up affecting visibilization by reshaping industries, technologies, and visual practices. In 2001, nine telecom competitors existed in the country, but half a decade later, less than half remained. By 2005, the market is overwhelmingly dominated by Telcel, a member of the Carso Group (a telecommunications and financial holding company established by Carlos Slim and his wife), which owns 75% of the market; its closest competitor is the Spanish company Telefónica Movistar, which holds 14%. As with the television industry of this time, the telecommunications market is open for competition but is effectively a duopoly. (Ibid., 66). These data become especially relevant when considering what informs and inspires some core aspects of Eve Gil's futuristic Mexico in *Virtus* (of Chap. 4), where Slim and the owner of Televisa become important characters. They also inform the final story under analysis in this study, "Él piensa que algo no encaja," by Guillermo Lavín, which metaphorizes the smartphone in the form of augmented reality glasses in order to critique how its overuse ushers in an era of "fake news."

Such impressive growth invariably causes ripple effects throughout the culture and inspires cultural texts. Let us consider José Woldenberg's column in the cultural magazine *Nexos* from April 2014 (Table 1.1), a creative, non-fiction text that registers the extent of the smartphone's impact in Mexico. It also takes the form of a list poem.

What begins with more banal observations of the media replaced by the smartphone—a watch, mail, camera, newspaper, etc.—turns back on itself

Table 1.1 The poem 'El iPhone es:' by José Woldenberg

El iPhone es:

- Teléfono, faltaba más.
- Correo.
- Mensajería.
- Reloj.
- Agenda.
- Cámara fotográfica.
- Archivo.
- Periódicos.
- Tienda.
- GPS.
- Calendario.
- Previsor del clima.
- Mapas.
- Cuaderno de notas.
- Cine portátil.
- Juegos.
- Videocámara.
- Rocola.
- Twitter.
- Brújula.
- Directorio.
- Internet.
- Sucedáneo del correo, la mensajería, el reloj, la agenda, la cámara, el archivo…
- Sombrero de mago.
- Acompañante.
- Camarada dócil.
- Terapia contra la soledad.
- Causa de la terapia contra la soledad.
- Un mundo en sí mismo.
- Enajenante, diría un mamón.
- Luciérnaga en el cine.
- Plaga en el teatro.
- Calamidad en los salones de clase, conferencias, mesas redondas.
- Pantalla hipnótica.
- Sustituto de la amistad.
- Diseño cuidado, esbelto, fino, mágico.
- ¿El fin de las conversaciones privadas?
- Chuchería en expansión
- Símbolo de status.
- Causal de divorcio.
- Obstáculo para la conversación.
- Como hijo único, aparato mimado.
- Heraldo de los nuevos tiempos.
- Libertad que atenaza.
- "Hermoso y maldito", diría Scott Fitzgerald.
- Tela de araña.
- Puente expedito.
- Como dormir, imprescindible.
- La cadena del perro, cuando la jala su amo.
- La cuerda del ahorcado.
- Trampa letal.
- Similar al abismo, a la nada, al vacío… cuando se pierde o descompone.
- "Lo de hoy".

The iPhone is:

- A telephone, of course.
- Mail.
- Messaging.
- Watch.
- Schedule.
- Photographic camera.
- Storage.
- Newspapers.
- Store.
- GPS.
- Calendar.
- Climate predictor.
- Notepad.
- Portable cinema.
- Games.
- Video camera.
- Jukebox.
- Twitter.
- Compass.
- Phonebook.
- Internet.
- Replacement of mail, messaging, clock, schedule, camera, storage…
- Wizard's hat.
- Companion.
- Docile colleague.
- Therapy against loneliness.
- Cause of therapy against loneliness.
- A world in itself.
- Alienating, an egghead would say.
- Lightening bug in the cinema.
- Plague in the theater.
- Calamity in classrooms, conferences, roundtables.
- Hypnotic screen.
- Substitute for friendship.
- Careful design, svelte, fine, magical.
- The end of personal conversations?
- Ever expanding gadget.
- Status symbol
- Cause of divorce.
- Obstacle for conversation.
- Like an only child, spoiled device.
- Herald of the new era.
- Liberty that tortures.
- "Beautiful and damned," Scott Fitzgerald would say.
- Spider web.
- Unobstructed bridge.
- Like sleeping, essential.
- A dog's leash, when pulled along by its owner.
- The rope of the hanged.
- Lethal trap.
- Similar to the abyss, to nothing, to the void…when it gets lost or breaks.
- "The latest thing."

to relate how this device has supplanted these real media in a process of remediation, or "by presenting themselves as refashioned and improved versions of other media" (Bolter and Grusin 2000, 15–16). In the latter half of the text where the metaphorical descriptions dominate, the centrality and impact of the smartphone on human subjectivity becomes clear in lines like "companion," "therapy against loneliness," "cause of therapy against loneliness," "a world in itself," "friendship substitute," "spider web," "like sleeping, essential," "a dog's leash, when pulled along by its owner." While it is clear that "hypnotic screen" is the description most directly aligned with some of the specular fictions treated in this monograph, the metaphors succeed in capturing the multitudinous ways in which the device has become the key visual technology in articulating the latest scopic regime of Mexico in the 2010s. This becomes very relevant for understanding the sociocultural and economic backdrop to the final story in this monograph, Guillermo Lavín's story "Él piensa que algo no encaja" which foregrounds virtual glasses as a metaphor for the smartphone. Published in 2014 (the same year as the list poem), the story offers a harsh criticism of the fake news that circulates on smartphones and social media apps, which bring about a post-truth state of affairs. As such, the story also signals a broader epistemological rupture, due in large part to the power of algorithms that have contributed to the perceived demise of a broadly shared consensus of basic truths regarding how the world and society functions.

Chapter Trajectory and Overview

The corpus under analysis here is grouped both chronologically and thematically. The impetus for keeping the works in this order is to demonstrate as discretely as possible how literary representations of vision and visual technologies have responded to alterations to the visual sphere over this relatively short, but dynamic, time frame (1993–2014). Beyond this linear presentation, each chapter presents a scopic regime, with the male gaze, televisuality, and the visuality of cybernetics (computers and smartphones) corresponding to each of the three main chapters.

In Chap. 2, the male gaze pierces through as the dominant marker of the visual regime. Porcayo's seminal cyberpunk novel *La primera calle de la soledad* (*PCS*) from 1993 takes on renewed meaning when comparing it to its sister story that appears in 1997, "Esferas de visión," which shares continuities of setting and characters in the same fictional universe. *PCS*'s discourse on gender—that of hetero-patriarchy—is significant enough to consider on its own terms (and remarkable in the way this aspect of the novel has gone uncommented upon for so long), but it comes into stark relief when considering its sister story published four years later. Both carry substantial themes regarding the eye and ocular prosthetic, with the gaze-as-male (in *PCS*) and lack of an eye as fundamental to female subjectivity in the story. The analysis begins by noting a contradiction in the novel where the male cyberpunk protagonist El Zorro obtains an ocular prosthetic after losing an eye, which endows him with the power to hack and resist the dominant powers of several multinational corporations that wish to enlist them into their ranks. The incongruity arises when considering El Zorro's prosthesis in light of Nicholas Mirzoeff's recent work on the history and meaning of the term "visuality." The protagonist embodies a "right to look," or countervisuality, which has traditionally been aligned with a feminist project. I argue that the gaze, when connected to a broader social imaginary in Mexico, reveals its transmedial nature, along with the widespread ramifications for gender relations. From here, Irmgard Emmelheinz's notion of the "spectacularization of femininity," which connects all females as subject to the male gaze under neoliberalism, helps to explain this phenomenon and links the science-fiction narratives under discussion to broader social and economic concerns. The focus then turns to "Esferas de visión" in order to analyze how female cyborgs are expressed in the same fictional world. This story presents a nameless, female, posthuman protagonist as traumatized from loss of her eye in the start of the story, for which trauma studies helps frame this interpretation. Following this, Sigmund Freud's repetition and compulsion aids in explaining the driving psychic force of her unresolved trauma. The female cyborg's permanent loss of an eye recalls Jacques Lacan's conceptualization of lack, along with its binary opposite, the phallus, as constitutive of subject formation. This theory serves to guide an understanding of the gender dynamics in both Porcayo narratives, with the female cyborg's lacking an eye as an *objet petit a* in "Esferas de visión," compared to *PCS*'s *phall*-ocular(prosthetic)centrism. In the end, when taken together both stories suggest that Mexican cyborgs do not transcend their biological sexes, as theorized by Donna Haraway or Rosi Braidotti, but rather that the characters are bound by them. It also intimates that technologies affect genders differently, endowing the male while incarnating the female as lack.

Chapter 3 examines a televisual scopic regime present in two key narratives by Pepe Rojo, whose work in the 1990s has come to be associated with the Mexican cyberpunk movement. His narratives, consisting of the now classic short story "Ruido gris" (1996) and his lesser studied novel first published in 2000, *Punto cero* (2012), present a televisuality—as opposed to virtual reality—as a dominant feature of the optical regime during the last half of the decade. To do this, a discussion is necessary to understand how NAFTA affected the television industry by ushering in an era of ratings from the Nielsen Company of the United States, privatizing the long-standing public broadcast station, installing a duopoly between Televisa and TV Azteca, which in turn increased competition of hyperviolent, reality television shows. The similarities between actual 90s shows and the fictional one in Rojo's story illuminates and critiques these processes via a metaphorized, near-future dystopia set in a megalopolis where ocular journalists receive payment for seeking and filming acts of aggression and gratuitous violence—in order to be broadcast. Another factor is at play, one which goes beyond interpreting the strong elements in this story that indicate social anomie, alienation, and a loss of identity; my reading argues that Rojo posits something more than these problems: he is suggesting that the posthuman subject's body is en route to disappearing due to an increase in presence and massive proliferation of screens in the neoliberal period. His little-known essay, "Tócame, estoy enfermo," informs both narratives and shows the influence on the author's thinking of European postmodern thinkers like Paul Virilio, Jean Baudrillard, and Slavoj ŽiŽek, among many others. He follows the notion in vogue in the 1990s to assert that the end of the human in the posthuman equates to the obsolescence of the body (performance artists Stelarc is a notable example). Gore is another way to point to the body in decline in the story, which brings about an engagement with Sayak Valencia's recent conceptualization of hegemonic modes of perception that are implicit in hyperviolence and its mediatic consumption. Moving on to *Punto cero*, Rojo engages with the private sphere of one's living space in order to highlight the psycho-social effects of television news programs. I discuss how televisuality pervades the entire narrative, even becoming part of its formal innovation, by incorporating symbols and signposting into its narration. Mis-identifications of one's self-image and bodily dis-locations present in the narrative evoke a Lacanian reading, which in turn prompts a review of the substantial influence that the French psychoanalyst has had on Rojo's life and writings. Finally, the novel also presents what Anne Friedberg characterized as "detemporalized subjectivities" in order to explain how visual media of film and television increasingly manipulate and reconfigure one's subjective experience of time, resulting in the primary cause of what Frederic Jameson characterized as a loss of historicity as a hallmark of the postmodern condition.

For Chap. 4, a cybernetic scopic regime appears in Eve Gil's *Virtus* (2008) and Guillermo Lavín's short story "Él piensa que algo no encaja" (2014). Gil's novel abounds with visual motifs, but the analysis here anchors upon the figure of President Wagner, along with the virtualized social sphere of the futuristic Mexico. Wagner's extreme good looks, his association with celebrity culture and telenovelas, and his being replaced by his hologram double after his physical death, make the novel an ideal specular fiction. Given that the fictional president shares an uncanny likeness with real-life President Enrique Peña Nieto, who was elected to office in 2012, especially his telegenic nature, a comparison reveals numerous similarities. Several Mexican media critics labelled Peña Nieto a "telepresident" with a reality-show administration, prompting a review of the history and context of political marketing in contemporary Mexico in order to help us understand how political power came to rely upon the rapid expansion of moving audio-visual image. From here, I compare the social plane described in Gil's dystopia to Guy Debord's *Society of the Spectacle* (1968); it is a place inundated with images, celebrity culture, advertising, etc. such that capital, in the form of an image, becomes a social relation among people—one suffused with capital, fetishization, and alienation. However, *Virtus* also updates Debord's theory to account for its evolution in the second half of the twentieth century, one which involves a hypermediated realm of megaspectacles and interactive spectacle. The second story treated is "Él piensa que algo no encaja" (2014) due to its visual technology of "virtual glasses," which are spectacles that enhance the users' field of vision such that nothing negative is visible: no trash on the streets, poverty has been eradicated, ugly people appear attractive, etc. These little, mobile, audio-visual technologies render the viewable world utopian and signal class difference. I read these devices as metaphorizing the rapid entrance and rise of the smartphone into Mexican society. These devices, along with the addictive social media apps like Facebook and Twitter, have been instrumental in bringing about the rise and viral circulation of fake news; this pernicious political and social phenomenon appears to the main character in the story after he himself is shot and paralyzed but can find no mention of event in news coverage about the shooting. As such, the story suggests how smartphones have contributed to a post-truth milieu in the 2010s. Lavín's virtual glasses confirm bias and legitimate an ideological perspective—that of the Mexican bourgeoisie of late neoliberalism—producing a distorted world in a pleasurable enough way such that one not need to engage with the world and try to change it.

This book aims to intervene in various fields. My monograph brings attention to a period and aesthetic of literary production in Mexico—cyberpunk and post-cyberpunk—that has not received enough scholarly attention to date within Science Fiction Studies of the region of Latin America. It builds upon what has been analyzed in order to give a fuller and more complete understanding of its inclinations and articulations. In this way, my monograph reinterprets brings forth frequently overlooked novels and stories and resituates them under various critical frameworks and approaches offered by visual culture studies, television and media studies, Global Studies and the effects wrought by neoliberalism. Within Mexican Studies, it carves out a unique and original space by focusing exclusively on a science fiction literary corpus whose principal thematic concerns center around the visual realm (of the e-image)—an area often considered antithetical to writing and textuality. During the past 20 years, a good deal of attention has been given in visual culture in Mexico, prompting prompted the emergence of an ample body of scholarship that has attended almost exclusively to the production of artefacts within the visual arts, such as photography, film, painting, digital images, etc. (Sánchez Prado 2011). However, this monograph foregrounds authors whose exclusively textual works capture these shifts as they are unfolding in the country. As such, this study highlights how these works register the impacts of visual technologies in innovative ways, by either making visual elements the rhetorical and thematic foci of their narratives, or by mimicking the subjective effects brought about these technologies and integrating them into their narrative discourse. These works do this in order to compete with a social plane where the electronic screen, along with its moving audio-visual image, is ascending toward dominance throughout much of society. In other words, there exists a kind of rivalry between the screen and the page in which the page absorbs the presence and effects of the screen in order to vie for its continued relevance. For this reason, my monograph also brings to visual culture studies what is often overlooked in the frame of analysis: visual objects and technologies represented through literary expression. The visceral, engaging, and critical nature of these texts deserve further scrutiny due in part to the urgency of their expressions, which in retrospect can now be read as speaking to the present of the country in the 1990s through the 2010s. However, it is worth mentioning that this monograph also adds to the Literary Studies in several ways, given numerous close readings, many of which are informed by literary theory. Finally, this investigation dialogues with Gender Studies in the country, given the way in which the materialization of new scopic regimes necessarily implicates gender and the gaze.

Works Cited

Abraham, Carlos, ed. 2013. *Cuentos fantásticos argentinos del siglo XIX*. Madrid: La biblioteca del laberinto.

Aguilar Benítez, Ismael. 1999. La flexibilidad como estrategia frente a la rotación de personal en la industria maquiladora del televisor. *Estudios Sociológicos* 17 (49): 215–237.

Agustín, José. 1990. *Tragicomedia mexicana: 3. La vida en México de 1982 a 1994.* México: Planeta.

Air Quality Life Index. n.d. Mexico City: ProAire (1990). https://aqli.epic.uchicago.edu/policy-impacts/mexico-city-proaire-1990/. Accessed 16 August 2022.

Amparán, Francisco. 1994. Ex machina. In *Más allá de lo imaginado III: antología de ciencia ficción mexicana*, ed. Frederico Schaffler González, 14–25. México, DF: Consejo Nacional para la Cultura y las Artes.

Bell, Andrea, Miguel Ángel Fernández-Delgado, Elizabeth Ginway, Yolanda Molina-Gavilán, Luis Pestarini, and Juan Carlos Toledano Redondo. 2007. Chronology of Latin American Science Fiction, 1775–2005. *Science Fiction Studies* 34 (3): 369–431.

Bellatin, Mario. 2017. *Carta sobre los ciegos para uso de los que pueden ver*. México, DF: Alfaguara.

Bojórquez, Daniela. 2014. *Óptica sanguínea*. Consejo Nacional Para La Cultura y Las Artes, Dirección General De Publicaciones.

Bolter, David, and Richard Grusin. 2000. *Remediation: Understanding New Media*. Cambridge, MA: MIT Press.

Bonina, Carla, and Judith Mariscal. 2008. Mobile Communication in Mexico: Policy and Popular Dimensions. 2008. In *Handbook of Mobile Communication Studies*, ed. James Katz, 65–78. Cambridge, MA: MIT Press.

Braidotti, Rosi. 2013. *The Posthuman*. Cambridge: Polity Press.

Brea, José Luis. 2010. *Las tres eras de la imagen: Imagen-materia, film, e-image*. Madrid: Akal.

Brown, J. Andrew. 2010. *Cyborgs in Latin America*. New York: Palgrave Macmillan.

Bull, Michael, Paul Gilroy, David Howes, and Douglas Kahn. 2006. Introducing Sensory Studies. *Senses and Society* 1 (1): 5–7.

Butler, Judith. 1990. *Gender Trouble: Feminism and the Subversion of Identity*. New York, NY: Routledge.
Capanna, Pablo. 2007. *Ciencia ficción, utopía y mercado*. Buenos Aires: Puerto de Palos.
Castells, Manuel. 1996. *The Rise of the Network Society*. Malden, MA: Blackwell.
———. 1997. *The Power of Identity*. Malden, MA: Blackwell.
———. 2000. *End of Millennium*. Oxford: Blackwell Publishers.
Castells, Pau, and Jan Stryjak. 2021. Country Overview: Mexico. GSMA Association. https://www.gsma.com/latinamerica/wp-content/uploads/2016/06/report-mexico2016-EN.pdf.
Castillo, Deborah, and Liliana Colanzi. 2018. Introduction: Animals That from a Long Way Off Look Like Flies. In *Latin American Speculative Fiction*, ed. Debra Castillo and Liliana Colanzi, 7–13. Vashon Island, WA: Paradoxa.
Cervantes, Sandra. 2010. Tijuana apantalla como capital de la TV. El economista.com. https://www.eleconomista.com.mx/empresas/Tijuana-apantalla-como-capital-de-la-TV-20101116-0100.html.
Chimal, Alberto. 2018. On Latin American Speculative Fiction. *Latin American Literature Today*. https://latinamericanliteraturetoday.org/2018/05/latin-american-speculative-fiction-alberto-chimal/.
Collins, Suzanne. 2008. *The Hunger Games*. New York: Scholastic Press.
Dalton, David. 2018. *Mestizo Modernity: Race, Technology, and the Body in Post-Revolutionary Mexico*. Gainesville, FL: University of Florida Press.
———. 2023. *Robo Sacer: Necroliberalism and Cyborg Resistance in Mexican and Chicanx Dystopias*. Nashville, TN: Vanderbilt University Press.
Davies, William, and Sarah Kember. 2018. *Economic Science Fictions. Economic Science Fictions*. Cambridge, MA: The MIT Press.
Diccionario de la lengua española. 2001. Especular. In *Diccionario de la lengua española*, 976. Madrid: Editorial Espasa Calpe.
Elizondo, Salvador. 1967. *Farabeuf o, la crónica de un instante*. México: Joaquín Mortiz.
Flood, Alison. 2009. Philip Roth Predicts Novel Will Be Minority Cult within 25 Years. *The Guardian*, October 26. https://www.theguardian.com/books/2009/oct/26/philip-roth-novel-minority-cult.
Fornazzari, Alessandro. 2013. *Speculative Fictions: Chilean Culture, Economics, and the Neoliberal Transition*. Pittsburgh, PA: University of Pittsburgh Press.
García, Hernán. 2012. Tecnociencia y cibercultura en México: Hackers en el cuento cyberpunk mexicano. *Revista Iberoamericana* 78 (238): 329–348.
———. 2017. Hacia una poética de la tecnología periférica: Post-cyberpunk y picaresca 2.0 en *Sleep dealer* de Alex Rivera. *Revista Iberoamericana* 83 (259–260): 327–344. https://doi.org/10.5195/reviberoamer.2017.7503.
———. 2018. Texto y contexto del cyberpunk mexicano en la década del noventa. *Alambique. Revista académica de ciencia ficción y fantasía / Jornal acadêmico*

de ficção científica e fantasía 5 (2). Article 5. https://doi.org/10.5038/2167-6577.5.2.5. https://digitalcommons.usf.edu/alambique/vol5/iss2/5.

García Canclini, Néstor, and Déborah Holtz. 1994. *Los nuevos espectadores: cine, televisión, y video en México*. México, DF: IMCINE, Consejo Nacional para la Cultura y las Artes, Dirección General de Publicaciones.

Getino, Octavio. 1990. *Impacto del video en el espacio audiovisual latinoamericano*. Lima, Perú: Instituto Para América Latina.

Gil, Eve. 2008. *Virtus*. México, DF: Jus.

Ginway, Elizabeth. 2020. *Cyborgs, Sexuality, and the Undead: The Body in Mexican and Brazilian Speculative Fiction*. Nashville, TN: Vanderbilt University Press.

Ginway, Elizabeth, and J. Andrew Brown. 2012. *Latin American Science Fiction: Theory and Practice*. New York: Palgrave Macmillan.

González, Maielis. 2018. Latin America and Cyberpunk: Notes Toward a Poetics of the Subgenre on Our Continent. In *Latin American Speculative Fiction*, ed. Debra Castillo and Liliana Colanzi, 211–231. Vashon Island, WA: Paradoxa.

Gorton, Kirstin. 2012. Television as a Global Visual Medium. In *The Handbook of Visual Culture*, ed. Ian Heywood, Barry Sandywell, Michael Gardiner, Nadarajan Gunalan, and Catherine M. Soussloff, 464–479. London: Berg.

Gramsci, Antonio. 1971. In *Selections from the Prison Notebooks of Antonio Gramsci*, ed. Quintin Hoare and Geoffrey Nowell-Smith. New York: International Publishers.

Hardt, Michael. 1998. The Global Society of Control. *Discourse* 20 (3): 139–152.

Harper, Douglas. 2001. Online Etymology Dictionary. https://www.etymonline.com/.

Heywood, Ian, and Barry Sandwell. 2012. Critical Approaches to the Study of Visual Culture: An Introduction to the Handbook. In *The Handbook of Visual Culture*, ed. Ian Heywood, Barry Sandywell, Michael Gardiner, Nadarajan Gunalan, and Catherine M. Soussloff, 1–56. London: Berg.

Instituto Nacional de Estadística y Geografía (INEGI). 2015. *Instituto Nacional de Estadística y Geografía (INEGI)*. https://www.inegi.org.mx/programas/dutih/2019/default.html#Tabulados. Accessed 8 May 2015.

Jameson, Fredric. 1991. *Postmodernism, or, the Cultural Logic of Late Capitalism*. Durham, NC: Duke University Press.

Jay, Martin. 1988. Scopic Regimes of Modernity. In *Vision and Visuality*, ed. Hal Foster, 3–23. Seattle, WA: Bay Press.

Kelly, James P., and John Kessel. 2007. Hacking Cyberpunk. In *Rewired: The Post-Cyberpunk Anthology*, ed. James Patrick Kelly and John Kessel, vii–xv. San Francisco, CA: Tachyon Publications.

Kurlat Ares, Silvia. 2021. Science Fiction in Latin America: Reading a Hidden Landscape. In *Peter Lang Companion to Latin American Science Fiction*, ed. Silvia Kurlat Ares and Ezequiel de Rosso, 3–17. New York: Peter Lang.

Lavín, Guillermo. 2014. El piensa que algo no encaja. In *Futuros por cruzar: Cuentos de ciencia ficción de la frontera México-Estados Unidos*, ed. Gabriel Trujillo, 125–132. México: Universidad Autónoma de Baja California.

Le Guin, Ursula K. 1976. *The Left Hand of Darkness*. New York: Ace Books.

López Dávila, Irak. 2006. Information Society and e-Government the Mexican Experience. INFOTEC, Federal Government of Mexico. https://www.itu.int/osg/spu/digitalbridges/materials/davila_paper.pdf.

López Martín, Lola. 2011. (Fanta)ciencia ficción hispanoamericana: teoría y definición del género. In *Lo fantástico en Hispanoamérica*, ed. Alton Honores and Pampa Polga Arán, 95–115. Cuerpo de la metáfora: Lima.

López-Lozano, Miguel. 2008. *Utopian Dreams, Apocalyptic Nightmares: Globalization in Recent Mexican and Chicano Narrative*. West Lafayette, IN: Purdue University Press.

de los Ríos, Valeria. 2011. *Espectros de luz*. Santiago de Chile: Editorial Cuarto Propio.

Maguire, Emily. 2021. From Technological Realism to the Science-Fictional Turn in Latin American Literature (1985–2017). In *Peter Lang Companion to Latin American Science Fiction*, ed. Silvia Kurlat Ares and Ezequiel de Rosso, 169–181. New York: Peter Lang.

Marecek, Jeanne, Mary Crawford, and Danielle Popp. 2004. On the Construction of Gender, Sex, and Sexualities. In *The Psychology of Gender*, ed. Alice Hendrickson, Anne Beall, and Robert J. Sernberg, 192–216. New York: Guilford Press.

McCaffery, Larry. 1991. *Storming the Reality Studio: A Casebook of Cyberpunk and Postmodern Science Fiction*. Durham, NC: Duke University Press.

McLuhan, Marshall. 1964. *Understanding Media: The Extensions of Man*. New York: McGraw Hill.

Metz, Christian. 1982. *The Imaginary Signifier: Psychoanalysis and the Cinema*. Trans. Celia Britton, Annwyl Williams, Ben Brewster, and Alfred Guzzetti. Bloomington, IN: Indiana University Press.

Mirzoeff, Nicholas. 1999. *Introduction to Visual Culture*. London: Routledge.

———. 2002. The Subject of Visual Culture. In *The Visual Culture Reader*, ed. Nicholas Mirzoeff, 3–101. London: Routledge.

Mitchell, W.J.T. 2002. There Are No Visual Media. In *The Visual Culture Reader*, ed. Nicholas Mirzoeff, 86–101. London: Routledge.

Montiel, Mauricio. 2001. *La penumbra inconveniente*. Barcelona: El Acantilado.

Nettel, Guadalupe. 2011. *El cuerpo en que nací*. Barcelona: Anagrama.

Núñez, Rogelio. 2006. Untitled. In *Here is Tijuana!* ed. Fiamma Montezemolo, Rene Peralta, and Heriberto Yépez. London: Black Dog Pub.

Ong, Walter. 1991. The Shifting Sensorium. In *The Varieties of Sensory Experience: A Sourcebook in the Anthropology of the Senses*, ed. David Howes, 25–30. Toronto: University of Toronto Press.

Parfit, Michael. 1996. Tijuana and the Border: Magnet of Opportunity. *National Geographic*, 94–107, August, 1996.
Porcayo, Gerardo. 1993. *La primera calle de la soledad*. México, DF: Consejo Nacional para la Cultura y las Artes.
———. Esferas de visión. 1997. *Silicio en la memoria*. Mexico City, Mexico: Ramon Llaca y Cía.
Potter, Sara Anne. 2013 Disturbing Muses: Gender, Technology and Resistance in Mexican Avant-Garde Cultures. PhD diss., Washington University.
Ramírez, José Luis. n.d. Cyberpunk: El movimiento en México. *Ciencia ficción mexicana*. http://comunidades.com.mx/cfm/?cve=11:09.
Rojo, Pepe. 1996. Ruido gris. México, DF: Universidad Autónoma Metropolitana.
———. 2012. *Punto cero*. México, DF: Editorial Resistencia.
———. n.d. La basura es un punto de vista. tierraadentro.cultura.gob.mx. Conaculta. https://www.tierraadentro.cultura.gob.mx/la-basura-es-un-punto-de-vista/.
de Rosso, Ezequiel. 2012. La línea de sombra: Literatura latinoamericana y ciencia-ficción en tres novelas contemporáneas. *Revista Iberoamericana* 78 (238): 311–328. https://doi.org/10.5195/reviberoamer.2012.6902.
San Diego/Tijuana Manufacturing in the Information Age: Charts. 2004. San Diego Dialogue. http://www.sandiegodialogue.org/cb_research.htm. Accessed 7 April 2014.
Sánchez, Guillém, and Eduardo Gallego. 2003. ¿Qué es la ciencia ficción? *Sitio de Ciencia-Ficción*. com. https://www.ciencia-ficcion.com/opinion/op00842.htm.
Sánchez Prado, Ignacio. 2011. Estrategias para mirar la nación. El giro visual de los estudios culturales mexicanos en lengua inglesa. *Mexican Studies/Estudios Mexicanos* 27 (2): 449–469.
Schwarz, Mauricio-José. 1991. La pequeña guerra. In *Escenas de la realidad virtual*, 127–136. México, DF: Claves Latinoamericanas.
Sinclair, John. 1996. Mexico, Brazil, and the Latin World. In *New Patterns in Global Television: Peripheral Vision*, ed. John Sinclair, Elizabeth Jacka, and Stuart Cunningham, 21–35. Oxford: Oxford University Press.
———. 1999. *Latin American Television: A Global View*. Oxford: Oxford University Press.
Sobchack, Vivian. 1994. The Scene of the Screen: Envisioning Cinematic and Electronic 'Presence'. In *Materialities of Communication*, ed. Hans Ulrich Gumbrecths and K. Ludwig Pfeiffer, 83–106. Stanford, CA: Stanford University Press.
Soler Frost, Pablo. 1993. *La mano derecha: (novela con fotografías)*. México, DF: J. Mortiz.
Spiegal, Simon. 2008. Things Made Strange: On the Concept of "Estrangement" in Science Fiction Theory. *Science Fiction Studies* 35 (3): 369–385.

Sterling, Bruce. 1988. *Mirrorshades: The Cyberpunk Anthology*. New York: Berkley Pub. Group.

Suvin, Darko. 1972. On the Poetics of the Science Fiction Genre. *College English* 34 (3): 372–382.

Televisión en México. 2009. *Bien común, Numeralia* (Portal de estadística universitaria de UNAM) 170 (February): 7–10. http://www.fundacionpreciado.org.mx/biencomun/bc170/Numeralia.pdf. Accessed 20 November 2014.

de Teresa, Adriana. 1996. *Farabeuf: escritura e imagen*. México, DF: Universidad Nacional Autónoma de México, Coordinación de Humanidades, Dirección General de Publicaciones.

Thirión, Jordy, and Rubén Espinoza. 2006. Changing Patterns in Mexican Society and Technology Policy (1990-2003): Still Far from Economic Development. In *Changing Structure of Mexico: Political, Social, and Economic Prospects*, ed. Laura Randall, 197–210. New York: M.E. Sharpe.

Toussaint, Florence. 1998. *Televisión sin fronteras*. México, DF: Siglo VeintiunoEditores.

Trujillo Muñoz, Gabriel. 2000. *Biografías del futuro: La ciencia ficción mexicana y sus autores*. Mexicali: Universidad Autónoma de Baja California.

Tunis, Courtney. 2007. "scopic, vocative." *Theories of Media: Keyword Glossaries*. The University of Chicago. https://csmt.uchicago.edu/glossary2004/scopic-vocative.htm. Accessed 10 June 2021.

Villoro, Juan. 2005. *El disparo de argón*. Barcelona: Editorial Anagrama.

Winthrop-Young, Geoffrey. 1994. Undead Networks: Information Processing and Media Boundary Conflicts in Dracula. In *Literature and Science*, ed. Donald Bruce and Anthony Purdy, 105–125. Amsterdam: Rodopi.

Woldenberg, José. 2014. El iPhone. *Nexos*. April 1. https://www.nexos.com.mx/?p=19944. Accessed 13 June 2021.

World Information Society Report. 2007. *Beyond WSIS*, 3. https://www.itu.int/osg/spu/publications/worldinformationsociety/2007/WISR07_full-free.pdf. Accessed 9 May 2015.

CHAPTER 2

Where is my Eye? Gendered Cyborgs, the Male Gaze, and Lack in *La primera calle de la soledad* [*The First Street of Solitude*] and "Esferas de visión" ["Spheres of Vision"]

> La mirada masculina maltrata a los cuerpos femeninos, [que] puede ser vinculado con la realidad. Libia Brenda[1]
>
> [The male gaze mistreats feminine bodies, which can be linked to reality.]

No other author in Mexico represents science fiction literature, especially cyberpunk, as boldly or enthusiastically as Gerardo Porcayo. One of its first practitioners and most ardent proponents, his involvement in the subgenre dates back to the late 1980s and continues in one form or another into the present[2]—an impressive feat considering some its participants saw the movement in the country as tired and effectively over as

[1] Libia Brenda said this on July 13, 2020 as a panelist for a virtual class session on science fiction written by Latin American women. The course title was *Ciencia ficción latinoamericana: la potencia de un futuro propio,* taught by Dr. Rodrigo Bastidas Pérez.

[2] Hernán García has documented Mexican cyberpunk well, citing around ten authors and anthologies that have been published in the past 15 years that broadly pertain to cyberpunk or post-cyberpunk narratives. See "Texto y contexto del cyberpunk mexicano en la década del noventa" (2018) for details. Several prominent examples relevant to mention here are Eve Gil's *Virtus* (2008), analyzed in this monograph in Chap. 4; Gerardo Porcayo's own novel *Plasma Exprés* (2017); and the assembled but never-published *Antología cyberpunk mexicano* (2013).

S. C. Tobin, *Vision, Technology, and Subjectivity in Mexican Cyberpunk Literature*, Studies in Global Science Fiction,
https://doi.org/10.1007/978-3-031-31156-7_2

early as 1998 (H. García 2018, 10). This chapter focuses on how Porcayo's work in the 1990s registers key aspects of this shifting visuality under neoliberalism by imagining how male and female genders have been impacted by visual technologies in different and differentiated ways. Taken together, the novel *La primera calle de la soledad* [*The First Street of Solitude*] (1993) and its accompanying short story "Esferas de visión" [Spheres of Vision] (1997) become exemplary specular fictions in that they present markedly gendered cyborgs whose difference is largely anchored upon explicitly optical motifs: visual technologies coupled with the locus of visual perception—the eyes—as a site of struggle between the posthuman subject, gendered identity, and multinational capitalistic forces. As I will argue, these two texts demonstrate more than just hetero-patriarchal fantasies at work in the country's cyberpunk; they link to several socio-political phenomena operating in contemporary Mexico, such as the spectacularization of femininity and a particularly Mexican male gaze cast by, and constitutive of, neoliberal masculinities. They also show how techno-vision is synonymous with sexually differentiated power, and lend themselves to both a Freudian and Lacanian readings of the phallus and lack for subject constitution between genders.

When juxtaposed, these two narratives highlight a glaring disparity between the constructions of their respective male and female cyborgs: in the novel, the hero protagonist hacker (and cyber-spy) struggles to subvert the hegemonic powers of a multinational capitalist order by leveraging the visual ability and cybernetic access that his ocular prosthesis provides; in the short story, the female protagonist, also a cyborg, is traumatized by her lost eye, which she futilely spends the duration of the story seeking. Unlike her male cyborg counterpart in the novel, instead of a protruding visual enhancement over her left eye, she overs it with a black patch, marking her as lack of the phallus. These potent posthuman allegories, written under a neoliberalizing Mexico in the 1990s, signal at least one prevailing cultural attitude toward gender and technology as articulated from one male author's perspective (albeit an important, influential one within the literary subgenre). This point takes on increasing relevance considering that young male urbanites comprised 100% of the Mexican cyberpunk literary movement, while women were wholly excluded as authors. The scopic regime promoted by these two works imagines a Mexico where only one gender—men—has the right to look in contestation to hegemonic power. It is worth remembering that Porcayo himself said that cyberpunk was a kind of x-ray to diagnose Mexico in the 1990s:

"una actitud literaria, una manera de decodificación apropiada al momento en que vivimos" (Porcayo 1997, 7) [a literary attitude, a manner of decoding reality suited to the times we live in].[3] If this be the case, then the issue of gender—in both the actual cyberpunk movement comprised of male-only authors,[4] and within the representation of genders in numerous works that frequently overlooked, denigrated, and objectified women—reveals a sizable blind spot within the development of cyberpunk.[5]

To this end, it merits acknowledging upfront that Porcayo, who many consider the premier Mexican cyberpunk author, rigidly reproduces the gender binary in his fiction. In all of what he produced in the original self-aware cyberpunk movement of the 1990s, as well as his more recent post-cyberpunk forays in the 2010s, Porcayo reinforces this male-female duality rather than questions it. In *Cyborgs, Sexuality, and the Undead*, Elizabeth Ginway briefly acknowledges the Mexican cyberpunks' standard offering of homosocial worlds comprised of hacking, crime, espionage, and violence (2020, 55–56) before she offers an extensive analysis of female cyborgs that appear during the neoliberal era that, in fact, trouble staid notions of gender. Porcayo's writing consistently insists upon and

[3] A frequently cited quote from Luis Ramírez helps elucidate this reality and the focus of Mexican cyberpunk critique: "Aunque pienso que no se trataba de que ya escribiéramos cyberpunk, de hecho, supongo que sucedió lo siguiente: nosotros abordamos el presente del México de los noventa -crisis económica, globalización, revolución, violencia urbana, narcotráfico, internet, apertura comercial, la estúpida creencia de que habíamos dejado el tercer mundo y estábamos a punto de pertenecer al primero- y ese presente, es el mismo que los escritores etiquetados cyberpunk en los Estados Unidos, vivieron diez años antes" (n.d. "Cyberpunk…", 4) ["We addressed Mexico's present in the 1990s, the economic crisis, globalization, revolution, urban violence, drug trafficking, the Internet, trade liberalization, the stupid belief we had put the Third World behind us and were about to be part of the First World, and that present was the same reality so-called cyberpunk authors in the United States had experienced ten years before us."]

[4] This is not to say there were no women writers who produced works considered to be science fiction during the time of the cyberpunk movement; authors like Cecilia Eudave, Karen Chacek, Gabriela Rábago Palafox, and Blanca Mart, among others, were around and publishing in the genre. Additionally, some women formed a peripheral part of the cyberpunk movement in providing graphic design in fanzines like *Sub* and *Número*, as well as editing services—secondary and minor roles. The point is that both groups of women were not active, contributing members of the movement's vision.

[5] As of this writing, this trend has reversed, with the visibility of women writing in science fiction, horror and fantasy in Mexico, Latin America and Spain, has exploded with numerous anthologies, scholarly works and journalistic articles, as well as courses and symposia specifically dedicated to the topic.

reinforces this duality rather than calling it into question, thereby helping to buoy and maintain hegemonic representations of gender—a fact that is not all the surprising given that the literary movement was comprised exclusively of male authors. My aim with this comparative analysis between two Porcayo works, beyond bringing to light his wholly unstudied short story, is to juxtapose two posthuman protagonists that exist in the same fictional universe—one male and the other female—in order to dissect how their genders are constructed and show some of the underlying psychological mechanisms at play. Gender exists on a broad spectrum in which the male-female binary remains a construct installed and maintained by a heteronormative patriarchy; Porcayo's texts remain beholden to this binary.

Porcayo: An Emblem of Mexican Cyberpunk

Gerardo Porcayo's profile—amply covered in multiple biographical accounts of numerous scholarly papers and journalistic pieces, along with his writing and contribution to promoting the Mexican SF scene—makes him an emblematic figure of Mexican cyberpunk. He is widely considered one of its founders from the 1990s, along with other proponents such as Isidro Ávila and José Luis Zarate. According to chronicler and science-fiction author Gabriel Trujillo Muñoz, Porcayo is "el escritor nacional más representativo del cyberpunk que aquí se escribe" [the most representative writer of cyberpunk in the nation] and that he was well ahead of his time, saying "con él comienza la ciencia ficción del nuevo milenio" (2000, 283) [With him the science fiction of the new millennium begins]. Along with his extensive corpus of literary production that includes numerous short stories and several novels, Porcayo was instrumental as an ardent promoter of SF production within Mexico in multiple ways. First, he, along with Zarate, created the *Premio Puebla de Ciencia Ficción* in 1984, which instantly became a cohering national event for science fiction authors on an annual basis, giving them an official literary space within which to meet and recognize outstanding works from the year. Ignacio Sánchez Prado has cited the importance of this event in institutionalizing science fiction as a visible literary movement within Mexico: it provided the springboard that launched most major SF writers born in the 1960s, as well as spurred the creation of the Fondo Editorial Tierra Adentro, a government-funded publishing company through CONACULTA that aimed at publishing writers under 35 years old. It became "the first institutional vehicle for the publication of SF within the larger frame of Mexican literature" (Sánchez

Prado 2012, 115). As this intermingling between writers became a yearly event, it helped generate another venue central to the cyberpunk movement and of which Porcayo was an important figure: fanzines. In the 1990s, these became a vital conduit thought which SF in the country was distributed and circulated among its authors and readers. The first of these was *Prolepsis* in 1991, created by Porcayo and Celine Armenta, and consisted of a two-page zine with six-point font that attempted to cram as much writing as it could fit on an 8 ½ x 11" sheet, equivalent to the fine print in legal documentation (Zarate n.d. "Fanzinerosos"). Porcayo also created the second electronic fanzine *La langosta se ha posado* in 1992, which is still in existence online as of this writing.[6] Cyberpunk in Mexico began to take form by the mid-1990s; attesting to this are the two compilations released that cemented the subgenre: *Cuentos compactos: Cyberpunk* [*Compact Stories: Cyberpunk*] (Ramírez 1997) and *Silicio en la memoria* [*Silicon in Memory*] (1997), both compiled by Porcayo himself. Fast forwarding 20 years, we see he is still writing in the post-/cyberpunk register with *Plasma Express* (2017) and *Volver a la piel* [Return to Skin] (2019). From all the above, it is clear that Porcayo was not merely an important author of cyberpunk SF in the country, but arguably *the* central figure in the overall maintenance and promotion of the genre by carrying the largest flag longer and farther than any other person. Considering his influential status makes focusing on his narratives a worthwhile pursuit for this study.

Porcayo's novel *La primera calle de la soledad* (hereafter *PCS*), published in 1993, is the first cyberpunk novel known to appear both in Mexico and throughout Latin America,[7] and its enduring impact can be seen in the significant interest that the North American academy has taken

[6] Other print fanzines included *Azoth*, *Fractal'zine*, *Umbrales* and *Sub*, among others. *Sub* arrived in the late-1990s and became one of the most high-quality 'zines within the movement, due in large part to the lower costs in printing and know-how of many tech-savvy SF writers and designers, such as Bernardo Fernandez ("BEF"), along with Pepe Rojo, Joselo Rangel, Ricardo Mejía Malacara, Rodrigo Cruz, et al. *Sub* stands for "Subgéneros de Subliteratura Subterranea" [Subgenres of the Subterranean Subliterature] touting the self-described marginal nature of SF production and consumption in Mexico. According to Zárate, it resembled a professional magazine with "textos excelentes, magníficos dibujos, una imaginativa diagramación, un diseño que...da envidia" [excellent texts, magnificent drawings, an imaginative layout, a design-worthy of envy] (n.d. "Fanzinerosos").

[7] However, the author did state that the idea began in 1988 (Trujillo Muñoz 2000, 286). Furthermore, Porcayo clearly had this on his mind as far back as 1984 when he published the short story "Sueño eléctrico" ["Electric Dream"], which received an Honorable Mention award at the first *Premio Puebla* in 1984 (n.d., "Cyberpunk..."). The term "electric dreams" is a central and recurring theme throughout the *PCS* universe and clearly references Phillip K Dick's influence in Porcayo's work.

in it within the 2010s. Also of note was the release of a third-edition in 2018—a rare feat in the country's science fiction literature—in order to coincide with its 25th anniversary of publication. Within science fiction circles in Mexico, and more broadly in Latin America, however, it has been known, read, and discussed for some time. Writing in 2000, Trujillo Muñoz called it

> La primera visión global, desde lo mexicano, de las expectativas computacionales del futuro y su impacto en las condiciones de vida de la humanidad en su conjunto, en las formas de poder y en la condición social que, desde estas nuevas tecnologías, evoluciona y se transforma en cada ser humano que toma contacto con ellas y las vive como propias. (2000, 286)
>
> [The first global vision, from a Mexican perspective, of the computational expectations of the future and the living conditions of humanity in its totality, in the forms of power and in the social condition that, from these new technologies, evolves and transforms each human being that comes into contact with them and lives them as their own.]

This novel embodies the ethos of science fiction production in the country within a globalizing Mexico under NAFTA by creating a narrative dystopia comprised of a severely eroded social order whose protagonist becomes its hacker-cum-cyborg protagonist that struggles to contest the hegemonic power of this era—the multinational corporation.

Within the last decade, scholars working in North America have interpreted the novel from various angles. Juan Ignacio Muñoz Zapata argues that it contains such narrative complexity that the novel involves a self-reflexivity so extreme that the narrative becomes "a metaphor of a metaphor" (2010, 192), and concludes the fiction should be read as a prime example of a critical dystopia.[8] In a similar vein, Hernán García classifies the novel as a Barthesian writerly text in that it requires an active reader to reconstruct the highly fragmented narrative into a coherent, sequential whole (2014, 6). In addition, his reading centers upon the representation of the male cyborg protagonist by focusing on how cybernetic technology and the posthuman body are presented as a form of social control rather than as having a liberating role or potential; this critique may be the novel's most enduring interpretation and one that serves as metonymic to

[8] The turn from late nineteenth-century dystopias toward a critical dystopia was more nuanced than its originator of the simpler dystopia. It tends "to be less driven by celebration or despair, more open to complexities and ambiguities, and more encouraging of new riffs of personal and political maneuvers" (Moylan 2000, 182).

Mexico's cyberpunk expression as whole regarding the deleterious effects of technology to people. Miguel García looks toward the novel's representation of a decaying urban space as indicative and critical of the presence of multinational companies in the country, as well as its nostalgic view of pre-technological past via the classic science fictional trope of the apocalypse (2015, 139). Finally, Inés Ordiz reads the novel as exemplary of the neo-gothic. For her, the monstrosity of capitalism, the lack of comfort that technology brings, and a postmodern indeterminacy to reality, are traits that can be linked to the gothic. And unlike classic gothic where a barbaric past irrupts into the ostensibly civilized present, *PCS* reconfigures this temporal disruption to show how a hyper-technologized future can be problematic (2016, 2). Finally, Ginway considers the cyborg body in the novel as an example of the baroque ethos—a paradoxical subaltern tactic in which subjects both resist and conform to dominant powers in order to survive. She notes that Mexican (and Brazilian) cyborg bodies tend to not dissolve into virtuality (often the case in the North), but rather remain. This remainder is a reminder of the enduring neoliberal trauma to the body politic (56). These five investigations signal the importance and narrative complexity of Porcayo's work,[9] as it relates to both the literary cyberpunk movement within the country, as well as its connections with the larger socio-economic and cultural changes brought about under neoliberalism.

What has been surprisingly overlooked and unstudied up to this point is the novel's gender politics. For the case in this analysis, this specifically involves how the novel's attitude toward gender relates to visual technologies, subjectivity, the eye and the gaze—all of which work together to make it a specular fiction. In addition, these five scholars treat the novel as a standalone work,[10] not taking into consideration its related companion story, "Esferas de visión," which appeared several years after the novel in the cyberpunk anthology *Silicio en la memoria* (1997). The novel and

[9] As of this writing, one other scholarly text focuses on the novel, although to a lesser degree of depth: Vanessa Ramírez's "El espacio urbano del cyberpunk en *La primera calle de la soledad*" (2019).

[10] By standalone, I mean not in conjunction with any other Porcayo stories that pertain to the same fictional universe. However, Miguel García's article, "Urbes corruptoras y visiones apocalípticas en dos novelas ciberpunk latinoamericanas" (2015) discusses urban space and apocalypse alongside another novel by Brazilian Fausto Fawcett's *Santa Clara Poltergeist*.

short story belong to the same fictional universe[11] by sharing continuities in terms of character depiction, attention to institutional powers, and spatio-temporal setting. Most importantly, they thematically express a concern regarding vision and the gendered cyborg body; this lays bare at least one major thread of prevailing cyberpunk attitudes of the time—heteronormative patriarchy and misogyny—and corresponds to this broader scopic regime occurring in Mexico under neoliberalism that is perceptible within its cyberpunk literature.

The publication of "Esferas de visión" follows the novel by four years but articulates even more pointedly the anxiety brought forth by an increasingly imposing mediascape, which necessarily involved a receding organic vision being supplanted even further by visual technologies. In other words, the processes by which people see in Mexico at this time is changing insofar as the presence of screens—primarily those of television, along with a nascent appearance of the computer and its screen—begin to notably increase throughout the country, most intensely in urban areas. With the human sensorium shifting further, these two works appear at key moments of these changes occurring in Mexico's visual sphere. In the story, the female cyborg's absence of an ocular prosthesis and the narrative's total focus on the loss of her left eye correlates to an increase in the number of screens present in the country in 1997 when the story was written and published. As covered in detail in the introduction, neoliberal reforms began as early as the 1980s under the De la Madrid administration, and increased intensity under Salinas in 1988, only becoming officially enacted into in 1994. This means over 10 years of significant reforms were underway by the time the short story is written and published. This span of years is not insignificant in relation to visual elements of each narrative. While the male cyborg in the novel also lacks his left eye, his vision becomes enhanced with an ocular prosthesis, endowed with what can be read as a technological protuberance, or phallus, that symbolizes power. The focus upon his eye is important to the narrative but not its central

[11] Three other Porcayo short stories also pertain to the same science fictional universe of *PCS* and "Esferas de visión": "Imágenes rotas, sueños de herrumbre" (1993), "Antenas sin marte" (2002) and "Colinas del viejo ser," (2002); the existence of these works underscores the enduring popularity of the original novel that spawned a total of four short-story addendums. These other three will not be treated here given that they do not focus upon issues central to vision and visuality, nor is the gender-technology link as prominent as in "Esferas de visión." Altogether, this makes them unfit to be considered within this analysis as specular fictions.

thematic preoccupation; in the short story, however, the loss of the eye becomes urgent from the first line to the last—not only its narrative framing device but also its primary topical concern. Taken together, these stories suggest that gendered subjects are affected differently from the proliferation of visual technologies around this time.

La primera calle de la soledad

The novel follows the hacker Oscar Martínez, nickname "El Zorro", who gets unwittingly recruited by Trip Corporation to help break the network of its rival competitor, *Laboratorios Mariano.* Both of these cyber-tech multinational corporations manufacture "sueños eléctricos" ("electric dreams"), a high-tech drug that functions as a type of mind control, often causing lifelike hallucinations in users that make real their anxieties and fears. El Zorro gets caught hacking on multiples occasions and gets turned over to one of the corporations, at which time he is obliged to break into the network of the other. To complicate matters, *Laboratorios Mariano* has a religion that it helps maintain, *Cristorrecepcionismo*, which has designed a program called *Asfódelo* ("the Asphodel") that has gained its own autonomy by realizing its basic function: to grant the wishes of the "electric dreams" users. The novel's spatial setting occurs in Monterrey, Mexico City and the Moon, where colonial penitentiaries have been set up and a rebellion breaks out toward the end of the narrative. The fiction is set in a futuristic time never specified in the text but intimated in various ways, such as the trip to "Tycho's City" (title originally in English) on the Moon that occurs in the novel's second section, or in the various references to the previous century. Some examples include the following: the video game salon where "El visor de espacio virtual está mostrando un nutrido grupo de robots primitivos, historia argumental salida de los viejos *pulps* del siglo pasado" (1993, 83) [The virtual space viewer is showing a large group of primitive robots, a storyline taken from the old pulps of the last century]; the appearance of "una bala calibre 45, salida de un rústico revólver del siglo pasado" (1993, 109) [a forty-five caliber bullet, shot from a rustic revolver from the previous century]; numerous references to twentieth-century figures both real and fictional, such as H.P. Lovecraft (1993, 116), Isaac Asimov (1993, 135) and *Frankenstein* (1993, 189). In these last instances, the novel engages in self-awareness of its generic register, and employs a degree of intertextuality.

Ocular Prosthesis: Confusion, Ambivalence, and Sight as Site of Struggle

The initial moments of the narrative introduce El Zorro's ocular prosthesis in a way that is imbued with confusion and obfuscation. In the second chapter, "Arribo" ["Arrival"], the heterodiegetic narrator introduces his arrival to the metropolis as a return after having lived elsewhere for over five years. He carries with him and assortment of gear, among which are mentioned his signature weapon, a dagger, his "lapbody" (a laptop), a CD full of terabytes of programs and data useful for purposes of hacking networks, false credentials and a "modificador retinal" (1993, 14) [retinal modifier]. Immediately after, the narrator states: "Extrae una tarjeta de crédito—que lo identifica como Ernesto García, un nombre más, un eslabón de su larga cadena—y la rasga contra el sensor de la entrada" (1993, 14) [He pulls out a credit card—which identifies him as Ernesto García, just another name, a link in a larger chain—and swipes it against the sensor of the entrance]. Here we are introduced to the protagonist as armed with information technology, weapons and his visual prosthesis, and then immediately after, his identity is given and admitted to be false. So, the narrative presents him at once as an uncertain identity, lending an air of mystery to his persona while also intimating the possibility of doubt and unreliability in this character. As he travels along in the silent metro wagon, he enters into the city around midnight and becomes swallowed up by the night and its electric lights, exemplified in the following passage. "Mañana empezará la acción. Ahora solo se deja engullir por las automatizadas mandíbulas del vagón. Avance sin ruido. Neones que acuden a su encuentro. Subliminales en enormes pantallas sobre los edificios" (1993, 14) [Tomorrow the action starts. For now, he lets himself be gobbled up by the train car's jaws. It advances silently. Neon lights encountered. Subliminal advertising across enormous screens covering buildings]. The dense description of omnipresent lights and screens here commences potently, reminiscent of the futuristic cityscape of Los Angeles in the year 2019 as represented in Ridley Scott's *Blade Runner* (1982), wrapping the protagonist in a vortex of visual technologies that both enhances the natural body's functioning via his retinal modifier and engulf it within its urban setting. This character is narratively flanked in visual obfuscation that suppresses his true identity. The city he enters into as well as the novel he inhabits is first and foremost a metropolis overrun with electric, visual stimulation—a motif of cyberpunk.

This theme continues when he returns to the bar El sueño de la gaviota (Seagull's Dream) that he used to frequent years ago when he lived there. He recognizes the bartender but this is not mutual. El Zorro claims that if it were not for "la nueva cicatriz que se abre paso desde el superciliar izquierdo hasta el pómulo del mismo lado y por lo rojizo del objetivo de su prótesis," (1993, 15) [the new scar that goes from his left eyebrow to his cheek on the same side and for the reddish color of his ocular prosthesis], then the bartender might not have recognized him. As in the second chapter, the visual technology that he uses to modify and enhance his own organic vision causes such a change in his own outward appearance that others are incapable of identifying him. This suggests that these particular visual technologies with a cybernetic base insert themselves within social relations in such a strong mediating capacity that they can distort and deceive intersubjective familiarity and recognition. That is, they can make recognizing one another a difficult task, adding distance between them.

Just as El Zorro's identity is initially shrouded in obfuscation, so too is the backstory of his acquisition of the ocular prosthesis veiled in an ambiguous mixture of contrasting sentiments and uncertainties. In a flashback, the narrator recalls how El Zorro came to acquire his prosthesis device. Faced with using his hacking skills for the benefit of corporate bureaucracy, he feels he has no other choice but to turn to the black market to make money—an event that echoes the vibrant informal economy exacerbated by neoliberal reforms that, as a reaction, have attracted many Mexicans (Biles 2008, 542). Once inside the black-market world, he begins plagiarizing the "electric dreams" transformed into masterpiece works of art from a company named Artdream, and soon he becomes obsessed with creating these artificial dreams in large measure because of their high profitability and tax-exempt status. At the same time, Trip Corporation begins designing a competing product which is the culmination of electric dreams and a highly developed virtual space, or virtual fantasies. El Zorro locks himself in a networked room in the *Micros de La Universidad del Tercer Milenio* where he spends over 55 hours attempting to hack Trip Corporation's corporate network in order to access their electric dreams product. While copying all the data necessary to aid him in his venture, an explosion rips through the room where he was hacking. "La ausencia del dolor, el ojo izquierdo que ha dejado de *captar imágenes*, el derecho registrando una hemorragia tremenda, un operativo militar extraordinario, su *deck* destruido y el cable conector roto a medias..."

(Porcayo 1993, 23; emphasis added in first sentence) [The absence of pain, the left eye that ceased *capturing images*, the right one registering a tremendous hemorrhage, an extraordinary military operative, his deck destroyed and the connector cable broken in two…]. He wakes up four days later in complete darkness, and spends another four in a holding cell being tortured before a Trip Corporation committee. They forcefully recruit him for a special group of hacker specialists in a group called "CTP" (Circuito Tecnodelectivo Profesional, or Professional Technodelinquent Circuit), and he feels he has no choice but to join them. In doing so, they repair his injuries from the blast by replacing his eye and part of his cranium "con lo más avanzado en biomecánica. Agregaron una interfase experimental" (1993, 23) [with the most advanced biomechanical technology. They added an experimental interface.], thereby furthering the fusion between the organic and metal and deepening his ties to cyborg identity. This visual technology is forced upon him—or more precisely, forced *into* his body—without his consent, and he is effectively recruited into a world he did not choose to be a part of, one which does so explicitly for the exploitation of his skilled labor.

El Zorro's ocular prosthesis also sets up a binary between organic/natural and inorganic/cyber-technological vision that spawns two distinct modes of visual perception, which has occasioned some discussion from one scholar of the novel. Juan Ignacio Muñoz Zapata invokes Scott Bukatman's observation that cyborg vision has become a contemporary sci-fi trope that more broadly represents a mediated vision brought on by television. In *Robocop*, for example, the scan lines that are superimposed on the screen come from the point of view of the protagonist signify "a technologized, cyborg vision" that can be read as signaling "a switch from film to video signals the onset of a mediated vision or even a mediated subjectivity" (Bukatman 1993, 254). Following this, Muñoz Zapata suggests that the shift from film to video in Latin America occurring in the 1980s and 1990s resulted in a similar kind of double vision that El Zorro's enhanced vision represents: "If ocular prosthesis is a new device of informatics and post-modern and late-capitalist mythology, the naked eye can observe the problem of adequacy and incompletion of the Modernity project in the subcontinent" (2010, 196). This astute reading succeeds in bolstering his argument for classifying the novel as a critical dystopia, as well as understanding El Zorro's ultimate desire to return to less technologically dominated life. However, considering the El Zorro's ocular prosthesis in *PCS* alongside its companion story "Esferas de visión" brings forth an even clearer and more marked desire for organic life/vision, while also revealing a sizable gap between each work's cyborg protagonist and their respective gender constructions. One way to understand this gap involves placing *PCS* into dialogue with a historically grounded sense of visuality in relation to heroic narratives.

The Right to Look: Male Visuality versus Female Countervisuality

The struggle for El Zorro to acquire technological vision in his left eye through his ocular prosthesis exposes a tension present within visual culture studies as it relates to narratives like *PCS*. In Nicholas Mirzoeff's *The Right to Look: A Counterhistory of Visuality* (2011), the author recovers the original meaning of "visuality" coined by Thomas Carlyle in the 1840s when he employed the term as it relates to heroic leadership. This usage differs from the more standard academic employment within visual culture studies to mean wide-ranging experience of visual experience in all possible modes; in this section, its meaning is understood in Mirzoeff's historical account of the term. In the past, vision, which was synonymous with heroic leadership, came to mean how history was visualized in order to affirm and maintain autocratic authority. "In this form, visualizing is the production of visuality, meaning the making of the processes of history perceptible to authority" (Mirzoeff 2011, 475). In this sense, visuality proper is a process related to the victors in historical struggles that create (or visualize) and re-create (sustain visuality) their authority, which results in being that which is deemed right, good, natural and thus, ultimately, aesthetic.[12] Visuality has thus historically aligned with authority and its continual process to assert itself as being invested with power within the higher social order. The reaction to the force of visuality is a countervisuality, or the right to look, which constantly attempts to assert its own right to be visible—or recognized by authority. He states: "The autonomy claimed by the right to look has thus been, and continues to be, opposed by the authority of visuality" (Mirzoeff 2011, 474). The binary Mirzoeff puts forth—visuality versus the right to look/countervisuality—conceptualizes the visual

[12] Each of his tripartite division of "complexes of visuality" involves classifying, separating and finally aestheticizing. He writes: "[Visuality] makes this separated classification seem right and hence aesthetic," noting that this classifying action is attributable to Foucault's notion of the "nomination of the visible" (Mirzoeff 2011, 3).

not strictly as a sensorial perception but a mode of discursive practice that is "formed by a set of relations combining information, imagination, and insight into a rendition of physical and psychic space" (2011, 476). The origins of this term, perhaps unsurprisingly, were attributed to the hero alone and thus associated with masculinity, whereas its counterpoint—the right to look—was primarily held to be that which was denominated as non-masculine categorical markers, such as feminine, lesbian, queer, etc. Countervisuality is, then, very much aligned with the feminist project (Mirzoeff 2011, 478).

When considering how El Zorro in the novel consistently enacts the right to look—both as a sensorial perception through his ocular prosthesis and as a psycho-social subject position of resistance to structural powers—he therefore becomes an agent for countervisuality. He attempts to assert his own autonomy in the face of the structural forces of Trip Corp. and *Laboratorios Mariano* that continually compete with each other and maintain their control over him and the ocular prosthesis he sees through. But, in doing so, his actions problematize Mirzoeff's framework. First, the novel's protagonist utilizes the few female characters solely for his own benefit; they are mere pawns along the path in his heroic journey. Second, he proposes to reassert himself—a warrior masculinity—as a model substitute to the dominant powers, thus further marginalizing the already sidelined, female characters in the novel. By attempting to assert his right to look—a countervisuality—in order to enact his ability to fight against multinational corporations in Mexico, he asserts his own autonomy and resistance in the face of oppression; but in so doing, he disregards the female characters, undermining the feminist project that countervisuality represents. If El Zorro can be viewed as an agent of countervisuality in *PCS*, then he does so at the price of excluding and invisibilizing others, particularly women, thereby denying the possibility for them to seek out and enact their own autonomy. This point reveals a blind spot in Porcayo's cyberpunk stories, insofar as they are meant to critique and diagnose the neoliberal scenario underway in Mexico at the time of their writing.

Female Characters in *PCS*: From the Male Gaze to the Spectacularization of Femininity

PCS foregrounds an array of gendered, visual practices in marked ways, as this section explores. Most specifically, Porcayo's writing carries such a heterosexually masculine, aggressive quality that it spills over into many aspects of the novel itself, aiding in the way it structures the gender relations between the male protagonist and the secondary, female characters. Of the numerous ways this occurs, one noteworthy aspect is the way the narrative focalization frequently privileges the ocularisation mode of perception, bringing the male gaze to the narrative forefront and making it central to the fiction's gender politics. In total, the novel offers representations of four female characters, all of which are silenced, abused or used for scopic or sexual pleasure by the male characters who overwhelmingly populate the narrative. Even the omniscient narrator, which ostensibly offers an objective representation of the narrative world, wanders into descriptions that resemble a kind of entranced and lustful staring at the few women who appear—most notably Nataly Deneux, El Zorro's main romantic interest during the action of the novel. In the following quote, we are introduced to her, in her role as a site locator for the *Cristorrecepcionismo* religious group strategically planning their entry into the Moon:

> Su nombre es Nataly. [...] Sus ojos azules, su cabello artificialmente naranja en un corte del siglo pasado: pequeño alrededor, largo en la cúspide. Viste un ajustado mono de material *stretch* color plata que, en una ventana triangular, permite observar nacimiento y curva de los senos. Dos aberturas ovaladas, más abajo, muestran una buena porción de las caderas.
>
> —Tengo preparados cuatro emplazamientos para el operativo—gesto torcido, retador; una mujer en la extensión de la palabra, segura de sí misma, de su potencialidad sexual—... (1993, 63)
>
> [Her name is Nataly. [...] Her blue eyes, her hair a dyed orange in a cut style from last century: a short bowl cut, long on top. Dressed in a fitted one-piece of silver stretch material that, in a triangular window, allows the beginning and curve of the breasts to be seen. Two oval openings, lower, show a sizable portion of her hips.
>
> "I have prepared four locations for the operation," with a twisted, challenging gesture; a woman in the full meaning of the word, sure of herself, of her sexual potentiality...]

Here the narrator plainly intermingles Nataly's purpose within the plot while restricting the internal focalization upon her body, a verbal act akin to a cinematic camera slowly panning down to emphasize the exterior appearance, while she offers relevant plot information. The character's body is given primacy over her role in the narrative, and the narrator's focalization suggests a heterosexually masculine gaze due to the emphasis in perceptual mode of ocularisation. It is worth pausing to consider how Gérard Genette's original theory of focalization responded to the narratological question of "Who sees the story?" which was later critiqued for being too vision centric. In order to account for other senses within narration, he changed the question to "Who perceives in the story?" in his *Narrative Discourse Revisited* (1988). To this end, he created five modes of narratological perception: ocularisation (sight), auricularisation (sound), gustativisation (taste), olfactivisation (smell) and tactivilisation (touch) (Jahn 2008, 174). When Nataly appears in the novel, what moves to the fore in character description is her appearance, relying heavily on ocularisation. What is more, Nataly is a French-speaking Swiss, noted by the narrator's describing her slight accent (Porcayo 1993, 63) and the multiple instances throughout when she utters "chéri" to Zorro as a term of endearment—a point that further contributes to her exoticization. The following chapter in the novel makes clear that her heterosexuality links with El Zorro, when she helps nurse him back to consciousness after he loses consciousness. The narration describes her "labios generosos" [full lips] and "pechos turgentes contra su coraza de supervivencia" [turgid breasts against her upper body armor] and finally, as their bodies meet, "los senos danzan el rito del encuentro. Cálidos, firmes, extraños y, por lo mismo, mortalmente eficaces" (Porcayo 1993, 69) [the breasts dance the rhythm of the encounter. Warm, firm, strange, and so mortally efficient]. This—the only significant detailed description of sexual coupling in the novel, heterosexual or otherwise—quickly devolves into cliché, but not before detailing Nataly in another round of narrative ocularization, mixed with the tactivilisation mode. Nataly's initial usefulness in the narrative is to give sexual satisfaction to El Zorro, although shortly after she becomes a replacement for Clara, El Zorro's first love.

These relations between the gaze and gender immediately invoke parallels with previous scholarship. For example, one is immediately reminded of Laura Mulvey's groundbreaking essay from 1975, "Visual Pleasure and Narrative Cinema" (2000), which offers a psychoanalytic reading of the cinematic perspectives provided in much classic Hollywood cinema, revealing what Mulvey conceives to be unconscious nature of the gaze as masculine.[13] The larger aim of her analysis attempts to dismantle the key structuring component in these classic films and deconstruct its seemingly natural quality in order to uncover the mechanism by which the camera lens becomes a complicit mediator in the objectification of women and their representation. For Mulvey, the gaze in this cinema is overwhelmingly male.

Porcayo's work of Mexican cyberpunk, often cited as one of the most representative of the movement, reproduces—through literature—a male gaze similar to that identified by Mulvey. Despite some of the more obvious differences of the objects of focus here—such as the place and time of Mulvey's analysis and Porcayo's works, as well as the different medium through which the gaze is articulated—a core component of her examination aids in helping us understand aspects of the male gaze in Porcayo's narrative. She observes: "In their traditional exhibitionist role women are simultaneously looked at and displayed, with their appearance coded for strong visual and erotic impact so that they can be said to connote to-be-looked-at-ness" (Mulvey 2000, 487). Nataly's role in *PCS* is that of erotic object, standing above all else as a projection of male desire of El Zorro, and presumably as well as a good number of readers of the novel. In this sense, just as Mulvey showed how Hollywood's Golden Age of Cinema created films designed for male viewers, Mexican cyberpunk of the 90s brought forth numerous novels and short stories made with male readers in mind. Given that Mexican cyberpunk was entirely comprised of male authors without exception, some may say that such a movement that puts forth representations of women gazed upon as objectified and sexualized is to be expected, and this assessment would be correct. To be clear, my argument here does not claim that all cyberpunk texts reflect this gaze or a particularly indignant representation of women, because a number of cyberpunk authors represented female subjects in more dignified and less scopophilic ways, such as Gerardo Sifuentes, José Luis Ramirez, Caín Curi, Juan Hernández Luna, and Pepe Rojo, to name several. Rather, there does exist a certain tendency within cyberpunk that engages with the

[13] Mulvey draws from Freud and Lacan to explain the psychoanalytical underpinnings of why the (Golden Age of Hollywood) gaze is male. The male character/camera/spectator triad that visually focuses on a woman on screen hides the connotation of her lack of a penis, which in turn threatens castration to male subject. From here, two routes are possible: voyeurism or fetishistic scopophilia (2000, 489).

gaze, as this chapter highlights. There is also a larger socio-cultural phenomenon operating here, one that exceeds its production within a cyberpunk literature wholly authored by men, and merits a deeper interrogation as part and parcel of Mexican culture as patriarchal in nature. The prevalence of such a scopophilic gaze that is present in this literary expression presents itself across a variety of media forms around the same time; this transmedial male gaze reveals itself to be a key practice of looking within the country—one which aids in signifying this particular scopic regime. In short, it is expansive, diffuse, and a significant part of Mexico's contemporary visual practices.

In order to demonstrate how the male gaze in Porcayo's literature connects to the larger science fictional and contemporary imaginary in which he participates and feeds from, as well as to link this gaze to the actual Mexican field of vision, a first consideration resides in the imagistic world he inhabits and helped to promote and sustain. Numerous examples abound of images of female characters whose primary purpose is for male scopophilic pleasure. Consider the cover of the book *Ginecoides, las hembras de los androides* (2003), a Mexican short-story anthology from 2004 comprised of only female authors of science fiction and fantasy literature—unique for its time. On it, a curvaceous, scantily clad, fair-skinned woman with a face mostly covered by a helmet and visor, dons a long, laser rifle in her left hand while her right hand rests on the door of a glossy, futuristic car. Her face remains largely covered and unseen, revealing only her nose and lips, her body wears the equivalent of an otherworldly bikini. This image presents a woman to be looked at for pleasure by heterosexual men, carrying an implicit message that all women possess this to-be-looked-at-ness.[14] This painting, originally done by Mexican artist Racrufi (Raúl Cruz) in 1994 and titled "Vigilante," circulated around the time of publication of Porcayo's novel, revealing even more of her skin and barely covering her breasts and genitalia; it renders her practically nude. A good

[14] As might be expected, a volume that specializes in visibilizing female authors of sci-fi and fantasy—the first of its kind in Mexico—and ends up presenting such an undignified representation of a woman on its cover was not well received among some of its contributors and allies. For example, contributor and editor Libia Brenda, along with Gabriela Damián Miravete, both expressed their disappointment and disgust with the cover in a conversation with me in Mexico City during the first Estéticas de Ciencia Ficción symposium in 2017. Brenda also noted how no contributing author was consulted regarding the cover by the anthologizer Jorge Cubría—a fact which only underscores the long-standing marginalized nature of women in the science fiction genre in Mexico.

amount of Racrufi's art work abounds in spectacularizing women for the male gaze. The woman who dons the cover of *Ginecoides* looks to be a prototype for another series of paintings with eroticized and nearly naked women adorned in futuristic techno-garb. Starting in the year 1997 until 2006, a total of 12 paintings appear that place this same woman, or women with very similar features, as the focus of a series of paintings.[15] Of note is that in one third of these, the character continues to a wear a kind of helmet that virtually covers her whole face, invisibilizing her facial features and fully foregrounding her body's exaggerated and unrealistic proportions that appeal to hetero-patriarchal fantasies.

Beyond these sci-fi paintings and book covers, more instances in other media demonstrate the breadth of the presence of the Mexican male gaze around this time. In particular, science fiction zines and comics don similar depictions of women. In the fifth issue of the zine *Sub* in 2002, Porcayo's own story "Rue Chair" (2003) comes accompanied with a woman wearing a helmet, fully covering her face, while her torso reveals bare breasts on a withering female body whose right arm is severed around the elbow, which offers up abjection. Subsequent pages feature a close-up of a breast and a nipple. The preceding story, written by Humberto Pérez Mortera, carries the title "mi virgen" and tells of a mentally challenged male narrator who went out on the town with his favorite prostitute. The accompanying image reveals a busty, three-legged woman whose body is pierced through a sword, and above her head it reads "Mi puta" [my whore]. Finally, in the realm of comics, several noteworthy instances of this same gaze resides in *Pulpo Comics*, an anthology of science-fiction comics from 2004 with different authors. The cover shows a bikini-clad woman who looks like an amalgamation between Lorena Velázquez from the b-movie classic *La nave de los monstruos*[16] and Princess Leia from *Star Wars*, but instead of Jabba the Hut being her captor, an enormous octopus dominates the image, towering above her and wrapping a tentacle around her body. Porcayo's own story "Paz y rutina" [Peace and Routine] gets illustrated by Bernardo Fernández in *Monorama* (2007). It contains an adaptation of the famous Marilyn Monroe shot from Billy Wilder's film *Some Like it Hot* (1959) where she works to keep her dress covering her legs and

[15] See Raúl Cruz's website at racrufi7.wixsite.com/racrufi. Some of the titles are *Archer*, *Angel*, *Armed*, *Intervention*, *Insect*, *Floating Power*, *Provider*.

[16] For an in-depth discussion of Lorena Velázquez, one of the first, impactful symbols of female star power in early science fiction and lucha libre films, see "The Star Power of Lorena Velázquez in Lucha Libre Cinema" by David Dalton (2022).

thighs from the wind blowing up through a grate of the subway below. In this story, Monroe is an android whose only narrative purpose is to sexually satisfy the male protagonist; she picks him up and carries him toward a bed, but once he demands to be let down and she does not obey his order, the protagonist rips her head from her body. This final example adds a hyper-violent act to the dominating male gaze. This handful of examples that foregrounds scopophilia across various Mexican science fiction media from the era show to what extent this gaze exists prominently around this time, accentuating a phenomenon proper to neoliberalism that Irmgard Emmelheinz calls the "espectacularización de la feminidad" (2016, 226) ["the spectacularization of femininity"].

Emmelheinz's useful concept connects all female subjects, including those described in detail above, to neoliberal masculinities and the gaze. She sees the former as a result of a mixture of relations among men in which they ritualize and objectify women, and are associated with violence, domination and barbarism (2016, 224)—qualities that describe virtually all the male characters in Porcayo's novel. For the gaze, she states: "Con la espectacularización de la feminidad, una vez que su esencia vital es sacrificada para su aparición, el maniquí cobra vida. Animada por la mirada, la subjetividad del maniquí es su espectacularización. Su visualización equivale al devenir ser" (2016, 226) [With the spectacularization of femininity, once a woman's vital essence is sacrificed for her appearance, the mannequin comes to life. Animated by the gaze, the mannequin's subjectivity is her spectacularization. Her visualization is her becoming.] Just as Nataly does in *PCS*, women are obliged to contend with this crucial subjectifying component of their *to-be-looked-at* nature.

Few other practices in contemporary culture help elucidate this phenomenon more than female weather forecasters, or *chicas del clima*, on Mexican television. This phenomenon started around the year 2000 when new competition in the television industry began competing with the heretofore monopoly Televisa (see Chap. 3 for details of these changes). The result here saw the weather forecast—traditionally given in a straightforward manner and delivered by men— eclipsed by young female presenters[17] in a clear attempt to boost ratings. The success of this move saw

[17] Even as of 2016, men give forecasts very infrequently—only for emergency weather situations, according to Abimael Salas, chief meteorologist at Multimedios y Milenio Televisión ("El encanto de…" 2016). This unfortunate state of affairs clearly reinforces the patriarchal structure where men are given the "serious" jobs and women relegated to being mere showpieces for the mundane tasks.

virtually all the channels switching to this format, which eventually became a Mexican standard in television. To give one prominent example of how the spectacularization of femininity and the male gaze is present both in Mexican society and in Porcayo's novel, one need only hear the words of Gabriela Lozoya, a female weather presenter for Televisa in 2016. She said: "Es importante tener un buen físico. Yo me pongo en la piel de un espectador y si veo a alguien feo, ¡pues le cambio! Hay hombres que me ponen en silencio y no más me están viendo" [It's important to have a good physique. I put myself in the place of a spectator and if I see someone ugly, then I change the channel! There are men that put me on mute and only watch me] ("El Encanto..." 2016). Lozoya is one of numerous women subjected to the animating forces of this gaze. 25-year-old Yanet García of Televisa in Monterrey became one of the first viral sensations on the internet regarding her presentation of the weather along with her physique, which she maintained through diet and exercise. In August of 2015, two male presenters invited her on their morning show *Gente Regia* in order to display her like an alluring object or glamorous commodity ("Las medidas de Yanet Garcia..." 2015); the centerpiece of her visit was their taking measurements of her curves on live television and discussing her sizes in amazement, as she smiled and blushed. In this revealing example, the process of spectacularization of femininity is on full display in the young female presenters of weather—both during the presentation of weather and other shows. It is this process that Porcayo's novel captures decades earlier through his own narrator in *PCS*.

Other Female Characters: Woman-as-Abject and Warrior/Neoliberal Masculinities

Returning to the novel, the representation of other female characters becomes instrumental in completing the analysis of its gender politics. As the fiction progresses, Nataly's presence is increasingly rivaled by Clara's absence. Clara is El Zorro's first, ardent love who represents an idyllic past that he met around the time when he was becoming entrenched in hacking and electric dreams. She interrupts the narrative quite frequently when El Zorro is feeling particularly alone or nostalgic, usually as an entire paragraph break written elliptically, such as "Clara..." (1993, 18, 19, 25, 45, 48, 61, 62, 97, 99, 151). As a character, she is wholly silenced and relegated to Zorro's pre-cyborg past, surfacing in his hallucinations and dreams. The first and most horrifying such occasion comes after El Zorro gets captured by Rioja "Bata Blanca," a mastermind of *Laboratorios Mariano* who injects an undescribed fluid into his neck. In the following chapter, El Zorro awakes sweating in an unknown desert area, causing some disorientation in him as a character (as well as for the reader), since the place has hitherto been undiscovered. He eventually comes across a house that he enters when a fetid odor immediately strikes him. He finds Clara, whose body is severely and actively decomposing, yet is still conscious despite worms crawling in and out of her cheeks and ants marching in and around her eyes. He realizes he is hallucinating due to whatever chemical Rioja injected into him, but this does not stop the scene from unfolding. Rioja himself appears with a massive erection and begins to taunt Zorro by grabbing Clara away from him and ripping off her face's lips and her nipples, framing Clara in horrific tortuous acts, signifying woman as object-turned-abject. He begins to rape the decomposing Clara while Zorro screams in uncontrollable jealously.

> Bata Blanca hace caso omiso de sus reclamos. Poco a poco la voz de Clara ha cesado. Bata Blanca fornica con un esqueleto con sexo. Ha engullido toda la carne.
>
> Los gritos del Zorro dejan de ser entendibles. La locura lo posee.
>
> Ahora, incluso, el esqueleto de Clara ha desaparecido, solo queda un órgano que se mueve arriba y abajo del sexo de Bata Blanca. (1993, 41)
>
> [White Robe ignores his screams. Little by little Clara's voice has ceased. White Robe fornicates with a skeleton with genitals. He has wolfed down all her flesh.
>
> Zorro's screams cease to be comprehensible. Insanity possesses him.
>
> Now, even, Clara's skeleton has disappeared, leaving behind only her sexual organ that moves up and down on Bata Blanca's genitals.]

In this brief description, which foregrounds the two modes of narrative perception of ocularisation and auricularisation, Clara is presented as abject throughout the hallucination and ultimately reduced to her sexual organ. Inés Ordíz's study of the abject in Porcayo's novel correctly characterizes this section as "una repulsiva imagen de lo más puramente abyecta" (2016, 125) [a repulsive image of the most purely abject nature], which recurs to Julia Kristeva's (1982) theorization of the abject as a necessary structuring component of the Other, further bolsters the gender binary in the novel. Given her representation as abject, Clara remains metonymically reduced to her sexual difference as object within this hallucination. It should be emphasized that her rape in this section is imaginary and thus not diegetically real within the narrative (although later El Zorro discovers that she was in fact gang-raped by Rioja's men in another place and time that precedes the fiction [1993, 61]). Despite any who might defend this sequence as one whose sole purpose is to portray the antagonists as decidedly evil in order to provoke extreme rage in El Zorro and the reader, it nevertheless reduces woman to an abject, sexually differentiated object; taken in the larger context of how poorly women are represented in the novel, it follows a consistent pattern of throughout the narrative in its hetero-patriarchal structuring of gender relations.

The only other two women remaining in the novel are Wanda, a female prostitute, and Anka, a lesbian friend of Nataly's. Wanda's role is brief and largely inconsequential, but also telling in its brevity. As soon as she appears she is described solely by her hair color—a brunette—and ends up being used by El Zorro to be put in contact with a Scotsman who attempts to repair Zorro's ocular prosthesis when damaged. She is killed off after being discovered during the operation, reduced to "una masa informe de huesos, sangre y carne chamuscada" (1993, 90) [a formless mass of bones, blood and burnt flesh] and ultimately relegated to the abject realm. El Zorro seeks out Nataly's friend Anka when he urgently needs a place to stay toward the end of the novel. He barges into her apartment by force, demands that she not go to work, and effectively kidnaps her while he hides out. In the few exchanges they have, she reveals her connection to Nataly by saying she fell in love with her, and thought she might be a lesbian like her, but never dared to inquire. She is quickly dropped from the novel, but the inclusion of a fourth female character being homosexual and attracted to the main object of the male gaze in the novel, rounds out the novel's depiction of the female gender.

In total, the female characters that populate this novel symbolize (i) an idyllic absence (Clara), (ii) an abject, sexually-differentiated object (Clara), (iii) sculpted, sexualized *to-be-looked-at* bodies (Nataly, Wanda), (iv) a sexualized and expendable prostitute (Wanda), or (v) an inclusion of heterosexual male lesbian fantasy (Anka). Taken together, they function narratively as mere markers of the protagonist in his mythic, cyber-hacking journey made only possible through his ocular prosthesis. This type of masculinity maps onto a neoliberal masculinity while also evidencing features of other archetypal models recurrent in science fiction. Following Linda Wright's inquiry into different variations of male types present in the genre, several key kinds include the warrior, civil and scientific masculinities. Of these, El Zorro's traits most clearly reflect the warrior, "one of the oldest and most persistent hegemonic ideals...of masculinity" (2010, 5).

Warrior masculinities teach other men and boys that the use of violence is justified when engaged in the fight between good and evil, and that the victor of the narrative's expression of what is good and right will always triumph. Along the journey, their dedication to the fight by the use of violence will be rewarded with "the love of, and sexual access to, women," along with the respect, comradery and/or apprehensiveness of other men (Wright 2010, 5). Indeed, El Zorro receives overt acknowledgement of his adherence to this model just after he awakens from the hallucinatory electric dream that brought him the decomposing, abject Clara and Bata Blanca. In a discussion about the surge of mysticism and religious fanaticism taking root all around him, the narrator describes him thus:

> Las creencias místicas jamás anidaron en el Zorro. No se lo permitió. En la marea inhumana y desorganizada que siempre llenó su vida, no hubo tiempo para detenerse en esos vanos islotes que siempre surgen de la esperanza de una vida eterna. Él había elegido otro camino. El del *guerrero*. (1993, 48 my emphasis)
>
> [Mystic beliefs had never taken hold in Zorro. He didn't allow it. In the inhumane and disorganized tide that had always filled his life, there was no time to stop and rest on those vain small islands that surface in the hope of eternal life. He had chosen a different path. That of *warrior*.]

This description explicitly characterizes El Zorro as embodying the warrior masculinity, further describing his not even having time enough to stop and consider the promises of religious salvation. Strong parallels exist between Wright's warrior masculinity of science fiction and elements of Emmelheinz's masculinities produced in the neoliberal era. According to Wright, warrior masculinities provide love and sexual access to women as a byproduct of their valor and struggle against nefarious forces, whereas for Emmelheinz, the neoliberal era has produced some Mexican masculinities as dominant and violent both verbally and physically, and as ritually objectifying women, among other traits (224). El Zorro straddles both, typifying strong characteristics within each, forging a new archetypal hero within Mexican cyberpunk that embodies some core ideals of neoliberal masculinities.

"Esferas de visión" ["Spheres of Vision"]

As mentioned earlier, this short story appeared in the 1998 cyberpunk anthology from Mexico, *Silicio en la memoria*, with Porcayo compiling and writing the prologue. It included other important cyberpunk authors such as Pepe Rojo (see Chap. 3), Bernardo Fernández, Gerardo Sifuentes and José Luis Zárate, et al. This compilation surfaced four years after Porcayo's novel 1993 *La primera calle de la soledad*, and shows just how much momentum the tendency gained within Mexican sci-fi in such a short period of time. In retrospect, it can be seen as the Mexican cyberpunk movement in full flex—with its most developed statement of what it was and what it represented.

"Esferas de visión" merits to be read as a companion piece to *PCS* for a variety of reasons. As indicated earlier, narrative voice and temporal setting align, as evidenced by the reappearance of the new religion from the novel, *Cristorrecepcionismo*, along with the drug "electric dreams" designed by Trip Corporation. But what sets the story apart, and makes it a particularly worthwhile vehicle to compare to the novel, is its rhetorically decrying of the loss of organic vision in a potent, condensed articulation under six pages in length—imbuing its visual discourse with an urgency not found in the novel. The female cyborg protagonist's urgency to recover her loss of sight in one eye benefits from a psychoanalytic framing and interpretation, given its strong parallel with a Freudian understanding of castration, mourning, and a compulsion to repeat. Finally, if *PCS* contains numerous references to visual technologies (among which the most important is El Zorro's ocular prosthesis) and the narrator's articulation of a male gaze, "Esferas de visión" foregrounds the deprivation of visual perception upon subjectivity, along with an array of innovative visual technologies that fail to replace the natural ability to see. Since the story is protagonized by a female cyborg in the same world that El Zorro inhabits, and both of them have lost an eye, comparing them brings the gender politics of Porcayo's cyberpunk fiction into stark relief.

"Where is my eye?" Female Cyborg's Deficient Eye as Wound, Trauma, and Neurosis

The essential expression of "Esferas de visión" is that of a startled female cyborg whose very psychological instability stems from the loss of her eye—from a fundamental, corporeal deficiency—that she goes in search of. The event catalyzes the story's conflict of her monomaniacal-turned-violent search for a way to recover her natural vision—in an attempt to become whole again. The exclamation "¡Mi ojo, mi otro ojo!" [My eye! My other eye!] opens and closes the story, thereby making it a vehement framing device that fundamentally laments the loss of organic vision. The protagonist, who remains nameless throughout the story, awakes from a hibernatory sleep on board a small submarine named Rogue, shouting these words. She awakes alone and, in the end, returns alone, shouting the same words. This exact expression recurs verbatim another eight times throughout the text for a total of 10 lamentations (1997, 150, 152, 153, 155, 156, 157), along with other extensive references to eyes, visual perception more generally, images, mirrors and screens. This title's sphere references most prominently the organic ocular object that she has lost or had removed from her (a point which is unclear from the heterodiegetic narrator's description at the story's outset): "'¡Mi ojo, mi otro ojo!' Así suelen empezar todos sus sueños y pesadillas. Toda su realidad" (1997, 150) [My eye! My other eye! So begin all her dreams and nightmares. All her reality.]

The memory of the original traumatic event—the violent act of having an eye removed—pervades her character throughout the story, and what the reader encounters in her is a subjectivity beset by traumatic neurosis. Contemporary Trauma Studies, founded largely by Sigmund Freud's psychoanalytic writing, understands trauma as a "severely disruptive experience that profoundly impacts the self's emotional organization and perception of the external world" (Balaev 2018, 360). It is theorized that the original event is not what is experienced, but rather the memory of it, which becomes repressed in the unconscious and returns to dominate the subject's conscious state in many potential forms, such as fragmenting the psyche and continually disturbing it in myriad ways (Balaev 2018, 360). In the case of Porcayo's female cyborg, she demonstrates a clear "compulsion to repeat" (Freud 1920, 14) the memory of the original traumatic event by constantly uttering the signifier that references her lost organ: "¡Mi ojo, mi otro ojo!". Save for one brief exception towards the end, this short outburst constitutes the only words she says aloud throughout. Repetition also occurs in the opening and closing actions of the story: in the beginning, she hibernates in the Rogue circling the floating city, and in the end, she returns to hibernate as the submarine circles the city on a daily, weekly, monthly, or even yearly basis before this cycle is broken (1997, 152). Her words and her actions are caught within a loop as her traumatic neurosis dominates her psyche and finds no resolution by the story's end.

She wears a patch over her eyeless socket in order to cover her traumatic wound, and she has an eye tattooed in the gap between and just above her breasts, as if to lament and never forget its loss.[18] This image of an eye is distinct from her natural eye in that it is "gris y frío, de una objetividad que ya no posee en su visión...en ninguna de sus visiones" (1997, 150) [gray and cold, with an objectivity that she no longer possesses in her own vision...in none of her visions]. Here, the narrator plays on two signifieds of "vision" in the title, one being her perceptual loss of sight caused by the lack of an eye, and the other referring to her recurring hallucinations that pervade her. The tattoo symbolizing lack that is placed just between her bosom corresponds to the area of her heart, the symbolic locus of feelings and emotion. The psychological instability she demonstrates throughout the story also receives additional description: "—Mi ojo, mi otro ojo-gruñe dentro de su esquizofrenia inducida" (1997, 155) ["'My eye, my other eye,' she groans in her induced schizophrenic state"], associating her mental condition to psychotic disorders characterized by distortions of reality, disturbances of thought and language, and withdrawal from social contact. Additionally, by beginning the tale in this way— "'¡Mi ojo, mi otro ojo!' Así suelen empezar todos sus sueños y pesadillas. Toda su realidad," (1997, 150) ["My eye! My other eye! All her dreams and nightmares usually begin this way. All her reality"]—there is a semantic uncertainty as to the boundary between her diegetic voice within the narration that screams this phrase aloud in the space of the submarine, and the possibility that this occurs in her dreams or nightmares during sleep. Since it is "all her reality," perhaps this distinction does not matter, since her entire life—whether asleep or conscious—is affected by the trauma caused by the loss of her eye. In all, this condition underscores the depth and severity of the loss of vision to her psyche.

Awaking into consciousness and remembering the loss of her eye provokes an extensive, obsessive search for it, which, like *PCS*, offers two distinct modes of visual perception for the protagonist. She connects to the controls of the submarine Rogue via the socket in her head, thereby facilitating her ability to command the vessel and bring it to surface. But

[18] An image inspired by this story was rendered by the artist Ponce and included in the second issue of the fanzine *Sub*, published in 1996.

this is only possible through the cybernetic enhancements which give her augmented control and enhanced visibility of the aquatic vessel:

> Un submarino biplaza de tonos amarillos y múltiples brazos robot. Visión insecta. Mira atrás, adelante, a un costado, al otro, arriba, abajo. No hay extrañeza en la transición, sus ojos cámara registran óxido, tuberías inservibles, la línea de flotación, inclinada y demasiado hundida en esa particular latitud. Sus ojos sonar, sus ojos radar, exploran océano y tierra en busca de peligro, roedores, patrullas y parias. (1997, 151)
>
> [A two-seater, yellow-toned submarine with multiple robot arms. Insect vision. She looks back, forward, to a side, then the other, above and below. There is no strangeness in the transition, her camera eyes register rust, unusable tubes, the flotation line, inclined and too sunken in at that particular latitude. Her sonar eyes, her sonar eyes, radar eyes, explore the ocean and land in search of danger, rodents, patrols and outcasts.]

Here, she is a cyborg fully integrated into the electronic circuits of the submarine. In this state, her sensory perception—most particularly her vision—not only functions without loss but is augmented, as when the narrator describes her visual sense in the plural and synaesthetically with her camera, sonar, and radar eyes—even comparing it to the compound eye proper to insect vision. It is not only as if she never lost her eye while connected to the submarine, but also that she possesses extra-sensory perception by being able to perceive beyond her normal visual function when using the submarine's computer. This human-machine hybridity appears fluid and augmentative of the protagonist's physical capabilities. But shortly after, she surfaces in the submarine to find that she has been circling a city-island surrounded by water, and it is here where she disconnects from the cybernetic system: "Después, vuelve a tener un solo ojo. No hay confusión. Es real lo que mira" (1997, 151) [After, she goes back to having only one eye. There is no confusion. What she sees is real.] The city has been devastated by *Cristorrecepcionismo* invaders, the same high-tech transnational religious institution from the novel *PCS* that helped start a massive war on the Earth and Moon. This reinforces the harsh duality created by a mediated vision, reminding us of Muñoz Zapata's assessment of *PCS*: when she sees without the prosthetic enhancements that connects her to the submarine's controls, she sees with only one eye and organically, and is therefore able to see in an unmediated manner the destruction of her home. The mediation of the cybernetic enhancement—or the mediated subjectivity according to Bukatman and Muñoz Zapata's usage—provides her with all the privileges of a technologically enhanced vision, save for one central difference: the apparatus itself. El Zorro's prosthesis covers his left eye, which allows him mobility on Earth, in space and on the Moon during his warrior journey, but the female cyborg protagonist's prosthesis is an entire underwater craft, restricting her movement to bodies of water. The Rogue itself is technically a corporeal prosthesis that restores her lost visual function and augments the limits of her bodily capabilities, but at the cost of severely reducing her mobility on land. Within the first two pages of the story, the comparison among both posthuman protagonists signals a profound technological and subjective inequality fundamentally marked by their respective genders.

Once the Rogue docks, the remainder of the story continues to deepen this inequality by narrating the female protagonist's monomaniacal search for her lost eye. She walks among the ruins of her home, and carries numerous guns to take revenge upon whomever took her eye. The day after her first night there, she comes across a group of emaciated outcasts among the wreckage, and asks: "Mi ojo. ¿Dónde está mi otro ojo?" [My eye. Where is my other eye?], and upon receiving no reply, "sus armas [vomitan] muerte," (1997, 153) [her guns vomited death] laying waste to them all. Returning to her submarine, she stumbles upon an alarm for the city along the way, which she activates and attracts three jets and two submarines to come to investigate, also initiating more bomb raids on the city. She watches with a rabid interest, and eventually locates a weak survivor from the jet attack who appears to be a pilot ejected from his plane before it crashed. After a brief discussion where he attempts to convince her to convert to *Cristorrecepcionismo*, the Christ figure of the new religion first introduced in *PCS*, she cuts out his eye with her "*gerber* de combate" (emphasis in original) ["hunting knife"].[19] Returning to the submarine, she attempts to replace her eye with his: "Maniobra con sus dedos la esfera visual, trata de adaptarla a su cuenca. Insiste. Hasta que el ojo se pudre, se vuelve líquido pestilente" (1997, 156) [she handles the visual sphere with her fingers, trying to adapt it in the socket. She keeps at it. Until the eye decomposes, turning into a pestilent liquid]. With this, she sets the submarine on auto-pilot to circle around the floating city and sinks back into her profound hibernation. As these events reveal, compared to El Zorro the female cyborg is markedly different in her ability to control her situa-

[19] A word specific to Mexico tied to the brand Gerber, which sells an array of large hunting knives akin to the one used by the character Rambo in his films.

tion. She exhibits irrational, neurotic behavior in her obsessive search for her eye, even murdering and dismembering along the way. It is important to underscore that for the duration of the story, she is eyeless. Its violent removal is vaguely suggested as prior to the plot, but this is never specified or detailed; additionally, the circularity of this short narrative implies that she will perform these actions again. As such, her eyeless-ness can also be interpreted as an underlying condition to her character, indicating that she signifies lack. Going further, when juxtaposed next to El Zorro in *PCS*, her lack of an eye signals her lack of a phallus; she is the product of castration with all the consequences this entails.

Male Retro-Cyborgs with Phall-ocular Prosthesis versus Female Cyborgs Who Lack

This lack becomes a salient difference when comparing both protagonists as cyborgs. Consider *The Cyborg Handbook*'s useful taxonomy of cyborg types that sheds light upon Porcayo's characters. In its introductory chapter, the cyborg is divided into a series of subcategories. For example, there is not just one generic cyborg, but rather a panoply of types that possess different possible configurations of how cybernetic machines and human organisms meld together.[20] Seeing where Porcayo's cyborgs fit into this categorization is revealing, particularly when considering their gender-technology coupling. In *PCS*, because El Zorro loses his eye in an explosion and has it restored as an ocular prosthesis, he would be considered a retro-cyborg, or "one whose prosthetic-cybernetic transformation was designed to restore some lost form" (Gray 1995, 14). But his female counterpart does not have a prosthesis installed and vision in her left eye restored, nor is she even conferred a poor substitute like a glass eye. Rather, without a prosthesis or ersatz eye she ultimately signifies a deficiency in this sense, unlike El Zorro, whose lacking eye receives a visibly protruding and functional replacement. She carries with her multiple guns, her massive hunting knife, and is even integrated into the submarine's circuit via the socket in her cranium that allows her to control the vessel and makes "su cuerpo [...] más" (1997, 150–151) [her body ... more]. At best, she is a semi-cyborg, or an organism that is only intermittently cyborg (Gray 1995, 14), when she interfaces and hibernates in the

[20] The different kinds include neo-, proto-, retro-, pseudo-, mega-, meta-, multi-, semi-, hyper-, omni- (Gray 1995, 14).

submarine. But she ends the story the same as at the beginning: a being whose subjectivity is founded upon the loss of her eye, by this fundamental lack. The narrator even states this explicitly that her lost eye is "una carencia que se ha transformado en emblema de su ser" (1997, 150) [a lack that has transformed into an emblem of her being]. She may be endowed with technology as a means to extend her human capacities when part of the submarine, but she is ultimately unable to assimilate it to help either repair the lost vision of her eye or find a workable alternative.

The short story's articulation of a fundamental lack caused by a lost eye recalls Lacan's conceptualization of lack and its binary opposite, the phallus, as constitutive of subject formation, a theory which aids us in understanding the gender dynamic in Porcayo's narratives. As Kaja Silverman notes, "The phallus is a signifier for the cultural privileges and positive values which define male subjectivity within patriarchal society, but from which the female subject remains isolated" (1983, 183). Since our female protagonist does not acquire a retinal modifier like El Zorro in the novel, she is isolated and blocked from being able to access the same tool as her male counterpart. The device can therefore be read as imbued with substantial social and gendered value—as an imaginary phallus that confers to the possessor status, access, agency, and power. In this sense, the ocular prosthesis that is so central to *PCS*'s plot and theme becomes a *phall*ocular prothesis: a metaphor that aids in signaling gender disparities of this period. Who sees, and who is allowed to see, becomes more marked when compared to the female cyborg in "Esferas de visión." She seeks out her lost eye, which becomes a kind of *petit objet a*—a lost object that she goes in search of but never finds. Given the repetition present in her actions and in the plot's elliptical chronology that ends where it begins (indicating the cycle may repeat, possibly ad infinitum), the lost object is not only unlocatable from the outset, but it will remain so. It is ultimately unattainable. In both cases, the phallocular prosthesis—El Zorro's acquiring and commanding it, the female cyborg impeded from obtaining it—can be read as a structuring force in both narratives, one which signals the structural inequality of gendered social relations in the country. Muñoz Zapata rightly points out that *PCS* is a novel about Mexican patriarchy in which, following Lacan, "woman is not included in the enunciated or grammatical subject of patriarchal society's Symbolic order" (2010, 200). But placing *PCS* alongside "Esferas de visión" goes one step further, showing just how deep this heteropatriarchy goes by revealing how the woman—the female cyborg protagonist—is not allowed to be a technologically enhanced seeing subject, unlike El Zorro. The gender divide remains stark in Porcayo's cyberpunk imaginary.

By way of conclusion, I want to highlight the peculiar cybernetic-specular device that aids in asserting the short story's futuristic nature, while at the same time hybridizing two objects that have become the site of widespread contemplation: the mirror and the screen. This occurs on the first page when she awakes from hibernation and looks at herself. She appears in front of a mirror and repeats her lamentation, "¡Mi ojo, mi otro ojo!," while looking at her returned image. But oddly, the mirror that returns her reflection does not offer a simple and reliable inversion, as mirrors do. She touches her fingers to the specular device "buscando tocar los electrones que pululan más abajo y se ordenan, devolviéndole una imagen fiel y corregida, no inversa..." (1997, 151) [looking for electrons that swarm beneath and reorder themselves, returning to her a faithful and corrected image, not an inverse one]. The mirror here is an object different from the standard one which commonly returns an inverted reflection of its onlooker. Porcayo's mirror is alive with an active display that simultaneously returns an image that is both somehow sufficiently accurate *and* "corrected." The following paragraph clarifies that this is indeed a "pantalla-espejo" [screen-mirror] (1997, 151)—immediately evoking a fusion of these two objects as a key site for subject construction. No longer does it merely reflect the object or person placed in front of it, rather it actively captures and displays them while adjusting and improving their image in real time. This screen-mirror proposes an image-device that is capable of modifying its replication on-the-fly—a kind of instantaneous digital rendering via Photoshop that is capable of being accurate enough to allow for self-recognition, while at the same time making instantaneous enhancements that improve how the subject sees him or herself. Considering Lacan's conceptualization of the mirror stage as situating "the agency of the ego, before its social determination, in a fictional direction," (2006, 2), then Porcayo's screen-mirror performs a double fictionalization for the subject. If looking into a mirror is already fictional for the subject since s/he identifies her or his self with the returned imago (the Gestalt they see in their reflection), then a mirror that further modifies the reflection by superimposing a happy emotional state atop what is seen introduces another distancing process into the matrix of identification. Unfortunately for the female protagonist, this device appears to have no palliative effect on her sense of self. Regardless, this fascinating idea melds the mirror with the digital screen into a hybrid-mediating device where the subject's imagined sense of self is altered via visual technologies.[21] It is Lacanian's mirror stage filtered through Baudrillard's simulacra, an object that underscores the pervasiveness and potential pitfalls of the digital screen in constructing identities.

Finally, how do *PCS* and "Esferas de visión" signal a scopic regime in contemporary Mexico? As this chapter has argued, *PCS* indicates that the gaze is largely male during the neoliberal period. Of course, it would be imprecise to say before NAFTA the gaze was not male, especially in the science fiction genre in film where we can point to numerous examples from Mexico's Golden Age of Cinema, as well as after, that reproduce the psycho-social phenomenon described by Mulvey's analysis. Some examples include *Santo versus la invasión de los marcianos* (1966), *Blue Demon y las invasoras* (1968), *El vampiro y el sexo* (1969) y *El macho biónico* (1981), *Dos nacos en el planeta de las mujeres* (1989), the last four of which had softcore porn versions available. It would be more precise to think of the male gaze, long present in the society, as being exacerbated in this new era due to a proliferation of television and computer screens occurring around this time (see Chap. 3 for details). Along with this increase of screen presence, the spectacularization of femininity, or the effect of a male gaze that structures women as its object, begins to increase in intensity as well, as exemplified in the array of images that connects *las chicas del clima* to the sexualized representations of female bodies of art, comics, fanzine graphic illustrations, and Porcayo's own female characters in *PCS*. When "Esferas de visión" appears four years after *PCS*, the loss of organic vision is more pronounced, and it therefore becomes a central thematic preoccupation. This short story registers this loss more pointedly than the accompanying novel, and its being published four years later may be read as a further diminishing of this natural vision that occurs at the

[21] In an interesting fiction-meets-reality twist, in 2013 some researchers at the University of Tokyo created just this device, a mirror that alters one's facial expression. The device is called an "incendiary reflection" that tracks a person's facial expressions and then alters them just slightly but upturning the corners of their mouth and crinkling the area around their eyes to make them appear happier than they actually are when they look at themselves in the mirror. The point is that if they look happier, they will also feel happier, so that they will consume more items while shopping (Waldman 2013). This is actually based upon a "facial feedback theory" that essentially claims that how a face appears may come to bear greatly upon their subjective experience of life, i.e. the more one forces themselves to smile, the happier one actually becomes.

helm of the expansive transnational media complex and the subsequent changes the country experienced. That is to say, if at first *PCS* acknowledges a loss of organic vision, then "Esferas de visión," by emphasizing the loss of vision so severely throughout, seems to suggest that these changes deepened and continued to reverberate far into the national psyche. They also signal a deep structural difference between how gender and visual technologies operate in Mexican society around his time.

Works Cited

Antología cyberpunk mexicano. 2013. Clarimonda Drunk Ediciones. Unpublished.

Balaev, Michelle. 2018. Trauma Studies. In *A Companion to Literary Theory*, ed. David H. Richter, 360–371. West Sussex: Wiley Blackwell.

Biles, James J. 2008. Informal Work and Livelihoods in Mexico: Getting by or Getting Ahead? *The Professional Geographer* 60 (4): 541–555.

Bukatman, Scott. 1993. *Terminal Identity: The Virtual Subject in Postmodern Science Fiction*. Durham, NC: Duke University Press.

Cubria, Jorge. 2003. *Ginecoides, las hembras de los androides: cuentos de ciencia ficción y fantasia por mujeres mexicanas*. Ed. Jorge Cubría. México: Grupo Editorial Lumen.

Dalton, David. 2022. On Virgins, Malinches, and Chicas Modernas: The Star Power of Lorena Velázquez in Lucha Libre Cinema. In *The Lost Cinema of Mexico: From Lucha Libre to Cine Familiar and Other Churros*, ed. Olivia Cosentino and Brian Price, 62–87. Gainesville, FL: University of Florida Press.

El encanto de las "chicas del clima" en la TV mexicana. 2016. *La Vanguardia*, January 6. https://vanguardia.com.mx/show/el-encanto-de-las-chicas-del-clima-en-la-tv-mexicana-JMVG3049770. Accessed 1 December 2018.

Emmelheinz, Irmgard. 2016. *La tiranía del sentido común: La reconversión neoliberal de México*. Paradiso Editores.

Fernández, Bernardo. 2007. *Monorama*. México: Editorial Resistencia.

Freud, Sigmund. 1920. *Beyond the Pleasure Principle*. London: Norton.

García, Hernán. 2014. Carne eres y en máquina te convertirás: El cuerpo posthumano en *La primera calle de la soledad* de Gerardo Porcayo. *Polifonía: Revista Académica De Estudios Hispánicos* 4: 4–23. https://www.apsu.edu/polifonia/v4/2014-garcia.pdf.

García, Miguel. 2015. Urbes corruptoras y visiones apocalípticas en dos novelas ciberpunk latinoamericanas. *Chasqui* 44 (2): 138–148.

García, Hernán. 2018. Texto y contexto del cyberpunk mexicano en la década del noventa. Alambique. *Revista académica de ciencia ficción y fantasía / Jornal acadêmico de ficção científica e fantasía* 5 (2): Article 5. https://doi.org/10.5038/2167-6577.5.2.5. https://digitalcommons.usf.edu/alambique/vol5/iss2/5.

Genette, Gérard. 1988. *Narrative Discourse Revisited*. Trans. Jane E. Lewin. Ithaca, NY: Cornell University Press.

Ginway, Elizabeth. 2020. *Cyborgs, Sexuality, and the Undead: The Body in Mexican and Brazilian Speculative Fiction*. Nashville, TN: Vanderbilt University Press.

Gray, Chris Hables, ed. 1995. *The Cyborg Handbook*. London: Routledge.

Jahn, Manfred. 2008. Focalization. In *Routledge Encyclopedia of Narrative Theory*, ed. David Herman, Manfred Jahn, and Marie-Laure Ryan, 173–177. London: Routledge.

Kristeva, Julia. 1982. *Powers of Horror. An Essay on Abjection*. Trans. Louis-Ferdinand Célice. New York: Columbia University Press.

Lacan, Jacques. 2006. *Écrits: The First Complete Edition in English*. Trans. Bruce Fink in Collaboration with Héloïse Fink and Russell Grigg. New York: W.W. Norton & Co.

Las medidas de Yanet Garcia Gente Regia 04-Ago-2015 Full HD. YouTube, Uploaded by Yanet Garcia www.youtube.com/watch?v=ulKHFbBxrXM. Accessed 9 August 2015.

Mirzoeff, Nicholas. 2011. *The Right to Look: A Counterhistory of Visuality*. Durham, NC: Duke University Press.

Moylan, Tom. 2000. *Scraps of the Untainted Sky: Science Fiction, Utopia, Dystopia*. Boulder, CO: Westview Press.

Mulvey, Laura. 2000. Visual Pleasure and Narrative Cinema. In *Film and Theory: An Anthology*, ed. Robert Stam and Toby Miller, 483–494. Malden, MA: Blackwell.

Muñoz Zapata, Juan Ignacio. 2010. Narrative and Dystopian Forms of Life in Mexican Cyberpunk Novel *La primera calle de la soledad*. In *Science Fiction, Imperialism and the Third World*, ed. Ericka Hoagland and Reema Sarwal, 188–201. Jefferson, NC: McFarland.

Ordiz, Inés. 2016. De-construcciones y ciber-construcciones del cuerpo gótico y ciencia ficción en *La primera calle de la soledad* de Gerardo Horacio Porcayo. In *Territorios de la imaginación: poéticas ficcionales de lo insólito en España y México, special issue of Brumal. Revista e investigación sobre lo Fantástico*, ed. María Gutiérrez Campelo, 121–130. León: Universidad de León.

Porcayo, Gerardo. 1993. *La primera calle de la soledad*. México: Consejo Nacional para la Cultura y las Artes.

———. 1996. Esferas de visión. *Sub* (fanzine), eds. Pepe Rojo, Joselo Rangel, Ricardo Mejía Malacara, Rodrigo Cruz, and Bernardo Fernández 'Bef': 8–12.

———. Esferas de visión. 1997. *Silicio en la memoria*. Mexico City, Mexico: Ramon Llaca y Cía.

———. 2003. Rue Chair. *Sub* (fanzine), eds. Pepe Rojo, Jóselo Rangel, Ricardo Mejía Malacara, Rodrigo Cruz and Bernardo Fernández 'Bef': 59–64.

———. 2017. *Plasma Express*. Ciudad de México: Planeta Mexicana.

———. 2019. *Volver a la piel*. Cuidad de México: Fondo de Cultura Económica.

Ramírez, José Luis. 1997. *Cuentos compactos: cyberpunk*. México: Fractal.

Ramírez, Vanessa. 2019. El espacio urbano del cyberpunk en *La primera calle de la soledad*. *Metáforas del aire* 2 (1): 106–120.

Ramírez, José Luis. n.d. Cyberpunk: El movimiento en México. *Ciencia ficción mexicana*. http://comunidades.com.mx/cfm/?cve=11:09. Accessed 4 May 2013.

Sánchez Prado, Ignacio M. 2012. Ending the World with Words: Bernardo Fernández (BEF) and the Institutionalization of Science Fiction in Mexico. In *Latin American Science Fiction: Theory and Practice*, ed. Elizabeth Ginway and Andrew Brown, 111–132. New York: Palgrave Macmillan.

Scott, Ridley. 1982. *Blade Runner*. Warner Bros.

Silverman, Kaja. 1983. *The Subject of Semiotics*. New York: Oxford University Press.

Trujillo Muñoz, Gabriel. 2000. *Biografías del futuro: La ciencia ficción mexicana y sus autores*. Mexicali: Universidad Autónoma de Baja California.

Waldman, Katy. 2013. Fake Mirrors May Soon Ensnare Shoppers in Web of Lies. *Slate*, August https://slate.com/human-interest/2013/08/incendiary-reflection-mirrors-make-you-look-happier-than-you-are-so-you-buy-stuff.html. Accessed 2 March 2015.

Wright, Linda. 2010. Talking About Men: Conversations About Men and Masculinities in Recent Gender-Bending Science Fiction. PhD diss., University of Ballarat.

Zárate, José Luis. n.d. Fanzinerosos. *Ciencia Ficción Mexicana*. ciencia-ficcion.com.mx. http://comunidades.com.mx/cfm/?cve=11:14. Accessed 29 October 2014.

CHAPTER 3

Televisual Subjectivities: Mediatic Ultraviolence and Disappearing Bodies in "Ruido gris" ["Gray Noise"] and *Punto cero* [Point Zero] by Pepe Rojo

We are getting closer and closer to the point where the social world is primarily described—and in a sense prescribed—by television. Pierre Bourdieu (1998, 22)

Dentro de la pupila de Ray, un cuadrado deforme. Adentro del cuadrado, la imagen de la televisión. En la imagen de la televisión, la cara de Ray. En la cara de Ray, sus pupilas. Dentro de las pupilas, un cuadro deforme. Pepe Rojo, *Punto cero* (2012, 104)

[Inside Ray's pupil, a deformed square. Inside the square, the image of the television. In the television's image, Ray's face. On Ray's face, his pupils. Inside his pupils, a deformed square.]

Pepe Rojo: A Cyberpunk Seer

Pepe Rojo has been profoundly affected by changes in the visuality of contemporary Mexico. His writing expresses an urgency regarding the country's visual practices and technological mediations that signal a greater transformation occurring in his nation's visual sphere within the globalized era. Many of his compositions abound in jarring visual motifs: eyes are removed, altered, replaced or operated upon; mirrors are frequently the site of elusive or deceptive identifications; electronic screens—almost always those of television—become charged narrative forces, some with a

S. C. Tobin, *Vision, Technology, and Subjectivity in Mexican Cyberpunk Literature*, Studies in Global Science Fiction,
https://doi.org/10.1007/978-3-031-31156-7_3

gravitational pull. Even when the overarching themes in his fiction do not directly engage it, the subject matter surfaces noticeably, as if exhibiting instances of a minor symptom of a larger underlying cause. In the quote above taken from Rojo's only novel, *Punto cero*, the narrator describes the protagonist Ray as he sits in his apartment watching television. The description here interweaves his eyes with television recursively in a *mise-en-abyme* where the focalization of narrative description makes it difficult to discern where the locus of visual perception—the eye—is separate from its focus, the television screen. The quote foregrounds not only the role that this medium plays in the field of vision of Mexico, but it also emphasizes the eye-television coupling as a key component in the formation of subjects. Writing around the same time as Rojo but in reference to her own postmodern Argentina, Beatriz Sarlo pointed out that "society is now televisual; we live in a 'state of television'" (1994, 70), indicating that much of contemporary life is becoming increasingly filtered and experienced through this audio-visual technology that has become so prevalent and influential in popular thinking and visual practices. Similarly, Rojo's literarily imagined Mexico also shows a prominent and urgent preoccupation regarding tele-visuality such that it seeps into nearly all areas of his work.[1]

In the chapter that follows, I contend that most all of Rojo's science fiction writing foregrounds vision as a central site for subject constitution powerfully mediated by television—what I am dubbing "televisual subjectivities." In the corpus selected here of the short story "Ruido gris" ["Gray Noise"] (1996) and novel *Punto cero* [Point Zero] (first published in 2000; second edition in 2012), Rojo's writing posits many ideas, such as: televisual/mediatic violence increases the perception of violence society-wide; the competitiveness in the media industries in Mexico—loosed by neoliberal capitalism—bears down upon all practitioners and affects all viewers, contributing to social anomie via isolation, alienation, depression and suicide; watching television abounds with mis-recognitions and dis-locations to the human subject-viewer; this visual practice scrambles the subject's sense of temporality; and finally, that body in the postmodern era—what some have

[1] Here are some examples of his other work where visual themes appear but are not as central to the two works treated in this chapter: "Conversaciones con Yoni Rei", "Y de pronto," and "El deseo y su cura" from *Yonke*; "El presidente sin órganos," "Dos años," and "Apariciones," "Tócame, estoy enfermo" from *interrupciones*; "Imag/Esp/Ecies: Random notes Towards a Zoology," and "Estroboscopía."

deemed "media society," (Jameson 1991, 3)—is in the process of becoming obsolete and even is on its way to vanishing. Given this, one key objective of this chapter is to demonstrate how the role of vision in Rojo's two central texts is linked to the televisual—not the cybernetic, as the case often associated with Mexican cyberpunks. This characteristic parallels actual transformations occurring on the ground in Mexico in the 1990s.

What consequences for subjectivity flow from this social plane overrun with screens and spectacle more generally? In "Ruido gris"," he establishes his conception of a cyborg body that is connected *not* to a decentralized cybernetic informational network, but rather functions as a bridge between the viewing public and the unidirectional televisual broadcast source. In *Punto cero*, the television ultimately consumes the protagonist into its screen,[2] disappearing him. This imposing televisuality is what creates anxiety and alienation within the subjects of his stories. Far removed from any rational, autonomous, self-directing, liberal humanist subject, the protagonists in his stories become the specific site of domination by this visual practice, undergirded by the larger media sphere comprised of multinational corporations. Unsurprisingly, television in his novel becomes a central locus of advertising and the commodification and consumption of globalized products. In addition, while Rojo's creative work is frequently informed by European theorists such as Jacques Lacan and Paul Virilio, his literary representations also retain strong undercurrents of contemporary events and social realities coming from his local environment. This makes his writing not merely a copy of contemporary Northern theories circulating around the time and overlaying them on top of a Mexican context, but rather one imbued with core elements of Mexican social realities of the 1990s. In this way, Rojo's writing continues the epistemological inflection established in the critical view that Latin American science fiction is primarily hybrid in its articulation (Paz 2008, 100–101; Haywood Ferreira 2018). That is, rather than incorporate settings or icons from the Global North's science fiction cannon and fuse these with local or national themes informed by historical circumstances, Rojo often takes theoretical concepts from the North and hybridizes these with local considerations. Nevertheless, before delving into the aforementioned thematic and theoretical concerns regarding televisual subjectivities in his narratives, I would like to start by positioning him in the science fiction context from which

[2] A very similar scene occurs in David Cronenberg's *Videodrome*, which Rojo cites in his essay "Tócame, estoy enfermo" (2009b), and clearly is a key influence in Rojo's thinking.

he emerged in order show how he articulates a unique visuality that is unmistakably televisual, as well as Mexican.

Much like what happened in the United States a decade earlier, the Mexican cyberpunk writers often took as their mythic trope the hacker immersed within a dystopian cybernetic setting where the screen was almost always that of a computer monitor, and its social space imagined was often that of a deceptive virtual reality[3]—powerful, recurring symbols of the early days of the internet (which still exist today in more evolved forms). As quoted in the introduction, Hernán García's extensive exploration of the cyberpunk movement details many of these core motifs, with the most pertinent being its "entorno de la realidad virtual como vía de perdición" (2012, 334) [generally environment of virtual reality as a road to perdition].

The cybernetic signified so commonly associated with the movement certainly had a connection most visibly in the media as early as 1994 when the Ejército Zapatista de Liberación Nacional (EZLN) leveraged the global communicative capabilities of the Internet via its web page to broadcast its message of resistance against the Mexican federal government and the multinational forces behind neoliberalism put into practice via NAFTA, helping to label it the first postmodern revolution or rebellion (Carrigan 2001, 417). *Hackitivismo* also existed in some parts of the country, gaining notoriety and momentum as a result of the EZLN's

[3] This is also what characterized US cyberpunk in the mid-1980s. Following up the brief mention of the subgenre in the introduction, it appeared in William Gibson's *Neuromancer* (1984) as a literary movement and by the time cyberpunk story compilation *Mirrorshades* came out in 1986, some of its writers were already speaking of its death as a movement. Curiously, some Mexican cyberpunk authors, such as Rodrigo Pardo and others, have stated that they wrote cyberpunk stories before knowing of or having read Gibson or other US cyberpunk. According to Luis Ramírez: "Por ese entonces varios escritores contaban la ciencia ficción desde una perspectiva que (debido a que no eran fáciles de encontrar las obras de Gibson, [Bruce] Sterling y otros, y no estaban, por lo tanto, muy difundidas), parecían propuestas sin abordar. Es el caso de Rodrigo Pardo -que obtiene el Premio Puebla en 1996, con un híbrido cyberpunk/hombres lobo-, quien asegura que él ya escribía cyberpunk antes de conocer el trabajo de Gibson. Eso nos pasó a muchos" (n.d. "Cyberpunk…") [At that time some writers told science fiction from a perspective that seemed like unchartered territory (due to the fact that it was not easy to finds works by Gibson, [Bruce] Sterling, and others, and they were not as such well known). That was the case with Rodrigo Pardo—who won the Puebla Prize in 1996 with a hybrid cyberpunk/wolfman story—who claims that he wrote cyberpunk before knowing Gibson's work. That happened to many of us.]. While some of the roots of Mexican cyberpunk have been said to be traceable as far back as Porcayo's short story "Sueño eléctrico" (1984) and José Luís Zárate's "Análogos y therbligs" (1986), this was not a self-aware movement labelled cyberpunk until the mid-1990s.

utilization of the Web as a tool of resistance and social justice; they helped the political Left by using subversion tactics such as defacing other political parties' or corporations' web pages with messages that run counter to their own, and providing servers to host alternative sources of information in order to offer a different viewpoint to the traditional media outlets (Lizama 2006). H. García's research into this area has brought to light the importance of this diffuse and overlooked literary cyberpunk movement in its critique of the social, economic and political effects of NAFTA and neoliberal dogma on the country, especially from the vantage of the youth within the generic register of science fiction. His contribution from a technoscientific perspective to the field of cultural and Mexican studies that focuses on science fiction cannot be understated.

However, given that H. García's broad focus pertained to mapping the corpus of Mexican cyberpunk short stories and novels, he did not dedicate as much time to the projective nature of such works—their lack of correspondence to actual conditions within the country—which I will discuss. By this I mean that a cybernetically connected Mexico on any significant scale in the 1990s and into the 2000s remains difficult to envision. As reviewed in the introduction, Mexico's efforts to transform into an information society have been sluggish at best. In 2006, the World Information Society Report, which rates 166 participatory countries using different benchmarks[4] for classifying them as an information society, ranked Mexico as 66 in the World Ranking; in the Americas, it reached only 15 (of the potential 18 Hispanic countries), despite having the largest Spanish-speaking population of any of those nations, around 107 million at the time. Between 2003 and 2006, between 12 and 18% of the population nationwide were Internet users (López Dávila 2006, 1), which undoubtedly means that even fewer regularly used the internet during the peak period of Mexican cyberpunk literary production a decade earlier, the mid- to late-1990s. All of this signals the fact that, no matter the cyber-thematic within the cyberpunk movement, at that time the country was far from achieving any significant informatization of society. Miriam Herrera Aguilar's 1998 assessment concluded that Mexico could increase its

[4] These were determined by various indicators that equal the Digital Opportunity Index (DOI), and is comprised by factors such as percentage of population that use a mobile telephone, mobile telephone tariff rates, internet access tariff rates, proportion of households with a computer, proportion of households with access to Internet at home, proportion of individuals that use the Internet, ratio of fixed broadband consumers, etc. ("World Information..." 2007).

industrialization but has a long way to go to becoming post-industrial—one whose majority of the economy is based on services, knowledge production, information: "México no tiene grandes posibilidades de ser una sociedad postindustrial, ya que tiene problemas prioritarios por resolver en los planos económico y educativo que son los principales factores a desarrollar para pasar a este estadio" (1998, 73) [Mexico does not possess great chances of becoming a postindustrial society, since it has more pressing problems to resolve in the areas of economy and education, which are the principal factors it needs to develop in order to move on to this next stage]. Given this, at its most developed, the cyberpunk movement, with its deceptive virtual reality and recurring figures of rebellious hackers and lethal cyborg mercenaries armed with prosthetics, was in this respect strongly notional rather than a reflection of their social reality. And rarely throughout the cyberpunk corpus is television a foundational theme or formative rhetorical device, except in Rojo's work; his stories more accurately reflect the larger social reality occurring within visual practices. It bears repeating from the introduction that *Numeralia*, a statistical journal published by UNAM, placed television in around 96–97% of the urban homes throughout the country in the mid-2000s, making it by far the most widely-utilized audio-visual technology ("Televisión en México" 2009, 7).

Of all the cyberpunk writers, then, Rojo's work remains unique as the singular expression of the heightened and pervasive televisuality that characterizes Mexico of the 1990s—when it was written. Televisuality, understood here broadly as the subject's psychological experience mediated through the audio-visual technology of television and all its related phenomenon,[5] persists as a hard kernel of his creative literary production. This motif also reflects the larger transformation happening within the country's mediasphere at this time: the neoliberalization of the television industry and all its subsequent consequences: an increase in multinational partnerships in the industry which resulted in a notable increase of imported, foreign—mostly US—programming, a heightened reliance upon ratings as a measure of gauging audience viewership and by extension the cost of commercial advertising, an increase in commodity circulation brought on by NAFTA, an upsurge in reality-style television programs (inspired by and modeled after this new genre coming from the United States and Europe), and a growth in the material production of television

[5] This is not to be confused with John Caldwell's appropriation of the term in his 1995 book (also called *Televisuality*) to describe a characteristic excess of style proper to US television starting in the 1980s.

screens in the maquiladoras (particularly in Tijuana where Rojo lives). It bears repeating that, as covered in the introduction, Tijuana earned the label the "television capital of the world" (Cervantes 2010), and, in a literal sense, televisions have become a part of Tijuana's material foundation. One could witness this phenomena walking about the city around this time stumbling upon a makeshift layer of steps that had solidified into the landscape, as photographer Rogelio Núñez's snapshot "Untitled" shows in *Here is Tijuana!* (2006, 168). What is more, discarded television screens also provided material building blocks for artist Fernando Miranda's tower of found objects, a work which partly inspired Rojo himself to write an essay titled "La basura es un punto de vista" (n.d.). All of the aforementioned factors impacted most potently the visuality of Mexico throughout the 1990s, which is primarily a televisuality; Rojo's work critically reflects this televisuality, meriting closer examination.

"Ruido gris": Ocular Cyborgs and Reality TV

"Ruido gris" begins with a buzzing in the protagonist's head that cannot let him fall asleep. It is a residue of the traumatic event that precedes as well as pervades the entire narrative: his raw, unmediated vision has been altered and partially taken over by an unnamed media company via a surgical operation that it helped pay for. A camera is attached to his right eye's retina and a microphone to his vocal chords to allow his eyes and mouth to transmit his subjective visual and auditory experience back to the media company; he has become an "ocular reporter." The contract with the company controls his days, as he is required to seek out newsworthy events that are sensationalist and hyper-violent for recording or live transmission. A raw first-person perspective is captured from his right eye and sounds from the microphone in his throat are either recorded for later editing and compiling within various programs, such as the reality TV news show *Rojo digital*, or, if the report has enough interest for the media company, what he sees, hears and says will be broadcast live directly out to thousands of viewers. Thus, his vision is no longer solely an organic function of his body, nor is it his wholly his own; he has been converted into a (tele)visual cyborg. His previous sensorial functions of seeing and listening have been converted into a form of labor in the service of a mass media corporation that contractually obligates his services six hours per day, seven days per week. In terms of the story's narrative strategy, the first-person narration thrusts the reader immediately into the imagined subjective point of view of a protagonist whose observing body has antecedently become a bridge between the mass media broadcast and the protagonist's audio-visual sensorial experience. The body and, most acutely, the eyes have become the site of the exercise of power at the helm of the media company whose principal aim is profit by increasing ratings and viewership (Martin 2015, 214; Shafer 2017, 86, Dalton 2019, 7), which causes a profound alienation in the protagonist (Fernandez-L'Hoeste 2017, 496; H. García 2011, 138), among other consequences. Other scholars have noted how, in this story, this line of work causes a loss of identity (Martin 204).

All of these readings of the story's protagonist in relation to his work prove valid and instructive in connecting to the social anomie wrought by neoliberalism in Mexico in the 1990s, but my interpretation reveals how Rojo is articulating something beyond alienation or loss of identity. The Tijuana author is postulating how a (post)human subject is on his or her way to disappearing due to an increasing presence and massive proliferation of screens during the neoliberal period. In this sense, Hector Fernández-L'Hoeste is correct in stating that "Ruido gris" marks a transformation in the sensibility in the modern era (2017, 496), although my reading goes farther by interpreting it through Rojo's own essay "Tócame, estoy enfermo," which helps to explain his conception of the human, the body, and subjectivity around this time—especially his interpretation of these elements in relation to electronic media and screens. This essay, more than any other non-fictional text from the author, shows his affinity for European (mostly French) theory and his influences from universal science fiction authors and other popular culture figures, all of which substantially inform the construction of the ocular reporter. We will return to this topic after discussing the story's representation of a multinational media corporation and how its use of ratings links with actual neoliberal policy of the 90s.

In "Ruido gris," the media corporation's presence, which is all-powerful and constant-yet-unseen, persists as the central antagonistic force. Its existence predates and outlasts the protagonist within the story's timeline, making it a profound, enduring entity within the character's life that rivals—and even surpasses—the impact of the lack of parental presence; H. García has read this substitutional functioning of the corporation[6] as

[6] In addition, H. García rightly points out that the media company appears as an amalgam of a maquiladora and a factory- or government-like entity that organizes most core aspects of the life of its workers or citizens (2011, 109).

taking on the role of "adoptive parents" (2011, 113).[7] But it is more than this: as a narrative actant within the story's diegesis, its omnipresence remains paradoxically elusive, a kind of dark matter that controls his daily life's direction in multiple ways, but manages to escape being seen by him as a physically existing institution. It is sensed only peripherally—through the protagonist's reporting of seeing the red, green, or yellow light that illuminates within his right eye and is connected to the camera, indicating that his vision is being recorded, on standby, or is being broadcast live, respectively. The company's presence can also be sensed non-visually by the protagonist, i.e. heard in the gray noise that buzzes between his eyes signaling the operating of the transmitting device, as well as the occasional voice in his ear of a program director that communicates with him from the station. The most notable such voice is "Rud," the nickname given for one with which he develops a rapport; Rud even gives the protagonist his own nickname, "el Desencantado" (1996, 43) [the Disenchanted One] toward the end of the story. The contract with the company controls his days, as he is required to seek out newsworthy events that are sensationalist and hyper-violent for recording or live transmission. Thus, the tale's central narrative conflict rests on an anonymous, invisible—yet omnipotent and pervasive—media corporation that not only overtakes the visual capacities of the individual subject, but exploits him (as well as other ocular journalists) for profit. Grace Martin interprets the main criticism in the story as directed toward the "media industry…for its unequal practices and disproportionate power over society" (2015, 213). She astutely recognizes that what Rojo portrays here is less the form of a panoptic surveillance society via Foucault where the few observe the many, but rather a complementary "viewer society" where the many watch the few;[8] the cyborg journalist performs the function of both a surveillance agent of other citizens as well as a surveilled subject by the corporation itself (2015, 201). However, on this point it is worth asking: how exactly are the ocular reporter's surveilling actions deterring the citizens he finds and records?

[7] This stance goes even further in Rojo's story "Conversaciones con Yoni Rei" (1998), where parents exchange their unwanted children with the generically named, multinational corporation Telcor International for credit to be used for shopping. Telcor uses these children as subjects for experiments (69). The tragicomic protagonist Yoni Rei of the title reveals himself to be a sad, irreverent, perverse, and increasingly monstrous cyborg as the story progresses.

[8] See Thomas Mathiesen's article about the synoptic society "The Viewer Society: Michel Foucault's 'Panopticon' Revisited" (1997).

In most instances, he does observe them and record or broadcast them, but his actions never appear to alter anyone's behavior within society (the Foucaultian interpretation of Bentham's Panopticon in modernity). In "Ruido gris," there is no internalization of rules or regulations, nor rehabilitation of those observed; to the contrary, the ocular journalist's presence ultimately intervenes in scenes that contribute to causing harm to citizens. Finally, Shafer properly recognizes that, while the media corporation is the mechanism that extends technological control over its employees, the real dehumanizing force is the neoliberal apparatus "that employs such technology for mass consumption" (2017, 87).

Television under NAFTA: The Rise of Ratings, Competition, and Mediatic Violence

While it is true that the story critiques both the media industry and neoliberalism, the latter is the economic system that shapes, conditions, and maintains the functioning of the media industry as it exists in "Ruido gris," underscoring its larger importance. To continue the aforementioned simile, neoliberalism acts as the politico-economic dark matter that (de-) regulates how the media industry and their news programs function. David Dalton biopolitical reading suggests that this economic system can be understood as "necroliberal," given that it is set up in such a way as to seek out and exploit death for financial gain (2019, 7). This useful theorization helps explain some of the effects that the market has brought about both in the story as well as in the Mexican televisual industry in the 1990s, and undoubtedly, death, ratings, and profit abound in "Ruido gris." Some scholars have pointed out that a suicide book ends the narrative (H. García 2011, 103; Martin 2015, 215; Dalton 2019, 20), but it is more precise to consider the seemingly small details that open and close the tale: the buzz and electricity hum of the (presumably gray) internal noise that he hears from the equipment installed in his head (1996, 7 and 45). In the first paragraph, the narrator links this noise first and foremost to the buzzing sound lights make when turned on at once in a shopping mall: "Mi cabeza es como un *mall* vacío" (1996, 7) [My head is like a vacant mall], underscoring commodification and the body. At the end, after he finishes narrating his fantasized suicide, the story closes with "Y quizá, solamente quizá, me olvidaría del zumbido por primera vez" (1996, 45) [And maybe, just maybe, I would forget about the buzzing sound for once.] The sound—a simile linked to the spaces of consumption typical of advanced capitalism—predates, pervades, and plagues the protagonist's phenomenological experience of the world.

What drives home this link between neoliberal capitalism and violence in "Ruido gris" is the importance of the ratings system which gauges viewership and sets prices for advertisement revenues. The incentive for the ocular journalist to seek out and report on increasingly sensational events, which are most frequently comprised of hyper-violent or gory spectacle, is motivated by the de-regulatory framework imposed upon the company to its increase in audience viewership, and therefore its ratings. This clearly parallels a larger shift in how television began to function in the 1990s, succumbing to the logic of the market as the prime mover of value. Here, higher viewership equals higher ratings, which in turn result in higher commercial advertisement revenues—the key source of television capital revenue. Throughout the short story, the term—"ratings," written in English—surfaces in six separate instances (1996, 13, 14, 22, 35, 38, 41), all of which signal this factor as the key arbiter of value in this business. This signifier appears directly linked to violent spectacle as the guiding principle—or marker of the free-market (de-)regulatory framework—of how an ocular journalist should go about his job: always seek out violent acts; the more violent, the higher the ratings. To give just one example from the text, after a policeman is shot in the head from behind during the interview, the ocular reporter comments during his live broadcast: "'Al parecer', comento al aire, 'todavía quedaba un individuo escondido en el clóset y este descuido de la policía ha provocado que otro oficial pierda la vida.' Siempre es bueno criticar a las instituciones. Aumenta los *ratings*" (1996, 99) ["It seems," I comment on air, "that there was still one person hiding in the closet, and this carelessness by the police has cost yet another officer his life.' It's always good to criticize institutions. It raises the ratings."]. This expression, narrated off-air and only to the reader, reveals clearly what incentives actively guide his actions. Other moments in the narration when the ratings have become synonymous with bizarre and violent spectacle not only corroborate this link but show to what extent this logic becomes internalized in the seeing subject. He himself begins to imagine what the program director would say regarding ratings or how what he is recording will be received (1996, 104, 113, 116). The market, i.e. the viewers, become moving-image consumers in this new visual economy, reflecting changes that mirrored those occurring on the ground in Mexico around this time.[9]

This measuring of audience ratings was by no means a new invention at the time, given that the Nielsen ratings system began measuring audience viewership as early as the 1950s in the United States. Nevertheless, in the case of 1990s Mexico, there exists a unique confluence of factors that made the importance of ratings more noticeable and a key standardized measurement to viewing habits. First, The Nielsen Company entered Mexico in 1991 (Neilsen, n.d.)[10] and has since become the leading means of measuring viewership in television and radio. This service directly relates to the success or failure of programs that run on a particular channel; this is due almost exclusively to the role of ratings for setting advertising costs. Ratings are, in effect, what sets the exchange value in monetary terms for publicity in television. The higher the ratings, the higher the ad revenue. Second, in 1993 under new ownership TV Azteca began competing more successfully against Televisa, which lent an unprecedented importance to the ratings systems—given the previously uncontested monopoly of the latter. After purchasing the company, TV Azteca's owner Ricardo Salinas Pliego set an ambitious goal to reach 24% of the ad market within four years of operation. By 1997, it was able to surpass that and achieve 31% (Sutter 1997, 24)—quite an astounding figure given that Televisa had gone virtually uncontested since its inception as a company in 1955 (under

[9] Despite this reading, however, there exists a unique element to viewership and ratings worth considering: advertising in media markets inverts this idea that viewers are the consumers of televisual broadcast commodities, that they possess "consumer sovereignty" (qtd in Williams 2004, 89); this is because advertisers demand audiences from media companies in order to market to them, which then determines supply. As such, rather than viewers being consumers in this realm, they are actually the commodity sold to the companies advertising on television. This would be pertinent to any analysis of "Ruido gris" if commercials appeared anywhere in the text, but they are wholly absent. Commercials do not exist in this fictional world and can only be inferred as a background element driving the value of ratings. Therefore, this curious omission in the story leaves ratings as a kind of floating signifier that are not explicitly connected to the ratings system.

[10] This is according to the Nielsen Television Audience Measurement webpage, where the Introduction page confirms: "Since it was established in 1991, IBOPE has done a systematic, continuous and automated television ratings measurement in México" (Nielsen n.d.) 1991 is the year when set meters and diaries began collecting data (a more rudimentary form of collecting data), and in 1993 "people meters" were installed to achieve more precision. IBOPE refers to the parent company, Instituto Brasileiro de Opinião Pública e Estatística, a market research company established in the 1940s that expanded to numerous other countries in the 1980s and 1990s.

the name Telesistema Mexicano). The rating system came to be the key measurement in this era of heightened competition caused by the privatization of public channels and the subsequent rise of TV Azteca that resulted. "The point to keep in mind," state media scholars Omar Hernández and Emile McAnany, "is that market forces can have unforeseen political and cultural consequences. Thus, the new playing field in Mexican open-air television was made possible in the first place by the privatization efforts of the Salinas de Gortari administration, and the commercial interests of the market have been the main factors in shaping it to this day" (2001, 393). Pierre Bourdieu would also agree in his native France where his lecture-turned-book *On Television* (1998) becomes a scathing yet measured sociological criticism of television in the free-market age. He writes: "Pushed by competition for marketshare, television networks have greater and greater recourse to the tried and true formulas of tabloid journalism..." (Bourdieu 1998, 51)— an observation that parallels with Mexico's *nota roja* at this particular time. Bourdieu takes the pressure a step farther, asserting that an increased reliance upon ratings in television has a far-reaching effect that goes beyond its own mediatic boundaries of broadcast television:

> Through pressure from audience ratings, economic forces weigh on television, and through its effect on journalism, television weighs on newspapers and magazines, even the "purest" among them. The weight then falls on individual journalists, who little by little let themselves be drawn into television's orbit. In this way through the weight exerted by the journalistic field, the economy weighs on all fields of cultural production. (1998, 56)

Bourdieu asserts that television has come to affect nearly every sphere of journalism by its own increased pressure to garner, above all, higher ratings. Similarly, Rojo's writing most notably bears the imprint of television on his own literary production. In the case of Mexico in "Ruido gris," competitive ratings tied to news programming that actively looks to broadcast moving audiovisual images of extremely violent events become not only central features of this new visuality, but active agents that perpetuate the perception of violence within society, as detailed below.

Violence and sensationalist programming, along with competition and ratings, can also be linked to the new kinds of shows that resulted from the creation of TV Azteca. These factors result from larger changes covered in the introduction regarding neoliberal policy that reduced government expenditures and privatized national industries, as did the then state-run television company, Imevisión, in 1993. The selling of this company included two open-air channels, 13 and 7, 169 local stations and theatre chains (Hernandez and McAnany 394), and eventually paved the way for Televisión Azteca to be formed.[11] What this television channel brought was a challenge to the monopolistic practices that Televisa had enjoyed during 40 years of uncontested reign. In its first two years, TV Azteca was unafraid to challenge the status quo and the way that the industry had hitherto functioned, distributing lower-cost programming and selling very low-rate advertisement (Hernandez and McAnany 2001, 398). As Hernández and McAnany mention, the ideological atmosphere in Mexico at the time created the perfect opportunity for TV Azteca to challenge Televisa and gain market share. For one, it provided news that was deemed credible insofar as it was simply an alternative to Televisa, whose ties to the government have notoriously been strong. The long-standing media behemoth has often been seen as the main propaganda source for the State going back years. This tie between the company and the State was in no way a secret, given that Televisa's president Emilio Azcárraga once stated publicly that "yo soy un soldado del PRI" (Toussaint 1998, 113) ["I am a soldier of the PRI."]. Given the government's military engagement with the Zapatista uprising in 1994, the coverage on behalf of Televisa was considered so "one-sided in its pro-government stance that it shocked an audience already accustomed to biased reporting into buying record numbers of newspapers and magazines" (Hernández and McAnany 2001, 397). Despite public distrust of Televisa's news reports, TV Azteca's own new program *Hechos* still garnered low ratings from the moment of its purchase in 1993, due in large measure to the fact that channels 13 and 7 were once government-owned and operated and consequently the stigma attached to them had not yet changed. It was not until August of 1995 that TV Azteca launched a reality news, *nota roja* program that for the first time offered something different to the viewing public: *Ciudad desnuda*. It "so unabashedly set out to report the everyday violence found in Mexico City that its producers claimed that 'blood would drip from the TV sets.' The show caught on quickly and in little over a year it was pulling ratings consistently in the high teens" (Hernández and McAnany 2001, 398).

[11] This occurred after a suspicious bidding process that later implicated the owner of TV Azteca Ricardo Salinas Pliego of being gifted with favoritism, given the connection of his brother to the ex-president Raúl Salinas de Gortari at the time (Toussaint 1998, 133–134).

Ciudad desnuda bears a striking resemblance to *Rojo Digital*, the reality news program to which the protagonist in "Ruido gris" often contributes. In describing the opening sequence of the program's introduction, the protagonist relates in layered detail the scenes that comprise it:

> Hay una toma con mucho movimiento de un tiroteo en el centro de la ciudad, hasta que uno de los que están disparando voltea a ver a la cámara y aprieta el gatillo, la toma se sacude y parece que va cayendo al suelo. Todo empieza a inundarse de un líquido rojo que va llenando el lente. El ritmo empieza a acelerarse. Una toma desde el punto de vista de un conductor que choca contra un camión escolar. Una contrapicada de un sujeto que se avienta desde un edificio...El sacrificio de una vaca en un rastro. El asesinato de un político. Un accidente industrial donde un tipo pierde un brazo. Tomas de explosiones en las que incluso el reportero sale volando. Un secuestro en un avión, donde el terrorista dispara en la cabeza de un pasajero. Y así sucesivamente. (1996, 109)
>
> [There's an action sequence of a shootout downtown, till one of the people firing turns and sees the camera and presses the trigger; the camera shot jolts and seems to fall to the ground. Everything starts to flood, a red liquid's filling up the lens. The pace starts to pick up. A shot from the point of view of a driver who crashes into a school bus. A worm's-eye view of a guy throwing himself off a building... The sacrifice of a cow in a slaughterhouse. The assassination of a politician. An industrial accident where some guy loses an arm. Shots of explosions where even the reporter gets blown up. A skyjacking where the terrorist shoots a passenger in the head. And so on.]

These images of extreme violence continue to appear in such rapid succession that they begin to blur altogether in lines of red, yellow, and gray colors that spin into a ball like fireworks until the explosion that converts the ball into the show's logo *Rojo Digital.* The comparison between the programming of the actual *Ciudad desnuda* in which "blood would drip off the TV sets" and the opening scene to the fictional *Rojo Digital*, where violent images culminate into the diegetic blood slowly covering and then filling the screen, share this uncanny similarity. *Ciudad desnuda* was not the only show of this kind, but it had the largest impact in terms of ratings. It also should be understood as the first of many, since it spawned a number of spin-offs, both within Azteca and its competitor Televisa. These violently sensationalist reality-news programs became popular enough that by the first week of July in 1996, 31 hours were broadcast over 17 different shows throughout the open-air broadcast spectrum, many following in the shoes of the pioneering program *Ciudad desnuda* (Fadul 1996). This included programs like *Historias de la calle*, *Rescate 911*, *Expediente 13/22:30*: *Cámara y delito*, *Primer impacto edición nocturna*, *Fuera de ley* (Hallín 2000, 36). Televisa produced its own show *A sangre fría* to directly compete with TV Azteca. In all, between 1995 and 1997 the audience for these shows grew an astonishing 50%, reaching a fever pitch of popularity that amounted to high ratings for both Televisa and Azteca. By late 1997, President Ernesto Zedillo called upon TV executives to moderate the violence of these programs, which resulted in the termination of both *Ciudad desnuda* and *A sangre fría* shortly after. It is nevertheless noteworthy that by no means did this terminate all *nota roja* broadcasts, as they continue to be part of the media landscape to this day, particularly as narco-related violence has surged since Felipe Calderón's own War on Drugs that he launched in late 2006. It is also worth remembering Dalton's conceptualization of necroliberalism at play here, given that the economic system monetizes human death and suffering for profit (2019, 7), which helps to explain effect of the wholly deregulated "free" market on television programming.

Elizabeth Ginway has suggested that Rojo's classic story "foreshadow[s] addiction to news" (2020, 183), which undoubtedly rings true. If one takes into account the aforementioned context, it is clear that the author's acute perception to some core changes within the Mexican media industry allowed him to extrapolate these alterations into a near-dystopian future. Hyper-violent media within this shifting sensorium becomes one its most salient features.

Electricity Injections and the Vanishing Body

Setting aside ultra-violent television programs, the ratings system which gauges their popularity, incentivizes increased productions in a competitive marketplace, and the effects of NAFTA on the media industry that allowed this all to happen, one can read in "Ruido gris" another pointed critique that Rojo makes regarding televisual media, the body, and subjectivity. In order to articulate this, it is instructive to bring into this discussion a nonfictional text[12] by the author: "Tócame estoy enfermo."[13] Written in 2002[14] with an updated revision in 2009, this essay explicitly develops Rojo's conception of the posthuman, including abundant citations of thinkers and extensive footnotes throughout.[15] What most stands out about the text in relation to "Ruido gris" is Rojo's repeated reliance upon French theorist Paul Virilio. While Rojo's essay brims with ideas and quotes from numerous authors, theorists, philosophers, and other speculative fiction writers (all of which hail from the Global North without exception), Virilio remains one of the most cited. The essay focuses on interrogating the status of "la nueva carne" (2009b, 2) [the new flesh], a term Rojo borrows from filmmaker David Cronenberg to describe the appearance of the post-human, the new kind of human being that appears toward the end of the twentieth century and start of the twenty-first cen-

[12] Rojo has written a substantial number of nonfiction texts, including essays, manifestos, and other experimental, hybrid works. His 2009 book *i nte rrupciones* includes six essays (2009a), although his work can be found in a wide variety of publication outlets, from science fiction websites like *La langosta se ha posado* to independent cultural criticism in *Revista Replicante: periodismo digital, critica cultural* and in independent publisher *Tierra Adentro*'s website.

[13] Rojo wrote two non-fiction texts with the title "Tócame, estoy enfermo." The first, mentioned above and discussed in this chapter, initially appeared in the website run by Gerardo Porcayo *La langosta se ha posado* in 2002. In 2009, a revised version appeared, also in PDF form (without printed page numbers, but for which I am citing as the number of pages within the PDF) with extensive footnotes attached, and making the text rather lengthy at over 9000 words. The second text with the same title is much shorter and appears in the 2009 collection book *i nte rrupciones* with a mixture of essays, poems and short stories. Rojo argues something quite different and more Lacanian in the shorter essay: language is a virus to the human (2009a, 101).

[14] Given the year this essay was published, it joins a number of other nonfiction texts written by Mexicans regarding the posthuman, sharing numerous thematic affinities with them: *El cuerpo transformado: cyborgs y nuestra descendencia tecnológica en la realidad y en la ciencia ficción* (2001) by Naief Yehya, *La utopía de los seres posthumanos* (2004) by Luz María Sepúlveda, *El cuerpo post-humano en el arte y la cultura contemporánea* (2005) by Iván Mejía, and *Posthumano: la vida después del hombre* (2007) by Mauricio Bares. For more information, see my article "Does the Posthuman *Actually* Exist in Mexico? A Critique of the Essayistic Production on Posthumanist Discourse Written by Mexicans (2001–2007)" in *Posthumanism and Latin(x) American Science Fiction* (Tobin, 2022).

[15] The essay offers a hodgepodge of US and European thinkers and science fiction writers whose output focuses on media and subjectivity, such as J.G. Ballard, Jean Baudrillard, William Gibson, Marshall McLuhan, Steven Shaviro, Bruce Sterling, and Slavoj Žižek, among others. While not an academic text per se, its length, numerous citations, and overall depth of argumentation makes it a valid entry into essayistic discourse on the posthuman.

tury. For Rojo, one of the defining features of the change this figure has undergone—if not *the* defining feature—is due to the telecommunications revolution that occurred after World War Two and dominated the second half of the century. Television, computers, and handheld devices of the new era of telecommunication create a new dimension for human experience, which Virilio names the "terminal body" (Virlio 1994, 3), where the body is an endpoint in a network of global communications. In this increasingly prevalent dimension, light projects onto body, rendering it a kind of screen—a clear divergence with its cinematic predecessor where an immobile body watches moving images projected onto a screen in a darkened room. Rojo, citing Virilio, states: "Actualmente, y gracias a la tecnología de la información, somos pacientes mentales sujetos a una terapia de *electroshocks* light, constante e ininterrumpida. Somos seres que necesitan 'inyectarse electricidad' constantemente. Nuestros cuerpos físicos se desvanecen para poder vivir en la nueva dimensión de la telecomunicación" (Virilio 1997, 2) [Currently, and thanks to information technology, we are mental patients subjected to electroshocks of light therapy, constant and uninterrupted. We are beings that need to be injected with electricity constantly. Our bodies disappear in order to be able to live in the new dimension of telecommunication.][16] This operating premise underlies Rojo's ontological conception of the human: telecommunications are in the process of supplanting the body and rendering it obsolete. His thought here aligns well with the general thrust of certain postmodern and poststructuralist thinkers in vogue around the time that proclaimed the death of the subject and the end of the human. Adding to this a tendency to view the human subject as a "having a body" rather than "being a body," Rojo relies upon a Western tradition of Cartesian dualism that sees the mind as a discreet and separable entity, distinct from the body. His posthuman conception is underpinned by transhumanist premises (2009b, 13). However, he ultimately puts a nihilistic spin on this approach by stating that the only option left—after the radical changes in reproductive tech-

[16] Rojo also cites other concepts by Virilio in his essay, such as "retinal persistence," and "industrialization of perception" (2009b, 3), the "third interval" (2009b, 5), "endocolonization" (2009b, 9), and "vision without a gaze" (2009b, 11). Virilio's thought is vast and complex, and too much to adequately discuss here, but John Armitage succinctly describes the overarching thrust of the French theorist's thought when he writes that Virilio's work "traces the gradual but continuing disappearance of human subjectivity into technological systems" (1997, 201) Eventually, human visual perspective will be displaced by "vision machines" that see in place of the human. See Virilio's *The Vision Machine* (1994) for more information.

nologies that render the body largely unnecessary for sexual coupling—is through virus and contagion. That is to say, the only refuge left for humanity to remember what it felt like to be human is illness (Rojo 2009b, 14–15). Needless to say, this is quite a problematic assertion given that all non-human sentient life also experiences contagion, virus and illness at some level; what is more, most human and nonhuman life exists in symbiosis with bacteria, as is the case with the microbiome, without which humans and animals would not exist. Nonetheless, however knotty some of these assertions are, they remain core tenets that underlie Rojo's conceptualization of the human.

While the body in "Ruido gris" has not yet disappeared completely or been rendered obsolete, it is true that its status remains in notable decline due to its direct link with electronic communications and the televisual media apparatus. Throughout the unnamed megalopolis in the story numerous bodies reveal themselves to be part of this "new flesh." Some convulse from SECLE (Síndrome de exposión continua a la electricidad) [Constant Electric Exposure Syndrome, or CEES]—the disease of the new century, akin to AIDS[17] in the twentieth—where an ocular reporter gets "hooked" by looking at a monitor while transmitting live. Other bodies die from this, as in the famous Toynbee case where media extremists kidnap him and intentionally "hook" him while broadcasting the process until his heart explodes (Rojo 1996, 24). Numerous bodies and faces are highly malleable, with virtually all citizens undergoing plastic surgery so that the poor and adolescents are the only ugly ones, their socioeconomic status being immediately visible (Rojo 1996, 24). And one martyr of entertainment, Grayx, decides to make a commentary on the "despersonalización del cuerpo" (Rojo 1996, 36) [depersonalization of the body] by televising the surgical removal of his head, which remains connected via cables and wires to his body and remains fully functioning during the procedure. Perhaps nowhere is this more apparent than in el Desencantado's final major broadcast in the mall, where he finds himself in a terrorist situation and decides to not advise two security guards of a ticking bomb he comes across. In doing so, lets them die for the sake of ultra-violent live footage. The bomb explodes, sending him through the air, as he narrates: "No soy un cuerpo, soy una máquina que vuela por los aires, cuya única finalidad es grabar y grabar y grabar para que todo el mundo pueda ver lo

[17] Shafer reads this parallel as evidence that el Desencantado is representative of a queer figure/cyborg (2017, 90).

que no les gustaría vivir" (Rojo 1996, 33) [I'm not a body, I'm a machine soaring through the air, whose only purpose is to record and record and record so that the whole world can see what they wouldn't want to live.]. In the beginning of the story, the narrator also states something similar: "El cuerpo es una máquina insensata" (1996, 7) [The body is an absurd machine.] These narrative events, metaphor, and simile all articulate a human subject whose body is being overtaken by audio-visual electronic machinery, and whose self is waning in the process.

One hallmark of the body's resistance to its disappearing, according to Rojo in "Tócame, estoy enfermo," is increased visual representation of gore (2009b, 6), which abundantly appears throughout "Ruido gris." Whether it is through the recorded suicides that are so commonplace that they appear banal and don't make ocular journalists much money (1996, 9–10), the narrator's own frequent imagining of his own spectacular suicide (1996, 25, 35, 44–45), the brutal killing where he manages to capture a live close up of a police officer getting his head blown off (1996, 12), or the final scene in the mall where he films a bomb exploding two security guards (1996, 33), gore's centrality in the story is hard to ignore, and in no place is this clearer than the aforementioned opening sequence to *Rojo Digital*. It is in these narrative sequences that Rojo offers his assessment of the status of the body in steep decline, where the increased circulation and prevalence of hyper-violent, moving images is a signifier of the vanishing body in the postmodern era. Rojo insists that "El sensacionalismo gráfico en los medios de comunicación es el último mecanismo mediante el cual el mundo recuerda la existencia del cuerpo" (2009b, 6) [Graphic sensationalism in mass media is the ultimate mechanism through which the world remembers the existence of the body]. With these examples in mind, it bears reading "Ruido gris" as a vehicle to express Rojo's transhumanistic ontology on a more abstract plane, one less situated in a place and time that foregrounds a neoliberal Mexico, and that more emphatically expresses his conception of a vanishing subject.

What remains impressively prophetic about "Ruido gris," and likely explains why this story still resonates so strongly with readers[18] and scholars 25 years after its publication, goes beyond the increased proliferation of screens on the ground in Mexico (and throughout much of the world) where many people are increasingly living their lives in, through, and sur-

[18] I have taught this story numerous times in multiple courses about science fiction from Latin America, and a majority of students consistently rank this as their favorite.

rounded by screens. The rise in violence in Mexico during the neoliberal era, particularly after the sharp rise following Calderón's War on Drugs in 2006, has brought with it the complicity of the media sphere and the general indifference of the viewing public, both of which factor prominently in the story. H. García points out how programs like this help form new types of human beings habituated to mediatic violence (2011, 116–117), whereas Martin goes a step further and speaks of consumption of these violent images as rendering citizens passive, causing the homogenization and "idiotization" of society (2015, 213). Both scholars perceptively point out the receptive effects of such hyper-violent media images in the story, but it is Sayak Valencia's recent research that allows us to concretely link what has been happening on the ground in Mexico since the story was published, thereby revealing the true anticipative quality of "Ruido gris." Building upon her work on "gore capitalism," Valencia incorporates the role of mass media in Mexico in order to postulate that the bombardment of ultraviolent images of massacred bodies anesthetizes spectators and renders them indifferent, rather than spurning outrage and calls to action. This anesthetized reception is not random but rather "una consecuencia de la producción de ciertos modos de percepción hegemónicos de las imágenes que distribuyen un pacto escópico necropatriarcal a través de los medios de información, entretenimiento masivo, la publicidad y el consumo" (Pérez Flores 2020) [a consequence of the production of certain hegemonic modes of perception of the images that distribute a necropatriarchal scopic pact through the information media, entertainment, publicity and consumption.] Obviously, Valencia's work focuses on feminicide in Mexico when she considers the necropatriarchal scopic pact, but it seems clear that a similar effect appears to be at play in Rojo's story despite its lack of attention to gender. It is here were Dalton's "necroliberalism" reveals its utility by casting a broader theoretical framework beyond gender. In an economic system that monetizes human death and suffering for profit (2019, 7), Rojo's reveals a mediasphere where anesthesized viewers are a consequence of a dominant mode of reception of ultra-violent images that distribute a "necroliberal scopic pact" through various forms of media—and where television remains the most notable form. The overall effect of consuming such hyper-violent and gory images through media numbs the general viewing public and is a function of the larger ne(cr)oliberal economic system. The bottom line here is that Rojo's "Ruido gris" not only absorbed trends in television programs in his contemporary moment while critiquing the new ratings system brought about by neoliberal changes to the media industries, but he also accurately foresaw Mexico of the 2010s. Few other national authors can lay claim to such an enduring and potent tale—whether in science fiction or other genres.

Punto cero: Televisual Imaginaries and Split Subjects

If "Ruido gris" proposes a multitude of critiques of a hyper-visual public sphere and spends most of its narration outside in the public spaces of the social, Rojo's *Punto cero* shifts its space toward the private, interior place of home. In so doing, he explores some of the more psychological facets of televisuality. The text—his only published novel to date—has been virtually ignored by scholars since it was first published in 2000, despite finding enough of a public to merit being republished in 2012. According to the author, one significant reason it garnered a large enough audience to warrant its second edition was due to the key narrative event of a "virtual kidnapping," which presaged actual virtual kidnappings that are believed to have begun in Mexico around 2001, a year after *Punto cero* was originally published. These events, made possible with cellular phones, increased dramatically toward the end of the 2000 decade, affecting thousands of families and individuals throughout Mexico.[19] Beyond this fact, *Punto cero* continues to bear witness to the importance of television in 1990s Mexico by foregrounding televisuality in the narrative, making it at once its central thematic preoccupation and a source of its rhetorical innovation.

As of this printing, the only proper scholarly treatment of *Punto cero* comes from Antonio Córdoba's *Extranjero en tierra extraña: El género de la ciencia ficción en América Latina* (2011). His useful analysis of Rojo's novel brings it, along with other science fiction works from Mexican and

[19] A virtual kidnapping, also called telephonic extortion, consists of the criminal dialing a telephone number, often at random, and the person who picks up the phone hears a voice, usually a minor, screaming for help. The victim in a panic usually says the name of his or her son or daughter out loud, and the extortion begins, after the victim believes that their son or daughter has been kidnapped when in reality they have never even met the kidnappers. The ransom amount requested varies from as low as 500 pesos up to 20,000 dollars. The turnaround time is usually quick and minimizes the risk for the criminal. In the year 2001, only 10 cases were reported, but in 2007 that figure reached as many as 10,000 (Amescua Chávez 2010, 116). The "virtual" aspect to this event is facilitated by leveraging the anonymity of a telephone call to make the victim believe a loved one has been kidnapped and demands ransom to be saved. However, this is not the case of *Punto cero*, where the virtuality of the kidnapping occurs on television and not in the subjective experience of the protagonist who is supposedly kidnapped.

Argentine authors that comprise his corpus, into dialogue with recurring tropes and motifs from the region's longstanding engagement with fantastic literature (understood in the Todorovian sense of the term most frequently employed in the twentieth century).[20] Córdoba's linking Rojo's novel with the fantastic is apropos, given that this work hybridizes science fiction and the fantastic mode—a factor that lends credence to the specularity of the novel (more on this later). In particular, Córdoba reads *Punto cero* as a narrative that shares numerous parallels with the region's strong fantastic tradition, offering a kind of inversion of Julio Cortázar's protagonist in "La noche boca arriba" whose reality becomes upended by the story's end (2010, 531). Rather than awake and realize his dreams have become his nightmarish reality as in Cortázar's classic story, the protagonist in *Punto cero* realizes that his nightmarish, televisual reality can be avoided altogether by entering the television screen, thereby ostensibly escaping a horrific end. My reading of Rojo's novel delves into the psychoanalytic elements of the novel, especially in light of influence that Jacques Lacan has had on Rojo's life. Córdoba also calls *Punto cero* the most noteworthy work from the cyberpunk movement (2011, 41)—a claim that seems somewhat premature from our current vantage, given that amount of Mexican science fiction scholarship since that has shown significantly more attention given to two other novels: Gerardo Porcayo's *La primera calle de la soledad* (1993) and Bernardo Fernández's *Gel azul* (2007).

Delving deeper into the articulations made within the novel, we see several specific critiques: that television creates—rather than reports—social reality, that consumer society has attained a new level of pervasiveness in Mexico, that the body and subjectivity have become dis-located by the presence of television, and that television is strongly helping to produce a detemporalization of subjective experience, all of which will be the focus of this subsection.

The narrative centers on Ray Domínguez, a young twenty-something in a huge city who just moved out of his affluent parents' house for the first time. Just after he arrives to his new apartment, he finds out that, according to a television news program, he had been kidnapped earlier that morning at the bank. He, along with a small group of his friends, comes to categorically deny the images and messages broadcast on

[20] More precisely, this tendency can be understood as the "modern fantastic," according to Omar Nieto's *Teoría general de lo fantástico: Del fantástico clásico al posmoderno* (2015), where he offers a tripartite taxonomy between classic, modern, and postmodern types.

television due to his own subjective experience and memory of the morning of his reported kidnapping. His friends visit him in the flesh in his new apartment, all watching the news together with incredulity as the surveillance shows Ray's capture. While the captors demand a pricey ransom and his father, a well-known magnate, states that he will have trouble putting it together, Ray decides not to tell the authorities nor even leave his apartment.[21] Shortly after, his lived body experience in the apartment undergoes a serious (yet invisible) beating while in his bathroom. This traumatic event further confounds the situation, seeming to corroborate what the television reports—despite the fact that Ray is still living in his apartment and he believes he has not been kidnapped. Several weeks after the event, the television news reports the kidnapper's setting a deadline for the ransom; if it is not reached, the kidnapper's assert that it would result in the killing of Ray. The climax culminates with a countdown that eventually "disappears" Ray into the television screen—and out of his apartment, avoiding his own death by being transported to a different place altogether (a detail which the narrative never reveals). It bears remembering that this climax in which someone disappears into a television screen shares an uncanny similarity with Francisco José Amparán's story "Ex machina" (as discussed in the introduction); this is, indeed, an intriguing climactic replication, given that each author wrote his story from a different city and year within the country; such a commonality lends credence to the broader thesis of this monograph that contends Mexico in this era tends to produce specular fictions in its science fiction literature.

Television influences, pervades, and eventually determines the narrative such that we might even say that it inhabits the entire book. From beginning to end, televisual signs appear throughout, as in video remote-control symbols for *fast-forward* ">>" or *pause* "||", inter alia, which precede and interpolate larger sub-sections within the fiction. The book cover in the

[21] This particular plot point becomes the most difficult to suspend disbelief on, given the many suggestions of his friends and extreme ease with which he could make a phone call or just take a walk out of his apartment to anywhere to see how—or if—he is seen by others. The narrative gives no substantial justification as to Ray's motivations, only that the television seems to take away his desire to do anything other than watch it: "Ray piensa en llamar a la policía para dar cuenta de su situación con tal de poder utilizar de nuevo su tarjeta de crédito y comprar todas las cosas que se le antojan. Lo olvida tan pronto como cambia de canal" (2012, 114) [Ray thinks of calling the police in order to account for anything that would allow him to again use his credit card to buy all the things that he wants. He forgets as soon as he changes the channel].

original edition displays the title and the word "Power" above a symbol designating an on/off button for a television. Dialogues from commercials or television programs very frequently intrude into the narrative, becoming part of it as well, at times turning indistinguishable from the narration's heterodiegetic descriptions of the protagonist's thoughts.[22] There are a number of sections that attempt to mimic the experience of watching television and, on occasion, *zapping* (rapidly and frequently changing channels); this sometimes results in a seemingly incoherent pastiche of dialogue and description that ends the section simply with the word "Click," as if changing the channel. These previous examples suggest the book's employment of a strategy of "retrograde remediation," where a "newer medium is imitated and even absorbed by an older one" (Bolter and Grusin 2000, 147). In this case, we observe literature absorbing and attempting to emulate television. Equally important, television is the anchor of narrative conflict throughout: the plot's forward arc culminates into a kind of vortex that inexorably pulls the protagonist towards it, eventually and climactically sucking him wholly into the television screen and thus televisual space itself; the screen consumes him. Anne Friedberg and Raiford Guns propose that "Televisual space is both the space of the televisual and the changes produced by the televisual to space itself" (2004, 131), thereby extending the definition of simply locating where television is watched to the ways in which the meaning and use of space can be transformed by the device's presence.[23] Televisual space becomes an all-consuming actant in *Punto cero*, a point which underscores the transformational power of television on subjectivity. Consistent with "Ruido gris," the subjectivity put forth by this novel remains steadfastly one that is powerfully mediated by televisuality, maintaining certain parallels that respond to larger transformations occurring in the country at the time as discussed in the previous section.

[22] With the exception of the character Lucy, which carries a first-person narration, the majority of the novel is told with a third-person, omniscient narrator.

[23] For Raiford and Friedberg, this can include screens other than television. The notion of space refers to "the 'space' that is constructed, effaced, traversed, contained on, through, in, at and around a variety of screens" (2004, 131). They state that televisual space has a multitude of potential definitions and uses and does not refer exclusively to television as the electronic device that receives broadcast signals and displays them on a monitor, but could also include the screen spaces where other types of images cross the television screen, such as the video games and video art installations.

(MIS)IDENTIFICATIONS, CORPOREAL DIS-LOCATIONS, AND DEHISCENCE: THE SUBJECT SPLITS OPEN

From the novel's opening narrated scenes to the plot's culminating fantastic end, the televisual as experienced by Ray becomes, above all else, the site of a severe mis-identification that negates his own individually lived reality. In other words, what he sees upon the television screen reflects a truer reality than the one he lives out in his own apartment. This is most clearly articulated by the story's description of his kidnapping early on, just after he moves into his apartment and his friend Mauricio calls him to tell him to turn on the TV and watch the news.

> Ray se siente como un títere, quiere gritarle a la pantalla. Se ve a sí mismo, y no recuerda nada. Su réplica sale de la toma. Se descubre torpe, indefenso. Ajeno. *El nombre de la víctima es Raymundo Domínguez*, la foto de Ray llena la pantalla, *hijo del conocido empresario industrial Arturo Domínguez*. Ray se frota los ojos. A él no le pasó eso, y sin embargo, sería el primero en hacer una identificación positiva de sí mismo. (Rojo 2012, 9)
>
> [Ray feels like a puppet, wants to scream at the screen. He sees himself and does not remember anything. His replica leaves the frame of the shot. He feels himself to be clumsy, defenseless. Alien. *The name of the victim is Raymundo Domínguez*, the photo of Ray fills the screen, *son of the well-known industrial businessman Arturo Domínguez*. Ray rubs his eyes. That did not happen to him, and yet he would be the first to make a positive identification of himself.]

As the narration reveals forthrightly here, Ray feels so distanced from the person that the television news displays upon the screen that he describes it as alien. It is an identification in that he recognizes himself and, at the same time, it is a mis-identification in that he sees the television image of himself as a replica, an *other*. This odd and seemingly fantastic proposition is exactly what Jacques Lacan posits when he states that "the self is an other" (2006, 9). By this he implies that the very notion of identity to a subject comes not from some innate, indissoluble sense of unique individual-ness, but rather is a complex matrix of language and imagery that is fundamentally exterior to a person's psychic interior. In this sense, Ray's identification and simultaneous mis-identification of his screenic image reflects a common process that the human subject experiences on a constant basis (according to Lacan), and one which Rojo links strongly to the image-identifications on television.

It merits pausing for a moment to discuss the impact of Lacan on this novel in particular and Pepe Rojo's life more generally, given that the French psychoanalyst is likely Rojo's largest intellectual influence and the analysis here includes understanding some articulations of Lacan through this novel. In his personal life, Rojo was married with and had two children with Deyanira Torres, a Lacanaian psychoanalyst in Tijuana. Starting in the late 1990s and lasting until 2005, Rojo, along with Deyanira and other figures instrumental in the cyberpunk movement, Rojo spearheaded an urban intervention titled "TÚ NO EXISTES" where they placed stickers and posters throughout the public sphere: on public mailboxes, bus stop surfaces, the then-border wall between Tijuana and San Ysidro, the fence surrounding Tijuana's bullfighting stadium, on metro doors of the subway, on massive circular highway supports, on front doors to businesses that allowed it, etc. Beyond Tijuana, this occurred in numerous cities, such as D.F., Puebla, Torreón, Coatepec, and Xalapa. This provocative message, inspired largely by a Lacanian approach to subjectivity, intended to jar the reader-viewer into questioning how they have constructed their identity, by making them consider that the "I" they identify as themselves is fundamentally erroneous and/or elusive. Those who came upon the stickers presumably also considered themselves to be rational beings to some extent, and thus probably rejected the message outright. "¿Qué quieres decir que no existo? ¡Esto es una tontería!" [What do you mean I don't exist? This is stupid!] would likely be a common response. Since Lacan constructs his entire model of subjectivity around a void with an insatiable desire as *the* bedrock psychological condition, he explicitly denies rationality—and Descartes's cogito (1977, 1)— as a fundamental basis for subjecthood. The "TÚ NO EXISTES" messages sat alongside a seemingly endless array of eye-catching commercial advertisements that attempted to interpellate and position the subject as a consumer, and, in doing so, sought to counterbalance the dominant interpellative visual advertisements of advanced capitalism.

The French psychoanalyst's influence appears in much of Rojo's writing, but the most overt expression occurs in *Punto cero* where Lacan frames the novel by being the source of the first epigraph along with the title itself. Rojo opens the work by writing: "En el fondo, sin duda, se pinta el cuadro. El cuadro, es cierto, está en mi ojo. Pero yo estoy en el cuadro" (2012, 2) ["No doubt, in the depths of my eye, the picture is painted. The picture, certainly, is in my eye. But I am in the picture].[24] To further complement this information, Rojo adds a paraphrased quote on the opposite page, where the meaning of the title is addressed: "El punto cero, según Jacques Lacan, es el punto entre nuestros ojos donde se sitúa la función de borde y el corte que hace que nuestra mirada sea nuestra. Así se mira hacia afuera mirando hacia adentro. Es siempre un punto ciego donde no se sabe quién está viendo" (2012, 3) [The zero point, according to Jacques Lacan, is the point between our eyes where the function of the limit is situated that makes our gaze ours. In this way one looks outward looking back within. It is always a blind spot where it is not known who is seeing]. The former epigraph comes directly from Lacan's *The Four Fundamental Concepts of Psychoanalysis*, where he maps out the position of the subject in the dialectic of human visual perception. Through a series of diagrams and in his typical non-linear expressive style, Lacan positions the act of visual perception as something that is fundamentally structured by a process exterior to the seeing subject: the gaze. "This is the function that is found at the heart of the institution of the subject in the visible. What determines me, at the most profound level, in the visible, is the gaze that is outside. I see only from one point, but in my existence, I am looked at from all sides" (1998, 106). The gaze that is outside, then, is embodied in the look from others—but it is also powerfully and fundamentally attached to the value placed on the look from others *by* the subject. He states elsewhere using these words "the gaze I encounter…is not a seen gaze but a gaze imagined by me in the field of the Other" (Lacan 1998, 84). In other words, the fact that I believe someone is looking at me is far more important than whether or not they actually are looking at me. This implies that the gaze exists in multiple forms: it can initiate and emanate from another person's face and eyes that train themselves intently upon me; it can also, however, be felt in a more mysterious, enigmatic quality that somehow exceeds any individual gaze that descends upon me. In this

[24] In the original English translation of *The Four Fundamental Concepts of Psychoanalysis*, there is a negation included in the last sentence that completely inverts its meaning: "But I am *not* in the picture" (1998, 96; my emphasis). This would seem to be a very unfortunate translation error, taking into account the radical change of meaning for the sentence. This Spanish translation presumably comes the Paidos publication of Lacan's text from 1997. Given this, as well as for consistency's sake, I have chosen to keep the original translation that appears in the novel, rather than correct it and speculate how this came to be. In any case, taking into account how Lacan's overarching theory articulates a severely decentered subject, it strongly suggests that the "I" is not locatable in the picture.

latter sense, it is the subject-being-looked-at who assigns the value of the gaze in this inter-subjective relationship. Kaja Silverman has pointed out that "The gaze is the 'unapprehensible' agency through which we are socially ratified or negated as spectacle. It is Lacan's way of stressing that we depend upon the Other not only for our meaning and our desires, but also for our very confirmation of self. To 'be' is in effect to 'be seen'" (1996, 33). Descartes's "I think therefore I am" becomes "I desire (to be seen by the other) therefore I am" in Lacan.

This understanding of the gaze—both real and imagined—that is fundamentally exterior to the seeing subject helps elucidate how a series of mis-identifications with the screen can lead to dis-locations of the body in *Punto cero*. The image of a kidnapped Ray quickly disseminates throughout other mass media news outlets of radio and newspapers, and soon Ray's mis-identification of the screen's image manifests itself in the dislocation of his own lived body within his own apartment. This occurs when this core group of friends consisting of Mauricio, Andrea and Lucy finally all converge there: Ray goes into the bathroom and suddenly, mysteriously, begins to feel like he is being assaulted: first, a searing pain like an electric shock covers his hand, then a hard punch to his back, and finally, the sensation that his hand was placed between two bricks and stepped on, crushing the bones within (Rojo 2012, 63). It appears that he is physically feeling the effects of being tortured by his kidnappers, yet still remains physically present in his own apartment without seeing who the kidnappers are, or even ever having been kidnapped in the first place. This "virtual" beating leaves real scars on Ray's body, and it becomes a painful reminder that the reality of his mis-identified other on the television news is affecting his subjective experience within his apartment. The disconnection between what is lived within his body inside his apartment and what he sees with his own eyes on television is radical, and the novel's plot hinges upon this inexplicable, illogical, fantastic narrative event. After this first attack, Ray's friends see him and become immediately shocked and confused as to what happened, discussing what step to take next—whether they should call a doctor, the police, the media, or a lawyer. Their ensuing conversation about what he should do becomes heightened to the level almost of an argument when Ray becomes flustered and kicks them all out of his apartment. Thus, he resolves, in effect, to do nothing, and throughout the remainder of the novel, he does very little other than watch television to see what is supposedly occurring to him according to the televised news reports. He remains willingly immobile in his own apartment, not contacting any institutional and familial social support to tell them that he is, in fact, perfectly free and not kidnapped in his own apartment, but that it is the media that is incorrectly reporting his kidnapping on the screen. His life unfolds on his Samsung 20" screen, and he watches it, mesmerized. In this sense, the narrative effectively splits Ray into two characters: the Ray who was kidnapped at the bank in the morning and the spectator Ray who watches as his life unfolds on the television screen. Moments of physical abuse return several times, such as later when he's in the kitchen and he feels that suddenly his left hand has been ripped off: "Y entonces su mano izquierda le hizo dar un grito. Sentía como si la hubieran arrancado de tajo. El dolor era insoportable" (2012, 83) [And then his left hand made him scream. He felt as if someone had ripped it clean off. The pain was unbearable]. But his hand is still there attached to his arm; it is only that he cannot move it. He becomes utterly confounded trying to understand why this is happening to him. In order to have definitive proof that the irrational is occurring to him, he decides to stab his left hand with a knife to see if he experiences pain. The knife goes in and out of his hand; he hears the sound of a bone cracking; he finally begins sawing away between his fingers, but no sensation comes, nor does blood spill forth. His hand appears bloodless, and in frustration he begins stabbing it repeatedly. But alas, he feels no pain, and the narrator concludes the section by observing that in a rational world with its laws of cause and effect, order and reason—the one in which he thought he lived—this would not happen. All his rational presuppositions of how the world functions have failed: "...pero Newton, Descartes, la teoría de la evolución, la biología, la anatomía y la medicina, le dieron la espalda" (2012, 92) [...but Newton, Descartes, the theory of evolution, biology, anatomy and medicine, all turned their back on him]. It becomes even clearer, then, by dint of his own inexplicable corporeal experience that does not correspond to the basic governing laws of physics and physiology, that we are in the realm of a world without rational explanation, one which, as Todorov says, would correspond to different laws than the one which science describes. We are in the realm of the fantastic, suspended in the interstice between belief and disbelief of a supernatural occurrence (1975, 31).

This dis-location between the body's lived experience and the projected televised image remains the plot device through which the novel carries out its own discordant logic until the fantastic end. Two months after his kidnapping, his perpetrators finally offer the public ultimatum announced on the television screen: his family must deliver the ransom within 24 hours or Ray Domínguez will be killed. Thus, another potential meaning to the novel's title—the zero point—is suggested in its retrogressive countdown of those hours until the final zero when Ray, his body transforming into the static black, white, and gray colors like those of an untuned channel, finally disappears into the television.

> **cinco**
> Todo impedía que Ray llegara a la puerta. No había salida....
> **dos**
> Como de golpe, todo cayó. La opinión de los comentaristas de la televisión. Los consejos de belleza. La necesidad de un trabajo. La cárcel de recuerdos e imágenes que eran sus amigos....
> Dejó de correr. Se sentó sobre una caja y esperó a que todo pasara. Tocó el monitor. Su brazo atravesó la pantalla. Afuera, su cuerpo adquirió consistencia. Las luces disminuyeron su intensidad mientras Ray miraba su reflecto en el cristal del monitor.
> Había algo en la mano, dentro de la pantalla. Era el control remoto.
> Ray lo volteó hacia sí mismo y apretó varios botones a la vez.
> **Cero.** (Rojo 2012, 166)
> [**five**
> Everything prevented Ray from getting to the door. There was no exit...
> **two**
> Suddenly, everything fell. The opinion of the television commentators. The beauty advice. The necessity of a job. The prison of memories and images that were his friends...
> He stopped running. He sat on a box and waited for it all to happen. He touched the monitor. His arm went through the screen. Outside, his body acquired consistency. The lights lessened their intensity while Ray looked at his reflection in the crystal of the monitor.
> There was something in his hand, inside the screen. It was the remote control.
> Ray turned it around toward himself and pushed several buttons at the same time.
> **Zero**.]

In these, his final moments, Ray does something that shows his executing a minimal level of agency: he pushes several buttons on the remote control just before the zero point occurs. Rather than being wholly subsumed into the screen altogether without a fight of any kind, Ray does what most television spectators also do—he pushes some buttons in the hopes of changing the channel and thus of the televisual experience being projected upon the screen. This sudden, yet subtle, action appears to have had some effect, because the denouement reveals that he survived the whole ordeal.

Ray leaves a message on his friend Lucy's answering machine stating that he is okay, living in a rented room, his wounds are healing and for the moment he has no plans to return to the city (2012, 170). A funeral was held for him, however, which he hopes to hear more about when he and Lucy manage to connect. The novel ends with a double twist: the Ray that was kidnapped and whose life was made a news spectacle died, whereas the spectator Ray who watched in disbelief managed to escape his seemingly inexorable death, possibly by virtue of using the remote control on the television in the final seconds.

To further complicate matters, the narration further cements the text in a fantastic realm because the split Ray experiences throughout the novel becomes literalized and unexplained at the end. As Córdoba notes, given Lucy's own unstable identity and schizophrenic episodes at various points in the novel, the narration becomes wholly unreliable (2011, 247). The novel is, at once, science fictional with clear elements of cognitive estrangement in its one central cyberpunk motif of reality-virtual inversion, while leaving the reader ultimately stuck in the Todorovian fantastic realm of uncertainty regarding Ray's ontological status. The ramifications of this end foreground two possible conclusions. First, it demonstrates how generic distinctions are quite fluid in Mexican non-mimetic cultural production. As discussed in the introduction, science fiction from the region has often tended toward generic hybridity more than the United States or Europe, due in part to the fact that they have not developed robust markets as in the North. Without much market segmentation in the region, writers do not hesitate to cross genres given the absence of specific market considerations. Furthermore, the fantastic and science fiction are siblings, of sorts, given that they both emerged from the firmament of the Romantic period in the nineteenth century and often experienced overlap (López Martín 2011, 97). In the early twentieth, early fantastic stories by Amado Nervo, Horacio Quiroga, and Leopoldo Lugones, were all considered "strange" or fantastic short narratives, but today we commonly refer to them as science fiction (many of these were also specular fictions). This trend continued even as late as 1940 when Jorge Luis Borges, Adolfo Bioy Casares, and Silvina Ocampo anthologized *Antología de la literatura fantástica* and included numerous short stories of science fiction. It is worth noting that the same year Bioy Casares published *The Invention of Morel*, which is commonly considered the first science fiction masterpiece from the region. It is also profoundly specular and anticipatory. These examples demonstrate how the fantastic and science fiction were deeply intertwined in the region and help to explain the cultural tradition in which *Punto cero* participates. Finally, this generic fluidity has other ramifications with regard to the specular nature of the novel, lending further validity to the usage of the term specular, particularly as it relates to speculation and critically examining tele-visual practices.

Specular gains even more currency when further considering the psychoanalytic articulations in the novel, such as Ray articulating a Lacanian split subject. As previously discussed, his mis-identification of the projected *imago* on the television screen and consequent dis-located body both invoke Lacan's mirror stage. After Ray forces his friends out of his apartment and resolves to do nothing, he turns on the television to watch a news segment about his kidnapping where he, his father, a kidnapper's voice, and some old friends and coworkers that knew him make up a news piece that is narrated by a reporter. When he turns off the television, the novel's narrator reveals Ray's reaction as he looks at the empty screen: "Su primera reacción había sido desconfiar. Pero la certeza del reconocimiento, esa trampa lógica que provoca la identificación en el espejo, en cualquier reflejo, se había arrastrado entre sus pensamientos y no había poder humano que lograra exiliarla" (2012, 62) [His first reaction was to distrust. But the certainty of the recognition, that logical trap the causes the identification with the mirror, with whatever reflecting surface, had lodged itself in his brain and there was no way humanly possible to get it out]. Here, Rojo references the so-called mirror stage as described by Lacan whereby a baby sees his/her image returned in a mirror and identifies his/her self positively as that image. This has numerous effects in subject formation, such as it "situates the agency of the ego…in a fictional direction […]" (Lacan 1977, 1). It is fictional because the baby—and later on, adult—is never simply that reflected image whole (Gestalt), that *specular I* that is seen exterior to the baby early on, but rather much more fragmented and partial within his/her psychic experience. Thus, recognition of one's self as one's image is also, simultaneously, a mis-recognition. In doing so the subject undergoes a continual process of a double move that asserts the "mental permanence of the I" as well as does it "prefigure its alienating destination" (Lacan 1977, 2). This double move, then, produces a double: the person who looks into the mirror and identifies his or her imago (the *specular I*) with being who they think they are (the *social I*), an event that is reasserted and maintained as the baby grows and enters the symbolic (i.e., learns language) and is told how s/he is and who s/he is by his parents as well as others. By switching Lacan's mirror for a television screen, Rojo suggests that television plays a primary role in creating a fundamentally deceptive imaginary order that significantly constitutes the psycho-social subject in contemporary Mexico.

Another Lacanian element surfaces, but less explicitly. Along with this fictional, splintered direction that the subject's ego identity takes, for Lacan there is also a fundamental discordance within the core of the human subject's psychic experience such that it can never be or feel whole. This alteration is caused by "dehiscence" (Lacan 2006, 97), a medical term Lacan borrows to refer to a gaping, a rupture, or a splitting open—as in a surgical wound—that occurs in the subject. This is the Lacanian real erupting and breaking through. Much like Lacan's discussion of a baby that falls into a trap that causes identification with the mirror and his Gestalt, Ray falls into the trap of identification with the television during the news segment about his kidnapping. He then reflects upon the spectacle that is being made of his life:

> Las heridas en su mano todavía no cicatrizaban, y de hecho parecía sangrar un poco más. La mención de su nombre o la aparición de su rostro en la televisión parecía excitarlas, y se abrían un poco más para mostrar, orgullosas, la carne viva que pulsaba bajo la epidermis. Alguien estaba sufriendo y Ray no sabía quién. No había límite que mostrara dónde acababa él y dónde empezaba lo que decían de él en la televisión. Sólo estaban las heridas en su mano, sangrando lentamente, el golpe en la mandíbula y en la espalda punzando como recordatorio de lo frágil de su posición, su identidad y valor. (Rojo 2012, 63)
>
> [The wounds in his hand had not yet scarred, and in fact it seemed that his hand bled a little bit more. The mention of his name or the appearance of his face on television seemed to excite the wounds, and they opened up a little bit more to show, proudly, the live flesh that palpitated under the epidermis. Someone was suffering and Ray did not know who. There was no limit to show where he ended and where began what they said of him on television. There were only the wounds in his hand, slowly bleeding, the pain in his jaw and the stinging back as a reminder of the fragility of his position, his identity and worth.]

What the spectator Ray then experiences here is a radical and literal splitting of his subjectivity such that the *specular I*—or the reflective image of his whole body that he sees and recognizes on the screen—becomes so associated with the *social I* broadcast by the news reports that it becomes difficult for him to deny that it is him on the screen. After the phantom beating, his body experiences an intense dehiscence with regard to his wounds, which respond to the psychic experience of Ray watching the news broadcast of himself. The wounds of his flesh—or the real in Lacanian terms—seem to come alive, announce themselves, and split further open. There are other traces of Lacan in the text that support this position, such as later when the narrator describes Ray in his apartment, alone with the rapidly changing images that cross the television screen, that the only constant is the lack: "Ese vacío que llamamos individuo. Ahí estás tú, Ray" (2012, 69) [That lack that we call individual. There you are, Ray]. Ray is a blank subject that is constituted by and composed of images that come from the television. Nowhere is this more apparent than when he falls asleep at night watching television, and the narrator describes the image broadcast of the gray static-effect screen that occurs when it no longer receives a signal.

> La luz encuentra forma en la silueta de Ray, lo construye y define sus límites, inventa un cuerpo que parece emerger de unas cajas, le da forma a sus ojos, sombra a sus labios y una expresión de tranquilidad a su rostro sin cesar de moverse un segundo. La luz del monitor inventa a Ray. Su piel es estática; él es la pantalla. (Rojo 2012, 69)
>
> [The light takes form in the silhouette of Ray, it constructs him and defines his limits, it invents his body that seems to emerge from some boxes, it gives shape to his eyes, darkens his lips and an expression of tranquility on his face without stopping to move a second. The light of the monitor invents Ray. His skin is static; he is the screen.]

This particular description underscores one chief difference between filmic and televisual spectatorship: the source of light. Friedberg points out that, unlike in the cinema where the screen receives the light from the projector, in television, the screen itself is a source of light (2004, 136). *Punto cero* literalizes this key component of contemporary spectatorship occurring in Mexico to signal the importance of the televisual image at this time. In taking stock of how these changing practices of spectatorship affect the subject, Rojo constructs in Ray a Lacanian subject whose split nature becomes manifest in the screen of the television that broadcasts his life. The novel repeatedly stresses throughout the ineluctable draw of the television image—that the images it displays hold more truth than the subject's lived experience.

Detemporalization and Commodification

The other major way *Punto Cero* articulates a televisual subjectivity resides in its representation of a scrambled temporality. While the novel can be said to have an overall chronological arc that begins with Ray's kidnapping and ends with his death/escape, there are enough moments throughout of repetition, rewinding, and temporal slippages that attempt to emulate the subjective experience of time spent watching television. Early on, this is accomplished at first very subtly on pages 8 and page 12, both of which have repeated dialogues verbatim between Ray and his friend Mauricio. The first time occurs while Ray is sleeping in his house and the phone rings, which takes him seven rings to locate the phone amidst the chaos of his boxes lying about in his new apartment. The dialogue is brief:

> -Bueno.-¿Ray?-Sí, ¿quién habla?-Soy Mauricio, ¿qué haces ahí?-Aquí vivo. -¿Estás bien?-¿Para eso hablas a estas horas?-¿Ya conectaste la TV?-Sí.-Pues bueno, busca un noticiero, como vas. Te hablo en cinco minutos. (2012, 8)
>
> ["Hello.""Ray?""Yeah, who's calling?""This is Mauricio. What are you doing there?""I live here.""Are you okay?""You're calling me this late to ask me that?""Have you set up your TV?""Yes.""Well listen, look for a news channel. I will call you back in five minutes."]

After Mauricio tells Ray he will phone him back, the call never materializes in the narrative, but this exact conversation repeats itself three pages later after shifting the focalization to Mauricio, working the late shift at a pharmacy. The television is turned on while he works, and on it he sees the news announcing Ray's kidnapping earlier in the day; this in turn sparks the call to Ray in his new apartment, and the dialogue repeats itself. This particular scene, rewound slightly by several minutes, shifts the temporal layout of the narrative just briefly, creating an overlap in time. Under Mieke Bal's understanding of sequential ordering within narrative, this falls under internal retroversion. She describes this kind of narrative event thus:

> The repetition of a previously described event usually serves to change, or add to, the emphasis on the meaning of that event. The same event is presented as more, or less, pleasant, innocent, or important than we had previously believed it to be. It is thus both identical and different: the facts are the same, but their meaning has changed. The past receives a different significance. (1985, 61)

Indeed, the past receives a different meaning within the novel's presentation, shifting the focus to the originator of the phone call, Mauricio. But it also adds an additional significance: this internal retroversion early on reflects certain modes of repetition inherent in watching television, such as certain commercials often recurring several times within a specific time block, how a breaking news story is repeated often word for word several times throughout a broadcast, or rewinding a videocassette brings about an exact recurrence of dialogue. It also serves to set the model for chunks of the rest of the narrative, which become speckled with various, subtle forms of repetitions, rewindings, and other asynchronies. The narrative internalizes these forms of time-shifting. Temporally, one effect this has in *Punto cero* is to transmit a detemporalized world, or one where linear, cause-and-effect chronology has been shuffled just slightly. Dialogues do repeat themselves verbatim, but only with mechanical and electronic reproduction. And here, right at the beginning of the novel, there is a kink in the narrative's own sequential ordering, an inadvertent rewind that replays a portion of what has just occurred by shifting the focalization of characters. This becomes another instance where Bolter and Grusin's retrograde remediation occurs: the medium of literature attempts to emulate the medium of television.

This effect touches upon Anne Friedberg's notion of "detemporalized subjectivities," from *Window Shopping* (1993). In this book, she inserted herself into the then lively debate on the postmodern by asserting that it is in fact cinematic and televisual apparatuses and their effects produced upon subjects that are *constitutive* of the postmodern condition, not merely a symptom of it. Her position takes as its starting point Frederic Jameson's assertion that one fundamental aspect of postmodern subjectivity is the loss of historicity, or our inability to access and retain the past, condemning us to a live in a perpetual present (1993, 2). But, she notes, this critique goes farther back to Charles Baudelaire's reflections upon the introduction of the photographic camera and its effects: not only does the ability to capture images that perfectly reflect reality aid in retaining memory while also helping to preserve history, but they also begin to supplant memory. For Friedberg, Baudelaire's fear was that the photographic image and its social effects upon memory and history was also that it could efface history altogether; so, where memory and history become precarious aspects of this modernity (for Baudelaire) and postmodernity (for

Jameson), the principal cause for Western society's inability to access history is due in large part to the changes brought about by the modes of spectatorship occasioned by cinema and television. "Cinema and television—mechanical and electronic extensions of photography's capacity to transform our access to history and memory—have produced increasingly detemporalized subjectivities." She notes that the increase of these two visual forms has engendered an "increasingly derealized sense of 'presence' and identity" (Friedberg 1993, 2).

This detemporalization is very present in both of Rojo's stories treated here, but in different ways. For "Ruido gris," the protagonist bemoans a digital world brimming with electronic reproduction: "El futuro es una repetición constante de lo que ya has vivido, quizás algunos detalles puedan cambiar, quizá los actores sean diferentes, pero es lo mismo. Y cuando no lo has vivido, seguramente ya viste algo parecido en alguna película, en algún programa de TV o escuchaste algo parecido en una canción" (1996, 102) [The future is a constant repetition of what you've already lived, maybe some of the details have changed, maybe the actors are different, but it's the same. And when you haven't lived it, surely you saw something like it in a film, on a TV show or you listened to something like it in a song]. When the future becomes a repetition of the present, or full of mediatic experiences that you have already seen and thus "lived" in some vicarious audio-visually reproduced way, a subject's sense of time has been reconfigured. The connection here between the ocular journalist and Friedberg's theory point to very similar preoccupations regarding lived subjective time. In terms of *Punto cero*, this detemporalization becomes, from the very beginning, part and parcel of its literary structure with its temporal slippages, rewind-and-replay, and other repetitions that occur throughout.

In *Punto cero*, there also exists a connection between a detemporalized world brought on in part by televisual spectatorship and living in a world of constant and frequently reoccurring appearances of the commodity. The character who most personifies this is Ray's friend Andrea, whose own subjectivity becomes inescapably ensnared in the image-world of the commodity. She works at an advertising agency in the creative department, inventing ideas, slogans and images, most often for 30-second television commercial spots. In one of her first appearances in the novel, the narration describes the editing process for a Kas soft-drink commercial that she was in charge of creating.[25] The description from pages 17–20 involve an unusual amount of repetition, this time due solely to the narrative's attempt to objectively describe the editing process—as if looking at the screen. Take by take, each edited cut is described in the most economical of terms, interpolated by a quick line of dialogue, which, as soon becomes apparent, involves Andrea and the editor. There exists in this exchange a kind of collapse between the narrative's own textual description, which usually remains a distant third person omniscience, and its descent upon the editing screen—remaining tight upon each take described, breaking it down into its most essential events. This culminates on page 20 with a narration of the commercial in its finally edited form:

> Chavos, camiseta, shorts. Subir mueble, azul verde. Sudor. Músculos. Piernas de chava. Falda corta, ligera y un top. Delgada, estilizada. Curvas. Chavo, quejándose: *¿cuánto falta?* Contrapicada: Dos pisos. Uno, dos, toma impulso y la chava camina hacia el elevador. Escote, senos. Elevador. *Fuera de servicio.* Brazos en caderas, sudor. *Preferiría estar en otro lado.* Empujan. Jadear. Sube, muestra ropa interior. *Quisiera algo para este calor.* Saca un Kas, tira bolsas. Dejan de empujar. Voltean. Mueble. Desliza. Maceta rota. Chava, sonrojada: ¿quién me puede ayudar? Logo. Kas, el remedio para todos tus males. Los tres toman Kas: *¿cómo te llamas?* (2012, 28)
>
> [Guys, shirts, short. Moving a piece of furniture, blue green. Sweat. Muscles. Legs of a girl. Short, light skirt and a top. Slender, styled. Curves. Guy, complaining, *how much farther*? Low angle: Two floors. One, two, quick take and the girl walks toward the elevator. Cleavage, breasts. Elevator. *Out of service.* Arms on hips, sweat. *I would prefer to be somewhere else.* They push, pant. She goes up the stairs, shows underwear. *Maybe something for this heat.* She pulls out a Kas, throws her bags aside. They stop pushing.

[25] Kas is a soft-drink manufactured and sold by Pepsi-Co that was originally released in the Spanish market before entering Latin America in the 1990s. Predominantly sold in the largest markets in the region, Argentina and Brazil, it was not until it entered Mexico in 1994 that it reached a moderate degree of success. Leveraging the power of cross-marketing, the drink was sold with the promotional help of the song "Dame más," played by the Argentine group The Sacados, itself a full-length, four-minute musical video-cum-Kas commercial located on a beach with many surfing shots, the singer belting out verses while the choruses involves ample takes of young, attractive people swilling Kas and smiling. Also, other advertisements were known for employing highly stereotyped gendered depictions, often with a slim, attractive, head-turning young woman whose body becomes the object of young male gazers who look onward. This last one clearly influences Rojo's introduction of Andrea, as the description parallels the stereotyped model just described. ("Kas" 2009).

> Turn around. Furniture. Slides. Plant pot breaks. Girl, smiling ¿who can help me? Logo. Kas, the cure for all your maladies. The three drink a Kas. *What's your name?]*

The televisual linguistic markers are incorporated into the narrative description in an attempt to emulate the jargon and rapid impact of the commercial's visual flow. The text becomes focused solely upon what appears on the editing screen. The linguistic register here, attempting to emulate the brief, visual images of recorded takes in a commercial, reinforces the way in which literature tries to compete with, absorb, and emulate its visual rival.

Later, Andrea, upon arriving at Ray's house, finds herself in a situation that eerily repeats the commercial she conceived of and created: Two strapping young men are moving a piece of furniture up the stairs, and since there is no elevator in Ray's building, she must wait for them to finish moving the furniture. As she does, they ask, "¿Cómo te llamas?" Andrea gets lightheaded with the mirroring of commercial fantasy and her real-life situation. She looks in her purse for a Kas but finds nothing. Again, the text repeats the commercial but in her life—only this time without internal reconversions of exact dialogue. This becomes part of a motif in the novel, as Andrea creates or imagines other commercials, only to find herself caught up within a similar—but real—situation later (2012, 93, 141, 173). The difference is in their endings: in all three of these sequences, where the commercial draws back to show the logo superimposed on top of the characters in their happy ending, in Andrea's life no such ending occurs. Clearly the commentary suggests how real life misses the commercial sheen of marketing fantasies, which is required by its own time restrictions and ideological practice of selling a commodity through a short burst of constructed audio-visual imagery. But this narrative strategy also reinforces the detemporalized nature of the characters, especially one who works in the world of commercial marketing.

In addition to the internal retroversion and repetitions of commodities in the narrative, *Punto cero*'s language contains many ephemeral, economic descriptions and even symbols that most attempt to emulate its televisual referent. The novel reads like a screenplay—not only because of the inclusion of short extra-textual markers of "Fade In," "La escena es así," and "corte a," to name three—but also in its own sparing prose throughout, as in the Kas commercial narration above, or other places where the text tries to capture the fragmentary syntactic experience of watching/listening to Ray's television.[26] Whether depicting characters, narrating events or imitating the narrations of television (commercials, live news broadcast, talk shows, or zapping), the novel's expressive style remains frugal. Despite the fact that many of Rojo's stories seem preoccupied with media to one degree or another, *Punto cero* remains the one that attempts the broadest and deepest criticism through a multiplicity of strategies of internal retroversions, repetitions, an inundation of commercial marketing discourse—all integral aspects to the televisual and subjectivity. Literarily, it does not make for the most sophisticated of descriptions, nor does it immediately engage with other prime examples of classic lettered works of ekphrasis where the literary description attempts to paint its likened picture. But it does mimic and reflect a key moment when this novel was written: fleeting, ephemeral e-images that appear and disappear upon the screen with increasing rapidity that contribute to, as Rojo suggests, the construction of split subjectivities. The television becomes central throughout the narrative and in its fantastic all-consuming end, a point which underscores its rise in presence and centrality in Mexico in the 1990s.

Between the private space of Ray's home and the psychic interior of his subjectivity, along with the cyborg reporter of "Ruido Gris" out seeking the hyperviolent spectacle in the public and consumer spaces of the streets and shopping malls, Pepe Rojo carves a singular niche in both the movement associated with him—Mexican cyberpunk—as well as authors more broadly in the country. Rarely have authors absorbed changes to the visual sphere in such an overt manner throughout this or any other period in the country. This is largely due to two key factors. First, the political and economic changes occasioned by the neoliberal treaty caused numerous transformations in how the media industry, most visibly in the way televisual

[26] Rojo's story "Conversaciones con Yoni Rei" also incorporates televisual vernacular in its discourse. The story attempts to emulate a mediatic structure throughout by framing the story within the context of a television script. It both commences and closes with a framing device that employs textual markers: "Fade in" (written in English) begins the narration whereas "Fade out" closes it. This frames the story with an explicit ideal reader in mind as a televisual spectator. Throughout the story, text maintains this structure with other scene descriptions that mimic scriptwriting conventions, such as "(Aplausos)" ["Applause"] (1998, 68, 71, 80, 82, "(Sollozos)" ["Sobs"] (1998, 70, 75), "("Risas)" ["Laughs"] (1998, 76) and various "Corte a" ["Cut to"] a different scene—all in order to either give the text a script-like format or the story a television-like reading experience where the reader is immersed in a literary world that emulates a televisual world of sensationalist reality TV.

media industry functioned, bringing competition to Televisa with TV Azteca. This, along with a ratings system that increased competition for advertisers and brought about a certain kind of violent programming, resulted in a sharp increase in ultraviolent reality TV programs that "Ruido gris" absorbs and mimics. The ultimate condemnation of the story is an economic system that, as Dalton contends, is necroliberal, monetizing death and human suffering (2019, 7, 9). *Punto cero* also borrows from this convention by basing the narrative on a virtual kidnapping that becomes mediatic news spectacle that seeks higher ratings, but the interior, private space of Ray's apartment becomes metonymic of his psychic interior experience of his own kidnapping. This introduces the second factor: Rojo's use of cultural theory as inspiration to create his novel's core structure. The novel as it is presented would likely have not been conceived were it not for Jacques Lacan's psychoanalytic theory of subjectivity, which suggests that the subject is fundamentally split and erroneously constituted by exterior images that constitute the subject's imaginary and aid in creating a false sense of self. Other theorists' ideas appear in his work, but none as prevalent as Lacan. In all, both "Ruido gris" and *Punto cero* remain key specular fictions that appear in a key moment for Mexico's changing visual sphere.

Works Cited

Amescua Chávez, Cristina. 2010. El secuestro virtual en el continuum de la violencia: Visibilizar lo que se oscurece. *Trace* 57: 111–127.

Armitage, John. 1997. Accelerated Aesthetics: Paul Virilio's *The Vision Machine*. *Angelaki: Journal of Theoretical Humanities* 2 (3): 199–209.

Bal, Mieke. 1985. *Narratology: Introduction to the Theory of Narrative*. Toronto: University of Toronto Press.

Bolter, David, and Richard Grusin. 2000. *Remediation: Understanding New Media*. Cambridge, MA: MIT Press.

Bourdieu, Pierre. 1998. *On Television*. Trans. Priscilla Ferguson. New York: New Press.

Caldwell, John T. 1995. *Televisuality: Style, Crisis, and Authority in American Television*. New Brunswick, NJ: Rutgers University Press.

Carrigan, Anna. 2001. Chiapas: The First Postmodern Revolution. In *In Our Word Is Our Weapon*, ed. J. Ponce de Léon, 71–98. Toronto: Seven Stories Press.

Cervantes, Sandra. 2010. *Tijuana apantalla como capital de la TV*. El economista.com. https://www.eleconomista.com.mx/empresas/Tijuana-apantalla-como-capital-de-la-TV-20101116-0100.html.

Córdoba, Antonio. 2011. *¿Extranjero en tierra extraña?: El género de la ciencia ficción en América Latina*. Sevilla: Universidad de Sevilla.

Cortázar, Julio. 2010. *Cuentos completos*. Vol. 1. Madrid: Alfaguara.

Dalton, David. 2019. El consumo de la muerte en las televisiones nacionales: necroliberalismo y la nación cyborg en *Ruido Gris* de Pepe Rojo. *Balajú. Revista de Cultura y Comunicación de la Universidad Veracruzana* 6 (11): 3–28.

Fadul, Maria Ligia. 1996. La pantalla televisa se pinta de rojo. *Nexos*, August 1.

Fernández, Bernardo. 2007. *Gel azul*. México: Suma de Letras.

Fernández-L'Hoeste, Hector. 2017. El futuro en cuentos: De ovnis e implantes oculares en la ciencia ficción mexicana. *Revista Iberoamericana* 83 (259): 483–499.

Friedberg, Anne. 1993. *Window Shopping: Cinema and the Postmodern*. Berkeley, CA: University of California Press.

Friedberg, Anne, and Raiford Guns. 2004. Televisual Space. *Journal of Visual Culture* 30 (2): 131–132.

García, Hernán. 2011. La globalización desfigurada o la post-globalización imaginada: La estética cyberpunk (post)mexicana. PhD diss., University of Kansas.

———. 2012. Tecnociencia y cibercultura en México: Hackers en el cuento cyberpunk mexicano. *Revista Iberoamericana* 78 (238–239): 329–348.

Gibson, William. 1984. *Neuromancer*. New York: Ace Books.

Ginway, Elizabeth. 2020. *Cyborgs, Sexuality, and the Undead: The Body in Mexican and Brazilian Speculative Fiction*. Nashville, TN: Vanderbilt University Press.

Hallín, Daniel C. 2000. La nota roja: periodismo popular y transición a la democracia en México. *América Latina Hoy: Revista de Ciencias Sociales (Salamanca)* 25: 35–43.

Haywood Ferreira, Rachel. 2018. La ciencia ficción latinoamericana tiende a la hibridez. YouTube, uploaded by Simon Bolivar Andean University, Ecuador Headquarters. https://www.youtube.com/watch?v=TMaaZiuaxPg. Accessed 14 July 2022.

Hernández, Omar, and Emile McAnany. 2001. Cultural Industries in the Free Trade Age: A Look at Mexican Television. In *Fragments of a Golden Age: The Politics of Culture in Mexico Since 1940*, ed. Gilbert M. Joseph, Anne Rubenstein, and Eric Zolov, 389–414. Durham, NC: Duke University Press.

Herrera Aguilar, Miriam. 1998. Determinismo tecnológico o no. In *Espacios de comunicación*, ed. Javier Esteinou Madrid, 69–78. México: Universidad Iberoamericana.

Jameson, Fredric. 1991. *Postmodernism, or, the Cultural Logic of Late Capitalism*. Durham, NC: Duke University Press.

"Kas." 2009. *Wikipedia: The Free Encyclopedia*. Wikimedia Foundation, Inc. Web. Accessed May 15 2015.

Lacan, Jacques. 1977. The Mirror Stage as Formative of the Function of the I as Revealed in Psychoanalytic Experience. In *Écrits: A Selection*, 1–7. New York: Norton.

———. 1998. *The Four Fundamental Concepts of Psycho-analysis*. New York: W.W. Norton.

———. 2006. *Écrits: The First Complete Edition in English*. Trans. Bruce Fink in collaboration with Héloïse Fink and Russell Grigg. New York: W.W. Norton & Co.

Lizama, Jorge Alberto. 2006. Hackers México, del Hack-Zapatismo a Raza Mexicana. In *Comunicación cybermedios: Promoción y difusión de la cibercultura, el cyberpunk y el hacktivismo*, October 5. https://cybermedios.org/2006/10/05/hackers-mexico-del-hack-zapatismo-a-raza-mexicana/. Accessed 15 May 2015.

López Dávila, Irak. 2006. Information Society and e-Government the Mexican Experience. INFOTEC, Federal Government of Mexico. https://www.itu.int/osg/spu/digitalbridges/materials/davila_paper.pdf.

López Martín, Lola. 2011 (Fanta)ciencia ficción hispanoamericana: Teoría y definición del género. In *Lo fantástico en Hispanoamérica*, 95–115. Lima: Cuerpo de la metáfora.

Martin, Grace. 2015. For the Love of Robots: Posthumanism in Latin American Science Fiction Between 1960–1999. PhD diss., University of Kentucky.

Mathiesen, Thomas. 1997. The Viewer Society: Michel Foucault's "Panopticon" Revisited. *Theoretical Criminology* 1 (2): 215–234.

Nieto, Omar. 2015. *Teoría general de lo fantástico: del fantástico clásico al posmoderno*. México, D.F: UACM, Universidad Autonoma de la Ciudad de México.

Nielsen Television Audience Measurement. n.d.. https://www.nielsentam.tv/. Accessed January 1 2023.

Núñez, Rogelio. 2006. Untitled. In *Here Is Tijuana!* ed. Fiamma Montezemolo, Rene Peralta, and Heriberto Yépez. London: Black Dog Pub.

Paz, Mariano. 2008. South of the Future: An Overview of Latin American Science Fiction Cinema. *Science Fiction Film and Television* 1 (1): 81–103.

Pérez Flores, Ana Laura. 2020 Sobre los cuerpos y la imagen. Entrevista a Sayek Valencia. *Contraficciones*, dossier #11, Jan. 16. http://correspondenciascine.com/2020/01/sobre-los-cuerpos-y-la-imagen-entrevista-a-sayak-valencia/. Accessed 13 August 2020.

Porcayo, Gerardo. 1993. *La primera calle de la soledad*. México, D.F: Consejo Nacional para la Cultura y las Artes.

Ramírez, José Luis. n.d. Cyberpunk: El movimiento en México. *Ciencia ficción mexicana*. http://comunidades.com.mx/cfm/?cve=11:09. Accessed 4 May 2013.

Rojo, Pepe. 1996. *Ruido gris*. México: Universidad Autónoma Metropolitana.

———. 1998. *Yonke*. México: Times.

———. 2009a. *Interrupciones*. Tijuana, BC: Nortestación.

———. 2009b. *¡Tócame! estoy enfermo*. n.p.: *La langosta se ha posado*.

———. 2012. *Punto cero*. México: Editorial Resistencia.

———. n.d. *La basura es un punto de vista*. tierraadentro.cultura.gob.mx. Conaculta. https://www.tierraadentro.cultura.gob.mx/la-basura-es-un-punto-de-vista/.

Sarlo, Beatriz. 1994. *Escenas de la vida posmoderna: Intelectuales, arte y videocultura en la Argentina*. Buenos Aires: Ariel.

Shafer, Alexander Phillip. 2017. Queering Bodies: Aliens, Cyborgs, and Spacemen in Mexican and Argentine Science Fiction. PhD diss., University of California, Riverside.

Silverman, Kaja. 1996. *The Threshold of the Visible World*. New York: Routledge.

Sutter, Mary. 1997. Mexican Acquisition Executives Are Looking in Part to Mipcom. *Variety*, September 22.

Televisión en México. 2009. *Bien común, Numeralia* (Portal de estadística universitaria de UNAM) 170 (February): 7–10. http://www.fundacionpreciado.org.mx/biencomun/bc170/Numeralia.pdf. Accessed 20 November 2014.

Tobin, Stephen. 2022. Does the Posthuman *Actually* Exist in Mexico? A Critique of the Essayistic Production on Posthumanist Discourse Written by Mexicans (2001–2007). In *Posthumanism and Latin(x) American Science Fiction*, ed. Antonio Córdoba and Emily Maguire. New York: Palgrave Macmillan.

Todorov, Tzvetan. 1975. *The Fantastic: A Structural Approach to a Literary Genre*. Ithaca, New York: Cornell UP.

Toussaint, Florence. 1998. *Televisión sin fronteras*. México: Siglo Veintiuno Editores.

Virilio, Paul. 1994. *The Vision Machine*. Bloomington, IN: Indiana University Press.

———. 1997. *Open Sky*. London: Verso.

Williams, Kevin. 2004. *Understanding Media Theory*. New York: Arnold.

World Information Society Report. 2007. *Beyond WSIS*, 3. https://www.itu.int/osg/spu/publications/worldinformationsociety/2007/WISR07_full-free.pdf. Accessed 9 May 2015.

CHAPTER 4

Fake Presidents and Fake News: Holograms and Virtual Lenses in Eve Gil's *Virtus* and Guillermo Lavín's "Él piensa que algo no encaja" ["He Thinks Something is Off"]

> Antes las televisiones estaban al servicio del presidente, pero ahora el presidente está al servicio de las televisiones. Alejandro Alfonzo, Communication Consultant for UNESCO
>
> [Before television was at the service of the president, but now the president is at the service of television.]

As the 2000s began in Mexico, the presence of computers and their screens increased significantly. The first decade of the new millennium brings about some variation of what the country's cyberpunk literature most frequently imagined in the 1990s as "virtual reality as a road to perdition" (H. García 2017, 334). As in US cyberpunk, the trope of virtual reality frequently signals an immersive sensorial experience available to users through the interactive use of digital technology, often occurring in cyberspace.[1] In *Neuromancer*, William Gibson referred to virtual reality as a "consensual hallucination" (1986, 51), which underpinned the thematic model of the delusion that would be common to so many narratives of this

[1] For a comprehensive genealogy of virtual reality and cyberspace that considers narratives from the Global North and South, see Teresa López-Pellisa's *Patologías de la realidad virtual* (2015).

S. C. Tobin, *Vision, Technology, and Subjectivity in Mexican Cyberpunk Literature*, Studies in Global Science Fiction,
https://doi.org/10.1007/978-3-031-31156-7_4

subgenre in the 1980s and 1990s—both in the United States and Mexico. This frame of virtual-reality-as-deception becomes a hallmark for this chapter's analysis of the novel *Virtus: El espectáculo más grande del mundo* [*Virtus: The Biggest Spectacle in the World*] and the short story "Él piensa que algo no encaja" [He Thinks Something is Off], although each feature different narrative actants. The deceptive virtualized reality portrayed in Eve Gil's novel involves cyborg citizens immersed in the presence of interactive avatars of famous telenovela actors and other celebrities, along with an omnipresent hologram of the president. In Guillermo Lavín's short story, the specular techno-device is comprised of virtual glasses that distort the users' phenomenological experience with his or her environment. While these aspects allow us to qualify both these narratives as specular fictions, they also correspond to different visual media underpinned by digital technology: computers in the 2000s, and smartphones in the 2010s. It is important to remember that scopic regimes exist simultaneously. The televisual regime so dominant in the 1990s remains strong into the 2000s and 2010s with the added emergence in these decades of computers and smartphones which go on to become notable signifiers in the broader visual field of the country. It is for this reason that television remains substantially present in each of these works. Finally, as with the other specular fictions in this study, both narratives in this chapter remain steadfastly anchored to the specific presents of their creation, absorbing the shifting sensorium in Mexico and framing and imagining their dystopias largely around these particular technologies. These works also peer into the future and prefigure key events or phenomena that occur after their respective publications.

As presented in the introduction, the first two decades of the twenty-first century see two significant changes in Mexico's field of vision that enable it to cohere into a cybernetic scopic regime. The first alteration regards the discernible proliferation of computers, which around the time Gil was writing her novel had a little over 20% presence in homes throughout the country; however, only 10% of these were connected to the Internet ("World Information…" 2007). While significantly lower than comparable countries in the region (like Brazil with 74% of household computers connected to internet), perceptible change is noticeable, especially in urban areas; one can begin to actually see how this transformation takes root—much more so than during the time in the 1990s when the cyberpunk movement was happening and the presence of computers in households was negligible. This burgeoning cybernetic milieu, overlapping with an overpoweringly televisual substrate of the country, marks the place and time from where and when Gil finds inspiration and material for speculation in her novel of political fiction *Virtus.* Among numerous other visual references in her work, the holographic president Jesús Wagner becomes the nexus through which her socio-political critique rests. Months after the author's novel was published, the iPhone entered Mexico in the summer of 2008. Whatever lack the country may have had with regard to the digital divide in the 2000s, smartphones quickly filled moved to fill the gap, predominantly in urban areas where this device overtook the country and its visual field by storm over the next half decade.[2] By the time Lavín publishes "Él piensa que algo no encaja" in 2014, these intelligent, mobile, telecommunication devices have achieved a rapid, expansive penetration, with at least half of all cellphone users reporting owning one (Castells and Stryjak 2021, 5). This new, internet-connected, small-screened, and inherently mobile visual technology adds yet another specular device upon which Lavín draws inspiration with his virtual glasses in order to metaphorize the smartphone. In all, these three technologies—television, computers, and smartphones—become the cornerstone of the electronic-image scopic regime of twenty-first century Mexico.

Virtus: From Virtualization to Blackout

The fiction is largely retold through the voice of the narrator-protagonist Juana Inés, who opens the preface of her manuscript by speaking of the Third War that is still underway and was initiated by the character "el Ventrílocuo" [the Ventriloquist] to whom she compares totalitarian dictators like Hitler and Stalin (Gil 2008, 8–9). The forthcoming text, she tells in the prologue, is an essay and not an autobiography, and her stated objective is above all to denounce what has come to be known as a domestic apocalypse specific to Mexico. After the prologue, the narrative begins with a flashback as Juana Inés recounts the blackout—or "devirtualization"— which occurred while she was at school and only eight years old. As described in the opening of this monograph, the second chapter

[2] The urban-rural population division has been around 80%–20% in the twenty-first century, with rural and often indigenous areas still suffering from extreme levels of poverty and lack of access to all kinds of resources, including cellular technology (Castells and Stryjak 2021, 9).

achieves a disorienting effect by placing the reader in the first moments of this blackout in media res, thrown into utter darkness and lacking all the context that expositions often provide. This first-person narration offers a limited point of view, which curtails the reader's knowledge of what is happening in this strange, perplexing, and suddenly ominous place full of screaming children in a location devoid of any illumination. From there, the plot then backs up further in time in order to provide the context of how this came to be possible, discussing how the technology, people, and private and public institutions came together to create such a world of virtualization, a.k.a. *Proyecto V.* One central character, constructed gradually throughout the subsequent chapters, includes Jesús Martín Wagner, who rose to power during the *sexenio* 2018–2024, and whose presidency ushered *Proyecto V.* into Mexican society. His image goes from being simply an accessible picture that circulates widely in many social spaces throughout the country during political campaigns to a ubiquitous moving audiovisual presence circulating across all of the virtualized society during his presidency; after he unexpectedly dies of a heart attack in the penultimate chapter, he "lives on" in the form of a talking hologram so lifelike that no citizen suspects he died.

Behind Wagner resides the enigmatic, largely anonymous Ventriloquist, a unified group character that acts as puppeteer and makes all the decisions for the president—including who becomes president and whom he should marry. As the novel's central but publicly elusive antagonist, the Ventriloquist represents a number of the elites that possess total control over the political direction of the country. The narrative intersperses details about how Juana Inés came to survive the blackout, offers personal details as to how she acquired her name inspired by Sor Juana Inés de la Cruz and her relationship to her mother and grandfather, along with major moments of the history of how virtualization came to be, thereby achieving a degree of narrative fragmentation; thus, two distinct narrative perspectives concatenate the fabula: one is the limited, first-person voice of our female protagonist, while the other offers a third-person omniscient narration that details key background scenes of how *Proyecto V.* came to be through the machinations of the Ventriloquist. We learn that Juana Inés's mother died, along with the rest of the cyborg population, due to a virus that brought the whole system down. Anyone who had a lectochip installed in their person—essentially the entire country—had the inadvertent result of initiating an automatic corporeal decomposition of the body 72 hours after disconnection. Juana Inés survives by being rescued by Dr. Linos

Pound, a physicist who never succumbed to the virtualization process, and who helped her de-virtualize properly in order to avoid death. The end of the text reveals that, in the aftermath, they found 413 survivors in all Mexico—or .02% of the entire population—and that Juana Inés was put in charge of the Project to Restore Reality. She dates her self-described written essay—the novel that we are reading—in October of 2068, which temporally places the narrative events from around 2020 through to the 2060s (Gil 2008, 122). Taken as a whole, the post-cyberpunk novel is at once dystopian, considering the events leading up to the blackout, and ultimately post-apocalyptic in the narration's present that frames Juana Inés's retelling. At the same time, the novel is a lightly disguised politico-economic satire of the late neoliberal Mexico that was being imagined and written shortly after Felipe Calderón launched his War on Drugs in late 2006.[3]

The cybernetic scopic regime imagined in *Virtus* involves a multifaceted visual sphere which comprises "the largest spectacle in the world" alluded to in the novel's subtitle. This includes the numerous institutional and material elements. For one, the prime mover is a hyper-neoliberalized media and telecommunications industry that sets the groundwork for *Proyecto V*. Later, two cutting-edge speculative technologies are required: DAVID (Digital Audio Interactive Decoder) and the lectochip. DAVID is an interactive cybernetic-television hybrid technology that evolved from a combination of flat-screen televisions as well as the interactive television systems that emerged in the mid-1990s. DAVIDs were placed throughout Mexico similar to how network routers are today: in homes and in public spaces throughout the country in order to allow a continual, connected access point to the broadcast source, akin to today's wireless networks. The original source of the broadcast comes from the Planta Virtualizadora ("Virtualized Plant") in Bridge City (formerly known as Tijuana). The

[3] Eve Gil explicitly acknowledges this in the epilogue. "Ciencia ficción…es solo un pretexto, una licencia que me tomo y una etiqueta para describir en pocas palabras la inefable esencia de una novela que disfraza de ironía el dolor y la indignación en que tiene su origen. Se trata, en realidad, de una metáfora fantástica de lo que actualmente acontece en…México…que necesitaba narrar, criticar, justificar, entender y explicar sin tener que escribir <<otro-libro-más-de-política>>" (2008, 123–124) [Science fiction…is only a pretext, a license and a label that I am taking to describe in a few words the ineffable essence of a novel that ironically dresses itself up in pain and indignation of its origin. In reality, this is about a fantastic metaphor of what is actually happening in Mexico that I needed to narrate, criticize, justify, understand, and explain without having to write "one-more-book-about-politics"].

lectochip is a tiny, seed-sized microchip inserted into the body which augments some human capacities. The government provided this device for free and touted it as being painless in its installation and instantaneous in its functioning (Gil 2008, 79). Once inserted into the human body, it facilitates a number of augmentations in the human subject's sensorial and intellectual capacity. Most importantly, it offers the ability to see and hear what the DAVID broadcasts or projects in space, effectively removing any need for other external devices (that extend the human senses via earplugs, a headset, and contact lenses/glasses, as in the virtual reality environments popularized in the late 1990s). The lectochip essentially replaces all of this cumbersome techno-baggage in one very small chip, making it fully internalized into the body such that it cannot be detected from outside. It considerably enhances the subject's perception of the projected images and holograms by up to 200 times that of analogue photography. In addition, the chip offers an artificial memory extension that endows any user with a highly advanced level of *lectoescritura*, or the ability to understand five languages, immediately upon insertion. These devices provide the user-spectator-citizen with high-definition vision and the ability to constantly intermingle with the overlaid, virtualized, interactive digital AV-images throughout society. Now that the newly converted cyborg citizens can access and interact with this virtualized society, the regime requires a celebrity *star system* that populates this virtual space, replete with telenovela actresses and telegenic politicians. The final visual element is a virtualized president whose ubiquitous image is eventually substituted with a hologram after he dies. Examples of all these elements pervade the novel in every chapter and make this literarily imagined Mexico the enormous spectacle evoked in the novel's subtitle, with many elements drawing upon the place and time in which the author wrote. *Virtus* is, therefore, an exemplary specular fiction of the 2000s.

The Society of the Spectacle in *Virtus*

Many of the aforementioned elements merit being read in conjunction with Guy Debord's *The Society of the Spectacle* (1967). The ample number of connections between both texts suggests that the French neo-Marxist's thought remains useful for analyzing Gil's futuristic representation of Mexico. It is useful to note that although the novel's subtitle references spectacle, it never mentions the manifesto within its narrative; however, it does mention numerous allusions to other thinkers and their theories or specific works, such as Giovanni Sartori's *Homo videns: la sociedad teledirigida* (Gil 2008, 102), Clément Rosset's *L'objet singulier* (Gil 2008, 108), Vivian Abenshushan (Gil 2008, 40), and Régis Debray's "videosphere" (Gil 2008, 29, 89). The latter author, an intellectual best known for fighting alongside Che Guevara in Bolivia in the 1960s, later produced an extensive body of media theory,[4] part of which clearly helped Gil to conceptualize the virtual president in *Virtus*. Debray's notion of the videosphere becomes particularly helpful when considering how president Jesús Wagner appears in the novel, which will be discussed in the next section.

All of aforementioned thinkers overtly signal the epistemological framework that helped shape Gil's own intellectual influences as the novel was being written; curiously enough, however, neither Debord, Jean Baudrillard nor Umberto Eco are cited—all important thinkers regarding the emergence of technologically mediated subjective experience within advanced capitalist consumer societies. For example, Eco's contribution to the discourse of the hyperreal from the 1970s was foundational in the milieu of postmodern thinking on authenticity in an era when instances of copies begin to outnumber and supplant real, aura-inherent people, objects, or experiences (be they historical figures, works of art, or even natural habitats). One hallmark of this era for Eco is the visual primacy of simulacra, where reality has been replaced by visual perception. Writing about Ripley's Believe it or Not Museums as a metonym of this new hyperreal era, he claimed that authenticity "is not historical, but visual. Everything looks real, and therefore it is real" (1986, 16)—even if it had never existed previously. Hence, the importance of the fantasy world of Disneyland/Disney World on both Eco and Baudrillard's discussion of the hyperreal (1986) and simulacra (1994). For his part, Baudrillard boldly asserted that commodity consumption has evolved to such an advanced stage such that people no longer consume proper commodities/produced objects, but rather they consume signs, images, and information (2005, 218–219); the real has been supplanted by these simulacra to such a pervasive extent that access to unmediated reality is irrevocably lost. Despite the fact that Baudrillard and Debord shared numerous affinities in their

[4] Debray's theory, called mediology, seeks to understand how changes in social configurations form in relation to the materiality of communication media.

thinking,[5] I maintain that Debord's spectacle remains the most productive framework through which to analyze *Virtus*'s literarily imagined visual field, largely due to commonalities among the novel and the theory. Debord theorizes how capital imbues the world of the image and ultimately colonizes culture more broadly—without losing all sense of meaning (as in Baudrillard). Gil's narrative articulates a futuristic world very similar to this. Debord sees spectacle as an evolution of Marx's conceptualization of the commodity, where commodities are still produced and based upon a capitalist mode of production. This element aligns more clearly with Mexico, given the country's uneven (post-)modernization via NAFTA, where much of the production of goods still take place, especially in maquiladoras. Debord's framework also retains a core emphasis on how mass media entertainment has reconfigured society in the service of capital. In addition, Debord contemplates the political nature of spectacle, which befits the Mexican political scene around the time the novel was being written by anticipating the rise of Enrique Peña Nieto. What is perhaps most fruitful is the way in which aspects of *Virtus* not only dialogues with Debord within a Mexican context, but how it also updates several components of the French thinker's theory for the first decade of the twenty-first century in the hemisphere.

Debord's fundamental insight resides in characterizing mass media—especially electronic media—as a fundamentally new and pervasive force of late capitalism (the mid-twentieth century), associating it with consumer society, and its resulting effects upon subjectivities. With his thesis—"The spectacle is capital accumulated to such a degree that it becomes an image" (2010, paragraph 34)—he asserts that this advanced mode of capitalist production has become organized around consumption, and that, as such, it requires a qualitative and quantitative shift into a reliance upon the

[5] In his earlier work, Baudrillard shared a common neo-Marxist framework with Debord and the Situationists, one which links the historical development of capitalism to the evolution of the commodity toward a consumer society, but he (Baudrillard) splits with them in the mid-to-late 1970s when he theorizes that the sign has broken free from its referent within consumer society and people consume signs, images, and information rather than commodities linked to existing objects. Best and Kellner signal two significant ruptures in their thinking: (i) spectacle still implies a subject-object distinction, which Baudrillard sees as being effaced in a hyperreal postmodern capitalist world, and (ii) Debord's insistence that spectacle is an extension of the commodity form does not reflect the extent to which capitalism has evolved, which, according to Baudrillard has become radically more abstract such that all original referents are lost (Best and Kellner, n.d., 7).

media and entertainment industries in order to create the desires necessary to sustain such high levels of a consumer-based economy. The social plane is therefore inundated with spectacle—or extensive imagery from advertising, product placement in television, films, deliberately arranged public relations events, and a plethora of celebrities within an expanding star system—all of which sell the image of a lifestyle that requires a dependence upon commodities and their fetishization (following Marx).[6] As a result, the spectacle as a fetishism of the commodity and the image results in widespread alienation throughout all sectors of society, as Debord states throughout his essay, and most acutely in the section titled "Separation Perfected." Therefore, the spectacle is more than simply commercial images circulating in society, it is also "a social relation among people mediated by images" (Debord 2010, paragraph 4). This connection shows how the spectacle relates to subjectivities in people, but its pervasiveness is even more universal than this. As media critics Steven Best and Douglas Kellner have pointed out, the spectacle has two interrelated meanings.

> In one sense, it refers to a media and consumer society, organized around the consumption of images, commodities, and staged events. But the concept also refers to the vast institutional and technical apparatus of contemporary capitalism, to all the methods power employs, outside of direct force, to relegate subjects to passivity and to obscure the nature and effects of capitalism's power and deprivations. (n.d. "Debord...", 132)

Spectacle is thus more encompassing than subjects' viewing and "consuming" of images; it involves an extensive assemblage that includes the institutions, corporations, organizations, methods, and psycho-social processes that underlie much of the machinery of the capitalist system. One key premise in Debord's thinking is that he insists that spectacle demands "passive acceptance...by its monopoly of appearance" (2010, paragraph 12). This claim is akin to Theodor Adorno's and Max Horkheimer's description of the culture industry as "mass deception," where spectators are mere receptacles of the ideologies portrayed in the moving audiovisual

[6] Marx's commodity fetishism asserts a mystic quality to commodities that spreads to social relations more broadly, due to the fact that people see a commodity and are blinded to the use value behind it; rather, they see the exchange value—its price in money—and fetishize for what it is. In his own words, he states that "the productions of the human brain appear as independent beings endowed with life, and entering into relation both with one another and the human race. Social relations among people are based upon the commodity" (2009, 83).

images of Hollywood Golden-Era films or advertising in radio (2007, 409), and had no agential capacity to resist what they saw as cultural imperialism. However, more recent media-reception theory has yielded a more nuanced understanding of how media functions within society when compared to both these accounts; together, they embody what has been dubbed by critics the "hypodermic needle model" due to being rudimentary, unsophisticated, and naïve (Williams 2004, 171) and suffer from multiple interpretive problems regarding how communication and persuasion actually function.[7] In spite of this more sophisticated understanding of how communication within media operates, cultural depictions of unidirectional media apparatuses that meet no resistance from spectators persist, as in Eve Gil's *Virtus*. Her novel offers numerous parallels to Debord's own assessment of an emerging postmodern, mid-century France, while also updating his appraisal to account for changes in visual technologies, their pervasiveness, and their local-national articulation within the social and political spheres in neoliberal Mexico. When scrutinizing these aspects in more detail, her narrative at its core presents a contradictory view of spectacle: she both updates Debord's spectacle in productive and innovative ways—revealing interactive spectacle and megaspectacles within a cybernetic scopic regime—while also reaching a similar conclusion regarding how viewing subjects passively accept the spectacle's specular monopoly. The more things change, the more they stay the same.

President as Apparition Rather than as Politician

The fictional figure of President Wagner can be read as signaling a contemporary crisis of faith in the also contemporary market-oriented politics. His metonymic character is the culmination of a lineage of actual presidents from the neoliberal era up to the time when the novel was written—Miguel de la Madrid (1982–1988), Carlos Salinas (1988–1994), Ernesto Zedillo (1994–2000), Vicente Fox (2000–2006), Felipe Calderón (2006–2012)—all of which endorsed and helped maintain the neoliberal

[7] Sometimes also called the "magic bullet" or "transmission belt" theory, Melvin de Fleur and Sandra Ball-Rokeach describe it thus: "media messages are received in a uniform way by every member of the audience and that immediate and direct responses are triggered by such stimuli" (1989, 164). Kevin Williams notes that this theory does not take into account intervening influences between the media and its consumers. It also negates the audience any agency to interpret, discard, or distort the media messages received (2004, 170–171).

political-economic policies adopted and promoted by the state. It therefore follows that the president in *Virtus*, conceived of in 2008 by Eve Gil around the period that Ignacio Sánchez Prado has deemed "late neoliberalism" (2019, 95), is portrayed as a puppet of neoliberal capitalist interests that are themselves incarnated by The Ventriloquist. This latter character, described with an ambiguous identity and portrayed as a largely secret cabal that consists of powerful and elite leaders of multinational corporations, most explicitly in the telecommunications and media industry (2008, 39–49), makes key decisions for President Wagner in order to maintain power. The character of the president looms large over the narrative, appearing in every chapter in one form or another, beginning with the revelation of his mysterious origins, his technocratic education as an economist in the United Kingdom and United States, and continuing with his rise to political power and conversion into a highly stylized and curated image, his image's ubiquity in the mass media throughout the country and the related fetishization of his image, his staged wedding that becomes a national and international spectacle, his instrumentality in the virtualization of Mexican society, only to culminate in his untimely heart attack at the age of 33, and his subsequent replacement by a hologram—in a move that the public does not notice. He becomes a pure and empty synthetic image by the end of the novel. Wagner's transformation into pure image underscores just how much, in an era of advanced capitalism and mediatic presence on television and other visual media, actual presidents rely upon the extreme and constant attention given to the visual in order to maintain power. This reminds us of W.J.T. Mitchell's assessment that "politics, especially in a society that aspires to democratic values, is also deeply connected with issues of representation and mediation, not only the formal linkages between 'representatives' and constituencies, but also the production of political power through the use of media" (1994, 3). *Virtus* underscores this indispensable mechanism of producing political power through the creation and circulation of visual and audiovisual imagery throughout the social sphere.

To make this possible, the narrative endows Wagner with several key traits. First, he is portrayed as a puppet to late-capital interests by emphasizing how his character is as bereft of opinion and agency, and second, how his most immediately apprehensible attribute as a politician is his good looks, which lends him a usefulness within political spectacle. While he entrances and delights an adoring and onlooking citizenry, behind the media representation of him he is revealed to be inept and incompetent—a generally clownish person incapable of leading a nation on his own accord. The narrator Juana Inés tells us repeatedly that his exceptional aesthetic appearance makes him the ideal leader, as in "Naturalmente, Wagner se limitaba a ser guapo y encantador" (2008, 51) [Naturally, Wagner was limited to being handsome and charming]. References to his good looks recur throughout the novel: as young, athletic, or angelic (2008, 28, 35, 36, 52, 53, 54, 93); as handsome (2008, 29, 53, 98, 103); as the sexiest man in the world (2008, 29, 57, 65, 73). His looks are so striking that Juana Inés refers to him as genetically perfect (2008, 25) and the "Seducer of the Country," going so far as to suspect that he might be a telenovela actor chosen by The Ventriloquist for the role of president (2008, 28). Despite his official published biography that explains his origins—born in Bridge City/Tijuana, educated abroad in the United States and having obtained a degree in economics in the United Kingdom—our narrator also doubts the veracity of Wagner's personal story, conjecturing that he might have been created genetically in a laboratory for the purposes of installing the virtual dictatorship of the larger narrative (2008, 29).

His appearance's primacy is underscored by his vacuous rhetoric. It is no exaggeration to point out that his character does not utter a single line of dialogue that indicates a modicum of political savvy or intelligence. This particular point recurs to Debray's mediology theory when which claims that in the the era of the videosphere "la relación prevalece sobre el contenido y la enunciación cuenta más que el enunciado. Lo importante es el contacto, no el discurso" (1995, 127) [the act of communication is more important than content, and the act of enunciation counts for more than the statement enounced. What is fundamental is contact not discourse]. If contact, enunciation, and connection have primacy over discourse, analysis and reason, then in *Virtus* communication subverts content in order to launch a biting critique of the contemporary political situation. President Wagner's speeches tend to ramble on in fixed sound-bites that repeat time and again platitudes that comfort and reassure the populace while at the same time conveying little to no actual information: "Su discurso, que podía dejarse escuchar en cualquier momento del día y en cualquier rincón virtualizado, estaba hecho de pregones al bienestar, la hermandad y el orgullo de pertenecer a la sociedad (o Proyecto de sociedad) más avanzada de la tierra" (Gil 2008, 30) [His speeches, which could be heard at any moment of the day in any virtualized corner, was comprised of proclamations of well-being, the brotherhood and pride of belonging to the most advanced society (or Project of society) on Earth]. Elsewhere, vacuous rhetoric flows from his mouth during speeches (2008, 29, 30, 31, 48, 49, 52, 109) and government television spots (2008, 77–79), when he repeats platitudes and banal phrases obligated by the role of being president. There is also a continued reassertion of the President's constitutional legitimacy: "¡Éste es un mensaje del President Legítimo y Constitucional quien democráticamente les ordena prestar atención a este comunicado legítimo…" and repeated mentions of similar terms, either by the President himself or Juana Inés describing his speech (2008, 29–30, 31, 47, 49, 65, 78). These become hallmarks of President Wagner's continually projected image, both literal and figurative, and they foreground the importance of, above all else, the audio-visual image over the discursive or symbolic content of his pronounced words.

Unsurprisingly, others made decisions for him (Gil 2008, 54). Juana Inés later states that "No tenía la mínima injerencia en la toma de decisiones. Quien decidía era el Ventrílocuo" (2008, 51) [He did not have minimal influence in the taking of decisions. Who made the decisions was the Ventriloquist]. Beyond the references quoted here, Juana Inés also makes similarly worded claims elsewhere (2008, 52, 59, 113). What is more, the novel demonstrates Wagner's political and agential impotence by showing how the Ventriloquist negates Wagner's wish to marry to a voluptuous telenovela actress named Desdemona Tart. Once it becomes clear that the young and single president has become smitten with this woman whom they feel is undignified to be the First Lady, they take it upon themselves to pre-select a respectable female for him (2008, 51–59), thereby taking away his ability to choose his own mate.

All of the aforementioned elements recall how Walter Benjamin, at the start of "Theses on Philosophy of History," invokes the true report of the automaton dressed in Turkish attire that played chess and wowed audiences by allegedly being able to beat them. The Mechanical Turk's intelligence was actually attributable to a dwarf that could fit inside the contraption and make moves that the Turk appeared to be making (1969, 253). In the first part of *Virtus* described above, Wagner takes on characteristics of the Turk being controlled by the actions of another hidden entity, this time not a dwarf but elite giants, embodied in the character named the Ventriloquist. It could be argued that all presidents and heads of state, especially in the modern and postmodern eras, rely upon hundreds, if not thousands, of people that help get them elected: more often than not, the rhetoric of their speeches is not their own, as they are most frequently drafted by speechwriters; even most of their actions are strategically designed by consultants and other advisers. In this sense, many presidents largely exhibit traits akin to a puppet. But what sets apart Eve Gil's President Wagner is how after his death his character becomes supplanted by a hologram—the corporeal referent is erased and replaced with a perfect simulation that is indistinguishable from his real, physical former self. He becomes a three-dimensional, moving audiovisual, virtual electronic image—a creation wholly designed and controlled by the Ventriloquist. If, before, the Ventriloquist scripted his words, made important decisions for his personal life, and created a highly stylized public image for him (controlling his "optics"—to employ a fitting, contemporary vernacular referring to a highly curated, mediatic perception of politicians by the public), after his death, the Ventriloquist advances to the final step in literally creating and controlling his projected and technologically-incarnated image in the form of a hologram. Since the Ventriloquist is an amalgamation of ultra-rich elites who own multinational corporations in the country, the novel suggests that a holographic President Wagner by the end of the novel is entirely a product of advanced capitalist business interests in Mexico. Such a political figure may be the most apt imagistic distillation of neoliberal politics, a point which Debord himself intimated in his follow-up essay *Comments on the Society of the Spectacle*, published over 20 years after his original critique. In it, the French theorist recognizes the neoliberal turn, that "integration of the state and economy is the most evident trend of the century," (1990, 12) an observation which applies as much, if not more so, to Mexico than any other Latin American country around this time. Debord also suggested that "technological innovation…has greatly reinforced spectacular authority" (1990, 12).

Toward the end of the novel, Wagner's death and subsequent conversion into a holographic image is the apogee of the novel's association of the presidency with visual mediation. This culminating logic is preceded by numerous supporting points in the narrative. For example, the start of the process of *Proyecto V.* begins with the presidential campaign of Wagner (approximately 40 years prior to when Juana Inés is penning the narrative in the early 2060s) (Gil 2008, 25); without him, the virtualization of the entire country would not have been possible. Regarding his own personal image and its importance, "Imagen ante todo" (2008, 57) [Image above all] is the guiding directive from the Ventriloquist for President Wagner early in his initial presidential term, emphasizing how his image is paramount to attaining political power. His highly curated appearance becomes broadcast across the nation in *Proyecto V.*, accessible to all, such that the more Wagner ascends the ladder, the more his image precedes him; consequently, the more he starts to *become* an image in the experience of the citizen-subject-spectators: "...la imagen del joven mandatario proyectada en los nuevos rascacielos reflectantes, cuya señal alcanzaba a divisarse con claridad hasta los barrios más remotos y olvidados" (2008, 52) [...the image of the young head of state projected on the new reflective skyscrapers, whose signal reached far enough to be made out with clarity in the more remote and forgotten neighborhoods]. This description reminds us of the words of cultural critic Carlos Monsiváis noting that "a politician only comes into existence when his first political ad" appears (2013, 123), and later after an "avalanche of [television] images, [the person in politics] shall be an apparition rather than a politician" (Ibid.). Further, Wagner's marriage to the carefully selected First Lady-to-be Lena Christian becomes the "Wedding of the Century" (Gil 2008, 73)—a media spectacle broadcast live nationally and internationally, providing yet more proliferation of his image throughout the country and beyond. This event helps solidify his status of president-as-celebrity and president-as-spectacle, described as such:

> La Catedral estaba sitiada de militares que, con todo y exosqueletos, se bastaban apenas para contener a la turbamulta eufórica que se conformaba apenas con presenciar los pormenores a través del inconmensurable plasma instalado a miles de pies de altura, por encima de las cúpulas, y que llamaba a gritos a su Presidente-Ídolo, a su Presidente-dios... (2008, 73–74)
>
> [The Cathedral was surrounded by soldiers that, outfitted with exoskeletons and all, had their hands full in controlling the euphoric crowd that barely could contain itself watching details presented through the incommensurable plasma screen situated thousands of feet high, above the cupulas, and shouted screams to their Idol President, to their President-god.]

Beyond the enormous multitude of adoring fans that surround the Cathedral watching the massive plasma television that towers high above them, an untold number of other spectators sit and watch from a distance at home in the traditional format of open-air live broadcast throughout the nation, making it a spectacle in Debord's original conception of the term. But the event is also later re-staged in a television studio in order to create a digitalized and virtualized version as a commemorative item, to be bought and sold throughout the world in Charlie Boy's stores (Gil 2008, 73). Thus, the narrative goes one step farther by turning the spectacled event—which is already a fetishized image-commodity according to

Debord—into a literal commodity. It becomes doubly commoditized, further reinforcing how the event is reduced to the logic of commodity spectacle. Given this aspect, along with the enormity of the event's reach, the wedding itself clearly represents a "megaspectacle"—a further evolution of its original conception. Best and Kellner describe this as a "significant escalation of the spectacle in size, range, and intensity" (n.d. "Debord…" 135).

The megaspectacle wedding is one of the novel's several references that suggests similarities between the fictional President Wagner's likeness to an actual contemporary political figure in Mexico. President Enrique Peña Nieto was president from 2012 to 2018—four years after *Virtus* was published. The novel's first (and only, as of this writing) edition was in March, 2008, one month before Peña Nieto, who at the time was governor of the State of Mexico, met his future wife, Angélica Rivera, a former telenovela actress also commonly known as "La Gaviota." They met in his PRI offices where they discussed her role in participating in the State of Mexico's "300 Compromisos Cumplidos," [300 Fulfilled Promises] a political public relations campaign to which she lent her easily recognizable face; she soon became a representative image aligned with the State of Mexico. Their relationship soon became romantic, and within five months, he asked for her hand in marriage. Before the official proposal, however, the scandal involving the couple and Pope Benedict XVI at the Vatican brought about scrutiny regarding political and televisual news reporting from Televisa. Peña Nieto presented Gaviota to the Pope by stating she would be his future wife near a hot microphone. The story was picked up by Channel 2, which divulged the news that, up to that point, had not been revealed. Their wedding occurred in late November of 2010, under the admiring gaze of crowds that lined the streets amidst paparazzi and numerous photographic and video cameras: a real-life mediatic spectacle within the life of a Mexican politician who was, by then, running for the office of President. These events have since been interpreted as an unprecedented fusion between politics and telenovela, which underscores the critical and prognostic value that *Virtus* brings to bear in its socio-political critique. According to scholar Sergio Aguayo (2013), it was the channel Televisa that made an extraordinary telenovela story of Peña Nieto's life.

> Es una historia de telenovela, porque tiene todos los contenidos que le permite identificarse con grandes segmentos de la población. Su noviazgo con la Gaviota, una actriz de Televisa, guapa, exitosa, divorciada y él, viudo, que

> buscan la felicidad en contra de enormes obstáculos. Y no hay que olvidar que el 20% de las familias en México son encabezadas por madres solteras o padres solos. Y el desenlace de esa telenovela en diciembre de 2009 es extraordinario. Imagínense como setting El Vaticano, y frente al Benedicto XVI Enrique Peña Nieto anunciándole a su santidad, 'le presento a quien va a ser mi mujer'. Y de casualidad está un micrófono y una cámara grabando en el momento en el cual se difunde. (Aguayo 2013, "Tejemaneje - La inteligencia..." 2:55–4:02)
>
> [It is a telenovela story, because it has all the elements that encourage identification with big segments of the population. His engagement with la Gaviota, a Televisa actress, pretty, successful, divorced, and him, widowed, looking for happiness against enormous obstacles. And we cannot forget that 20% of Mexican families are headed by single mothers or fathers. And the denouement of that telenovela in December of 2009 is extraordinary. Imagine as a setting the Vatican, and Peña Nieto announcing himself to his holiness Benedict XVI by saying, 'I introduce to you the woman who will be my wife.' And coincidentally there happens to be a microphone and camera recording at that very moment, broadcasting.]

Aguayo refers to Peña Nieto's mediatic intelligence, or the way in which the he uses mass media and in particular, television, through a strong alliance with Televisa, in order to construct a very familiar and compelling narrative with which many Mexicans are able to easily connect. However, the event was repudiated by many, including those in Peña Nieto's own party, such as María de Ángeles Moreno, a PRI senator: "Nadie tiene razón ni necesidad de anunciar en Roma y en el Vaticano, y ante el papa, que se va a casar. Es un asunto privado" (Villamil 2012, 69) [Nobody has the right nor the necessity to announce in Rome and in the Vatican, and before the Pope, that they are going to marry. It is a private matter.] Although Aguayo cites the outcome of this telenovela as this meeting between the Pope, the then-governor, and his future wife, he overlooks the relationship's mediatic hyping in the wedding, which appeared across the magazine tabloid covers such as *Quien* with titles such as "La boda más esperada" [The most anticipated wedding] ("La boda..." 2010). The parallel here with the fictional president is clear, to which the title of the sixth chapter in the novel attests: "AHORA SÍ, LA BODA DEL SIGLO" [FINALLY, THE WEDDING OF THE CENTURY]. In this sense, a kind of *telenovelazation* of the lives of the real Peña Nieto and fictional Martín Wagner show the image of his personal life spectacularized for social recognition and finally, political gain. The highly curated appearance of both their lives supersedes the importance of any substantive element regarding their abilities to perform and fulfill their civic duties. Investigative journalist Jenaro Villamil contends that Peña Nieto's wedding demonstrated the early pact between Peña Nieto and Televisa as a way to control a narrative surrounding him in a time when he was careful in making political moves; in 2010, when governing the State of Mexico, he needed a distraction from the controversial electoral reforms put forth, and the relationship that culminated in the wedding spectacle provided the perfect cover for this. (Villamil "La telenovela 2012" 2010b). Two years later in 2012, Villamil's reporting leads him to publish *Peña Nieto: El gran montaje* [*Peña Nieto: The Great Montage*], a book that highlights the way in which this politician uses his private life in conjunction with mass media, particularly television, to manufacture political power. The fact that Peña Nieto and Rivera separated shortly after leaving office in 2018, and then publicly announced their divorce a year later, lends even more credence to the belief that their relationship was possibly staged in order to establish a compelling telenovela-esque narrative as part of a broader campaign strategy to increase electability. As investigative reporter Daniel Lizárraga stated: "Este divorcio es como si se hubiera acabado el contrato, o la novela" (Gallón 2019) [This divorce makes it seem like the contract or the soap opera season ended].

Political Marketing and the Actual Secretaries of State

Beyond the spectacle of the wedding, another qualitative change occurs in Mexican politics' use of the moving audio-visual image during the neoliberal era, one worth reviewing in order to shed light on how the actual country has inspired the futuristic fictionalization in Gil's novel. The history of *mercadotécnia política*, or political marketing, stretches back farther than can be covered in the scope of this study, but one of the key transformations it ushered in merits further scrutiny—the curation of politicians' images and the increased circulation of images in the mediasphere in Mexico. Indeed, the science fictional imaginary detailed in *Virtus* is largely responding to and drawing from this mediasphere in order to extrapolate the effects of such changes in the future.

It is difficult to pinpoint with certainty when political marketing came to play such a critical role in Mexico, but José Rúas Araújo, a political scientist specializing in media, has studied this and suggests some important moments. According to him, this urgency to tightly control politician's projected mediatic image begins in the aftermath of the 1988 elections when the PRI suffered some major losses and politicians realized that they had neglected to consider how media could be leveraged to strategic ends (2011, 48). Although in the 1980s and 1990s Mexican politicians began to increasingly rely on political consultants, it was not until the 2000 election that this notably changed. In the late 1990s two presidential candidates hired two major political consultants from the United States: Vicente Fox retained the services of Dick Morris, and his PRI opponent, Francisco Labastida, hired James Carville, both of whom had worked on Bill Clinton's successful 1992 and 1996 presidential campaigns (Rúas Araujo 2011, 49). The trend here clearly shows that the political consultants hired in Mexico tended to be foreign and the majority largely hailed from the United States (although those from Spain are visible). This boom in political consultants has led to the situation where these professionals earn exorbitant amounts of money themselves, often more than the candidates who hire them. Javier González Rodríguez, who consulted for Partido de la Revolución Democrática (PRD) earned 548,408 pesos (roughly US $35,000) in the month of October 2012 alone, whereas Peña Nieto earned 204,825 pesos (roughly US$13,146), during that time just under 2.5 times that of his consultant. Considered over the span of years, these numbers come to be quite surprising. In the years ranging from 2006 to 2013, the newspaper *La Vanguardia* revealed that seven more political advisers that individually earned between six and eight million pesos from consulting (US$385,000–$513,000) ("Asesores políticos..." 2014), a fact which unambiguously indicates how a political image consultancy became a lucrative profession in the 2000s.

Political marketing also means big business for the mass media industry, especially television. In a survey conducted in 2003, 84% of Mexican citizens answered that they got information about political issues through television and radio, and 10% through the printed press (Rúas Araújo 2011, 44). This demand has attracted the "supply" of candidates such that 60–70% of their campaign budgets have gone solely to television. Vicente Fox spent up to 4/5 of his budget on this particular medium, and was considered by some to be the most dynamic in photo opportunities of all the previous candidates combined. The television industry also benefitted greatly from supplying this demand: in the 2006 election year alone, Televisa brought in US$65,000,000 and TV Azteca US $50,000,000, around 80% of the total money spent on television campaign adverts (Rúas

Araujo 2011, 47). This link takes on even greater significance with Peña Nieto, since for his 2012 campaign he signed an unprecedented multimillion-peso agreement with TV Promo and Radar Servicios Especializados, both of which linked to Alejandro Quintero, the vice president of Business Development at Televisa (Villamil 2011). The connection between PRI and Televisa has long been acknowledged and even admitted to by Televisa's founder Emilio Azcárraga Milmo, who once famously said in 1990, "Yo soy un soldado del PRI y del presidente" [I am a soldier of the PRI and the president]. Peña Nieto's marriages—both literal and figurative—to Angélica Rivera and to Televisa respectively, should not be met with any surprise. What is, however, notable is the excessive degree to which Peña Nieto flaunts his politics-cum-televisual-media union. One of the overall effects of the creation and maintenance of this electoral spectacle, according to Rúas Araújo, is that the images and attributes of candidates takes on such great importance that the political party they are affiliated with becomes marginalized or even obsolete in the process (2011, 44). The exclusive focus on the singular candidate alone, essentially ignoring his affiliation with his party, requires that his visual and thematic image be meticulously detailed and curated, often based on the ephemeral and the sensational. The strength and import of this audiovisual media is perhaps most eloquently described in the words of Mexican communication theorist Alejandro Alfonzo who stated that when "los consorcios televisivos han sustituido al Estado en su papel regulador, los verdaderos secretarios de Estado son los dueños de los medios; los jueces, los comentaristas; los generales, los directores de información, y la verdadera legitimidad (del país), la rige el poder mediático" (Pallais 2004) [when the television consortiums have substituted the State in its regulatory role, the actual secretaries of State are the owners of the media; the judges, the commentators, the generals, the directors of information, and the true legitimacy (of the country), are governed by mediatic power].

Alfonzo's criticism underscores the true antagonistic force of the novel's Ventriloquist, the ambiguously described group character comprised of the country's ruling elites. The instances where The Ventriloquist appears in the novel are numerous, yet the identities of the people that make up the unified group character are alluded to only one time, in Chap. 4, with two names clearly referring to owners of two mass(ive) media and telecommunications corporations in Mexico: Milo Karraz and Charlie Boy. Milo refers to some future offspring of one of the Azcárraga clan, likely a child of the then-current owner of Televisa, Emilio Azcárraga

Jean;[8] Charlie Boy clearly refers to Carlos Slim Helú, the telecommunications magnate, owner of Telmex and América Móvil, along with a host of related businesses. It bears remembering that Slim was not only the richest person in Latin America but also the world from 2010 to 2013 (Emspak 2023). The fact that the only two people explicitly named as part of the Ventriloquist refers obliquely to two of the richest and most powerful men in the country, and that these two men are instrumental in controlling the president, underscores the novel's critique of the expansive reach and influence that the mass media and telecommunications industries wield with regard to political power.

With this qualitative change in how political power functions in neoliberal Mexico, both with its intricate link to mass media and its extreme dependence upon a highly curated image of political figures (to the exclusion of other important factors like party affiliation, policy positions, etc.), the logic of this dynamic—that President Wagner is replaced with a talking holographic image of himself—culminates by the novel's end. But how are we to interpret the hologram itself? What are the qualities of this synthetic image? What kind of valuation do the people-spectator-subjects ascribe to it? To put it in the form of a question inspired by visual cultural theorist W.J.T. Mitchell, what does the hologram in *Virtus* want? The answer is multifaceted and includes numerous articulations made by the novel. For one, as I have been arguing so far in this chapter, the narrative conceptually posits Wagner as a union of Mexican politics and economics by replacing the presidential figure with a vacuous technological double, completely manufactured and maintained by capital interests. The political has been wholly subsumed or supplanted by the economic in the figure of President Wagner, and they are now indistinguishable from one another. The market now reigns over everything, including the political arena. The image, therefore, projects an intentionally deceptive political figure in order to

[8] The corporation's founder was Emilio Azcárraga Vidaurreta (president of the company 1955–1972), who began Telesistema Mexicano, comprised early on of a radio and several television stations. He was succeeded by Emilio Azcárraga Milmo (1972–1997), who incorporated the company known as Televisa by merging Telesistema Mexicano with the Monterrey station Televisión Independiente de México. He was followed by his son Emilio Azcárraga Jean (1997–2017), who was in charge of Televisa when Gil was writing *Virtus*. He left just before the process of the massive merger between Televisa and Univision began (negotiated in 2021 and made official in 2022). It is worth noting that new, unoriginal, and octosyllabic name, TelevisaUnivision, possesses the uncanny quality of some of *Virtus*'s own neologisms.

obtain control over the political process from the powerful position of the presidency. The manufacture and maintenance of political power is centered upon the creation and curation of the mediatic image.

Another valuation of the holographic Wagner employs idolatrous terms. The previous quotation that describes Wagner during the Wedding of the Century notes his idol-like and god-like adoration by the multitudes of adoring masses, and this occurs elsewhere, too. Early in his mandate, Juana Inés describes his "grandes y vivaces ojos celestes y su figura espigada y atlética de joven Mesías sin dolor" [large and vivacious celestial eyes and his slim and athletic figure of a young Messiah without pain]. (Gil 2008, 28). Later, as a hologram he is seen as omniscient (2008, 89, 108) and all powerful: "Jesús Martin pasó a convertirse en Dios omnipresente, visible pero inalcanzable, y por inalcanzable más próximo al deseo que al amor" (2008, 107) [Jesús Martin went on to become an omnipresent God, visible but unreachable, and, as such, therefore closer to desire than love.] The association with God here places Wagner in the most lasting tradition of reverance to images, and confers upon the hologram what Mitchell has described as the ultimate value given to images (2002, 13), while at the same time emphasizing the focus upon desire, which adds a fetishistic component to the process. Worship of him and his likeness abounds throughout much of the text, along with the portrayals of him as a deity, such as in his marriage to Lena, aka María Magdalena, or his "resurrection" as a hologram when Lena wakes for the first time since his transformation to notice him looking at her with his face covered in blood with a crown of thorns (Gil 2008, 105).

To this end, the hologram of Wagner is adored and exulted like an idol. Such adoration leads to numerous expressions depicting attitudes toward his virtually projected image from cultish devotion to fascistic rule. He remains in power in a "virtual dictatorship" (2008, 23, 95, 101, 118) for 26 years until the flashback blackout that begins the second chapter, killing over 99% of the population. *Virtus*'s narrator states in no uncertain terms the link between Wagner and fascism when she elaborates his backstory as a protégé of Spinoza Ruttman, a democratically elected president with fascistic tendencies who preceded Wagner by almost two decades; Ruttman initiated Wagner into politics by rearing and training him in how to maneuver the spotlight. Juana Inés frequently refers to Wagner's rule as totalitarian regime (2008, 8, 24) and a virtual dictatorship (2008, 23, 95, 101, 118), although this turn occurred after some years of Wagner's initial democratic election, the creation of the DAVID technology, and the modification of the Constitution to amend term limits. Despite the novel's critique of Mexican democracy in the 2000s that merits a comprehensive reading, largely owning to the fact that this occupies a substantial portion of Juana Inés's reflection, what interests me here is the connection between President Wagner's projected image and eventual totalitarian conversion. Here, they are one and the same, reminding us of Walter Benjamin's prediction of how the mechanically (cinematically) reproduced work of art would not alter only the human sensorium, but also give rise to mass political movements—especially fascistic ones (2009, 670–671). As the auratic nature of the work of art declines and degrades authenticity, it is replaced by mechanically reproduced copies which becomes inauthentic and hold exhibitionist value. This qualitative transformation of moving audio-visual technologies along with the human sensorium gives rise to mass political movements. Written during the rise of Hitler, the German thinker's central preoccupation was that "all efforts to render politics aesthetic culminate in one thing: war" (2009, 684), which turned out to be true with the Second World War. The main difference between Benjamin's assessment and Gil's regards the way in which the moving, audiovisual image has evolved to employ strategies where war is unnecessary. The Mexican aestheticization of politics within a cybernetic age requires an actor so handsomely entrancing and stupid that, once elected democratically, he can erode the system from within.

Portraying Wagner as a virtual dictator that was democratically elected and who maintains a high level of support parallels with a central advancement of Debord's thought on spectacle, politics, and economics. The French theorist initially conceptualized two distinct modes of spectacle: *diffuse*, which arises from advanced capitalist societies abundant with commodities, and *concentrated*, which emerges from totalitarian regimes, as he theorized in his initial treatise. But he conceptualizes a new evolution of these concepts in his follow-up essay from 1988, in which he conflates both forms into a single configuration: *integrated*. Societies with integrated spectacle hybridize both of these elements to create an even more pernicious form that possesses the following five characteristics: "incessant technological renewal; integration of state and economy; generalised secrecy; unanswerable lies; an eternal present" (Debord 1990, 11). Each element exists in one form or another with varying degrees of intensity in the novel's futuristic Mexico. Technological regeneration can be found in the lectochips and other speculative apparatuses that make virtualization possible, as well as in the hologram of President Wagner; the "integration of state and economy" parallels the fusion between the political figurehead Wagner and the country's business elites as represented by the Ventriloquist; a generalized secrecy exists throughout the political-economic realm with the Ventriloquist controlling all aspects of presidential politics, especially by concealing the creation, maintenance, and total control of the holographic President Wagner. Unanswerable lies echo throughout *Proyecto V.*, from Juana Inés's characterization of the society which has collapsed "todo discernimiento entre Verdad y Mentira" (Gil 2008, 26) [all discernment between Truth and Lie]; she maintains that that "se nos había condenado a vivir una Mentira" (2008, 24) [they had condemned us to live a lie]. The eternal present parallels a society strung out on entertainment and telenovela celebrity culture, always returning to the same trivialities that such a culture offers. In this way, *Virtus* signals integrated spectacle by conceiving of how each previous form evolves into a single fusion, articulating it in a local context that is at once rooted in its present and extrapolated into the near future. Debord's final facet regarding the eternal present allows us to move from the political realm of the novel to the social plane more broadly.

The Spectacle of the Social

Where do we see the more diffuse social elements of spectacle in *Virtus*'s textual representation of a futuristic society? The better question may be to ask where does spectacle not appear. The text teems with a Mexican iteration that permeates the narrative's *Proyecto V*, namely in the realm of pervasive advertising, education, and telenovelas. However, the nexus that connects the social plane to these areas is the subject's physical body. As mentioned at the beginning of this chapter, almost the entire population—99.98%—obtains lectochips inserted into their bodies in order to both augment their vision for virtualization, as well as endow them with linguistic capacities that enhance them to be able to instantly understand and speak numerous languages (thus skipping the arduous educational process required to acquire foreign languages). This move thereby transforms virtually all Mexicans into cyborgs, which would render them "cyborg citizens." In *Cyborg Citizen* (2002), Chris Hables Gray discusses the potentialities such a conversion can bring about, but he strongly warns of the grave dangers present. "Cyborg politics is about power…[which can be] both coercive and constructive. Coercive power can be incredibly augmented by cyborg technologies to our peril, so we need specific protections for the cyborg citizen. Constructive power, for cyborgs, arises from having information and controlling our technologies" (1995, 198). Gray's warning of this impeding danger of potential political power that tends toward the coercive holds parallels with Eve Gil's novel. As this section demonstrates, *Virtus*'s posthuman masses are anything but positive or democratic: they are a collective who are repeatedly distracted, entranced, image-addicted, stupefied, and wholly controlled by the spectacled oligarchic media apparatus. The lectochips that enhance their bodies and brains do not enable or increase liberal democratic activity in the country; instead they bring about an increase in biopolitical control of the population by The Ventriloquist via President Wagner. Gray suggests that, following Langdon Winner, that artifacts have a politics of their own. Those cyborgs that gain real citizenship have either "access, knowledge, or control as a result of their relationships to complex technologies," whereas those that do not become "technopeasants" (1995, 25). Indeed, in *Virtus* technopeasantry describes the social body (and individual bodies) in Mexico, where the lectochip and DAVID make possible the hyper-visual, totalitarian society.

The most overt indication of a Debordian society of the spectacle resides in the advertising images of multinational corporations and their products. These become the clearest hallmarks of spectacular society, with slightly altered but clear allusions to multinationals: such as the advertising for Woll-mart, Coka-coke, Pepsi Cale, Megasoft V, McDonaldland, etc., that adorn floating miniature planets near skyscrapers (Gil 2008, 16, 73). McDonaldland also appears as an official sponsor in Juana Inés's high school for virtualized shootout battles with adolescent schoolkids from Germany (2008, 12). This social state reveals not only how education has become fused with spectacle, but also how some keys aspects of this pedagogical method in this futuristic Mexico has transformed into *edutainment* (Gil 2008, 11)—a neologism signifying the fusion of education and entertainment. It therefore demonstrates the triumph of the latter in terms of the way that spectacle permeates previously untouched spheres of educational instruction. When the blackout that opens the novel occurs, Juana Inés narrates what is was like to be in this virtualized, always-connected school during that event. Such an experience understandably shocks all the children, as if they had been swallowed by a white whale (Gil 2008, 12). For the first time in their lives, the overlaid world of digital virtuality that comprised their daily experience had been removed, resulting in stupor, disorientation, and a profound sense of aloneness experienced by all: "La ausencia de imágenes nos reducía a un montón de niñitos asustados que buscábamos el calor de los demás cuerpos que, antes de esto, no nos habían interesado en lo absoluto" (2008, 13) [The absence of images reduced us to a bunch of scared little kids that sought the heat of other bodies that, before this, had not interested us in the least]. Shortly after this passage, Juana Inés reveals an underlying motivation behind the creation of *Proyecto V*:

> Uno de los fines de la virtualización era crear fuertes lazos emotivos entre humanos y avatares, de tal suerte que no experimentáramos necesidad de relacionarnos afectivamente entre nosotros, seres de carne y hueso pero sosos y aburridos en comparación con las maravillosas imágenes que se nos procuraban a toda hora. (2008, 13)
>
> [One of the goals of virtualization was to create strong emotional links between humans and avatars, such that we would not experience the need to relate affectively to each other, beings of flesh and bone but dull and boring compared to the marvelous images that surrounded us every hour.]

By giving such prominence to strong affective links between cyborg citizens and avatars—that is, virtualized, participatory, highly engaging audiovisual images—rather than real social relationships, *Virtus* comments upon the immense power of interactive spectacle to capture and maintain human attention at the expense of creating and maintaining real, interpersonal social relations. This biopolitical directive was so widespread that it even was practiced within the family unit, as demonstrated shortly after when Juana Inés reveals that her mother had never even kissed her once in her life; she did so only to comfort the scared, eight-year-old Juana Inés in the grave circumstances of the blackout.

Since the novel's publication, researchers have corroborated the numerous negative social consequences of spending too much time with digital screens. Sherry Turkle's important work *Reclaiming Conversation* (2015) draws on much of this research, showcasing how the use of smartphones and computers in young people often becomes overuse, resulting in a cascade of negative social and developmental outcomes. The largest and most pernicious effect is the lack of empathy that the use of cell phones brings about in much of a generation who have lived a significant portion of their lives in an existence mediated through screens. A lack of empathy for other people, an inability for self-reflection, an unwillingness for solitude (without screens), flight from boredom and avoiding interaction with others, all stem from overuse of computers and smartphones.[9] Turkle cites an impressive number of studies that underpin and inform her book occupying 50 pages of endnotes—too long to include here. However, here is one key quote that synthesizes a core thesis of her book:

> We've seen more and more research suggest that the always-on life erodes our capacity for empathy. Most dramatic to me is the study that found a 40 percent drop in empathy among college students in the past twenty years, as measured by standard psychological tests, a decline its authors suggested was due to students having less direct face-to-face contact with each other. We pay a price when we live our lives at a remove. (2015, 171)

This enormous drop in empathy was most perceptible within the decade of the 2000s—when Gil was writing *Virtus*. These effects capture well how the socio-visual plane of *Virtus* is situated with regard to the spectacle in Mexican society. A world without empathy also helps explain why she replicates the hypodermic needle theory of media reception where subjects remain passive within spectacle.

One of Gil's perspicacious strengths is her ability to allegorically capture these outcomes in the novel's setting of around the 2050s from the context of the early to mid-2000s (when she wrote the novel), when these devices were only beginning to be used and few studies or formal awareness existed regarding the more deleterious social effects of cybernetic technology. What is more, the link between spectacle and lack of connection with others comes to the fore here when Debord writes: "Technology is based on isolation, and the technical process isolates in turn. From the automobile to television, all the goods selected by the spectacular are also its weapons for a constant reinforcement of the conditions of isolation of 'lonely crowds'" (2010, paragraph 28). Debord's "lonely crowds" echo the always-connected and virtually immersed cyborg citizens of *Virtus* whose salient feature is their inability to socially connect with others.

Another example of spectacle that illuminates Mexico's strongest audiovisual export is the ongoing references to the Mexican telenovela in *Virtus*—a narrative element that abounds throughout much of the novel and becomes another clear hallmark for demonstrating local identity and sensibilities. Juana Inés recognizes that Mexico in this era is "una nación

[9] The study referred to here is "Changes in Dispositional Empathy in American College Students of Time: A Meta-Analysis" by Konrath, et al. (2011).

irremediablemente enganchada a la Barra de Telenovelas" (Gil 2008, 25) [a nation hopelessly hooked on telenovela programming], which can be read as an anodyne comment from an observer within the country that is also peripheral to this visual practice. But she also believes—and insists firmly— that President Wagner was, in fact, a telenovela actor playing the role of president (2008, 28). It is later revealed that his image consultants also worked with telenovela actors in order to create and maintain his best aesthetic appearance for the camera (2008, 36). Further, Wagner's previously discussed images cast upon skyscrapers throughout the country turn out to be highly-staged media events helmed by telenovela directors (2008, 52). What is more, Wagner falls in lust with Desdemona Tort, the actress in vogue at the time for her role in the program *Pícaras y licenciosas*; this turn causes such a scandal for the Ventriloquist that they begin a worldwide casting search for a dignified and appropriate partner with whom Wagner can be seen in public (2008, 53–55). While the presence of the telenovela makes the indelible mark of being one core component of Mexican televisual culture imprinted on the novel, one final example illuminates what media theorists Jesús Martín-Barbero and Germán Rey point out as a paradox of Latin American culture industries during globalization: "La inserción de producción latinoamericana [de telenovelas] en el mercado mundial tiene como contraparte un claro debilitamiento de su capacidad de diferenciación cultural" (1999, 91) [The insertion of Latin American [telenovela] production into the world market has as its counterpart a clear weakening of its ability to differentiate itself culturally.] Put simply, one effect of globalization on telenovelas in Latin America is that these programs are so similar that they seem essentially the same. We see this clearly in the novel as the narrator discusses both open-air channels—the not-so-veiled reference to and equivalent of the duopoly of Televisa and TV Azteca (as discussed in the Introduction):

> La legendaria avaricia de los titulares de broadcast y narrowcast los había llevado a implementar servicios y productos a cual más descabellados. Un ejemplo: la programación de los dos únicos sistemas de televisión abierta era prácticamente la misma. Variaban los conductores, los actores, las escenografías y, presumiblemente, los libretistas, pero mientras en un canal se trasmitía la telenovela de las seis, *Colegialas maliciosas*, en el equivalente de la competencia era posible contemplar actricitas igualmente jóvenes, guapas y semidesnudas en idéntico melodrama de título *La malicia de ser colegiala*... (Gil 2008, 39)

> [The legendary avarice of the narrowcast and broadcast owners brought them to implement service and products which were increasingly ridiculous. An example: the programming of the two only open-air broadcast television stations were practically the same. The anchors, actors, settings, and presumably, the scriptwriters varied, but while one channel broadcast the six-o'clock telenovela *Naughty Schoolgirls*, the competition's offering also featured actresses equally young, attractive and semi-nude in the identical melodrama titled *The Naughtiness of Being a Schoolgirl...*]

The narrator's comment illustrates well Martín-Barbero and Rey's critique of how televisual products in the globalized era are essentially indistinguishable from one another—are homogenous, which is the same phenomenon that plays out in Pepe Rojo's "Ruido gris" with regard to hyperviolent, reality TV news programs (discussed in Chap. 3). As Graham Murdock makes clear, the key difference here lies between plurality and diversity; while indeed the expansion of mass media industries and television programs under globalization undoubtedly expands the number of goods and products it offers, thereby allowing more choice, "many of them are versions of the same product in a variety of packages" (qtd. in Williams 2004, 81). What makes *Virtus* intriguing in this respect is how it goes further by taking this logic to its conclusion: rather than simply having two seemingly identical programs that exist in quasi-competition, a special service is created in the era of virtualization called *Mosaico* that fuses both together in one interactive spectacle during the era of *Proyecto V*. It offers "una ilusión de interactividad entre las actricitas de una y otra, [los espectadores] tenían posibilidad de ver cientos de nalgas y chichis en una sola toma, y hasta efectos de roces lésbicos entre las de allá y las de acá" (Gil 2008, 39). [an illusion of interactivity between actresses from one program to the other, (the spectators) had the possibility of seeing hundreds of asses and tits in one single take, including the effects of lesbian light-touches between actresses from one program with others from a different one.] While the male gaze does factor prominently in this overtly televisual aspect of the novel (and hearkens back to Porcayo's narratives examined in Chap. 2), showing a continuity—if not intensification—from one decade to the next, it is the interactivity that interests us here because it posits an advanced form of spectacle beyond Debord's original formulation. For *Mosaico*, two distinct programs fuse together into one interactive audiovisual experience where the user-spectator can interact with actresses from each telenovela, but with the next version of the program—*Mosaico 2.0*—the users' possibility for interactivity evolves even further by including another sense. Viewer-users can now also sniff the actresses who emit a variety of smells, be it sweat emitted from their breasts, perfumes applied to parts of their bodies, or the scent of the gum they are chewing—all of which is made possible by a perfume sponsor (Gil 2008, 39).

This olfactive move within interactive spectacle in the novel anticipates "scent branding," whose purpose is to associate a product with a scent in order to make it stand out in a saturated commodity market.[10] While the idea of adding smell as an additional sensory experience for spectating subjects and consumers is not new, it has become a legitimate marketing strategy in recent years—one backed by scientific studies in neurology that demonstrate anatomically why memory is more closely associated to smell than to any other human sense. Just as negative smells can be associated with negative memories, positive associations of smell can help strengthen the affective bond a consumer has to a brand and, in turn, increase sales. In one study, consumers who shopped in the presence of a simple scent spent 20% more on average than those that did not.[11] The point to keep in mind here is that this powerful interactive event that adds aroma-based marketing draws spectators even closer to a real sensorial encounter of being in the presence of celebrity. It also makes this consumer experience stand out in a social plane overrun with spectacles.

Interactive spectacle updates Debord's conceptualization by offering subjects the possibility of empowerment and creativity in allowing them to enact agency in the act of spectating, while, at the same time generating new ways for them to be further seduced and dominated by capital's clutches (Best and Kellner n.d. "Debord…", 144). For the former, one can think of how audiences, be they televisual or cybernetic, are now able to participate in interactive situations through instant polling, voting on performers, contestants, or issues of their preference, or commenting their

[10] Colleen Walsh summarizes: "For decades individuals and businesses have explored ways to harness the evocative power of smell. Think of the cologne or perfume worn by a former flame. And then there was AromaRama or Smell-O-Vision, brainchildren of the film industry of the 1950s that infused movie theaters with appropriate odors in an attempt pull viewers deeper into a story — and the most recent update, the decade-old 4DX system, which incorporates special effects into movie theaters, such as shaking seats, wind, rain, as well as smells. Several years ago, Harvard scientist David Edwards worked on a new technology that would allow iPhones to share scents as well as photos and texts" (Walsh 2020 "What the nose…").

[11] See the article "The Power of Simplicity: Processing Fluency and the Effects of Olfactory Cues on Retail Sales" by Herrmann et al. (2013).

reaction or opinion to real-time spectacle events; this allows their own voices to be heard, so to speak, and become more active within a given synchronous broadcast scenario. For the latter potential outcome, novel forms of seduction in integrated spectacle can intensify domination by further ensnaring subjects into spectacle's grip, be it through the numerous forms of overuse and addiction brought about by videogames, virtual reality, and social media, and some of the pernicious effects caused by such use. One widely discussed example of this has been negative self-images (Fardouly and Vartanian 2015), rates of depression, self-harm, and suicide that teenage girls and young-adult women strongly correlate to excessive social media use such that social psychologist Jonathan Haidt argues it should be considered a "substantial contributor" (2022a, 65).

The end result here is that many users spend an inordinate amount of time fully engaged with their screens, thereby absorbing and perpetuating all of the pitfalls involved in Debord's original prognosis that appearance overshadows substance. These real-world features of an advanced form of spectacle sketch out its possibilities, limits and overreach, but the critique that *Virtus* makes is entirely aimed at the pernicious effects. The novel's cyborg citizens are wholly duped by the spectacle, narcotized by the interactive, digital-virtual images within which they live. Examples of this trait abound in the narrative, as in the following descriptions. Here is Juana Inés describing the insidious social effects of *Proyecto V*.

> Nadie padecía ni se preocupaba por nada. Mientras en otros países sufrían violencia, matanzas, hambrunas y desastres naturales, nosotros interactuábamos con avatares de nuestros actores y actrices preferidos, o de los dioses del Olimpo, con la cara de alguno de éstos, y alimentábamos nuestros ojos con las más exquisitas visiones de los más fabulosos platillos del universo, sin percatarnos de que languidecíamos por desnutrición. (Gil 2008, 24)
>
> [No one suffered or worried about anything. While other countries suffered violence, massacres, starvation or natural disasters, we interacted with avatars of our favorite actors and actresses, or with Olympic gods—with the face of one of these, and we feasted our eyes on the most exquisite visions of the most fabulous dishes of the universe, without even noticing that we were languishing from malnutrition.]

In this passage, spectacle is shown as particularly destructive in its visually hypnotizing and narcotic powers that entrance the population to such a point that they remain unaware of their lack of proper nutrition, thereby circumventing their own ability to recognize their own basic needs while short-circuiting their ability to enact political agency to counter this lack. The following description also comes from Juana Inés as she describes how Dr. Lino felt like he as an outsider without a lectochip (and therefore not a participant in virtualization) when observing the goings on within society: "una multitud de locos asiéndose a objetos invisibles, conversando y besándose con seres ficticios, asombrados a perpetuidad ante apariciones maravillosas que un ojo en bruto no era capaz de captar ni remotamente" (2008, 95) [a multitude of lunatics holding onto invisible objects, conversing with and kissing fictious beings, perpetually amazed by marvelous apparitions that an natural eye was incapable of perceiving even remotely]. These aforementioned quotes that highlight interactive spectacle also signal an essential prevarication in the way Mexicans live their daily lives within spectacle: seeing, believing, and interacting within a virtualized reality—seemingly unable to do otherwise. Ultimately, the entire apparatus dispossesses them of their free will (Gil 2008, 7). Along these lines, Juana Inés also expresses how the masses within *Proyecto V* "se ha perdido todo discernmiento entre Verdad y Mentira" (2008, 26) [having lost all discernment between Truth and Lies]. Later, Juana Inés also notes that "se nos había condenado a vivir una Mentira" (2008, 24) [they condemned us to live a Lie], referring to the Ventriloquist as the ruling elites that created the largest spectacle in the world. In this context, the lie that she speaks of reminds us of Debord's original assessment of spectacle that "the true is a moment of the false" (1990, 9).

In all, *Proyecto V.* posits more advanced forms of spectacle: megaspectacle and interactive spectacle. Megaspectacles abound, especially in the political realm, headed by Jesús Wagner's telegenic good looks, his connections with telenovelas, the (televisual) mass media system, and advanced capitalist interests. Interactive spectacle ultimately renders the masses of cyborg citizenry as passive, manipulatable user-spectators. Rather than endowing them with the agency of being able to recognize their situation within virtualization and be able to resist within it (*détournement* in Debord's conceptualization), they become further ensnared in its clutches, most clearly demonstrated in *Mosaico 2.0*, along with the descriptions of everyday life where both children and adults are hypnotized by the marvelous images and interactive holographic avatars with which they interact. The Ventriloquist—the group character comprised of neoliberal elites—remains the prime mover and benefactor of this state of affairs, pulling the strings of Wagner's image and creating a hologram that maintains a virtual dictatorship for several decades. The only way out of virtualization is to either not have a lectochip installed (as with Dr. Linos), have it removed (as with Juana Inés), or for the entire system to crash. The latter does in fact occur—a virus crashes the system—and kills off 99.98% of the population, or all those without chips. At this point, the novel turns post-apocalyptic and condemns the entire political, economic, and mediatic apparatuses as being so pernicious in their functioning that it almost wipes an entire nation off the planet, suggesting the only way to fix the nation is to begin ex-nihilo. This provides even more proof to the now overused assertation, attributed to both Frederic Jameson and Slavoj ŽiŽek, that it is much easier to imagine the end of the world—or (post) national world, in this case—than an end to capitalism (Fisher 2009, 2). Finally, given the treatment of cyborg citizens in the novel, Gil postulates new stages of spectacle that, at the same time, relegates interactive subjects to the same sort of passive consumers as conceived by Debord in his 1967 treatise. It is as if the antiquated hypodermic needle model of media from the early and mid-twentieth century had merely laid atop newer technologies of information within cybernetics of the twenty-first century in order to realize a critique of the Mexican masses as incapable of resisting the maneuvers and machinations of late neoliberalism. In the end, the novel advances a powerful update on Debord's theory of spectacle regarding how it functions in a digital era, while simultaneously offering the same core critique that made his theory overly simplistic and hermeneutically deficient.

"Él piensa que algo no encaja" [He Thinks Something Is Off]

Six years after Eve Gil wrote *Virtus*, Guillermo Lavín's short story "Él piensa que algo no encaja" appears, and Mexico's visual field has markedly changed again. As detailed in the introduction to this book, as well as briefly at the beginning of this chapter, smartphones barely existed in 2008 accounting for less than 2% of all cellphone connections, but by 2015, this device comprised approximately 50–60% of the market—a dizzying increase that signals a rapid transformation in the country's field of vision (Castells and Stryjak 2021, 5). This notable scopic alteration as to *how* people look, *where* they look, and *what* they look at, is the core novum to Lavin's tale—a specular technology of virtual glasses that enhance users' visual perception when worn. Differently from *Virtus*'s augmented or virtualized reality where images are overlaid atop the raw reality in order to distract, hypnotize, and control the Mexican masses, these glasses provide enhanced and improved visual perception: any viewable object, landscape, or person that provokes a negative reaction in the viewing subject is automatically replaced with its polar opposite and renders a purely positive aesthetic response. So, when the glasses are worn, people who are overweight, old, and/or ugly become lean, young, and beautiful; a dirty and disorganized space is rendered clean and orderly, etc. In addition, they automatically detect when a user has downtime and is standing in line, which then prompts the wearer to put on the user's favorite television program so as to not have to endure "dead time." What is more, news programs offer modified, idealized news about to the political and social goings on in the country.

Interrogating the meaning of these glasses in Lavín's story makes it an exemplary specular fiction within the cybernetic scopic regime examined in this chapter—one that firmly anchors it in the 2010–2015 period when it was written. It is worthwhile to consider Google Glass as a real-world referent that may have contributed to Lavín's speculative technology. These glasses allow users to record their subjective point of view with audio and are equipped with digital-virtual lenses that offer some degree of augmented reality. What is more, the first prototype was introduced to the public in 2012 and was made available for public purchase in May of 2014—four months before the story appeared in *Futuros por cruzar: Cuentos de ciencia ficción de la frontera México-Estados Unidos* [Futures to Come: Science Fiction Stories from the Mexico-United States Border] (2014). The temporal correlation could not be stronger here. However, another real-world device factors into the story's extrapolation: here, virtual glasses allegorize the rapid proliferation of smartphones and the accompanying social effects in Mexico around this time. "Él piensa que algo no encaja" also anticipates by several years the arrival of the mediatic phenomenon now widely understood as "fake news"—but in a Mexican context. The term "fake news" became popularized shortly after the 2016 US presidential election to describe false news stories generated by or for a politically polarized audience with the goal of sowing doubt about political actors, denigrating their public persona and campaigns, thereby hindering their chances of becoming elected.[12] Yet, Lavín wrote his story in 2014, at least two years before "fake news" came to be understood in its current and popular usage. What the author is responding to, at least in part, regards Mexico's own informational ecosystem and the formidable marriage between mass media and politics, thereby complementing the critique laid forth by Gil's *Virtus*. Lavín's story serves the function of assessing fake news proper to Mexico in the 2010–2014 period, while also anticipating what comes shortly after in the 2016 US elections and has since spread throughout much of the developed world. In this sense, given that a good deal of scholarly discourse of science fiction considers whether texts are essentially predictive of the future or descriptive of its present, it is worth noting that "Él piensa que algo no encaja" performs both functions very well.

Lavín's story does not possess the more sophisticated prose of some of his other work, especially his most lauded and studied piece of cyberpunk short fiction, "Llegar a la orilla" (1994) ["Reaching the Shore"], but "Él piensa que algo no encaja" [He Thinks Something is Off] is no less instructive in its approach to (specular) technology and its critical stance toward the sociopolitical state of affairs in Mexico. Set along the US-Mexico border in an unnamed town in the state of Tamaulipas, the third-person

[12] During campaigns, fake news often becomes viral and spreads more rapidly than fact-checked news coming from legitimate news sources in both the corporate and non-profit media sectors (Vosoughi et al. 2018, 1146). Fake news was made possible via a broad array of cybernetic devices like smartphones, tablets, and computers, along with the social media software on websites and apps that enable the rapid dissemination of information. The wide-ranging social and political consequences of fake news were not only felt in the United States where the term was coined, but also quickly spread throughout significant parts of the globe, resulting in a total of 70 countries experiencing social media disinformation campaigns by at least one political party by 2019, a figure which doubled from the 28 in 2017 (Alba and Satariano 2019). Due in part to this trend, in the social sciences, there has been—and still is—a broader inquiry that has not yet reached a consensus into the pernicious social effects of social media and its deleterious psychological effects on users—one which exceeds the scope of the current discussion of this story. Suffice it to say, when Lavín wrote his story in 2014, there was not much mainstream discourse regarding the addictive nature of smartphones or the deleterious effects on users of social media sites/apps like Facebook or Twitter, but as of the early 2020s, the discursive zeitgeist of the moment views social media companies as pernicious players in news distribution and in the corruption of societal discourse. See Jonathan Haidt's impactful articles in *The Atlantic* "Why the Past Ten Years of American Life Have Been Uniquely Stupid" (2022a) and its follow-up "Yes, Social Media Really is Undermining Democracy" (2022b).

narrative begins in media res, with the main character Eddy bedridden in a hospital and something feels off; the narration recounts the events that led up to his hospitalization. In a flashback, the narrator relates how Eddy needed to renew his Visitor's Visa (Tarjeta de Cruce de la Frontera) in order to cross the border between the United States and Mexico rapidly and efficiently. He and his wife of over two decades would frequently cross to go shopping for higher quality and cheaper goods in the United States, but since his visa had lapsed, his wife had to cross the border alone (much to her dismay), while he began the paperwork to renew his visa. The bulk of the story narrates the events leading up to and including his visit to the US Customs Office in Mexico to renew his visa. After walking into the building alone while making numerous observations about his experience along the way, he exits and makes a video call to his wife, during which time he "sintió algo raro, como si la cabeza de un niño le golpeara en la espalda" (Lavín 2014, 130) [he felt something strange, as if a child's head had rammed into his back]. He passes out, wakes up in a hospital bed immobile and confused, before a doctor tells him he was caught in the crossfire of a cartel confrontation in which a stray bullet struck his spinal cord and that he is paralyzed him from the waist down. Incapable of moving, he quickly decides to put on his enhanced glasses and live through them; he is now unable to live without them, the narrator reveals.

What most interests us here is the story's core novum: this optical technology that occupies a central role in Eddy's and his wife's lives, along with the powerful subjective effects associated with their usage. At the discursive level, the glasses are almost always referred to as simply "glasses"; however, on one occasion they are referred to as "virtual glasses" (Lavín 2014, 125). Through this instance, along with descriptions of how they function, it becomes clear that these spectacles provide a visual enhancement to the world viewed through them: "desde que se popularizó el uso continuo de los lentes virtuales se acentuó nuestra forma de ver" (Ibid.) [since they became popularized the continued use of these virtual lenses enhanced our way of seeing.] This enhanced optical perception comes in two modes explicitly mentioned: Modo Visión Mejorada (2014, 130) [Improved Vision Mode] and Modo Omnisciente (2014, 132) [Omniscient Mode]. The latter option offers users the ability to intimately share their perspectives with others users, as when Eddy accesses his wife's point of view in a real-time phone call after waking in the hospital bed and discovering that he has been paralyzed. She had crossed the border to go shopping before the tourist rush, so Eddy "accompanies" her virtually through the glasses to a restaurant. This immersive audio-visual experience allows him to feel that he is there—that he is her, in a sense—experiencing the subjective positions she embodies and the movements that her body makes; in turn, he feels happy that she is letting him live a little through her, since he is now unable to walk. This suggests a form of intervisuality between subjects that is made possible through this speculative technology. The story stops shortly after this event, suggesting it is likely that much of his life will be lived through the virtual glasses of others from this point on.

The other enhancement, Improved Vision Mode, occupies the bulk of the tale and offers its most substantive critique that can be read as allegorizing the effects on society and individuals of the massive influx of smartphones into Mexico, along with the concomitant fake news phenomenon to which it contributed. Improved Vision Mode impacts the story in the most significant manner. This first such instance occurs early on when the protagonist is alone with his wife at home, both watching their favorite television shows through their glasses in the living room: she is lying on the couch looking toward the ceiling and enjoying her telenovelas, while he sits in a nearby chair and watches a violent American action series. They are, as Sherry Turkle terms it, alone together (2011). Eddy removes his glasses to adjust them and quickly looks over at her as the narrator comments: "Estaba engordando. Ambos están engordando. Mucho. Él se colocó de inmediato los lentes, para ignorar el envejecimiento y la atrofia de la belleza" (2014, 127) [She was getting fat. Both are getting fat. Very fat. He put back on his glasses immediately in order to ignore this aging and the atrophy of beauty.] The glasses here are explicitly used to block out an unpleasant reality reflected by the obesity epidemic in Mexican society that occurs in the neoliberal period, as numerous commenters and studies has pointed out.[13] The story does not delve into whether this is a result of personal choice and agency, but focuses rather on how it is much easier to ignore this reality through an immersive visual technology that encourages facile distraction.

This enhanced visual perception recurs a week later when Eddy goes to process his visa renewal. Upon entering the building with his glasses on, he notices pleasant smells, but then immediately needs to remove his glasses.

[13] See Gálvez's *Eating Nafta* (2018), Secretaría de la Salud (2013); Friel et al. (2013); Mazzocchi et al. (2012).

> Se quitó los lentes unos instantes, debido a que se empañaron. La realidad se le mostró tal cual: el edificio mal pintado, descascarado, el piso deteriorado por décadas de uso continuo, pero, sobre todo, lo peor: ver de golpe a la multitud, una insufrible cantidad de gente mal vestida que se movía en los pasillos, formaba colas, gente que huele mal, gente de las afueras que viene a suplicar que les reasignen el agua, les pavimenten la calle, que iluminen con lámparas las calles, que les regalen láminas de cinc para techar sus casas. Esa gente no usa los lentes. No los pueden pagar, ni el dispositivo ni el software y sus actualizaciones constantes, ni la conectividad permanente. Se colocó de nuevo los lentes para huir de aquello. El olor a sudor reconcentrado desapareció. "Gracias, bendita tecnología", pensó. (2014, 128)
>
> [He took off his glasses for a second because they had become foggy. Reality showed itself as it really was: the poorly painted building, peeling walls, the floor worn from decades of continual use, but more than anything, the worst part: seeing the masses, an insufferable quantity of poorly dressed people that moved in the hallways, getting in line, people who smelled bad, people that came from far away to beg for them to turn their water back on, pave the street, illuminate their streets with lamps, gift them zinc sheets to cover their houses with a roof. Those people don't use the glasses. They can't afford them, not the device nor the software nor the constant updates, nor the permanent connectivity. He put the glasses back on to flee from it all. The odor of intensely concentrated sweat disappeared. "Thanks, blessed technology," he thought.]

Several aspects stand out in this passage—two related to the visual and another that pertains to the olfactive. First, it makes clear what was suggested in the previous scene with his wife: wearing these glasses distorts the protagonist's visual perception by idealizing the surroundings that a viewing subject perceives through them. It is only through the absence of a technologically modified vision that viewing subjects can truly perceive and apprehend the social reality surrounding them, which in this case is an agglomeration of unclean, poorly dressed, and smelly citizens that are there to solicit various government services to better their quality of life. Second, socioeconomic class starkly arrives to the narrative by way of contrast. Prior to this, one can notice smaller details regarding the couple's middle-class lifestyle accentuated by consumption, largely described through the technological objects like the virtual glasses and the electric car Eddy drives, but it is not until this paragraph that a juxtaposition between those who do and do not wear virtual glasses foregrounds class difference. Not only do the glasses themselves signal class by being a marker of social status, but those that are able to afford them visually perceive Mexican society in ways that differ from those that do not. Eddy's initial positive impression of the government building quickly vanishes after he removes them, and, he is able to ignore what he perceives to be the unpleasant reality by simply putting them back on—just as he did with his aging and expanding wife in the domestic scene alluded to before.

The aforementioned passage also articulates that these glasses modify a user's perception of scents. How this is technologically and physiologically possible remains unexplained at this juncture, but we do learn shortly after that his spectacles come with smell sensors that block out unpleasant odors (2014, 129). Eddy finally arrives to process his visa and is presented with a young, attractive, and flirtatious brunette woman, which the narrator remarks as showing off cleavage from her well-endowed chest. Because he must undergo an ocular scan for security purposes, he removes his glasses: "La joven y hermosa muchacha se convirtió en una desaliñada vieja, monstruosamente gorda, cuando obedeció su orden de quitarse los lentes para el chequeo. (2014, 129) [The pretty, young woman turned into a disheveled old woman, monstrously fat, when he obeyed her order to take off the glasses for the scan.]. Due to her obesity, she is so large that they barely fit in the small office where the scan is performed.

> Casi no cabían juntos en la pequeña oficina destinada a la comprobación de identidades. El sobrepeso de ambos entorpecía los movimientos. Ella apestaba a frituras; él a loción Adler, fresca y novedosa. Aguantó la respiración lo más que pudo, hasta que concluyó el escaneo y pudo acomodar de nuevo las lentes y reajustar los sensores olfativos. Con el documento en la bolsa, la infalibilidad de transitar entre gente desagradable y olores inmundos le pareció un bálsamo para las molestias que sufría. (Lavín 2014, 129)
>
> [They almost did not fit in the small office designed for identification verification. The excess weight of both of them made moving around awkward. She smelled like fried food; he like Adler cream, fresh and new. He tolerated breathing as long as he could, until the scan finished and he could put back on the lenses and readjust the olfactory sensors. With the document in his bag, the inevitability of moving among unpleasant people and awful smells seemed to him like a comfort for the annoyance he underwent.]

Up until this point, it is assumed these are mere glasses that do not affect the nose, but here it becomes explicit that smell sensors accompany and connect to the glasses (but with no further explanation on how they function). If before the class difference between Eddy and the poor and othered masses he finds himself among is merely suggested, here this distinction becomes central to the narrator's description of the scene by underscoring smell as a marker. Lavín's choice to add this additional novum to the story connects with recent scientific research as to how class affects one's sense of smell. A 2018 study of a variety of Brazilians in São Paulo from different classes, races, and levels of education found that "[i]ndividuals of lower socioeconomic status performed significantly worse than those of higher socioeconomic status on 20 of the 40 odorant items. Socioeconomic status is significantly associated with influence in the ability to identify odors" (Fornazieri et al. 2019, 84). While the factors contributing to this stark variation in the ability to smell—in function of class—merit further examination, as the authors of the study acknowledge,[14] this component of Lavín's story provides yet another instance in this monograph where a technoscientific speculation in a Mexican science fiction narrative captures how a complex social and physiological phenomenon operates in the realm of the senses. Eddy not only visually perceives the social plane in which he moves with class informing his perception, but he also smells differently than those that surround him. Smell, which often gets relegated as a more vulgar sense compared to sight (Shohat and Stam 2002, 55), strongly underpins his view of the world and his judgement of those that inhabit it. Alternately, it is assumed that the poor are either not bothered by the collective odor to which they contribute, or cannot discern it. Regardless, they are unable to block it out due to their lack of financial means to acquire the glasses and smell sensors. In all, this element brings to mind the expression of seeing the world through rose-colored glasses—often cited to describe optimists who mainly see the positive points of people or places and therefore perceive them unrealistically—but with the additional element of olfaction. Due to Eddy's own secure socioeconomic position and materially comfortable status, he sees—and smells—the world through the rose-tinted glasses of the middle class.

Beyond how these glasses color Eddy's visual and olfactive senses to render the world more appealing to his socioeconomic position, they also

[14] It merits underscoring the fact that this study occurred only in an urban space and does not include rural subjects tested. The conclusion of this analysis has spurned the need to find to what extent other elements may be influencing such a distinction, such as "differential exposures to xenobiotic agents, cultural differences, familiarity with odors or their names, cognitive development, or other factors" (Fornazieri et al. 2019, 84). Having said this, the authors consider several factors that help explain why: higher levels of pollution, disadvantages regarding health and nutritional status, less exposure and familiarity to some odorants (Fornazieri et al. 2019, 86–87).

bring to him a kind of fake news which reinforces class-specific perception regarding the state of the nation. While waiting in line to renew his visa, his glasses detect his stillness and automatically begin playing his favorite television show for him to watch while waiting, but he prefers to watch a news program. He turns to his favorite news channel and happens upon a press-conference broadcast of gay actors from film and television that announce they have abandoned the homosexual lifestyle; they have discovered that heterosexuality was not something as wicked as they previously thought, but rather something they found pleasurable. Afterward, the anchorman appears on Eddy's virtual glasses' screen.

> El conductor del noticiero presentó a continuación un panorama del Popocatépetl y el resumen de noticias, donde el secretario de Seguridad de la Nación anunció que estaban ganando la guerra al crimen organizado; los secuestros descendieron un cincuenta por ciento, los enfrentamientos entre los cárteles son un fenómeno aislado, indigno de cuantificar en las estadísticas. En cuanto a la extorsión y el pago de piso, vamos mejorando. Eddy se sintió reconfortado. (Lavín 2014, 128)
>
> [The anchorman presented a view of the Popocatépetl [volcano] and summary of the news, in which the Secretary of National Security announced that they were winning the war against organized crime; kidnappings dropped by fifty percent, confrontations between cartels were an isolated occurrence such that he did not feel the need to quantify the statistics. Regarding extortion and the rent, we are improving. Eddy felt comforted.]

The country is undergoing sweeping, positive change. With organized crime, drug trafficking violence, and confrontations among cartels significantly down, one of the nation's most dangerous, widespread, enduring, and traumatizing social problems of the twenty-first era seems to be quickly disappearing. While the narrator informs us that this news comforts Eddy, the reader may be suspcious of this information, in part due to the fact that the protagonist's virtual glasses have already revealed two instances of enhanced, yet unrealistic, vision in displaying what Eddy subjectively sees through his glasses. Could a news program be an extension of Improved Vision Mode?

A superficial reading of Lavín's story could assume the news program is another idealized augmentation of Eddy's sense perception of the world provided by his spectacles, but a deeper look into the potential meanings of this section uncovers that it can be read as a curious form of fake news in the Mexican mediasphere. As previously mentioned, the term fake news[15] immediately conjures the politico-mediatic phenomenon that refers to the deceptive practice that was detected during the 2016 US Presidential election when numerous videos, articles, memes, graphics, and other forms of content that contained verifiably false information—often with aesthetics similar to that of the contents produced by legitimate news organizations—were intentionally created in order to sow confusion; the purpose was to foment doubt and/or denigrate political candidates and/or their parties in order to sufficiently sway public opinion and affect election outcomes. But, as early as 2012, Mexico was already experiencing their own version of fake news in the run-up to the presidential election, one that undoubtedly informs Lavín's fictional articulation of it, while at the same prefiguring what was to unfold several years later in the US context. Most notably, these instances of fake news include the so-called phenomena of the "Televisa controversy" and "Peñabots," both of which had at their center President Enrique Peña Nieto. The former regarded some scandalous revelations that Peña Nieto had been in cahoots with Televisa to obtain positive media coverage, whereas the latter included netbots on Twitter—automatized, robotic network programs which were deployed to thwart negative media coverage and increase the favorable perception of the candidate—with the aim of augmenting the overall image of the candidate's appearance within the mediatic space of social networks. Both of these strategies merit further consideration, given their heavy reliance upon visual technologies and practices to create and sustain themselves.

These scandals that incriminated Peña Nieto involved two key information leaks which occurred mere weeks before the presidential election: the Televisa controversy dropped on June 7th and the Peñabots were revealed on June 12th—both in *The Guardian* newspaper. These disclosures surfaced in the midst of the #YoSoy132 student protest movement, itself predicated upon a suspicion among tens of thousands of students nationwide that Peña Nieto was benefitting from biased media coverage (Tuckman, 2012). The documents, leaked on June 7th, demonstrated a

[15] In retrospect, this original understanding of the term seems rather narrow, as if bracketing the phenomenon in isolation from the broader media ecosystem to which fake news pertains. Shortly after fake news entered the lexicon, it gave way to discourse about the "post-truth" era following the election; some recent scholarship qualifies this era not as one simply consisting of misinformation but rather one of "alternative epistemology" that "does not conform to conventional standards of evidentiary support" (Lewandowsky et al. 2017, 356).

strategy in which Peña Nieto paid for favorable coverage, as evidenced in an extensive media budget between the Peña Nieto campaign and Televisa that listed different ways in which the station positively promoted the candidate's image in his first two years as governor of the State of Mexico (2005–2006), consisting of nearly 200 news reports, interviews with him or members of his team, and segments featured on their various news programs and channels (Carroll 2012).[16] The vast majority of the campaign's budget (88%) went to paying for airtime to run Televisa spots and segments on news programs, whereas the rest went to other media, such as magazines, and production costs. Another important leak was a communication strategy document that offered guidance on how Televisa would increase negative coverage of Andrés Manuel López Obrador during his 2006 campaign for president in order to diminish his chances of winning. Towards the end of Peña Nieto's term, it was later revealed that his government had spent hundreds of millions per year (US$2 billion over five years) on political advertising—far more than any president that preceded him; this effectively created a "presidential branding juggernaut capable of suppressing investigative articles, directing front pages and intimidating newsrooms that challenge it" (Ahmed 2017). While the Televisa controversy offered overt evidence of what many in the public already assumed to be the case—media bias strongly favoring one candidate or party—it is also worth noting that these examples operate within an economic milieu where politics and media have been been—and remain—tilted toward this outcome for many actors both political and journalistic. A *New York Times* investigative report demonstrated this, based upon dozens of interviews of editors, journalists, and media executives from Mexico, all offering damning testimony of this state of affairs regarding the country's ostensibly free press. The conclusion reached by the piece states unequivocally that there exists a "media landscape across Mexico in which federal and state officials routinely dictate the news, telling outlets what they should — and should

[16] It should be noted that Televisa has denied any collusion with any political parties. In a joint statement with *The Guardian* in February, 2013, they published that "Televisa has publicly and categorically denied the allegations of political bias. It also denies the authenticity of the documents provided to *The Guardian*." ("Guardian Statement..." 2012). They also published a refutation with six key ways in which the British news outlet's story lacked proof of shenanigans (Moctezuma 2012). However, many of the names and dates that were given by an unnamed source who claimed to have worked at Televisa and been present during key meetings where collusion occurred, appear consistent with other evidence that *The Guardian* outlet has fact-checked (Hodgson 2012).

not — report" (Ahmed 2017). With virtually all news outlets depending on public advertising money to survive, there exists a longstanding influential relationship where most journalism that tries to hold power to account—be it televisual or written—becomes thwarted, stultified, neutralized.[17] Even *La Jornada*, the outlet formed by leftist writers and intellectuals in the 1990s and has long been since considered a central voice of journalistic critique, has been coopted in a sense by being forced to accept advertising dollars from the federal government.[18] In all, the picture that comes forth, then, is that Peña Nieto is but one politician—albeit a particularly egregious one—in a vast terrain of political players and institutions that have essentially coopted the news media at the state and federal levels by becoming the major investor in advertising.

However, there is another way in which Peña Nieto has distinguished himself in a media landscape that transforms from one dominated by the televisual to one in which a cybernetic ecosystem rapidly emerges in politics: Peñabots. This strategy employed by the president materialized in two ways: the first during his 2012 presidential campaign, coinciding with the Televisa Maguey controversy, and the other consisted of frequent, multipronged schemes developed and deployed while president. Both relied extensively on utilizing Twitter to improve the perception of Peña Nieto in public opinion while also drowning out any negative coverage of him or his campaign/administration, thereby also elevating the perception of the state of the country, the job he was doing in leading it, and his overall image. Peñabots were first uncovered in late 2011 when Twitter accounts were discovered with identical posts using the same language, as if coordinated. Further, the accounts had all been created around the same time and only showered this identical praise for the candidate (Maguey 2011). By March, 2012 it was estimated that 20 to 30% of his Twitter followers were bots, according to Andrés Sepulveda, the digital media consultant who was paid US$600,000 and alleged that he deployed 30,000 bots to push trending topics that created false surges of excitement for the

[17] The article uncovers numerous examples of bribes, along with such a widespread internalization of the marriage between politics and media coverage that two-thirds of Mexican journalists admit to self-censorship (Ahmed 2017).

[18] According to the *New York Times* article, when *La Jornada* was on the brink of bankruptcy in the mid-2010s, "the government intervened, rescuing the publication with more than US$1 million in official advertising and, critics say, claiming its editorial independence in the process. 'Now they own them,' Marco Levario, director of the magazine *Etc.* said. 'The paper has been like a spokesman for the president.'" (Ahmed 2017).

candidate. After Peña Nieto won the election, an array of strategies was used in order to maintain appearances. These included the overwhelming use of hashtags in order to create confusion and made it harder for users to access information; spreading false news stories and other disinformation to delegitimize protests against the president; spam flooding in order to bury stories about how the president was embroiled in corruption; and launching bogus trending topics in order to compete with and eventually drown out legitimate trending topics (Velasquez Leiferman and Khrushcheva 2019). Taken together, the net effect of these strategies is one where the mediatic image of Peña Nieto projected across social media is altered and ultimately falsified in order to maintain an appearance of effectiveness. Given the number of scandals he was embroiled in throughout this tenure in office, any sustained, coordinated effort to lighten or suppress scandal contributed to an overall improvement in appearances.

This improvement of appearances, both in terms of the political leader and the state of the country, is precisely the kind of fake news proper to Mexico in the early 2010s that Lavín is channeling in "Él piensa que algo no encaja." Peña Nieto's multi-pronged approach to the creation and maintenance of his image included intentionally deceptive journalistic practices with the Televisa Controversy, along with the extensive social media campaign of the Peñabots, in order project an augmented persona of someone he was not, as well as an idealized version of the nation. Considering this, it is perhaps unsurprising that a high number of voices have characterized Peña Nieto as a televisual president. From Andrés Manuel López Obrador calling Peña Nieto a product of television in 2012 (Carroll 2012), to social scientists of communications debating this topic in scholarly journals, like "Peña Nieto and Televisa: A Construction of a President?" (Solis Delgado and Acosta) in 2015, or finally, to investigative reporter Jenaro Villamil's numerous books dedicated to the topic that span over a decade and have as their focus Peña Nieto and the televisual media, with titles like *El sexenio de Televisa* (2010a) [Televisa's Six-year Presidential Term] and *Si yo fuera presidente: el reality show de Peña Nieto* (2009) [If I were President: The Reality Show of Peña Nieto].[19] Thus, our

[19] Other relevant books of his include *La televisión que nos gobierna: modelo y estructura desde sus orígenes* (2005) [*The Television that Governs Us: Model and Structure from its Origens*]; *El sexenio de Televisa: conjuras del poder mediático* (2010a) [*Televisa's Term: Conspiracies of Mediatic Power*]; *Peña Nieto: El gran montaje* (2012) [*Peña Nieto: The Great Montage*]; *La caída del telepresidente: de la imposición de las reformas a la indignación social* (2015) [*The Fall of the Telepresident: From Imposing Reforms to Social Indignation*].

protagonist Eddy's comfort comes from being immersed in a mediasphere where the positive news stories are accentuated and the negative ones suppressed, resulting in the overall image of the country and its leadership as not simply idealized, but intentionally manipulated.

Following this falsely idealized image of the country, the story offers a depiction of virtual glasses that perform a similar function. They offer two distinct visual enhancements for users that can afford them: an Improved Vision Mode where all subjective visual and olfactive sensory perceptions are enhanced, and news programs offer spectator's an embellished and fabricated vision of the state of the country.[20] These spectacles have a clear referent outside the text in John Carpenter's *They Live* (1988), where sunglasses offer wearers the supernatural ability to specially see through them: anyone who puts on the glasses is able to truly apprehend the reality around them, seeing the real message behind advertising images, which largely consist of the directives: consume, marry and reproduce, and obey. Slavoj ŽiŽek interprets these glasses as "ideologico-critical spectacles" that allow the wearer to see the true reality behind an advanced capitalist, liberal democracy like the United States. Therefore, natural sight without the sunglasses functions as always-already ideological; we are always within ideology as part of our everyday experience (2008). But with the virtual glasses in Lavín's story, we see the opposite feature, they are "ideologico-augeo spectacles," in ŽiŽek's terms. Their purpose is to *not* see the true nature of things, to mask the unpleasant reality around them; take off the glasses, and unvarnished reality is there. Put them on and society and its individuals are rose-colored. This understanding of ideology is in line with Terry Eagleton's identification of it as "[signifying] ideas and beliefs which help to legitimate the interests of a ruling group or class specifically by distortion and dissimulation" (1991, 30), a definition, it should be noted,

[20] The criticism of this short story contains a very similar condemnation as Luis Estrada's film *La dictadura perfecta*, released in October 2014—the same year and month that the story was published. In the film, during a scene in which the characters discuss a coordinated media strategy to divert attention away from a political scandal, it is suggested that maybe reporting on the numerous killings and violent confrontations on the front page of the local newspaper will offer cover from the scandal. Carlos, the television producer in charge of curating the political image reacts to this suggestion as such: "Tenemos ordenes de arriba de ocultar todo este tipo de información para que la gente no piense que pasen este tipo de cosas. Además, los televidentes ya están hartos de las notas de sangre" (47:23) [We have orders from above to conceal all information of this kind so that people don't think these kinds of things happen. Furthermore, the audience is already sick of these kinds of violent pieces.]

that falls shy of Karl Marx's notion of ideology as false consciousness.[21] For Eddy in the story, these glasses confirm bias and legitimate an ideological perspective, distorting the world in a pleasurable enough way such that one not need to engage with the world and try to change it. Thus, ideology is worldview embodied in the virtual glasses, with a prepackaged set of ideas that pertains to class. One sees (and smells) the world according to one's socioeconomic class (thanks to the ability to able to access the proper visual technology), which in Eddy's case is the Mexican middle-class of late neoliberalism.

The final move that occurs in the story suggests that the virtual glasses Eddy wears may contribute to the broader epistemological break that has been discussed and accentuated in the wake of the fake news phenomenon in the United States and beyond. In this way, the story pivots from critiquing its own socio-political and mediatic milieu of the 2010s with Peña Nieto to prefiguring what some consider the most pernicious threat facing liberal democracies in the 2020s: fake news as part of a broader post-truth information ecosystem in which the curation of one's news feeds in social media platforms, driven by algorithms that tailor to each users' preferences and enable media silo-ing where large groups of people are rarely exposed to ideas that run contrary to their own worldview. As a result, any shared sense of empirically verifiable truth that lends itself to a broader, moderately stable sense of what collectively constitutes reality in a society withers away until no consensus exists. "Él piensa que algo no encaja" points toward this social state obliquely as the story ends and the full extent of the reach and subjective consequence of his glasses is fulfilled. The short work closes with the narrator describing Eddy lying in the hospital bed, having just recently found out that he had been paralyzed from the waist down:

> Más tarde, en lugar de ver los noticieros indaga en Internet, pues quiere saber cómo fue el enfrentamiento que le costó la movilidad de sus piernas, pero no encuentra la noticia. Duda un poco y supone que no usa los parámetros correctos en la búsqueda. Abandona la idea. "Como quiera que sea –reflexiona durante unos segundos—, algo no encaja". Luego vuelve a la serie de acción que tanto le gusta. (2014, 132)

[21] In Marx's view of false consciousness, the exploited and alienated workers within capitalism are convinced that the system works for them and will therefore not attempt to overturn it. He likens this naturalized deception to the resulting process of the camera obscura, which inverts captured reality for the spectator (2009, 42).

> [Later, instead of watching the news he checks the Internet, because he wants to know how did the encounter that cost him the mobility of his legs occur, but he cannot find the news story. He doubts for a second and assumes he did not use the correct parameters in his search. He gives up. "Whatever happened," he reflects for a few seconds, "something is off." Later, he returns the action series that he likes so much.]

Eddy's inability to find any reporting on the internet that corroborates his own subjective, lived experience leads to the line that titles the story—he thinks something is off. The truth about what happened to him, on the one hand, and the total lack of external acknowledgement of the event within the news, on the other, leads to a physio-cognitive dissonance that lasts for several seconds: a vacillation between knowing something to be true within his own traumatic, corporeal experience, followed by doubting this truth. The final line of the story shows the choice made—that he will just watch more television through his virtual glasses, rather than attempt to make known what happened to him. The whole episode of how he was shot and paralyzed from a stray bullet will be buried deep inside his own memory, eventually immersed beneath more layers of false memories brought about by Improved Vision Mode, fake-news reporting, and innumerous hours of spectacle. Therefore, the corporeal and epistemological truth of his own lived experience that caused the paralysis will be covered up such that even he will not be able to recall it. The event effectively did not happen, making it likely that even Eddy may deny that is was the stray bullet that caused his paralysis. In this way, the story suggests that alternative epistemologies are created in a spectacular, informational ecosystem.

Virtus and "Él piensa que algo no encaja" both share in their critique of core elements of the Mexican cybernetic scopic regime that emerges in the first two decades of the twenty-first century. The novel engages with Debord's theory while also furthering his assessment to consider functional changes for the digital age in the country. This includes interactive spectacle and megaspectacles in the social, economic, mass-mediatic, and political spheres. President Wagner's incarnation as a hologram distills the novel's strongest critique, which is that politicians are constructs wholly created by media industries and controlled by national elites, and that this is most perceptible—and powerful—in the visual realm. The novel rides the line between absorbing its then-present social and political milieu with telenovelas in the era of globalization and an increase in political marketing, while also prefiguring—if not outright predicting—transformations that occurred shortly after the novel was published with the rise of Peña Nieto. It is worth noting that author has acknowledged that she did not model Jesús Wagner on Peña Nieto, but rather on Vicente Fox (Stephen Tobin, WhatsApp message to author, Feb. 1, 2022), thereby making some of the parallels between Wagner and Peña Nieto uncanny. For "Él piensa que algo no encaja," spectacle continues to be part of the everyday socio-political fabric through the use of virtual glasses, but the most prominent feature is how the story perceives fake news in Mexico in the early 2010s with the rise of Peña Nieto immersed in scandals like the Televisa Controversy and Peñabots. Like Gil, Lavín's story is deeply embedded in the moment of its creation, while also anticipating the broader implications for modes of knowledge in everyday life with the rise of fake news and post-truth, all of which have been made possible only through cybernetic devices.

Works Cited

Adorno, Theodor, and Max Horkheimer. 2007. The Culture Industry as Mass Deception. In *The Cultural Studies Reader*, ed. Simon During, 405–415. London: Routledge.

Aguayo, Sergio. 2013. Tejemaneje - La inteligencia del presidente (Segunda parte). https://www.youtube.com/watch?v=KX6B4Y7mSdw. Accessed 5 June 2021.

Ahmed, Azam. 2017. Using Billions in Government Cash, Mexico Controls News Media. *The New York Times*, Dec. 25.

Alba, Davey, and Adam Satariano. 2019. At Least 70 Countries Have Had Disinformation Campaigns, Study Finds. *The New York Times*, Sept. 26. https://www.nytimes.com/2019/09/26/technology/government-disinformation-cyber-troops.html. Accessed 2 March 2021.

Asesores políticos, ¿con sueldo mayor al de Peña Nieto? Editorial. *Vanguardia*. 27 Jan. 2014. https://vanguardia.com.mx/noticias/nacional/2685576-asesores-politicos-con-sueldo-mayor-al-de-pena-nieto-BXVG2685576. Accessed 15 August 2022.

Baudrillard, Jean. 1994. *Simulacra and Simulation*. Ann Arbor, MI: University of Michigan Press.

———. 2005. *The System of Objects*. Trans. James Benedict. Croydown: Verso.

Benjamin, Walter. 1969. *Illuminations*. Trans. Harry Zohn. New York: Schocken Books.

———. 2009. The Work of Art in the Age of Mechanical Reproduction. In *Film Theory and Criticism: Introductory Readings*, ed. Leo Braudy and Marshall Cohen, 665–685. New York: Oxford University Press.

Best, Steven, and Douglas Kellner. n.d. Debord and the Postmodern Turn: New Stages of Spectacle. Author, private collection. Unpublished. 1–18.

Carpenter, John. 1988. *They Live*. Alive Films.

Carroll, Rory. 2012. Mexican Media Scandal: Televisa Condemns Guardian Reports. *The Guardian*, 27 June 2012. https://www.theguardian.com/media/2012/jun/27/mexico-media-scandal-televisa-condemns-guardian-report-intimidating. Accessed 15 March 2022.

Castells, Pau, and Jan Stryjak. 2021. Country Overview: Mexico. GSMA Association. https://www.gsma.com/latinamerica/wp-content/uploads/2016/06/report-mexico2016-EN.pdf.

Debord, Guy. 1990. *Comments on the Society of the Spectacle*. Trans. Malcolm Imrie. London: Verso.

———. 2010. *Society of the Spectacle*. Black & Red.

Debray, Régis. 1995. *El estado seductor: Las revoluciones mediológicas del poder*. Buenos Aires: Manantial.

Eagleton, Terry. 1991. *Ideology: An Introduction*. London: Verso.

Eco, Umberto. 1986. *Travels in Hyper Reality: Essays*. Translated from the Italian by William Weaver. San Diego: Harcourt Brace Jovanovich.

Emspak, Jesse. "How Carlos Slim Built His Fortune." *Investopedia*. Investopedia US. 3 Aug. 2022. Web. 2 Jan. 2023.

Estrada, Luis. 2014. *La dictadura perfecta*. Bandidos Films.

Fardouly, Jasmine, and Lenny R. Vartanian. 2015. Negative Comparisons about One's Appearance Mediate the Relationship between Facebook Usage and Body Image Concerns. *Body Image* 12 (1): 82–88. https://doi.org/10.1016/j.bodyim.2014.10.004. Accessed 4 February 2022.

Fisher, Mark. 2009. *Capitalist Realism: Is There No Alternative?* New Alresford: Zero Books.

de Fleur, Melvin, and Sandra Ball-Rockeach. 1989. *Theories of Mass Communication*. London: Longman.

Fornazieri, Marco, Richard Doty, Thiago Bezerra, Fabio de Rezende Pinna, Fernando Costa, Richard Voegels, and Laura Silveira-Moriyama. 2019. Relationship of Socioeconomic Status to Olfactory Function. *Physiology & Behavior* 198., Elsevier Inc: 84–89.

Friel, Sharon, Deborah Gleeson, Anne-Marie Thow, Ronald Labonte, David Stuckler, Adrian Kay, and Wendy Snowdon. 2013. A New Generation of Trade Policy: Potential Risks to Diet-Related Health from the Trans Pacific Partnership Agreement. *Globalization and Health* 9 (46): 1–7. https://doi.org/10.1186/1744-8603-9-46.

Gallón, Angélica. 2019. ¿El fin de un amor o de un contrato? Las polémicas que rodearon el matrimonio de Angélica Rivera y Peña Nieto. *Univisión Noticias*. 17 February. https://www.univision.com/noticias/trending/el-fin-de-un-amor-o-de-un-contrato-las-polemicas-que-rodearon-el-matrimonio-de-angelica-rivera-y-pena-nieto. Accessed 24 August 2022.

Gálvez, Alyshia. 2018. *Eating NAFTA: Trade, Food Policies, and the Destruction of Mexico.* Oakland, California: University of California Press.

García, Hernán. 2017. Hacia una poética de la tecnología periférica: Post-cyberpunk y picaresca 2.0 en *Sleep dealer* de Alex Rivera. *Revista Iberoamericana* 83 (259–260): 327–344. https://doi.org/10.5195/reviberoamer.2017.7503.

Gibson, William. 1986. *Neuromancer.* West Bloomfield, MI: Phantasia Press.

Gil, Eve. 2008. *Virtus: El espectáculo más grande del mundo.* México, DF: Jus.

Gray, Chris Hables, ed. 1995. *The Cyborg Handbook.* London: Routledge.

———. 2002. *Cyborg Citizen: Politics in the Posthuman Age.* London: Routledge.

Guardian Statement on Televisa Coverage. 2012. *The Guardian*, June 8. https://www.theguardian.com/world/2012/jun/08/guardian-statement-televisa. Accessed 13 January 2022.

Haidt, Jonathan. 2022a. Why the Past Ten Years of American Life Have Been Uniquely Stupid. *The Atlantic*, May: 54–66.

———. 2022b. Yes, Social Media Really Is Undermining Democracy. *The Atlantic*, July. https://www.theatlantic.com/ideas/archive/2022/07/social-media-harm-facebook-meta-response/670975/. Accessed 29 July 2022.

Herrmann, Andreas, Manja Zidansk, David E. Sprott, and Eric R. Spangenberg. 2013. The Power of Simplicity: Processing Fluency and the Effects of Olfactory Cues on Retail Sales. *Journal of Retailing* 89 (1): 30–43. https://doi.org/10.1016/j.jretai.2012.08.002.

Hodgson, Martin. 2012. Mexico's Televisa Files: how do we know they are genuine? *The Guardian*, 8 June 2012. https://www.theguardian.com/media/2012/jun/27/mexico-media-scandaltelevisa-condemns-guardian-report-intimidating. Accessed 15 March 2022.

Konrath, Sara H., Edward H. O'Brien, and Courtney Hsing. 2011. Changes in Dispositional Empathy in American College Students Over Time: A Meta-Analysis. *Personality and Social Psychology Review* 15 (2): 180–198. https://doi.org/10.1177/1088868310377395.

La boda más esperada. 2010. *Quien.* Grupo Expansión. Jan. 29.

Lavín, Guillermo. 2014. El piensa que algo no encaja. In *Futuros por cruzar: cuentos de ciencia ficción de la frontera México-Estados Unidos*, ed. Gabriel Trujillo, 125–132. Mexicali, BC: Universidad Autónoma de Baja California.

Lewandowsky, Stephan, Ullrich Ecker, and John Cook. 2017. Beyond Misinformation: Understanding and Coping with the "Post-Truth" Era. *Journal of Applied Research in Memory and Cognition* 6: 353–369. https://www.cssn.org/wp-content/uploads/2020/12/Beyond-Misinformation-Understanding-and-Coping-with-the-Post-Truth-Era-Stephan-Lewandowsky.pdf. Accessed 29 July 2022.

López-Pellisa, Teresa. 2015. *Patologías de la realidad virtual. Cibercultura y ciencia ficción.* Madrid: Fondo de Cultura Económica de España.

Maguey, Hugo. 2011. *Apenas lleva una semana y @EPN ya 'acarrea' en Twitter*. November 11, 2011. https://www.animalpolitico.com/sociedad/epn-es-el-mas-popular-pero-le-caimos-en-lamovida-y-a-sus-penabots#axzz2pexR2Ru3. Accessed 15 March 2022.

Martín-Barbero, Jesús, and Germán Rey. 1999. *Los ejercicios del ver: Hegemonía audiovisual y ficción televisiva*. Barcelona: Gedisa.

Marx, Karl. 2009. *Das Kapital: A Critique of Political Economy*. Washington, DC: Regnery Pub.

Mazzocchi, Mario, Bhavani Shankar, and Bruce Traill. 2012. *The Development of Global Diets Since ICN 1992: Influences of Agrifood Sector Trends and Policies*. FAO Commodity and Trade Policy Research Working Paper no. 34.

Mitchell, W.J.T. 1994. *Picture Theory: Essays on Verbal and Visual Representation*. Chicago, IL: University of Chicago Press.

———. 2002. The Surplus Value of Images. *Mosaic: An Interdisciplinary Critical Journal* 35 (3): 1–23.

Moctezuma, Regina. 2012. Documents Are No Proof of TV Dirty Tricks Claims. *The Guardian*, June 8. https://www.theguardian.com/world/2012/jun/08/documents-no-proof-tv-dirty-tricks-mexico. Accessed 5 January 2022.

Monsiváis, Carlos. 2013. And then Television Appeared Among the Mexicans. In *Technology and Culture in Twentieth-Century*, ed. Araceli Tinajero and J. Brian Freeman, 111–123. Tuscaloosa, AL: University of Alabama Press.

Pallais, María Lourdes. 2004. Antes, la TV estaba al servicio del presidente, ahora es al revés. *La Crónica*, September 22. No longer online. Accessed 1 May 2015.

Rúas Araújo, José. 2011. Escena política y mediática en México: Las elecciones presidenciales. *Revista de Investigaciones Políticas y Sociólogas* 11 (2): 43–58.

Sánchez Prado, Ignacio. 2019. Mont Neoliberal Periodization: The Mexican "Democratic Transition," from Austrian Libertarianism to the "War on Drugs". In *World Literature, Neoliberalism, and the Culture of Discontent*, ed. Sharae Deckard and Stephen Shapiro, 93–110. Cham: Springer International Publishing.

Secretaría de la Salud. 2013. *Estrategia nacional para la prevención del sobrepeso, la obesidad y la diabetes*. Mexico City: Impresora y Encuadernadora Progreso.

Shohat, Ella, and Robert Stam. 2002. Narrativizing Visual Culture: Towards a Polycentric Aesthetics. In *The Visual Culture Reader*, ed. Nicholas Mirzoeff, 37–59. London: Routledge.

Tobin, Stephen. Whatsapp message to Eve Gil. Feb. 7 2022.

Trujillo Muñoz, Gabriel. 2014. *Futuros por cruzar: cuentos de ciencia ficción de la frontera Méx ico-Estados Unidos*. Edited by Gabriel Trujillo Muñoz. Mexicali, Baja California, México: Universidad Autónoma de Baja California.

Tuckman, Jo. Mexicans Protest Against 'Media Bias.' *The Guardian*, 10 June 2012. https://www.theguardian.com/world/2012/jun/10/mexicans-protest-against-media-bias. Accessed 5 January 2022.

Turkle, Sherry. 2011. *Alone Together: Why We Expect More from Technology and Less from Each Other.* New York: Basic Books.

———. 2015. *Reclaiming Conversation: The Power of Talk in a Digital Age.* New York: Penguin Press.

Velasquez Leiferman, Tamara, and Nina Khrushcheva. 2019. Of Peñabots and Post-Truth: The Use of Bots and Trolls in an Online Disinformation Campaign in Mexico during the Peña Nieto Administration (2012–2018). December 23. https://www.academia.edu/41562107/Of_Pe%C3%B1abots_and_Post_Truth_The_Use_of_Bots_and_Trolls_in_Online_Disinformation_Campaigns_in_Mexico_During_the_Pe%C3%B1a_Nieto_Administration_2012_2018_. Accessed 22 March 2022.

Villamil, Jenaro. 2005. *La televisión que nos gobierna: modelo y estructura desde sus orígenes.* México, DF: Grijalbo.

———. 2009. *Si yo fuera presidente: el reality show de Peña Nieto.* México, DF: Grijalbo.

———. 2010a. *El sexenio de Televisa: Conjuras del poder mediático.* México, DF: Grijalbo.

———. 2010b. La telenovela 2012. *Proceso*, November 28. https://issuu.com/telenews/docs/proceso_1778. Accessed 30 August 2022.

———. 2011. Los asesores mercadológicos de Peña Nieto. *Homozapping*, August 10. https://jenarovillamil.wordpress.com/2011/08/10/los-asesores-mercadologicos-de-pena-nieto/. Accessed 1 May 2015.

———. 2012. *Peña Nieto: El gran montaje.* México, DF: Grijalbo.

———. 2015. *La caída del telepresidente: De la imposición de las reformas a la indignación social.* México, DF: Grijalbo.

Vosoughi, Soroush, Deb Roy, and Sinan Aral. 2018. The Spread of True and False News Online. *Science* 359 (6380): 1146–1151. https://doi.org/10.1126/science.aap9559.

Walsh, Colleen. 2020. What the Nose Knows. *The Harvard Gazette*, February 20. https://news.harvard.edu/gazette/story/2020/02/how-scent-emotion-and-memory-are-intertwined-and-exploited/. Accessed 25 February 2021.

Williams, Kevin. 2004. *Understanding Media Theory.* New York: Arnold.

World Information Society Report. 2007. *Beyond WSIS*, 3. https://www.itu.int/osg/spu/publications/worldinformationsociety/2007/WISR07_full-free.pdf. Accessed 9 May 2015.

ŽiŽek, Slavoj. 2008. Through the Glasses Darkly. *In These Times*, October 29. https://inthesetimes.com/article/through-the-glasses-darkly. Accessed March 15 2022.

CHAPTER 5

Conclusion: Specular Fictions in the Age of Embodied Internet

In the time since the researching of this book began in the early 2010s, more has happened to further increase the presence and centrality of the e-image transmitted on ever smaller and increasingly mobile screens. As Chap. 4 argued, the prevalence in smartphone usage in Mexico, Latin America, and throughout much of the rest of the world, has societies grappling with how to adapt to their overuse and distractions they pose, some deleterious effects of social media usage on its users, and the pernicious threats to democracy posed by fake news spreading more rapidly through them than real news, among other problems. New terms have appeared during this time in an attempt to articulate the social experience of the device's dominance: for example, the idea expressed of having "on-screen relationships," the neologism "screenagers" that describes teenagers' overuse of smartphones, or the compound noun of "screen time," which denotes time spent engaging with a screen. Furthermore, the lockdown caused by the coronavirus pandemic that began early in 2020 forced many in the globe to stay indoors for numerous months and essentially live much of their social and personal lives through screens. "Excessive screen time has become a grave concern," two public health researchers remarked in the summer of 2021 (Pandya and Lodha 2021, 1). Culling study data from countries like the United States, Canada, India, China, and Australia, they cite numerous analyses that corroborate their claim: Overall digital

S. C. Tobin, *Vision, Technology, and Subjectivity in Mexican Cyberpunk Literature*, Studies in Global Science Fiction, https://doi.org/10.1007/978-3-031-31156-7_5

device usage increased to 17.5 hours per day for heavy users and 30 hours per week for non-heavy users, and adults experienced a 60–80% increase compared to pre-pandemic times (Pandya and Lodha 2021, 4). This massive, semi-obligatory surge of interacting with screens for work, school, and socializing inaugurated the 2020s as an era in which the human lives not only with, but through screens. In a metaphoric sense, the heavy users crawl within and live inside screens and escape the real, giving the climax of Pepe Rojo's novel *Punto cero* in Chap. 3 increasing relevance as time passes. By the summertime of the first lockdown, another Latin American author, Alejandro Zambra, published a realist short story titled "Screen Time" in an issue of *The New York Times Magazine* (2020), which narrates the relationship between two young parents, their two-year-old, and their suddenly prominent relationship with television during lockdown. Among other elements this reveals, it definitely shows the continued relevance of the television screen throughout the world.

As of March, 2022, with the lockdown a thing of the past, the average Mexican spends almost nine hours looking at a screen of any kind. When considering just the time spent on computers and mobile phones, Mexico logs 4.37 hours per day on average, just below Brazil, Colombia, and Argentina in South America. Quite surprisingly, all of these countries possess more screen time than the average person in the United States on average. Furthermore, when considering social media usage, these rankings persist (Moody 2021). The other statistic that appears at once unexpected, yet fitting, regards the fact that Mexico is the country in the Western Hemisphere with the largest percentage of the population that uses the internet to stream television, at 97.9% (Moody 2021). While there can be no doubt that the ascent of screens is a global phenomenon, it is also true that it particularly affects Mexico as much if not more than most other countries within the Western Hemisphere. What is more, as Mexican journalist Monserrat Valle Vargas pointed out in a recent article that, at current trends, people will spend an average of nine years of their life looking at a smartphone screen (2020). All of these statistics help take stock of the enormity of this cybernetic scopic regime in which smartphones are playing an increasingly central role, one that rivals and will likely overtake television in being the main screen upon which eyes gaze. Along the way, these devices will devour and recycle older forms of media, split them into ever smaller chunks to be streamed on Instagram or Tik Tok (or whatever the next app in vogue is).

About a year and half after the lockdowns began in October, 2021, Facebook officially changed its name to Meta, along with an announcement of their overarching plans for the coming years. What started in the 2000s as a social media platform based on text, quickly moved on to include photos, and later videos. Mark Zuckerberg announced: “But this isn’t the end of the line. The next platform will be even more immersive—an embodied internet where you’re in the experience, not just looking at it” (2021). After numerous decades of theorizing and much ballyhoo from Silicon Valley and tech enthusiasts, the goal of the metaverse appears to finally offer an immersive social space of digital virtuality where many previously real social experiences with family and friends can be fully—some might say radically—replaced with the user-spectator-subject as an avatar. In Zuckerberg’s description, the intermediary component of the computer monitor, smartphone, or tablet will disappear, and finally, we will enter the screen like in Rojo’s *Punto cero*. Together, all participants will appear as holograms within this digitally created virtual space where everyday activities like working, shopping, playing, etc., will occur. “The defining quality of the metaverse will be a feeling of presence—like you are right there with another person or in another place,” he stated. Invoking Star-Trek vernacular, Zuckerberg affirms: “you will be able to teleport instantly as a hologram to be at the office without a commute, at a concert with friends, or in your parents’ living room to catch up,” thereby opening more opportunity for everyone regardless of where they live. The hologram-centric discourse in his announcement connects this relatively incipient visual technology with a posthuman imaginary in ways as yet unrealized in actuality. Worth noting here is the origin of the neologism: Neil Stephenson’s post-/cyberpunk novel *Snowcrash* (1992) coined the term “metaverse” referring to a place to which characters escape in order to flee the drudge and oppressive horrors of a hypercapitalist, massively unequal world in which pizza delivery employees can be killed for showing up late with a delivery and living in a 20'×30' storage unit is considered something of a luxury for the masses. The metaverse consists of this typical cyberpunk virtual-reality setting that is a haven for crime, virtual sex, addiction, and is, above all, an escape from the world. Considering this, it is incredible that the announcement of Meta’s forthcoming metaverse arrived with no discernable sense of irony, or, even a nod to the fact that the source material for what they aspire to create is an infernal social order in which few would want to exist. Some would argue that late neoliberalism increases the scope and contours of this vastly unequal social order more every day.

Any reservations about the metaverse could be interpreted as just more bourgeois ennui and/or paranoia from the Global North if it were not for the fact that, as of 2022, the estimated number of Facebook users in Mexico is just over 90 million—almost 70% of the population (Statista 2022, n.d.). It comprises more than half of all desktop social media visits in the country, and users of all ages look at it on smartphones; in early 2022, 60% of internet users used Facebook as a source of news, which, in considering the prefiguration of Guillermo Lavín's "Él piensa que algo no encaja" in Chap. 4, distributed the most amount of new misinformation (Statista 2022, n.d.). The undeniable impact on Mexico of this US-based, global social media platform continues strongly to this day, and will remain so for the foreseeable future. If the metaverse becomes realized even to a small degree envisioned by Zuckerberg and the other tech giants of Silicon Valley like Google and Apple, then for tens of millions, if not billions, of people, the screen will fade and the subject will fully enter the digitally constructed, interactive, immersive, audio-visual, virtual space. If one recalls that Facebook acquired Oculus in 2014 for $2 billion, banking on the technology to finally bring virtual reality mainstream. The Oculus device, a large, head-mounted display that looks like black, opaque scuba goggles that also cover the wearer's ears, became the crucial component in the product launch the same year Facebook acquired the company that created the device. The 2016 photo that Zuckerberg posted to his Facebook page is now iconic, and it shows a large conference room full of tech enthusiasts and journalists with Zuckerberg walking down the aisle in a t-shirt and jeans, his public-relations smile spread wide across his youthful face, as he looks upon a sea of masked men's heads (they are, indeed, all male). The man sitting just in front of him dons a thick frown under his Oculus device, suggesting underwhelm or discontent—a stark juxtaposition to Zuckerberg's ostensible jubilation. Make no mistake, some form of this inflection of a cybernetic scopic regime is coming, and if this photo is any indication, there will be happy rulers and many frowning users.

One larger signification of Meta, Oculus, and a social and interpersonal world lived through holograms and virtual reality is a qualitative expansion of a posthuman visuality. There is no doubt that the e-image that appears on television, computers, and smartphones participates in an extensive genealogy of other visual and communications technologies that preceded them. As such, our contemporary visuality discussed here undoubtedly links with film and even photographs, but something seems qualitatively different when the human subject is immersed within an audio-visual, haptic environment—a mixed reality milieu. A person is in two places at the same time: one physically and the other subjectively. To some extent this has always been true of the viewing subject when looking at screens with electronic images that constantly change—and especially smartphones that can transfix people walking or driving. But we make a significant leap forward when one is immersed within the digital virtuality that is interactive. As Kathy Cleland has convincingly argued, "our individual agency, cognition and subjectivity extends into, and through, our prosthetic digital technologies, the human subject is increasingly constituted as an assemblage of human-computer-communications networks" (2010, 75). In her article "Prosthetic Bodies and Virtual Cyborgs," she conceptualizes this posthuman visuality through extensive psychoanalytic and phenomenological accounts, along with numerous neuroscientific studies of mirror neurons and autoscopic phenomena, in order to offer a powerful demonstration of just how these mixed-reality environments are experienced in the brain (74). As such, we now have a relatively clear picture of what happens neurologically when one plays videogames or immerses themself in Zuckerberg's fantasy of the impending metaverse. The physical intermixes with digital virtuality in a complex amalgamation that makes clear the association of the body as integral to a larger media ecosystem, extended in the way McLuhan imagined the body as an extension of media (1964, 23, 72), and its cognitive processes linked with and through cybernetic computation and telecommunication circuits. A strong case, then, can be made for the hologram-avatar as a prosthetic body that is the "emerging paradigm for experience in the 21st century" (2010, 74). A fully realized posthuman visuality is central to this paradigm, one toward which the specular fictions of this monograph points.

Specular fictions continue to appear, especially in science fiction literature.[1] Most recently in Mexico, we can point to the young Andrea Chapela, whose *Ansibles, perfiladores y otras máquinas de ingenio* (2020) offers many stories with a cybernetic visual regime. In particular, the stories: "90% real," "Ahora lo sientes," and "Calculando recalculando" imply the screen, often in less of a thematically central way as in this monograph, and

[1] Several examples in Mexico and beyond are worth considering. The latter Within Mexico, Daniela L. Guzmán's "El cielo de los entrenadores Pokemón" can also be considered specular in the way it engages with these popular augmented reality figures. In Latin America, two stories from the recent anthology *Tercer mundo después del sol* from 2021 offer more examples of science-fiction literature thematically entangled with visual technologies, such as the post-cyberpunk "A través del avatar" by Argentina's Laura Ponce (2022), or "Un hombre en mi cama" by Ecuador's Solange Rodríguez Pappe (2021).

more pervasive in the background. These specular fictions articulate a more intimate relation with the screen in a less antagonistic manner. The short narrative “La persona que busca no está disponible” recounts how the female protagonist, who lives in New York, maintains her relationship with her mother, who lives in Mexico City, via something that sounds exactly like the metaverse. The major difference between the two is the interface, which in Chapela’s story only requires wearing contact lenses.

> Yo llevaba por lo menos dos años usando lentillas y aunque había sido horrible acostumbrarme a la picazón, valía totalmente la pena, el mundo no tenía sentido para mí sin ellas. ¿Quién necesitaba pantallas, paredes inteligentes y teléfonos cuando podía tener todo pegados a los ojos, desplegando imágenes tridimensionales a su alrededor? (2020, 145)
>
> I wore lenses for at least two years and although it had been awful to get used to the itching, it was totally worth it. The world did not make sense to me without them. Who needs screens, intelligent walls, and telephones when they could have everything glued to their eyes, giving off three dimensional images around them?

Later, she facilitates international communication between her and her mother by designing a “espacio de llamada” [calling space], a space of digital virtuality. “Hablamos todas las semanas en el espacio de llamada que es casi como estar frente a ella. ¿Para qué venir si con un pensamiento podemos vernos, hablarnos, como si estuviéramos en la misma ciudad” (2020, 148–149) [We spoke every week in the calling space that is almost like being in front of her. Why would she come here if, with nothing more than a thought, we can see each other, talk to each other, as if we were in the same city?] Indeed, Zuckerberg’s pronouncement that the metaverse has a “feeling of presence — like you are right there with another person or in another place” emulates Chapela’s description perfectly. The short fiction hinges largely upon a transhuman theme where her 90-year-old mother decides to not extend her life well into her hundreds, and she does this by consciously choosing to not have her failing organs replaced, as most everyone else does. But this theme is underpinned by the idea of whether or not these metaverse-like spaces can truly transcend one’s physical absence, or if Zuckerberg’s notion of teleporting can replace the real. The visual motif in this story makes it specular, but it also points to further possible directions in the science fiction of the 2020s and beyond. The screen is giving way to a more fully enveloping visuality, one where the subject is "in the experience, not just looking at it," to borrow Zuckerberg's phrasing.

This monograph concludes looking backward in order to consider the future of this specular literature. Around a decade ago when the idea for this monograph was a seedling, Erja Vettenranta suggested in *Technology and Culture in Twentieth-Century Mexico* that it may "still be too early to determine whether the contemporary digital culture will produce its own chief narrative form in the same manner that the novel characterizes the print culture of the last five centuries" (2013, 303). One potential avenue that this form may take includes the technocultural inquiries and posthuman science fiction short stories from writer and cultural critic Naief Yehya. "The printed word has one quality that the screen cannot offer," Yehya writes, "it gives us a respite to reflect, it allows us to take time to think and consider things" (qtd in Vettenranta 2013, 310). Considering both Vettenratta and Yehya's quotations here bring to mind that one possible answer to the former's unconcluded proposition. A narrative form that will vie for relevance in contemporary digital culture consists of specular fictions. In this era, it is becoming practically impossible to avoid the screen in the North and South for a large number of people, and as a result, authors use the printed word to bear witness to its dominance now as a lived experience. On the whole and across most cultures, people live their lives not only alongside but increasingly through screens. Visual events with the e-image will continue to their sharp and steady increase concomitant with the continued, vertiginous growth of smaller screen production, which are increasingly mobile and omnipresent, found now everywhere—on new refrigerators, on car dashboards, or as Art Mode TVs (televisions that double as works of art when not emitting shows, films, or commercials), among other places. And yes, VR-headsets, augmented-reality spectacles and contact lenses, and other wearable technology will gain currency and spread. All of these visual interfaces will continue to capture and inspire the critical imagination of science fiction authors for the foreseeable future.

Works Cited

Bastidas Pérez, Rodrigo. 2022. *El tercer mundo después del sol: antología de ciencia ficción latino-americana*. Barcelona: Minotauro.

Chapela, Andrea. 2020. *Ansibles, perfiladores y otras máquinas de ingenio*. Ciudad de México: Almadía Ediciones.

Cleland, Kathy. 2010. Prosthetic Bodies and Virtual Cyborgs. *Second Nature* 3: 74–101.

McLuhan, Marshall. 1964. *Understanding Media: The Extensions of Man.* New York: McGraw Hill.

Moody, Rebecca. 2021. Screen Time Statistics: Average Screen Time in the US vs. the Rest of the World. *Comparitech.* https://www.comparitech.com/tv-streaming/screen-time-statistics/. Accessed 24 August 2022.

Pandya, Apurvakumar, and Pragya Lodha. 2021. Social Connectedness, Excessive Screen Time During COVID-19 and Mental Health: A Review of Current Evidence. *Frontiers of Human Dynamics*, July 22. https://doi.org/10.3389/fhumd.2021.684137. Accessed 24 August 2022.

Statista. 2022. Facebook Usage Penetration in Mexico from 2018 to 2027. July 22. https://www.statista.com/statistics/553759/facebook-penetration-in-mexico/. Accessed on 29 August 2022.

Stephenson, Neal. 1992. *Snow Crash.* New York: Bantam Books.

Valle Vargas, Monseratt. 2020. Pasarás casi 9 años de tu vida viendo la pantalla del smartphone, según estudio. Xataka.com, November 23. https://www.xataka.com.mx/medicina-y-salud/pasaras-casi-9-anos-tu-vida-viendo-pantalla-smartphone-estudio. Accessed 24 August 2022.

Vettenranta, Erja. 2013. Cyborg Versus Homo Scribens: Mexican Literary Expressions in the Era of "Technoculture". In *Technology and Culture in Twentieth-Century*, ed. Araceli Tinajero and J. Brian Freeman, 303–315. Tuscaloosa, AL: University of Alabama Press.

Zambra, Alejandro. 2020. Screen Time. The New York Times Magazine, trans. Megan McDowell, July 12. https://www.nytimes.com/interactive/2020/07/07/magazine/alejandro-zambra-short-story.html?fbclid=IwAR1sJg-RWDIxLyebrI-dZwMKYm8y7fds81asdRIxv453RZ0teG_oW9bcN4M. Accessed 24 August 2022.

Zuckerberg, Mark. 2021. Founder's Letter. Facebook.com. October 28. https://about.fb.com/news/2021/10/founders-letter/. Accessed 26 August 2022.

Index[1]

A

B

C

[1] Note: Page numbers followed by 'n' refer to notes.

S. C. Tobin, *Vision, Technology, and Subjectivity in Mexican Cyberpunk Literature*, Studies in Global Science Fiction,
https://doi.org/10.1007/978-3-031-31156-7

Printed by Printforce, United Kingdom